St Clare's in Sussex

severe wrist pain
limited motion
swollen
Needs xray

NORTH RIVER

ALSO BY PETE HAMILL

NOVELS

A Killing for Christ

The Gift

Dirty Laundry

Flesh and Blood

The Deadly Piece

The Guns of Heaven

Loving Women

Snow in August

Forever

SHORT STORY COLLECTIONS

The Invisible City

Tokyo Sketches

JOURNALISM

Irrational Ravings

Tools as Art

Piecework

News Is a Verb

MEMOIR

A Drinking Life

Downtown: My Manhattan

BIOGRAPHY

Diego Rivera

Why Sinatra Matters

NORTH RIVER

A NOVEL

Pete Hamill

LITTLE, BROWN AND COMPANY
New York Boston London

Little, Brown and Company
Hachette Book Group USA
237 Park Avenue, New York, NY 10017

Visit our Web site at www.HachetteBookGroupUSA.com

First Edition: June 2007

Copyright acknowledgments appear on page 342.

Library of Congress Cataloging-in-Publication Data

Hamill, Pete.
North River : a novel / Pete Hamill. — 1st ed.
p. cm.
ISBN-13: 978-0-316-34058-8
ISBN-10: 0-316-34058-8
1. Physicians — Fiction. 2. Poor — Fiction. 3. Grief — Fiction. 4. Grandparent and child — Fiction. 5. Nineteen thirties — Fiction. 6. Manhattan (New York, N.Y.) — Fiction. I. Title.
PS3558.A423N67 2007
813'.54 — dc22 2006038088

10 9 8 7 6 5 4 3 2 1

RRD-C

Printed in the United States of America

In memory of

My brother Joe

who tried so hard

to make the world a better place

Love in full life and length, not love ideal,
No, nor ideal beauty, that fine name,
But something better still, so very real . . .

— GEORGE GORDON, LORD BYRON, 1818

NORTH RIVER

ONE

DELANEY KNEW HE'D BEEN IN THE DREAM BEFORE, KNEW FROM the hurting whiteness, the icy needles that closed his eyes, the silence, the force of the river wind. But knowing it was a dream did not ease his fear. As before, he waved his bare hands to push through the whiteness, but as before the whiteness was porous and he knew it was snow. As before, there was no horizon. As before, his feet floated through frozen powder. There was no ground beneath him. There was nothing to grip. No picket fence. No lamppost. And no people.

No friend.

No woman.

As before: just the driving force of the snow . . .

Then he was awake in the blue darkness. A sound. A bell. His hand clumsy with sleep, he lifted the black telephone on the night table. Still dead. Someone at the wrought iron gate below the stoop was jerking the old bell rope, making an urgent ding-dinging sound. A sound he had heard too many times. Shivering in cotton summertime pajamas, he threw off the covers. *Ding-ding-DING.* The window shade was raised a foot, the window two inches, part of Delaney's desire for fresh air on the coldest winter nights. Drifted snow covered the oaken sill. He raised the shade and could see the snow moving horizontally from the North River. The wind whined. A midnight snowfall was now a dawn blizzard. Ripping in from the west along Horatio Street. *Goddamn you, Monique! Answer the goddamned bell!* And remembered that his nurse was gone for the long New Year's holiday, off somewhere with her boyfriend. Delaney pulled a flannel robe over his shoulders and parted the dark blue drapes, as if obeying the orders of the downstairs bell. *Ding-ding. Ding-ding-DING.* He glanced at the clock. Six-seventeen. The bell demanding attention. On a day of morning sleep all over New York. He raised the window, its glass rimed with the cold. Snow blew harder across the sill. He poked his head into the driving snow and looked down. At the gate under the stoop, a man was pulling the rope attached to the bell. Delaney knew him. A man who looked like an icebox in an overcoat. Bootsie, they called him. Bootsie Cirillo. Snow was piled on his pearl-gray fedora and the shoulders of his dark blue overcoat. At the sound of the window rising, he had stepped back and was now looking up.

"Doc? Eddie Corso sent me, Doc." His voice was raspy. "He needs you. Right now."

"Give me five minutes," Delaney said.

"Make it t'ree."

Delaney sighed, closed the window, and dressed quickly in rough clothes. Thinking: These goddamned hoods are worse since the movies got sound. *Make it t'ree.* Christ, I'm too old for these guys. He pulled a sweater over his denim shirt, added a scarf and a cloth cap with a longshoreman's pin. A gift from Knocko Carmody of the dock wallopers' union. Delaney pulled on bridgemen's shoes and took his time lacing them. Then he pocketed keys, some dollar bills, picked up his worn black leather bag, and went down the hall stairs to go out through the gate under the stoop. The snow hit his face, again like needles. Again he closed his eyes. The dream, the goddamned dream . . . all the way from the last years of the nineteenth century.

"You took too much time, Doc," Bootsie said. "This is fucking *bad.*" He turned and shook the snow off his fedora and used it to brush powder off his shoulders. Snow was gathering on the roof and hood of the black Packard that was two feet from the curb. Bootsie jerked open the door on the passenger side, gesturing with his head for Delaney to get in, then moved around to take the wheel.

"We're late," he said.

"I did my best, Bootsie," Delaney said, sliding into the front seat and closing the door. The fat man started the car and pulled out, the snow rising loosely from the hood. Bootsie drove east on Horatio Street, the wind whipping hard behind them. There was no traffic. The car skidded on the turn at Hudson Street.

"Maybe I should walk," Delaney said.

"Eddie's maybe nine *blocks* from here."

"He's a thousand miles from here if you get us killed, Bootsie."

The fat man grunted, slowed down. The window was foggy from their breathing, and Bootsie took out a white silk handkerchief and wiped at it. Then handed the handkerchief to Delaney. The doctor wiped at the steamy front window on his side, then rolled the side window down an inch. Bootsie grunted.

"How come you don't got a car?" Bootsie said. "You could follow me."

"Can't afford it."

"Come on. You're a *doctor.*"

"That's why I can't afford it."

"These bust-outs around here, they don't pay?"

"They're poor, Bootsie. They still get sick."

The fat man turned, made a right and another right, heading toward Little Italy. A few kids were coming down from the tenements. One of them was carrying a surplice, its hem emerging below a wrapping of Christmas paper, the boy off to serve the seven o'clock mass at

Sacred Heart. As Delaney so often did, long ago. He noticed that up here the streetlights were still working. Another zone in the city grid. Another world.

"What happened to Eddie?"

"You'll find out."

"Maybe I could get ready if you told me what happened."

Bootsie sighed, pondered this, made another turn through the snow-packed streets. Parked cars were turning into immense white sculptures in the wind-driven snow.

"Mr. Corso got shot, maybe an hour ago."

"Where?"

"The stomach. Maybe the arm too. And maybe the hand. There's blood all over his fingers . . ."

"I mean, where'd it happen?"

"The club. We had a New Year's party, all the guys, the wives. A band too, and all the usual shit, noisemakers, funny hats. Most people go home, maybe t'ree in the morning. Some of the guys go over Chinatown to get laid. Then there's a card game, whiskey, a big pot. I cook up some breakfast, scramble eggs, sausage, the usual. Then in the door comes t'ree jaboneys, guns out. They don't say a word. They just start shooting. Then everybody's shooting. The t'ree shooters go down, but so does Mr. Corso. He's hurt real bad, but he says, 'Go throw these cocksuckers in the river.' I stay with him while the other guys haul the dead guys away. It's still dark, see? Nobody on the street. All the lights out. No cops. Nothing. Just the fucking snow."

He pulled up a few doors from the storefront housing the Good Men Social and Athletic Club. The street was empty. He and Delaney got out. Bootsie knocked on the door. Three fast raps, then two. A sallow man with dead eyes peered out, opened the door wider. Most of the lights were out.

"Took your fuckin' time," the sallow man said to Bootsie.

"Fast as I could, Carmine. It's a fuckin' *blizzard* out there."

The club was a mess of noisemakers, funny hats, overturned tables, and blood. Delaney could see smears through the blood where bodies had been dragged. Against the wall, Eddie Corso was lying on a cot. He smiled thinly when he saw Delaney.

"Medic, medic," he whispered, and then grinned in a bleary way.

There was blood on his face, probably from his wet crimson hand, but there was a huge spreading stain of blood on the white shirt.

"Jesus, it hurts like a bastard, Doc."

"You've been through worse."

He grinned. "Morphine, morphine . . ." The call of the trenches in the rain. "Please, Doc . . ."

Corso laughed and then moaned, and Delaney gave him what he needed. He swabbed his arm with cotton soaked in alcohol, prepared a syringe, then injected him with a shot of morphine. Corso winced, then sighed in a gargly way. Delaney ripped open the bloody shirt to look at the worst wound, then used pressure and tape to staunch the bleeding.

"You've got to go to a hospital, Eddie."

"A hospital? You nuts? You might as well drive me to the *Daily News*." His voice was quavering and whispery with morphine. "This can't get out. This —"

"I can't do what you need, Eddie," Delaney said. "You need a surgeon."

"You did it in the Argonne, Doc!"

"And botched it for too many guys."

"You didn't botch it for me!"

"You need a professional surgeon, Eddie. Someone whose right hand works right, not like mine. Someone at St. Vincent's."

"Anybody comes in shot, the nuns call the cops."

"Let me see what I can do," Delaney said. "Your phone working?"

"Yeah," Bootsie said. "Over there."

Delaney called St. Vincent's, identified himself, asked which surgeons were on duty, and held on. His eyes moved around the club, the blood and disorder, and Eddie Corso moaning, and the sallow man guarding the door, and Bootsie nibbling at some cake left on the bar. His gaze fell on the framed photographs of prizefighters and ballplayers, of old picnics, feasts, weddings, and then on the browning photograph of the remnant of the battalion. In a gouged field in France. All of them were still young, the farm boys and the city rats, and he could see Eddie Corso laughing like a man who'd won a lottery, always joking, as brave as any man Delaney had ever known. He saw himself too, off on the side, with his medic's armband, his face gaunt, a cigarette in his good right hand.

"Hello, hello," came the voice on the phone. "This is Dr. Zimmerman."

"Thank God," Delaney said, relieved that it was this particular young intern. "Jake, I need a big favor."

It was after eleven when Bootsie dropped him off at the house on Horatio Street. They had taken Eddie Corso through an old delivery entrance at the side of the hospital and hurried him into surgery. If he lived, there would be no records. If he died, it didn't matter. Around ten, Jake Zimmerman came out, young and bony and frazzled, and told Delaney with a nod and a thin smile that Eddie would survive. The nuns would bring him along after the operation, adhering to their own special vows of silence.

"By the way," Zimmerman said, "where'd your patient get those scars? One on the back, one on the leg?"

"The Argonne," Delaney said. "I sewed him up. That's why it looks so bad."

"The Argonne?"

"Yeah."

"You never told me that."

"It was a long time ago, Jake."

In another life.

Now he was on Horatio Street, with the snow still blowing hard.

Bootsie's exhausted breathing had fogged the windows. Delaney opened the door.

"Thanks, Bootsie," he said.

"Thank *you*, Doc."

Then he reached over and touched Delaney's arm.

"You're a good fuckin' man, Doc."

"I wish," Delaney said, and stepped into the driving snow.

He looked up at the small brick house, the one he'd been given at her death by Evelyn Langdon. Ten years ago now, in a good year, before the goddamned Depression. She was the last of the old Protestant families who had come to the street in the 1840s, fleeing cholera and the Irish, building their impregnable brick and brownstone fortresses. He had kept her alive until she was seventy-three. She had outlived her two children and all of her friends. When she died and the will was read, there was a note to Delaney, explaining that the house was now for him and his wife, Molly, and his daughter, Grace. *You have been my last and perhaps truest friend. Please use this house to enrich human life.*

Well, I did try, he thought as he opened the iron front gate under the stoop, remembering Evelyn's note. I tried, and too often failed. Most of all, I've failed those I loved the most.

Then he noticed the disturbed snow on the stoop itself, and, at the top, a fog rising on the tall glass windows of the vestibule. It was like Bootsie's fog in the car, a streaky, uneven fog made by breathing. He hurried up the steps, gripping the iron banister with his good left hand. Foot marks were drifted over with fresh snow. He glanced back to the street, but Bootsie was gone.

The vestibule door was unlocked. It was always unlocked, so that in bad weather the boy from Reilly's candy store could drop off the newspapers. In the left corner, he glimpsed the *Times,* the *News,* the *Mirror.* Maybe the footprints belonged to the newspaper boy. Maybe.

Then, pushing the door open a few inches, he saw the baby stroller. It was worn and ratty with age, strands of its wicker hood sprung and loose. Like something bought at a secondhand shop. Under a pile of covers, his head wrapped in a green scarf and a yellow wool hat, was a child.

He knew this boy with the wide, wary brown eyes. He had not seen him since the boy was six days old, another unformed infant huddled in the nursery of New York Hospital. But he had his mother's eyes, and her blond hair. That morning Grace had let him hold the boy, saying only that the boy's father, Rafael Santos of Cuernavaca, Mexico, was out running errands. She was not even seventeen that morning, his and Molly's only child. Now a child with a child. Smart, gifted, spoiled, but a child. Like ten thousand other young mothers in New York. When Delaney returned to the hospital, late the next morning, she and the baby were gone. Almost three years now. The postcards came for a while. From Key West. From Cuba. Later Grace wrote a longer letter from Mexico, telling Delaney and Molly that all three Santoses had boarded a ship to Veracruz, with stops along the way. *I tried calling before we left,* she wrote. *Nobody was home.* Molly read the letter first, then slapped it against Delaney's chest. "Spoiled rotten," she said. "By you." There were a few more letters, cryptic or guarded, as if Grace was afraid of having them read by anyone else. And then the letters stopped. It was like an erasure on a charcoal drawing. Grace was there in his life, and in Molly's, but not there. He never did meet the goddamned husband.

He unlocked the inner vestibule door and wheeled the silent boy into the hall, closing doors firmly behind him. His own bedroom was to the left on the street side, the former parlor converted long ago by some forgotten inhabitant, with the former bedroom now full of chairs and couches, looking out on the back garden. Sliding oak doors separated the rooms, but the parquet floors stretched from front windows to rear like a dense oaken plain. He gently freed the boy from the blankets, thinking: Goddamned swaddling clothes. The boy had a lighter version of his mother's dark blond hair, and he gazed up at Delaney in silence. And then Delaney saw the letter on the boy's lap. Addressed DADDY. Sealed. He dropped it on the bed. Thinking: I'll read this later, but not in front of the boy. I don't want him to see my rage. She will explain herself, of course, but I can't stop now. He slipped off his heavy clothes and felt a chilly dampness penetrating the room. Thinking: Build a fire. He lifted the child, breathing hard on the boy's cold cheeks. Then the boy moved his arms. His face looked as if he had a toothache.

"Mamá," he said, waving a freed hand toward the door. With an accent on the second syllable. "Mamá?"

"We'll find her, boy. Don't worry."

"Mamá?"

The boy was wearing a pale blue snowsuit with a dark blue sweater underneath, and Delaney removed it and then lifted him and placed him standing beside the bed, his feet planted on the threadbare Persian rug. Carlos. His name is Carlos. A good weight. Maybe twenty-nine, thirty pounds. A healthy weight. Clear skin too. Small white teeth. He smelled of milk. The boy stood there, a hand on the mattress, gazing around at the strange high-ceilinged room, with its electric lights rising from the channels of old gas lamps, the dark glazed paintings on the walls, the dresser that held Delaney's clothes. The boy was looking at the two framed photographs on top of the dresser. Delaney's wife, Molly, when she was twenty-five. Grace, when she was sixteen, about the time she met Rafael Santos somewhere out in the city. Delaney thought: The boy has intelligent eyes. Yes. His mother's eyes.

"Mamá!" the boy said, pointing. "*Mamá!*"

"Yes," Delaney said, "that's your mama."

The coals were ashen gray in the fireplace, and Delaney squatted, crumpled an old newspaper, built a small house of kindling, struck a match. He thought: What the hell is this, anyway? I've treated about three thousand kids this size, this age, but I don't know a goddamned thing about taking care of them. Not even for a day. I didn't even know how to take care of my own daughter when she was this boy's age. I went to the war instead. The boy watched him, his dark eyes widening as the flame erupted. He glanced back at the photograph, then looked again at the fire, as Delaney used a shovel to lift a few chunks of coal from the scuttle. Delaney felt his right shoulder begin to ache. Not from the cold. But he would have to do something to keep the boy warm in this large, drafty house. In the good years before the Crash, Delaney had installed a hot-water system in the house, not easy because it was built in 1840. Before he could convert the house to steam heat, the banks had failed, taking his money with them. The heat still belonged to the nineteenth century. Wood and paper and coal in a manteled fireplace. The boy seemed to love it, flexing his small hands for warmth. I've got to feed him too. But almost no restaurants would be open on New Year's Day. Not until tonight. He must need to eat. Christ, I need to eat. Breakfast. Christ, no: *lunch.*

"How about some food, Carlos?" Delaney said. "I think I've got cornflakes and eggs and stuff like that."

The boy looked at him blankly, and Delaney realized that he didn't understand the words. For almost three years, they had been in Mexico, where the boy's father had family and friends. They surely had spoken to him each day in Spanish, even Grace. So had the maids. And the cook. For Santos was not a peasant, according to Grace's meager letters. He came from money, as so many revolutionists did. Delaney knew a few words in the language, but he wished he and Molly had spent their European time in a land of vowels, instead of among the consonants of Vienna.

"Quiere . . . comer?" he said, making a spooning motion with his empty hand.

The boy nodded, Delaney took his hand. I'll have to keep him off these stairs. Have to buy some of those folding gates. I'll have to do a lot of things.

• • •

The boy ate two bowls of cornflakes and kept sipping from a cup of cocoa. He was watching Delaney, as if trying to understand who this strange man was. And where they were now, in this vast house. He started to imitate Delaney too, shifting his spoon awkwardly from hand to hand, the spoon too large, slopping the wet flakes on the table, spilling some milk. His mother must have fed him for too long. Or a maid. Spoiling him rotten. The boy was propped up on a cushion, and his eyes kept glancing from Delaney through the two kitchen windows to the yard. Glancing at the blinding whiteness.

"O," the boy said, gesturing with the spoon.

Delaney followed his gesture.

"O," the boy said.

Delaney smiled, suddenly understanding.

"Yes, that's snow."

Thinking: At least your mother found time to teach you one word of English. You probably never saw snow before this morning. And your mother waved a hand and said its name. Before abandoning you in a goddamned doorway.

"Want to see the snow?"

Delaney got up and lifted the boy off his cushion.

"Wait," he said, groping for the words of the Cuban orderlies at the hospital. Wait. What was the word? And said it: "Espérate."

Delaney climbed the hall stairs two at a time, retrieved the boy's wool cap and new hooded jacket with mittens attached, and came back down, again wearing his winter clothes. The boy was at a window, squinting at the glaring snow.

"Let's go," Delaney said, pulling on the jacket, shoving the boy's hands into the mittens, tying the hood under his chin. "Vamos, boy. Let's see the snow."

He opened the door leading to the outside shed. This was the place of everything that didn't fit anywhere else: shelves stacked with boxes of detergent; stacks of old magazines and newspapers, tied with twine; unused Christmas decorations; milk bottles; a rake hanging on a nail; a wide-bladed snow shovel; a large red toolbox. Most of the space was taken by Delaney's Arrow bicycle, its pedals and gears wrapped tightly in oiled cloth. He and the boy eased past the bicycle to a second door, leading to the yard. Delaney had to push hard on the door to move the piled snow.

Then it was before them, and the boy took a deep breath and exhaled. The North River wind was not as strong here, the buildings making a brick-walled fortress of the backyards. But it still had the magical power to whirl snow into small mountains, some of them taller than the boy. The rosebushes were blocky and irregular and white. And the olive tree, a gift from Mr. Nobiletti, the shoemaker, stood in its corner, wrapped for the winter in tar paper, so white it seemed like a giant ice-cream cone. The bases of the three fences had vanished under drifts. Delaney reached down and made a snowball.

"Snowball," he said, hefting it for the boy to see.

"O-baw," the boy said.

With his left hand, Delaney lobbed it toward the nearest fence, where it exploded in powder. He said, again, "Snowball!" The boy was awed. Delaney made another and threw it harder against the back fence. A snowy bas-relief fell off the fence. Now Delaney's lower right arm ached, though he had not used it for throwing. The boy pulled some snow off a small mountain and tried to make it into a ball. The first ball crumbled in his hands. Then he tried another, and this one was packed better, and he threw it about two feet and saw it vanish into another small mountain. He laughed in delight.

"O-baw!"

He made another snowball and threw it, and another and another. Always with the left hand. Delaney understood why he kept shifting spoons over his cornflakes. *Looks like we've got a southpaw here. Like his grandmother. Like Molly.*

"O-baw!" the boy squealed. "O-baw."

He looked at Delaney, as if trying to decide how far he could go. Delaney smiled. And then the boy dove into one of the snow mountains and rolled and pummeled the snow with his arms and kicked with his small legs.

"O! O! O! O!"

The boy fell asleep in his arms as he carried him up the stairs. Delaney laid him on his own unmade bed and removed the heavy clothes and the shoes. The boy came suddenly awake, his eyes taking in the strange room and Delaney's face. He didn't move and looked afraid.

"Mamá? Dónde está Mamá?"

"Don't worry. She's coming back."

Thinking: She'd better come back. Fast. I can't do this. He felt a wash of dread. Something out of rainy dawns with fixed bayonets. Thinking: I must read the letter. Afraid of it too. Thinking: I want to hit someone. Anyone. But not this boy.

"Everything's okay," Delaney said softly. "Todo bien, Carlos."

The boy's eyes moved around the room. His left hand went to his crotch.

"Oh, okay, I understand, come on."

He lifted the boy and took him to the bathroom between the bedroom and the living room. He lifted the seat and helped the boy stand on the ceramic rim of the toilet. Delaney thought: I need to get a box in here. A cheese box, low and flat and strong. I can paint it red. Or maybe yellow. What else do I need? What does the boy need that I cannot give him? When the boy was finished, Delaney showed him the chain for flushing and how to do it, and then turned on the hot water in the sink. He washed with a facecloth, and then the boy took the warm, wet cloth and washed his own face. Delaney dried him, lifted him, and took him back to the bed. He covered the boy with sheet and blanket, and the boy pushed his face into the pillow. He was still for a long moment. Then he sobbed.

"Mamá, Mamá, dónde está?" he murmured.

Delaney went to the boy and sat beside him. The boy's need and uncertainty — perhaps even fear — were almost tangible. He patted the boy on the back, swift, steady pats like an extra pulse, and spoke in a low voice. *It's all right, boy. You're safe here. You will eat. You will sleep. Your mama will be back.* But as the child's sobs ended, Delaney could sense unspoken questions rising in the warming air: Where am I, and who is this man, and where is my mother? He placed his hand firmly on the boy's back, steadying him the way he had steadied so many people who were injured, hurting, confused, and full of fear. On beds all over the neighborhood. At last the child fell into sleep.

The clock told Delaney it was two thirty-seven in the afternoon. The end of a very long morning. He stood up as silently as possible and put some fresh coals on the fire. And now? What now? The letter. I must read the letter from Grace. He fought off a shimmer of dread by thinking only of the immediate needs of the boy. I can lay out a bed for him on the floor, made of blankets and pillows, just for tonight. Or take him to one of the two bedrooms upstairs. But what if he wakes up in the dead of night? I can't have him roaming the stairs in the dark. Christ . . .

His own exhaustion was eating at him now. As he undressed and donned pajamas, he wondered about Eddie Corso. About who shot him and why. About whether he would live. As always, questions but no answers. He'd have to wait. The nuns had taken Eddie into their consoling hands. Now he had other things to do. Or one big thing. He had to read the fucking letter.

TWO

New Year's Eve.
Dear Daddy,

I am so sorry to do this to you. I hate doing this to me too, because I love this boy. But I've come to realize that I can't be his mother right now. My mind is a mess, as it has been for a long time, something you must know better than anyone. Something is sure to snap. I feel that I might do harm to myself, and to the boy. You don't need that to happen.

I remember the time you first took me to the Frick, when I was eleven, and I saw for the first time the Vermeer. It was an image of domestic perfection on the earth and it made me long for a life of such perfection. It also made me want to be a painter. To live in the safety of a studio, to create my own world. I seem to have failed at all that. When you wrote me last year about Momma's death, if that is what it is, I didn't answer because I was convinced that the world was basically shit. Only my son made me believe that it was worth going on.

His name is Carlos Zapata Santos. He answers to Carlito. He talks some good Spanish and a few words of English. His father's name is Rafael Santos, as you know. I don't know where Rafael is. He could be in Spain, which is where he said he was going, or in Moscow. I don't know. We've been apart for four months. I'm going to try to find him.

Carlito will be three on St. Patrick's Day. Día de San Patricio, as they say in Mexico. Viva Irlanda! He does not wet the bed. He takes a nap, una siesta, every afternoon, and he sleeps well at night. He's had a shot for smallpox and shots in Albuquerque for diphtheria and tetanus. He seems very healthy. You will know better than anyone what else he might need. He is very intelligent. He was never baptized. Ni modo, as the Mexicans say. No matter.

I don't know how much Carlos remembers his father. Even in Mexico, he saw very little of him, while Rafael was working at the Secretaría de Educación Popular, creating education programs for other people's children. Rafael left last July, saying he was going away to continue his revolutionary education and would send for me and Carlito later. He said he was going to Spain and then possibly to Moscow, and would bring his lessons back to Mexico. He never came back. He never sent for me. And so I must find him or go mad. I am, after all, my mother's daughter.

I stayed on with his family, a kind of prisoner, for three months, hoping to hear from him, and then took Carlito and slipped away in the night. I went to Taos in New Mexico, where some New York painters have settled, and I supported myself selling insipid landscapes to tourists. God help me, but I was so lonely I even had an affair with a watercolor painter! I should have come home to your house, but my vanity was too powerful. I couldn't even ask you for help. Until now.

Even now, I cannot knock on your door, cannot face you. Forgive me. Before everything else, I must find Rafael. Wherever he is. Carlito needs his father. I need my husband. After that, I can live a human life, in what I hope becomes a better world. Please, Daddy, try to understand. Please . . . If you call me selfish, or spoiled (as Mother so often did), fair enough. But understand that I must do this in order to live. And to give Carlito the life he deserves.

None of this is your fault. You were never anything but a wonderful, loving father. You gave me the gifts of art, of music, of literature, and above all, the example of simple human kindness. The way you have given so many gifts to the people of our neighborhood, comforting them, saving their lives. You taught by example. By doing. The problem was never you. The problem was me. I have some flaw in me, some kind of emptiness that can't be filled. At least not so far. I am almost twenty years old and nothing at all seems certain. There's something in me that causes me to hurt everyone who loves me.

I don't want to pass that flaw, whatever it is, to Carlito.

I ask only one thing. That you don't put him up for adoption. I realize that you have so many things to do, and so little money, but if he is adopted by someone, he'll vanish as surely as his father has. America is too big. So is New York. Please don't let him vanish. My first stop is Barcelona. I will check American Express every day. I will send you an address, and if you say that you are giving up on my son, I'll be on the next boat home.

I've saved almost eight hundred dollars and will use it to find Rafael, to come back with him, to try one final time to make something that can last, or to end it. Please forgive me for everything. I will love you for as long as I have life.

Your daughter, Grace

Delaney sat in the old worn chair beside the fireplace, the pages of the letter on his lap. He pictured his daughter out in the raging snow, pushing her son in a two-dollar stroller with the river wind at her back, and he thought of her life, and his own, and he began to weep.

He woke in the blue light of evening, to the boy's angry wailing for his mother. Delaney placed a hand on his shoulder, tapping rapidly and gently with his fingers, saying over and over that it was okay, boy, don't cry, boy, everything's gonna be okay. The boy then wept in a clogged way, punctuating his lament with a single word: Mamá.

Delaney switched on the lamp, took a tissue from beside the bed, and touched the boy, then placed the tissue at his nose. "Blow," he said. The boy froze for a moment, his eyes full of tears, rivulets of tears marking his cheeks. Delaney gestured with his own fingers at his nose. "Blow."

The boy blew. Once, then again. Then looked around at the strange world.

"Everything's okay," Delaney said, as the boy stared at him. "Todo bien."

The boy's lower lip jutted out, as if he would cry, then he seemed to gather himself. Delaney pointed at his own chest.

"I'm your Grandpa," he said. He jabbed his chest again. "Grandpa."

The boy whispered, "Ga'paw."

"That's right!" Delaney said, smiling. "Grandpa."

The boy smiled too.

"Ga'paw."

Delaney lifted him. "Let's get dressed." The boy's head was beside Delaney's ear.

"Co'flakes, Ga'paw . . ."

"No, something better than that." Delaney glanced at the front windows. The snow had nearly stopped. He tickled the boy and Carlito giggled. "How about spaghetti!"

Carlito couldn't figure out the word, but they washed and dressed and then went out to the evening streets together. The snow was lighter now. The boy's eyes widened. Hundreds of kids were pushing each other on sleds, throwing snowballs like warriors, climbing great piles of snow that had buried all the parked cars. Long dark blue shadows were cast by the tenement on the corner, that grim factory for making children, and criminals, and illness. But all was luminous in the general whiteness. The sidewalks were gone under the snow, and the only path was in the middle of the street. Adults hurried along with modest bags of groceries, fighting for traction, shouting at the snowballers for a cease-fire while they passed. Carlito stopped walking, the snow near his knees, and watched. Then he reached down and tried to pack a snowball, but the dry cold powder blew out of his small hands. His brow furrowed. "Take a little time," Delaney said, squatting and holding fresh snow tightly in his own hands until it annealed. "See, like this . . ." Then he packed a ball and handed it to Carlito. "*Now* you can throw it, boy," Delaney said, making a gesture. "Throw the snowball." Carlito heaved it awkwardly with his mittened left hand toward a snow mountain and laughed in delight. He grabbed more snow in both hands. "Wait," Delaney said. "Easy now. Pack it, and count. One, two, three, four, five — how's that?" The boy had his snowball now and then he threw it three feet into a snowbank and clapped both mittened hands. "*Hoe*-ball! *Hoe*-ball!"

Then Delaney got hit between the shoulder blades. He turned to the gang of young snipers and sappers and shouted, "Hold it, hold it! *Cease fire!*" His words were muffled by the snow and the ferocity of combat. The ambush artists shouted their taunts, and Carlito seemed alarmed. But Delaney laughed and lifted him with his left hand to his own shoulders. They hurried together out of no-man's-land, where nothing at all could remind the boy of his mother.

They made a right at Hudson Street, moving south on the wide avenue. No trains were in sight on the elevated railroad. The streetlights were out, telling Delaney that the storm had knocked out the electricity, which was why the El was not working and the phones were dead. The bars and food shops were open, with candles lighting their interiors, and the street itself was a kind of party, Horatio Street multiplied by a factor of ten. Not like Times Square the night before, if Times Square was as it always was on New Year's Eve. But close. More a downtown version of Brueghel. In a few Italian stores, including Nobiletti's shoemaking shop, the front pages of the *News* and *Mirror* had been taped to the inside of the front windows, showing La Guardia being sworn in at midnight. The headlines shouted: IT'S MAYOR FIORELLO and HERE'S THE MAYOR! And Delaney realized he had not yet read the newspapers. He wondered if any Republican had ever been honored this way in the history of Hudson Street, so deep in the heart of what his father always called Tammanyland. Certainly this was unique, because Fiorello was the city's first Italian mayor, fifty years after the first Italians came down the gangways onto Ellis Island. They called them Wops then, which stood for "without papers." Now one of them was the mayor of the greatest city in America. Tribal pride. But there were no other signs of politics on Hudson Street. There was only the snow and the kids and the sense of shared natural disaster, which always gave New York a special exuberance. And placed images into the very young, which would return in trembling dreams, as the Blizzard of '88 had returned to Delaney just this morning. Carlito would probably dream of this day for the rest of his life.

They finally reached Angela's restaurant at the moment when electricity returned to the western side of the street. Cheers erupted along with more barrages of snowballs, and Delaney lowered the boy and hurried with him into the restaurant. Thinking: Goddamn you, Grace, you should be here with us. You should be whispering to your son. This sweet baffled boy that you've abandoned to my incompetent arms. Goddamn it all to hell.

There were about a dozen customers at the tables, couples, parties of four, a few of them blowing out the emergency candles as the surging electricity reached Angela's. The aroma of garlic and oil filled the room, and from somewhere in the rear, beside the kitchen, an Italian radio station suddenly played music. At one corner table, four Tammany politicians poked glumly at their pasta, one of them smoking a cigarette while he ate. Delaney tried to remember the name of the presiding pol. A judge now. A friend of his father's. Since midnight, the Republicans, and that goddamned La Guardia, owned City Hall, and the pols' world was turned upside down. They all nodded at Delaney and looked curiously at Carlito.

In another corner was Knocko Carmody, his black derby hat firmly in place over his Irish face of pink cement. He had three union lieutenants with him. Delaney tipped his union cap to Knocko and the man's eyes brightened. He smiled, his fork wrapped with pasta, threw Delaney a thumbs-up with his free hand, and made a sign that they would talk later. They knew each other from grammar school, and during the past summer, Delaney had saved his wife from peritonitis when her appendix burst. He realized that half the crowd had been in his office at one time or another.

Then from the rear, an enormous smiling woman came forward to greet them, her makeup heavy, gold bangles bouncing from gold posts in her earlobes. She had immense breasts, and a button was open at the top of her blouse, showing her cleavage. Her olive skin was glazed with fine perspiration from the heat of the kitchen. A wide white apron was tied behind her back.

"Angela, Happy New Year!" Delaney said.

"Same to you, Doc," the woman said, her voice burred by tobacco. "And who's this little movie star?"

"My grandson. He's staying with me for a while."

"Whatta you mean, a while?" she said softly.

She gave Delaney a look that said: This must mean trouble.

Delaney shrugged. "I don't know yet."

Angela nodded, sighed, took them to a small corner table, where Delaney hung the boy's mackinaw on a wall peg and placed his own jacket and cap above it.

"Wait," Angela said. "I got a thing he can sit on."

She went into the back, past the kitchen, and returned with a high chair. She put the boy on the floor and tied a bib under his chin. She lifted the tray of the high chair, put the boy snugly into the seat, lowered the tray, then pushed the chair to the table. All in a few expert seconds. The boy was to Delaney's right, the perfect spot for a left-hander.

"You want some clams?" Angela said. "I got some in from Georgia. Just two days ago. Before the trains stopped wit' the snow."

"Let me think a minute," Delaney said. "I promised him spaghetti, so . . ."

"So I give him a kid portion, and you —"

"Why not? Spaghetti. With the clams . . ."

As they waited, the boy's brown eyes moved around the crowded room, with its haze of burnt nicotine, and the pictures on the ochre walls. The Bay of Naples. A view of Palermo. Both gauzy with nostalgia. Both painted by Fierro, the sign painter, who had a shop on Ninth Avenue, a Sicilian married to a Neapolitan in what some people called a mixed marriage. There were other pictures in Angela's gallery. A heroic painting of Garibaldi, brought over from the old country by a customer. A painting of flowers on green fields. Photographs of Angela when she was younger and thinner. Her family in the old country, a year before they took the ship to La Merica, where Angela was born a few doors away from Transfiguration Church on Mott Street. Mother and father were still alive, both patients of Delaney's. And there on the wall, standing alone, was Frankie Fischetti, the first kid from Hudson Street to be killed in the war. Carlito blinked, his eyes like a camera shutter, as if freezing each new thing he saw into memory. He had been taken by his mother to a world of many rooms.

A young waiter arrived with a basket of Italian bread, a fat slab of butter, a dish of olive oil. He rubbed the boy's blond hair and hurried away. The waiter was quickly replaced by Angela, carrying a bottle of Chianti.

"For the New Year," she whispered, so the Tammany boys would not hear. "And for Fiorello. Don't get use' to it."

She laughed and went away. Delaney poured an inch of the wine into his glass, tore off a crust of bread, and handed it to the boy.

"This is a restaurant, Carlito," Delaney said, waving a hand around the long room. "Where people come to eat."

The boy listened but said nothing, trying to decode this new, secret script. He must have learned some English in New Mexico, Delaney thought, while his mother peddled paintings of mountain ranges. He must have been in restaurants there, even with his mother saving every dollar for the search for her husband. He must know more than he lets on. The way his mother was when she was three. He must remember the watercolor painter too. The door opened and a pair of St. Vincent's interns came in, overcoats buttoned tight over green uniforms, their eyes frazzled and hungry. Neither man was Jake Zimmerman, savior of Eddie Corso. They stood by the door, eyeing a tiny empty table to their left, the last one in the place. Delaney recognized them from the hospital but couldn't remember their names. They smiled when they saw him, mouthed greetings for the New Year. Delaney beckoned to one of them, and the young man leaned over.

"How's that special patient of Dr. Zimmerman?"

The intern paused, then said: "Okay. He'll live. He doesn't exist, but he'll live."

"Good," Delaney said. "Had a rough twenty-four hours?"

"Everything. People falling in the snow and breaking arms, elbows, wrists, and heads. Old ladies tripping down stairs. Babies close to death 'cause there's no goddamned heat. Everything. Hell, you know how it is."

Delaney nodded. "Well, stay safe."

"Thanks, Dr. Delaney."

Yes, he knew how it was. He had interned at Bellevue, bigger and crazier than St. Vincent's. Before the war. They owned one of the first ambulances, after cars came to the city, but it didn't work in snow or ice, and not very well in rain. Thirty-six hours on, eighteen hours off. Just Delaney and a driver. The calls came from the police, and then they raced to the scene, to the man trapped in an elevator pit, to the woman who slashed her wrists after discovering she had a dose of the clap passed to her by her husband, the four-year-old boy whipped into unconsciousness by his father, the girl who gave birth in the vacant lot, her child strangled on the umbilical cord. He knew how it was. Caging emotion. Accepting numbness. Good training for a war. Or a marriage.

The door opened and two more Tammany guys arrived in search of consolation.

He'll live. Eddie Corso will live.

"Here ya go," said Angela, breaking his reverie with two bowls of spaghetti on a tray. She placed the larger one, dotted with clams, in front of Delaney. The boy stared at his bowl. It had no clams, but he did not ask why.

"I know it's a *real* New Year now," Delaney said. "Service by the boss."

He lifted his small glass of wine in a wordless toast and smiled.

"Like I said, Doc. Don't get use' to it."

The interns were seated now, and the room was noisier, a full house, with a steady murmur of talk, Puccini now playing on the hidden radio. It was like being at an opera where the audience talked though the performance. The murmur was punctuated by sudden bursts of laughter, except from the politicians.

"Spaghetti," Delaney said, pointing at the bowls.

"Bagetti," the boy said.

With his left hand, he tried to twirl the slippery strands of spaghetti on his fork, but they kept falling, and Delaney leaned over and cut them into smaller pieces. The boy stabbed at them with his fork and then grabbed a few strands and started chewing. He made a face — what is this taste? — and then decided he liked it, and tried again with the fork, and this time succeeded. Delaney smiled.

"Bagetti," the boy said. "No co'flake."

"*Right.* Spaghetti."

Chairs scraped on the floor, and Delaney turned. Knocko Carmody was approaching him, smiling. The others from his table were standing now too.

"Does this kid have a union card?" he said, his voice a growl but his eyes twinkling. The other three stayed back, as respectful as lieutenants to a general.

"He's coming to the hiring hall this summer, Knocko."

"Just bring him around. He gets a card, just showing up."

At the hard sound of Knocko's voice, Carlito stopped eating but then quickly resumed.

"Who's this?" Knocko whispered.

"My grandson."

"Grace's kid?"

"Yeah."

"And where's the beautiful Grace?"

"Away."

He said the word as if naming something permanent.

"Shit," Knocko said.

"Yeah."

They'd known each other too long to invent a story.

"You need some help, you know where to find me."

"Thanks, Knocko."

Out he went, into the snowy street. He was flanked by two of the men, and the third walked directly behind him. There was a clatter of dishes as the waiter cleared their table. Delaney glanced at Carlito. All the spaghetti was gone from his bowl. Some was on the checkered tablecloth, some on the bib or the floor. Delaney lifted a portion of his own pasta and placed it in the boy's bowl. He sipped his wine and finished eating. Angela returned with a wet cloth and began cleaning the boy's face and hands.

"This kid don't fool around," she said.

"He's an eater."

"He's gonna be pretty big," she said. "Look at them feet."

"With any luck."

Carlito must have sensed that they were talking about him, but he said nothing.

"I got something else for you," she said to the boy.

She waved at a waiter, made a spooning gesture. The waiter shouted something into the kitchen, then hurried over to take away the pasta dishes.

"You're gonna need help," Angela said, her face grave. "A lot of help."

"I know."

"You can't go running out on house calls carrying a three-year-old with you."

"I know." He laughed. "But you know what I really need first? I need a cheese box. The boy can't reach the bowl when he stands in front of it."

Angela laughed.

"I don't have one here, and the cheese store is closed. Wait'll to-morrow."

The waiter arrived with two dishes of vanilla ice cream and two spoons. The boy smiled. This was food he had seen before his journey to New York.

"You're gonna need a woman," Angela said.

He carried the boy part of the way on his shoulders, leaning into the wind, fighting to keep his balance, but bumping the boy up and down in a kind of dance. Carlito laughed in delight. Then he stopped laughing, and Delaney slipped him off his shoulders, saw that his eyes were closed, and held him close for the rest of the journey west on Horatio Street. A taxi pulled up in the center of the snow-packed street. A well-dressed man and woman stepped out. The Cottrells from next door. Both were Delaney's age. From 93 Horatio. His neighbors. They didn't look at him. They never did. Not since that summer afternoon four years earlier, when their son was knocked down by a speeding car driven by a drunk. At the sound of screeching brakes, Delaney rushed outside. He did what he could for the boy while an ambulance slogged through traffic from St. Vincent's. But it was too late. The boy was dead. Nine years old. The only boy among three sisters. The Cottrells chose to blame Delaney and never spoke to him again.

As the gate of the Cottrells' house clanged shut, he could feel the boy's warmth, and his vulnerability on this street in the perilous city. Don't worry, boy, he thought. I'll make everything work. Or die trying.

Later, by the light of candles, he sat in his big chair with a notebook in his lap. Through the open oak doors that separated the bedroom from the rear, he could hear the shallow breathing of the sleeping Carlito. He began to write down the things he would need. Maybe fit out one of the maids' rooms upstairs. A good bed. Clothes, guards for the stairs. Food. Including spaghetti. *Monique will help, after she returns tomorrow.* Money too. Money most of all. Not easy, at two dollars for a consultation, three for a house call.

This goddamned Depression. When will it ever end? He couldn't charge a patient who had sixty cents to last a week. He couldn't turn away anybody because of money, or the lack of it. He couldn't ever charge a veteran. Not ever. In the week before Christmas, he had earned forty-two goddamned dollars. And he paid Monique twenty.

He thought about applying for a loan. From St. Vincent's. Or some bank. Maybe one of the vested old Tammany pols knew a banker. That judge, whatever the hell his name was. But in all the years since his father had died, Delaney had asked them for nothing. Ah, Big Jim, would I even ask *you?* If you were here, would you come to my rescue? Could I even ask? He dozed, and saw himself filling in a form under the lipless stare of a bank manager.

Name	James Finbar Delaney.
Address	95 Horatio Street, New York, N.Y.
Age	47. Almost 48.
Date of birth	June 24, 1886. I was two during the Blizzard of '88.
Place of birth	New York, N.Y.
Names of parents	James Aloysius Delaney and wife Bridget George (both deceased)
Their country of origin	Ireland
Did they love each other?	Of course.
Did they love you?	With everything they had in them. In their own separate ways.
Other siblings	None alive. Two died when very young.
Marital status	Married, with an explanation
Name of spouse	Molly O'Brien (Delaney)
Her place of birth	Co. Antrim, Northern Ireland
Citizenship	American (naturalized: 1912)
How did you meet?	On a dock over at the North River. She was ill. I'm a doctor.
Issue	Daughter Grace, born July 1, 1914
Your education	Sacred Heart grammar school (graduated 1899) Xavier HS (graduated 1903) City College of N.Y. (graduated 1907) New York Medical School (graduated 1909) Internship, Bellevue Hospital, N.Y., 1909–1911 Johns Hopkins, 1911–1913 Postgraduate studies in surgery, Vienna, 1913–1914
Military service	United States Army (AEF medical corps), 1917–1919

Employer's name	Self-employed
Annual income	$1900–$2200 p.a. (avg.)
That's all?	It used to be more. Until 1929 . . .

Delaney could feel the banker's chilly rejection. He listened for the boy, who was breathing in a steady way.

Any persistent ailments? Heartbreak.

He lifted the candle and his daughter's letter. Time to go upstairs. To Molly's floor. The shrine of the past, soon to be filled with the future.

Delaney opened the small rooms first, two of them, with single windows facing the backyard. The rooms of the Irish maids, who served a haughty family long ago. The shades were drawn. In the light of the candle, he saw an old-fashioned lamp on a small table beside a bed. He lifted it and felt the weight of oil, turned up the wick, placed the candle against the wick. Orange light filled the room, along with the burnt, sour odor of stale oil. Thank you, Lord, for small miracles. He blew out the candle. There were paintings by Grace on the walls of each room, done while she was a teenaged girl at the Art Students League. A gypsy. A man with a turban. An old woman. The brushstrokes were bold. God, she was so confident then.

There was a bed for Grace in one of the low-ceilinged rooms, but the other was empty. When she was thirteen, that became her studio, with her ceramic tabletop and her easel and her tabouret. She loved that room, especially when morning light came streaming in. He noticed splatters of old paint on the floors, and opened the closet door to see her brushes and various jars and cups and tubes of paint. He lifted one tube of burnt sienna. It felt like iron.

He looked into the bathroom, saw the old tub with its lion's feet upon the tiles and the ceramic sink with its chipped edge. He turned the tap. The water flowed, rusty and coughing and then clear. When Grace made watercolors, she washed her brushes here. Never oils, she said. Because they would clog the drains. She soaked those brushes in turpentine, then used the faucet in the garden. Now on the top floor, the cold was total, like an apartment in Siberia. Delaney wished he had risked everything before the Crash to install steam heat. Each small room had a kerosene heater, and in the winter when they were all together here, Mr. Lanzano would lug the kerosene cans up the stairs without complaint, while his son helped deliver the blocks of ice through summer heat. The kerosene odor was awful, but Grace as a teenager said she loved it. *Oh, Daddy, it's so* real! How long did she live here? Eight years? No, seven. And is it the odor of kerosene that urges me even now, in blizzards, to sleep with the window open?

Delaney paused before unlocking the door to the large room at the front of the house. Molly's room. He hadn't opened this door since that August night when he heard her playing one of the preludes. She had been gone for a year then, and now it was January, which meant it was sixteen months since Molly vanished. Last August he was alone in bed in the vast oaken emptiness and hurried upstairs and opened the door. The music stopped. He called her name. Molly! O my Molly-O.

But she wasn't there. There was no sound at all in the empty house, except his own heavy breathing.

That night was twelve months after she had vanished, and tonight she still wasn't there. She might never be in this room again. This room that was her secret garden of books and music and dreams. Right up to the moment when she went down the stairs and started walking to the river, the breeze ruffling her blue dress. Other people saw her go, but I was out on house calls. Goddamn it all to hell.

He took a breath, exhaled, and went in.

The room was as it always was: wide, the ceiling higher than in the small maids' rooms in the rear. The hardwood floors looked gray under a coat of fine dust. The fireplace awaited a fire. The piano stood near the windows, properly grand in spite of the dust, filling the space between the windows. Delaney sat down on the wide sturdy bench and could see Molly's heroes, framed upon the wall. Mr. Bach. Mr. Mozart. Mr. Brahms. Mr. Scott Joplin. Mr. Arnold Schoenberg. In the years after the war, he was away so much on calls, or at the hospital doing grand rounds, or tending to patients, that she often played only for her masters

The wall on the right was stacked from floor to ceiling with his books and hers. Many of his were on the top shelves, near the ceiling, some going back to high school, dozens from Johns Hopkins before the war. The textbooks were filled with the medical ignorance of the day, now worthless rubbish that could not even be sold to the dealers on Fourth Avenue. And yet he could not throw them out. Once he loved them and learned from them. They were now like aging teachers whose time had passed. Then his eyes fell to the lower shelves, full of treasures. Dickens and Stevenson and Mark Twain. Conrad and Galsworthy, Henry James and Edith Wharton. On one shelf, Theodore Dreiser leaned against Dostoyevsky, and he remembered how sure he once was that they were snarling at each other, each filled with certainty. To their left, unable to soothe them, was the good Dr. Chekhov. With any luck, these books will be the patrimony of the boy. And who will teach him how to read?

There too was his chair, with its thick rounded arms and its ratty green brocaded covering. The place into which he would sink at the end of a fatiguing day. There he would read novels to know more about human beings, who were, after all, his basic subject, and still were. The medical books didn't tell such stories. Only novels did. Sometimes Molly would play a concert for him alone. When she wanted to annoy him, or irritate him for some infraction of decent manners, she would play Schoenberg, knowing that Schoenberg would always break his trance. When she wanted to move him into sleep, she played Brahms. She knew that men broken by war need lullabies. *O my Molly-O.*

He opened a closet filled with dusty luggage and Molly's old summer dresses, and lifted a small valise down from a high shelf. He turned a small key in the lock and clicked it open and then placed his daughter's letter into a folder with her other notes from distant places. The folder was on top of those from Molly. Letters Molly wrote to him in France. Earlier letters full of plans and hope. The 1918 letter sent to his hospital bed in Paris, as his ruined arm slowly healed. The letter telling him about his mother and father and how they had died in the influenza epidemic. Along with thirty thousand others in New York alone and millions all over the planet. Some of the older letters were full of longing for him, pulsing with love and desire. From the time before the slow darkness fell. Letters that made him bubble with happiness. Letters that made him weep. Only later, as time dragged and healing slowed and his stay in the French hospital was prolonged, only then did Molly's tone alter into icy anger. Have you forgotten you have a daughter? she wrote. Have you forgotten you have a wife? And why did you go to that stupid war anyway? You didn't have to go. You were never going to be drafted. You volunteered! Why? Over and over. Why? Those letters were there too. He clicked the valise shut, locked it, and placed it back on the shelf.

Then he lighted the candle again and shut down the oil lamp, locked the door behind him, and went down one flight to bed. His pajamas felt cold. He placed more coal on the fire and looked at the sleeping boy in his corner of the huge bed. There were no sounds from the street, as the silent neighborhood huddled under the smothering blankets of snow.

He slipped into bed in the dark.

O Molly. Come home, Molly. I need you now. Come and play for me. Come and play for this boy. Come home, my Molly-O.

THREE

THE WOMAN ARRIVED JUST BEFORE SEVEN O'CLOCK THE NEXT morning. At the first ring of the bell, Delaney was in the cellar, shoveling coal into the small boiler that heated the water. A flashlight was perched on a milk box. The sound of the bell first made him think it was Bootsie again. Some demand in the ringing. A feeling of alarm. And Monique was not yet at her desk. He closed the furnace door, laid down the shovel, grabbed the flashlight, and went up the darkened stairs, afraid the sound would wake the boy. But Carlito was already awake, sitting on the stairs near the bottom, his pajamas blotchy with urine. He must have tried, Delaney thought. He must have stood on the bowl and tried. The boy hugged Delaney's leg as if consumed with shame, and the doctor hefted him and carried him to the door under the stoop. This should take only a minute, boy, he whispered. Hug me to stay warm.

The woman stood beyond the gate, snow on her wool hat and shoulders. She was in her middle thirties, with olive skin, a longish nose, a strong jaw, a faint mustache. Her body looked heavy under her dark blue coat, and she was wearing men's boots. Her black eyes glistened. She was carrying a woolen bag and a cheese box.

"I'm Rose," she said in a gruff voice. "Angela sent me."

"Come in, Rose. Come in."

She stepped in as Delaney backed up, her feet crunching on the hard snow that had blown in through the night. She pulled the gate shut. Steam was easing from her heavy lips. She stomped her boots on the mat and, as Delaney held the vestibule door open, passed into the hallway. Delaney closed the second door behind her.

"This is him, huh?" she said, and smiled.

"This is Carlito."

She grinned more widely, showing hard white teeth, and turned to Delaney.

"Okay. Where's the bathtub?"

Still in bathrobe and work shirt, Delaney brushed his teeth and washed at the sink while water ran into the small bathtub. An old showerhead rose above the tub. Steam drifted from the running water, and he used his fingers to wipe a space in the fogged-out mirror. The bathroom door was still open, and he saw Rose drape her coat over a chair. She looked thinner in a long dark dress that went below her knees, over the men's boots. Then she pushed into the bathroom and placed the cheese box at the foot of the bowl. She removed the boy's clothes, dropped them on the floor, and wrapped him in a large beige towel to keep him warm. The boy's eyes were wide. What was this? *Who was this?* How many people were there in this world?

"Okay, get out," she said to Delaney. "Get dressed. I gotta wash this boy."

Delaney wiped his face, dried it, smiling as he shut the bathroom door behind him. He pulled on trousers, a clean shirt, socks, and boots. He could hear her low affectionate voice through the door:

"What a handsome boy. All nice and clean now, you're gonna be nice and clean. Hey, what's this thing? What you got there? Nice and clean now. And your hair? Gotta wash that too. Pretty blond hair. Can't wear it dirty."

Thank you, Rose. Thank you, Angela.

There was a slight New York curl in her voice, "doity" instead of "dirty." She dropped the *d* off every "and." The *h* was banished from "thing." She must be here a while. She's definitely not just off the boat. Then the telephone rang for the first time in many hours. He lifted it.

"Hey, it's me," Monique said. "I'm at the telephone company. I told them we need the goddamned phone. I told them, hey, the man's a *doctor,* people could die. Then I shot three guys at the front desk. *That* worked."

Delaney laughed.

"What would I do without you, Monique?"

"You'd be doing house calls, that's what. The patients must be going nuts trying to get through to you. I'll be there in maybe twenty minutes."

"I've got a surprise waiting for you."

"I don't like surprises."

"You might love this one."

"See you."

She hung up. He buttoned his shirt. How long have you been here, Monique? How long have you been nurse and secretary and bouncer? Since we laid out the office. Since before the goddamned Depression. Since Hoover was president. Since the time when Molly found her secret garden on the top floor, her aerie, her retreat. Away from Monique, who annoyed her with her energy or her precision or her daily presence. Away from the patients. Away from me. The bathroom door opened and Rose was there, smiling a lovely smile, her face glistening from the small steamy room, snuggling the boy with one arm to her generous breasts and lifting clothes from the stroller with her other hand. Carlito was smiling too, pointing a finger at Delaney, then curling it. She dressed him quickly in two shirts and corduroy trousers.

"Now, where's the kitchen?" she said.

Delaney led her downstairs again to the kitchen, the boy back in her arms.

"This is small," she said darkly.

He tried to explain how he needed space on this floor for a waiting area, a consulting room, a small bathroom for patients, but she wasn't really listening. They went into the kitchen and she put the boy down on a chair. And Carlito pointed to the pantry.

"Co'flay," he said.

"You want co'flakes? Okay, boy. "

How did she know co'flay was cornflakes? The telephone rang and Delaney hurried into the consulting room to answer it. Annie Haggerty. About her mother, around the corner on Lispenard Street. She was hurt. Bleeding and moaning.

"Where's your father, Annie?" he said, knowing he was talking to a girl who was about fourteen.

"Out."

"Is your mother awake?"

"Yeah."

"Is she bleeding?"

"Yeah."

"Where?"

"Face."

"Nose? Mouth? Ears?"

"Yeah."

"All of them?"

"Yeah."

"I'll be over as soon as I can. Keep talking to your mother, Annie. Keep her awake."

"Okay."

He wrote a note to himself: the name Haggerty, the word "blood."

He knew the building too well. The telephone rang again. *Hurry, Monique.* This was Larry Dorsey's wife. He was a saxophone player in some Times Square hotel.

"Doc, it's Larry. He got hurt New Year's Eve, some fight, drunks throwin' chairs. You know. He got hit on the head, but he won't go to St. Vincent's. Goddamned Irish, don't want to go to hospitals."

He took her address on Bank Street and then went to the kitchen.

"You get more calls than a bookmaker," Rose said. Her English is good, Delaney thought, but who is she? Carlito was delighted with his cornflakes.

"Many more."

She was going through the pantry.

"Not many pots and pans. The icebox is great, electric and all. But we gotta get some food in here for this boy."

"Yes, we do, Rose. Plenty of food. Maybe when my nurse, Monique, gets here, you can —"

"And we gotta get rid of that stroller," she said, pronouncing it "strolla." "That thing will give you a disease or something."

The telephone rang again.

The snow was piled high on Lispenard Street as Delaney trudged toward number 12, shifting his heavy leather bag from gloved hand to gloved hand. Today a change in routine. House calls in the morning or Mary Haggerty might die. Trucks were pushing for passage to the meat market, where Harry Haggerty was a butcher. Delaney knew the street well. Herman Melville had worked here, right in that building, waiting for ships to arrive so he could clerk the cargo. A job that he needed because nobody was buying his books. Even today nobody anywhere around here had heard of the white whale. Or Ahab. Or Queequeg. Or Melville himself . . . He climbed to the second floor and knocked.

"Yeah?" came the girl's voice.

"Dr. Delaney."

She unlocked the door and Delaney went in. The girl was trembling and pale, her hair frazzled, her eyes wet. There was an odor of excrement in the air.

"Where's your mother, Annie?"

She led him to the back bedroom, where the odor was stronger. The woman's face was swollen blue. Her husband had literally beaten the shit out of her. One eye was closed. The other was skittery with fear. Her nose had been pounded to the side.

"Annie," he said to the girl, "boil a pot of water, will you, dear?"

All the way to Bank Street on his second call, he struggled with his rage. The story was too familiar. Big tough Harry Haggerty had come home loaded, demanded his supper, and when his wife served it cold, he started pounding her. He had to punch real hard. After all, he only had seventy-five pounds on her. Then he passed out on the couch, and went off to work at dawn. Big tough guy. Knowing that the cops would do nothing. Just another domestic dispute. If she died, maybe they'd make an arrest. . . . Delaney had done what he could: cleaned the wounds, applied bandages, checked for broken bones, gave her some aspirin and a painkiller, and told Annie to hold ice to her face. She should come see him when the swelling went down, and they would discuss what to do about her broken nose. The wounds in her mind would need much more time, and he could do little to heal them. Physician, heal thyself . . .

Larry Dorsey was in bed in the first-floor flat on Bank Street. The place was spotless, the wood polished, no dust. Wallpaper from an earlier time still looked fresh. It was an apartment without children, except Larry. Delaney could see a piano in the living room, topped with framed photographs of Louis Armstrong, Duke Ellington, and Bix Beiderbecke. A gallery of heroes, just like Molly's, but with different names and faces. Louise was heavy, wearing full makeup, her face twitching.

"Look at that," she said, pointing to her husband's head. "That ain't kosher."

She was right. There was a bulge on the right temple. Larry was conscious, but when Delaney gently touched the lump, he pulled away in pain.

"That hurt," he said.

"Is it getting larger?" Delaney said to Louise.

"Yeah," Louise said. "When he come home last night, there wasn't even a bump."

Delaney leaned in close. "Listen, Larry, we gotta get you to St. Vincent's —"

"No hospital. Not for me. Not now, not never. Everyone I ever knew went to a hospital never came back. Including my father."

"Larry, you might have a fractured skull. You might have bleeding in the brain. We need X-rays. And I don't have an X-ray machine in my bag."

"Not a chance."

Delaney sighed in an exasperated way.

"Okay, I can't force you. But tell me this: Who's your favorite undertaker?"

Louise sobbed and turned away.

"Don't make jokes, Doc," Larry whispered.

"It's no joke, Larry."

Larry said nothing. Delaney put his hands on his hips, trying to look stern.

"Come on, you dope," he said. "I'll go with you. I want to hear you play 'Stardust' again."

Delaney and Louise walked him east on icy streets to St. Vincent's. Larry Dorsey grumbled all the way. The wind rose, and they shuddered together in their heavy winter clothes. Boys shoveled snow in front of the shops. An elevated train moved slowly along the tracks into a crowded platform. The street in front of the emergency room had been plowed since he'd taken Eddie Corso through the secret door a hundred feet away from this entrance. They walked in past an empty ambulance. Delaney explained the problem to a buxom nurse named McGuinness. He saw nuns like black haystacks walking the corridors beyond.

"Thanks, Dr. Delaney. We'll take care of it. Call later and we'll know what it is."

"Thanks, Miss McGuinness. Is Dr. Zimmerman on duty?"

"Wait, I'll get him."

Zimmerman emerged from an inner room, smiling, shaking hands with Delaney, while Dorsey was led away and a second nurse took notes from Louise. The two doctors stepped to the side. Zimmerman was in his twenties, skinny, freckled, with reddish hair and bulging, inquisitive eyes. He had some Lower East Side in his voice.

"Like Grand Central around here today," Zimmerman said. "They're all digging their way out and falling down with heart attacks."

"How's our patient?"

"He's a tough nut, all right. He keeps asking for morphine and then laughing."

"Can I see him?"

"Third floor, at the end."

Zimmerman turned to see a man with a white face being carried in by two younger men. Delaney touched the intern's sleeve.

"Thanks, Doctor."

"If we get caught," Zimmerman said, "we'll do the time together."

Eddie Corso was in a bed in his private room, covered with a heavy blanket, a transparent oxygen tent over his head. He needed a shave. To the side of the door was Bootsie, looking suspicious, even anxious, trying to appear casual by examining the state of his fingernails. The shade was drawn, a light burning on a side table. Delaney parted the flap of the tent.

"Morphine, morphine . . ."

"That's a bad old joke now, Eddie."

"So am I."

Palm down, Corso curled his fingers at Bootsie, and the fat man eased out the door to stand guard in the hall. Corso smiled weakly.

"Thanks, Doc. Again."

"Thank Dr. Zimmerman."

"I did. But it was you, Doc. Without you . . ."

"Enough already."

A longer pause.

"I hear you got someone staying with you at the house."

"I do. My grandson."

"Where'd his mother go?"

"I don't know. Maybe Russia."

"Russia? Is she nuts? There ain't enough snow right here for her?"

"The truth is, I'm not really sure where she is. I think Spain. Which means she has a passport, and had a ship to catch. I called Jackie Norris at the Harbor Police and asked for his help."

"He's a good cop. You didn't mention me, did you?"

"Never. Jackie says he'll do what he can."

"He always keeps his word."

Corso closed his eyes and looked as if he were drifting. Delaney came closer.

"You hurting, Eddie?"

He opened his eyes.

"Nah. Well, just a little. You got someone to help with this boy?"

"Angela sent me a woman."

"Good. She's a Wop, I hope?"

"I think she's Italian, but I don't know. I didn't ask."

"Angela sent her, she's a Wop. Good for you, with a kid on your hands. Otherwise, you wouldn't know what the fuck you were doing."

"That's for sure."

They were silent for a while.

"Your daughter Gracie don't come back, Doc, the kid could be there a long time."

"I've thought about that."

"How old is the boy?"

"Three in March. On St. Patrick's Day."

"Jesus Christ. Another goddamned Mick. And fifteen years from now, when you're an old man, he'll be graduatin' from high school."

Delaney laughed. "I thought about that too."

Corso seemed to be fading away by the second. Delaney thought he should call Zimmerman, maybe something . . .

"You got any money?" Corso said, coming back from where he had gone.

"Enough."

"Come on. Don't bullshit me, Doc. I know you spent a mint when Molly, you know . . ."

He didn't finish the sentence. The missing words were *took off*.

"I remember you put ads in the newspapers," Corso went on. "You had them leaflets on every lamppost from Twenty-third Street to the Battery. You hired some private dick. That must have took a lot of dough."

"I've got enough, Eddie. I saved some, I have patients. The boy won't starve."

"Las' time I was in your house, when I had that thing with malaria, I froze my nuts off. You don't have *steam heat*, Doc. That kid'll be runnin' around bare ass and —"

"The woman will watch him."

"Freezing her own ass off too."

Corso turned his head to the wall and sighed.

"How long's it been now?" he whispered. "Since Molly went —"

"Sixteen months," Delaney said.

"Christ."

Corso's hand moved to the flap of the tent, then fell to his side.

"I'm thinkin' of gettin' out of this thing."

"Good."

"I don't like the way the thing is going. Moving booze, runnin' clubs, that was one thing. That was *fun,* f' Chrissakes. But that's over. It died with Prohibition." A pause. "I don't like what some of these guys want to do now. And they don't like that I don't like it. Especially the fucking Neapolitani . . . bunch of cazzi. That Frankie Botts . . ."

He cleared some phlegm from his throat, and Delaney put a tissue to his mouth so he could spit it out. The sputum was pink.

"Besides, I got three grandchildren myself now, Doc. I sent them and their mother away this morning . . ."

"They're good kids. I delivered two of them, remember? And gave all three their shots."

"Right, right . . ." He closed his eyes again briefly. "I want to see *them* graduate from high school."

"And college too."

"Hey, wouldn't *that* be something? College. They'd be the first kids in the history of the Corso family to . . ."

They were both quiet for a while. Then Delaney said, "If you get out of . . . the business, what'll you do?"

"Maybe become a priest."

Delaney laughed.

"Nah. Maybe I'll move to Florida. Or out west someplace."

"You'd go nuts."

"I'd rather be nuts than dead."

Delaney moved slowly west, into a river wind. The snow was now ice, blackening in the streets like an untreated wound, and he could not feel his face. As always, in icy winter or torrid summer, he looked down at the two or three feet ahead of him, because when he gazed into the distance he felt he could never make it. As always, he fought off the things he had seen on his house calls, the need, the pain, the false comfort he had given to these hurt people. He was a doctor, but medicine was not an exact science. There was no cure for everything. As in life. The cause of death was always life. Across many years now, he had comforted people he knew would soon die. He hoped his consoling whispers would do them no harm. He hoped too that he could reduce their immediate pain. But he could not carry them around in his head like luggage. He had to examine them with all the intensity he could muster, do what he could, avoid harm, and then forget them.

He could not forget Eddie Corso. Eddie wasn't a patient. He was a friend, the friendship created in rain and blood. And now, slipping, tottering, pausing on the black ice, Delaney saw Eddie again in the driving rain of France, knee-deep in the water of the funk hole, canteens slung around his neck, his eyes wide and half-mad. He was going to the water hole at the foot of the cliff. Knowing the Germans were up there somewhere, knowing they had machine guns and potato mashers, knowing they had what the Americans didn't have: overcoats, boots, ammunition, food, and water. The Americans had tried catching water in stretched ponchos, but the Germans shot holes in them. And shot one of the soldiers too. The remnants of the battalion could not go back, ease away in retreat, because the Germans were there too, and later it would be said that they were a lost battalion. On that night they weren't a battalion anymore. And they were not lost. They were surrounded. But Eddie said he would go for the water, as dirty as it was, and he would frisk the dead for bread or hardtack hidden beneath their tunics. Delaney told him not to go. Eddie said even the Germans had to sleep, and it was better with the pounding darkness of the rain to go now. And so he went, up over the lip of the funk hole, a New York rat slithering through broken trees and gouged earth and unburied bodies, gripping the canteens so they would make no jangling noise. See ya, Eddie said. And was gone. Delaney heard nothing except the rain hammering around them, and the snoring of soldiers up and down the trench. Then the sky was lit up by a star shell, sending spears of light through the ruined forest like something from the Fourth of July, and then the machine gun opened up. *Brrrraaaap. Brrrraaaap.* The light burned itself out. And then there was silence. The men beside Delaney did not even stir. Then, away off, he heard moaning. And he grabbed the first aid kit and lifted himself out of the funk hole and went to look for Eddie. He found him on his back in a thicket, a dozen feet from the water hole. His eyes were wide. Fresh slippery blood, thin and watery in the rain, soaked his shoulder and his arms, and there was a hole torn in one of the canteens. At least one round in the back, and blood leaking over his boots from a leg wound. Holy Jesus, Doc, it hurts like a bastard. Delaney undraped the canteens and left them in the drowned mulchy leaves. Then he saw the wound in Eddie's leg and knew he could not walk. He grabbed him under the armpits, dragging him into the denser foliage and then turned him and heaved him onto his shoulders and carried him, slipping, falling, wet with blood, back to the line. One of the other doctors, Hardin from Oklahoma, hurried from another hole, and together they ripped open Eddie's clothes and cleaned the wounds as best they could with alcohol, and tied coarse tourniquets on the ripped thigh and the smashed shoulder, using strips of uniforms from the dead because there were no bandages left. The fuckin' pain, Doc, hurts like a fuckin' bitch. Delaney gave him a shot of morphine, his own hands trembling, and the rain falling hard, and after a few minutes Eddie looked dreamy. Delaney sat for a long time in silence, thinking that if relief did not come soon, Eddie would surely die. If relief did not come soon, they all would die. He would never see Molly again. He would not see the little girl Grace. He would not ever walk with them again beside the flowing summer waters of the North River.

And here he was, walking into a hard wind on Horatio Street, the North River in sight, and the house waiting for him at number 95. On the corner, he saw four young kids riding a familiar object up and down a snowy hill. The stroller. Rose didn't waste time. A narrow path had been shoveled through the snow along the sidewalk. And into the front yard too, right to the gate under the stoop. And where now is my little girl, who is now a woman? And where is my dear Molly-O?

There were seven patients waiting in the hall, two of them standing for lack of space on the bench. Three were reading the *Daily News*, and all looked relieved to see him, smiling tentatively or nodding in approval. Five of them were women. A normal day. "Give me a few minutes," he said, and eased into the consulting room. Monique was busy with files and mail. She smiled and told him to take off his coat and galoshes. "Or you'll end up a pneumonia case yourself."

He hung coat, hat, scarf on the oak clothes tree and sat down to peel away the galoshes. Heat flowed from a small kerosene stove out past Monique, near the low barred windows.

"Where's the boy?" Delaney said.

"Upstairs with Miss Verga. Rose. They're fixing the rooms. His room and her room."

"She's moving *in?*"

"Of course."

"I don't know anything about her, Monique."

She lifted a sheet of paper and glanced at her notes.

"Her name is Rose Verga. Angela told me that, at least, is true. She says she's thirty-two, so figure she's thirty-eight. She's from Agrigento in Sicily and went to school there for six years. Figure four. She can read and write. In English too, which she learns from the *Daily News* and a dictionary. She was married for a while after the war, but the guy died and she came here."

"Did she ever take care of children?"

"No. She worked in three sweatshops, sewing dresses. She cleaned offices nights down Wall Street, she was a waitress in different places, including a place run by Angela before she got her own joint."

"She never had children?"

"She says she can't."

He folded his arms and looked vacantly through the front windows at the street. Kids went running by, heading for the river.

"What do you think, Monique?"

She sighed.

"I don't know . . . She's a little sure of herself. But what the hell, give her a try. You can always can her if it don't work out."

The telephone rang.

"Dr. Delaney's office, how can I help you? Oh. Yes. He has office hours until four. Just come on over, Mrs. Gribbins."

Monique hung up.

"And what do we pay her?" Delaney said.

"She wanted ten dollars a week plus room and board. I got her to take eight, for the first few weeks, maybe months. Then we'll see."

"You're a hard woman, Monique," Delaney said. Then he sighed, and nodded at the door leading to the reception area. "Who's first?"

"You'd better try Mrs. Monaghan. If she's not already dead."

Mrs. Monaghan came into the small office, where Delaney sat behind his cluttered desk. She was about forty, had been in a few years earlier with a broken hand, after falling on ice. She had six children, the oldest only eleven, no husband, and worked in a movie house on Fourteenth Street. Her manner was breathless and tentative. She had kept her wool coat on, but she was still shaking. When the door closed, he asked her what was the matter, although he already knew.

"Oh, Dr. Delaney, it's been dreadful, dreadful. I woke up with the chills, with a fever, cold and burnin' at the same time. I had a dreadful pain here, in the right side of my chest, dreadful, dreadful. I went into the jakes and spat up guck with blood in it."

"Take off your coat."

She did. He took a sputum sample, then tapped with his finger on the right side of her chest, above her breasts. He listened with the stethoscope and heard the bubbly breathing start and stop. It was surely lobar pneumonia.

"You'll have to go to St. Vincent's, Mrs. Monaghan," he said softly. "You've got pneumonia."

"Sacred heart of God," she said, and moaned. "Oh, I can't go there, Dr. Delaney. I've got the children at home, I've got to work, I can barely walk, and, oh God, I can't go there. Please, Dr. Delaney, can't you give me something here?"

He told her there was no choice, that she had to go in, and he'd call for an ambulance if she couldn't walk, and he'd ask Monique to try to get some help with the children, and also call her job. She began to weep.

"If I go there, I'll die for sure," she said. "And all the weans'll be orphans."

"If you don't go, Mrs. Monaghan, you're sure to die."

And sobbing, trembling, tottering uncertainly, she went into the hall to wait for an ambulance. Delaney thought: I have to call the hospital and ask about Larry Dorsey too.

Then Frankie Randall came in, his face a pale yellow. He wished Delaney a belated Happy New Year and took his quinine for the malaria he'd contracted at a training camp in Louisiana in 1917. He was in and out, with nothing else to say. Then Mrs. Harris took a seat, big and blowsy, a pasty-faced veteran of the old bordellos behind the warehouses on the North River, and he gave her some mercury to help control the lingering presence of a disease of the trade. She went to pay Monique. Mickey Rearden was another malaria case. Unlike Frankie Randall, he liked to talk. He talked about the Giants' coming season and how great Bill Terry would be as a successor to John McGraw, playing *and* managing, and how it would be grand to be down in that Florida for the spring training when it started. Delaney was curt with him, briefly thinking about the boy and the need for money. For food and clothes and the woman named Rose. Mickey, please take the quinine and go, and for fuck's sake stop talking. I've got to earn some money.

He heard a banging, then heavy footsteps above him coming in from the top of the stairs. He opened the door and asked Monique what all the racket was about.

"The bed," she said. "For the boy. They're taking it up top."

"What bed?" he said. "I don't have any cash to pay for a bed."

"It's only a dollar," she said.

"You found a bed for a dollar?"

"Rose did. She called somebody and here it is, an hour later."

Delaney thought: Rose Verga doesn't fool around. He reached into his left pocket for money.

Monique said: "Can I tip the guys a quarter?"

When the last patient left, he hurried up the stairs, while Monique added up the fees and wrote numbers into the ledger book. He could hear Rose talking to the boy before he saw them.

"Okay, Carlo, you grab that end, yeah, right there, *then* you pull."

"That end," the boy said.

Delaney turned on the top landing and saw Rose and the boy on either side of the bed, pulling sheets tightly across the narrow mattress.

"Hey, Doctor," she said and smiled. "We doing good. He's workin' hard, this Carlo. He swept the floor all by himself."

The boy grinned in a shy way and stared at Delaney.

"What's *his* name?" Rose said to the boy and pointed at Delaney.

"Ga'paw."

"You remember! Gran'paw. You're smart, Carlos. That's your gran'paw, all right."

Delaney reached down and lifted the boy and hugged him. He was warm in his arms. Delaney held him tight and felt a little ice melting in his frozen heart.

"Ga'paw," the boy said.

Rose explained that the boy had a spiced ham sandwich for lunch and some mushroom soup, and she walked with Delaney outside the bedrooms to the upstairs bathroom. The cheese box was already in place. "I gotta paint that," she said. "A real good yellow. You know, like the sun." Towels were draped neatly on the rods of the holders, soap lay in a glass dish. Then they paused outside Molly's room.

"Rose, this room is locked," Delaney said in a soft, polite voice. "It has nothing to do with you. It's just —"

"This was your wife's room, right?" she said.

"Right," he said, thinking, Women know everything important. She glanced at Delaney with a dark gaze, tinged with pity.

"You want some food? I got soup in a pot, some good bread."

"I'll help myself."

"I can do it. Then I gotta go someplace and pick up clothes."

They went down the stairs together, Rose now holding the boy. The odor of kerosene got stronger. There were two more patients waiting on the bench, both women.

"Take care of them," Rose said. "I get the soup ready."

She put Carlito down and went through to the kitchen, the boy holding her skirt. Delaney saw the women patients: a heavy cold with a hacking cough, a twisted ankle. When they were gone, he walked back to the kitchen, and Rose ladled out some soup and laid the Italian loaf and a slab of butter on the table. He thanked her and she went out. The soup was tasty, the bread fresh, with a crisp seeded crust. The boy watched him eat.

"She's a nice woman, Rose is," he said to the boy. "You make sure you do what she says, because she will be very good to you."

The boy wore a serious face as Delaney spoke. Soon he would be fluent in English, and Italian too. Or Sicilian. How does the brain wire words? Why do the Swiss manage three languages, while most Americans have trouble with one? The telephone rang once, and then Monique poked her head in.

"Jackie Norris on the phone," she said. "He says you know what it's about."

He got up to go to his office. "Talk to this young man, will you?"

All cops had the same voice, clipped and laconic, and Jackie Norris had been a cop since he came back from the war. They exchanged hellos and Jackie then got right to it.

"Doc, your daughter, Grace, left New Year's Day on a Spanish freighter out of Hoboken. Bound for Barcelona, Spain. It arrives in, oh, ten days. Depending on the ocean. She had a U.S. passport, under her own name, and two pieces of luggage. She didn't use the married name you gave me."

"Is there any way I can send her a cable?"

"Of course. I mean there must be. Let me find out the details."

"No, Jackie. You have things to do."

"I'll find out."

"By the way," Delaney said, "how's the knee?"

"This weather, it kills me. Hard to sleep. Fucking Heinies . . ."

"Come by. I'll take a look."

"I can't for a while. We got a double homicide on Morton Street. They drafted me 'cause I know the neighborhood. A man and a woman, dead in his bed, and her husband on the lam. The usual shit."

"Anybody we know?"

"Nah. The dead guy's from Brooklyn, lived two months on Morton Street, a furnished room. The couple's Irish. Might be just off the boat. Love is wonderful."

"Well, stay off the ice, Jackie. And thanks."

In the kitchen, Carlos was gnawing on a crust of bread. He was sitting now on a plush red cushion, taken from the upstairs living room. He pointed to the snow in the yard.

"O," he said.

"Okay, lad. Let's finish eating first."

They played in the garden for a while, but it was hard to make snowballs from the iron crusts of old snow. Delaney could see the boarded-over back windows of the Logan house, right next door to the west, number 97 Horatio. Taller by a floor than his own. Brownstone, not brick, like a vagrant visiting from Gramercy Park. The windows on the street side were sealed too. Even the hard kids and the rummies avoided the place. They all believed that ghosts lurked within. Perhaps they did. Above all, the ghost of poor Jimmy Logan. He had grown rich in the good times after the war, import-export, the trade of the river; bought this house; added a second in the Poconos; had two cars and three daughters. Insisted that people call him James, not Jimmy. Suits from Brooks Brothers. Shoes from England. After the Crash, his stocks and bank accounts vanished. He got rid of the cars. Then one Friday, his business ended too, the movers carted away the furniture, and he came home and shot his wife, and two of the daughters, and himself. Jackie Norris helped clean up that mess too. So did Delaney, when Monique heard the shots. The story was all over the tabloids, and a judge ordered the house sealed until the youngest daughter, four years old, grew up. She was staying with relatives in New Jersey and would be a long time growing up. The house stood there now, part of the parenthesis within which Delaney lived. Ghosts to the left. Bitterness to the right. He looked away.

After a while, the boy began to shiver. They went back inside. Rose was coming in the front door with a battered suitcase and a shopping bag. She laid the bag on a chair beside the kitchen table. She was definitely moving in.

"Give me ten minutes, I unpack," she said. "Come on, Carlos."

The boy went up the stairs behind her, taking one step at a time. The house was getting fuller, and somehow richer.

Delaney went to his consulting room and worked on a cable. YOUR SON IS SAFE. HE WANTS TO KNOW WHEN YOU'RE COMING BACK. DAD. No, that was wrong, making her feel guilty. ALL IS FINE WITH CARLOS. I HIRED A WOMAN TO HELP CARE FOR HIM. WHEN WILL YOU RETURN? Too many words, too expensive. This is a cable. CARLOS FINE WOMAN HELPING WHEN YOU RETURN QUERY DAD. One, two, nine words. Better . . .

Monique came in.

"Three house calls waiting. Also the mail. Some bills for the electric, the telephone, the usual first-of-the-month stuff. I also gave Rose ten dollars for food. Hey, you look wiped out. Maybe you should grab a nap."

"Maybe."

"I mean, if you get sick, the whole thing stops."

He laughed. "I can't afford to stop now."

"You ain't kidding. You got ninety-seven dollars in the account, and now you gotta feed three people, plus coal and kerosene."

"Maybe I could tend bar after house calls."

"Maybe you could do a novena."

She turned and he held the text of the cable, the two early versions crossed out.

"If Jackie Norris calls with an address, send this, okay?"

She looked dubiously at the text and hurried away to answer the ringing telephone. He went up to see the boy. Carlito was sitting on the floor in Rose's room, watching her lay clothes neatly in the dresser drawers. The suitcase was open on the bed. On the small lamp table, an Italian-English dictionary was laid upon a copy of the *Daily News*. Just as Monique told him. Rose was smiling as she moved, and in the hard snow-bright light he noticed that she had a fine white scar from her left cheekbone to the lobe of her ear. The slice of a knife. It did not affect her smile, so he knew the blade had missed the crucial tendons.

"Looking good now," Rose said, her smile showing a slight overbite. She unfolded a framed photograph on a small easel and placed it on the dresser top. The frame was brass. "That's my mother, my father. My brothers, my sisters. There's me too."

The father was dressed in a badly-fitting black suit, starched collar, wide knotted tie, squinting sternly at the camera. The mother looked blank and uncomfortable in a dark skirt that reached her shoe tops. Rose was probably fourteen and resembled her mother. The oval shape of her head. The young men were all smiling, perhaps preening, their suits pressed, their shoes glistening with polish. The girls were glum, except for Rose, who was flashing her wonderful smile and her intelligent eyes. Delaney thought: She was thirty pounds lighter then and two inches shorter.

"It's a Sunday," Rose said. "My father's birthday. We all went to eat together. I'm fourteen. My brothers left after the picture, chasing girls." Beyond the Verga family there was a bay filled with anchored fishing boats and a distant line of mountains. "Long time ago."

After a melancholy moment, she turned her back on the photograph and took blouses from the suitcase and started hanging them in the shallow closet.

"You gotta get this boy some more clothes," she said. "I know the bargain places. Or up at Klein's, on Fourteen' Street. And that window in his room, it don't close right. I put the towel to close it up, see? So the boy don't catch a cold. And you, Dottore, go down and sleep a little, okay? You look terrible."

Wearing a bathrobe, Delaney slipped under the covers and fell into an hour of deep dreamless sleep. He came suddenly awake, rose quickly, brushed his teeth and washed, and then, feeling refreshed, went off into the blue twilight to make three house calls. When he returned, Bootsie was waiting in the hall. The fat man rose from the bench, wheezing slightly.

"You keep too many hours," Bootsie said. "Even your nurse went home."

Delaney opened the door to his office.

"How's the boss?"

"Much better. He wants to go home. He wants you to put in a word with that Zimmerman."

"He'll go home when he's ready. That's not up to me. What can I do for you, Bootsie?"

Bootsie took a long tan envelope from his jacket pocket and handed it to Delaney.

"Mister Corso sent you this."

He turned to go.

"Hold it a minute, Bootsie."

"Yeah."

"What did he say? What's his message?"

Bootsie smiled without humor.

"He said, you don't take it, he kills you."

He smiled again, then went out through the hall. Delaney heard the gate clang shut behind him. From the high floor he could hear the murmur of Rose's voice, talking with the boy. He closed the office door and laid the envelope on the green blotter of his desk. He sat looking at it for a long moment. Then he used a letter opener to slice through the seal.

There was no note. He spread the contents on the blotter. There they were: fifty one-hundred-dollar bills. Five thousand dollars in cash.

"God damn you, Eddie," Delaney whispered.

FOUR

At his desk, Delaney held the phone for a long time, while off in St. Vincent's one of the nuns went to find Zimmerman. The news on Larry Dorsey was good: no fracture, no brain damage. He'd be playing saxophone in another week. But it was Eddie Corso he wanted to know about. He heard granular rain lashing at the back window. It would either wash away the scabbed snow or glaze it with ice. He wanted the goddamned snow to be gone. He wanted to walk around the neighborhood with the boy, to give him some basic geography, to show him the North River. He wanted to tell him about springtime in New York, and how the bony trees would burst with leaves, and how the Giants would soon play ball in the Polo Grounds again. They would go together. The boy would be three on St. Patrick's Day, a good age to begin looking at the most beautiful of sports. He would explain to Carlito what a hot dog was too, and how it wasn't a dog at all. They would eat hot dogs while sitting together in the sun.

"Hello?"

"Zim, it's Delaney. How's our patient?"

"He's some tough old bastard," Zimmerman said. "He wants to leave tomorrow."

"What do you think?"

"Two more days, at least. He's healed well, the pain is almost gone, no signs of infection, but . . ."

"Want me to take a look?"

"If you like, but he seems . . . I don't know, a guy gets shot like he was, you think he'd stay in bed for a month."

"He's been shot before."

"I know. You told me, and I saw the scars. I don't know why you didn't become a surgeon."

"Someday I'll tell you all about it. Did he talk about anything else?"

"Well . . ."

"What do you mean? Well, what?"

A pause. A smothering hand on the phone at the other end, a lowering of the voice.

"He gave me some money," Zimmerman said. "He gave the nuns money too."

"And what did you do, Jake?"

"I told him to forget it. Then he told me if I didn't take it, he'd have me killed."

Delaney chuckled. "The nuns too?"

"That wouldn't scare them. Aren't they in, what do you goyim call it? A state of grace?"

"Yeah, they die, they go straight to Heaven. If you see a nun driving a car, get off the street."

"Anyway, I don't know what they did about the money. And I don't want to know."

"Neither do I."

"Try to come in and talk him down. He says he wants to drive to Florida."

"I'll call tomorrow. Thanks, Zim. For everything."

"Thank *you.*"

Delaney hung up the telephone and sat for a few minutes, staring at a framed browning photograph of his father standing with John McGraw, before the war. In the days when his father was Big Jim and Delaney was Little Jim, even though he was two inches taller than Big Jim. At that time a lot of people received cash in envelopes, almost certainly including Big Jim. He placed the bills back in the envelope and opened the wall safe where he kept his passport, the deed to the house, his marriage license, along with morphine and other dangerous items. He laid the envelope on top of the small pile, then twirled the dial to lock the safe. He put out the lights and closed the doors and went quietly up the stairs. The only sound from the top floor was Rose's light snoring. He went into his bedroom.

In the darkness, wrapped in a cotton nightshirt, the covers pulled tight, Delaney listened to the hard rain and could not sleep. He wished he had someone to talk to. Someone who could listen while he discussed the money. He wished he could explain how torn he was, how he was trying to balance the sudden presence of the boy in his life with the ancient sense of corruption that he was feeling about those five thousand dollars. Big Jim wouldn't think about it for a minute. He was Big Jim Delaney, district leader, ward heeler, and he knew how the world worked. He had never read Niccolò Machiavelli, but he had graduated from the University of Tammany Hall. He always said his favorite color was green, and not because he was Irish. Delaney's mother would have placed the child and his future before the legal concerns, knowing in her chilly way that what was legal was often not the same as what was moral. New York had taught her that, and so had Ireland. *You must be daft,* he could hear her saying. *You've helped thousands of people for free, not taking a bloody dime, and here is a gift that will make a boy's life more possible. Take it. It's yours. God sent it to you.*

With Eddie Corso's money, he could have the house steam-heated, putting heat into the arctic top floor without the stench of burnt kerosene. He could pay for clothes for the boy, warm winter clothes, lighter things for the summer. He could buy a small used car and do even more house calls and perhaps help even more people. There'd be no need for the bicycle, except for exercise. He could deliver the endless New York casualties to the doors of the hospital. Then he remembered dimly a phrase from a high school religion class, something about an "elastic conscience," and how its possession was the worst example of the sin of vanity. That's me, Delaney thought, here in this monk's bed. The man with the elastic conscience. . . . He wished he could pray, but all of that faith and belief and certainty had ended forever in the Argonne. After seeing true horror, no sane person could believe again in a benevolent God.

He could see and hear Izzy the Atheist at the bar in Finnegan's last summer, railing at all the big gods. Izzy, who was half Jewish, half Italian, full of sarcasm, his teeth yellow and framed by a biblical beard. "What kind of god tells a man to kill his son? Like Abraham and Isaac? I'll tell you what kind of a god! An egotistical, cruel, son of a bitch of a god!" Someone shouted at him to shut up. Izzy went on without fear. "God comes to me and tells me I gotta kill my son? To prove I *love* God? You know what I tell him? I tell him: Hey, pal, *go fuck yourself,* you fat-headed prick!"

Delaney smiled fondly in the darkness. Izzy the Atheist had lived in the trenches too, in the mud and shit and fear, and sometimes raved in Delaney's office, waiting for his quinine. He wasn't the only man, sound of body, who had a hole chopped out of his brain by what he saw. Nobody who had gone to France ever said a word to him. Those who tried to stop Izzy's ravings were all men who had stayed home. The vets knew that God was just another form of bullshit.

But if God was gone, or simply deaf to all cries for help, Delaney did wish that he could speak to his daughter, Grace. Urging her to return. Come and take your son, Grace. Do not hand me this cup. Come and retrieve him, and I'll give you Eddie Corso's five thousand dollars. Not as a bribe, but to give you a means to begin again here in New York with your son. With or without your man, the son of a bitch. You can pick up the pieces of your life, you can stretch canvas and mix paint and create. You can become again the woman you started to become when you were sixteen and seventeen, when the whole world awaited you. Goddamn you, Grace. And then he fought against his bitterness, trying to place it in a cage, and then to shrink it. He addressed himself out loud: "Stop it, stop this self-righteous horseshit." And thought of Grace at three years old, the age of the boy. And addressed himself. You put your marks on her too. You broke the balance. You went off to the goddamned war when you didn't have to go. You could have fought the call-up in 1917, claiming truthfully that you had two dependents. You didn't fight the draft. You went to the war and you were gone more than two years. When you returned, you were at once so numb and so busy trying to get back lost time and lost money that you had no time for that little girl. You were there, and you were not there. She learned to live without you. She needed you, because . . . because her mother was drifting into the cold numb isolation that came from rage. Or because all little girls need their father. Or because . . . But then you don't truly know why, do you? You weren't there. Grace needed you and you went to the war. You were sworn to do no harm, and then you went ahead and did it.

"Stop it."

He let the boy rise in his mind, with those bright intelligent brown eyes and his wonder at the snowy world. He could be here for three weeks or twenty years. There was no way of knowing. Grace was out wandering the dangerous world. Across oceans lurked dragons. The boy was here. The boy was alive. He was a fact, not an abstraction. He is asleep upstairs, while the cleansing rain falls on the city. *I can do for him what I did not do for Grace. I can take his hand. I can love him . . .*

After a while, Delaney fell asleep. And dreamed a dream almost as familiar as the older dream of snow. He was in a long gray concrete corridor, trying to find an exit. The dying, the injured, the wounded, were all around him, writhing, moaning, seething with pain. There were soldiers with tin pots on top of their heads and blood streaming from their eye sockets. Slum kids from Brooklyn and the Bronx and Hell's Kitchen stood at an angle to the wall, erupting with strands of yellow mucus. Old women pulled robes against shriveled bodies. There were bashed women and stabbed women and women crazy with disease. The floor was slippery with blood and shit and urine. Someone screamed for morphine. Many held out hands, demanding to be touched, to be healed, and he would not touch them.

Then he was awake, his heart pounding.

The clock said three-fifteen. He could hear a few cars making a tearing sound through the rain. The snow was surely gone.

Then he heard the music.

The piano.

Brahms.

He threw off the covers and reached for his robe in the chilly room. The music stopped. It was the melody she played that summer evening before going on her walk to the North River, never to return.

He dozed again in the silent bedroom and conjured images of Molly, with her lustrous black hair and her crooked grin. Molly at the Battery gazing at the October harbor and the lights glittering off the waves. Molly in Tony Pastor's on the Fourteenth Street Rialto, laughing at the comics and the jugglers, and later humming the melancholy ballads as they walked toward home. They're all sentimental rubbish, she said, but they get into your head. . . . Molly announcing she was pregnant that first time, her face transformed, radiant, luminous, and then the bitter tears when the child came too soon and was dead. He saw that it would have been a boy, but he did not tell her for more than a year. He saw her beside him on the streets of Vienna, joyous as they skipped together through the evening crowds to the opera house; or walking beside him across Central Park to the Metropolitan, where she stared at the Vermeer and said she could hear the Dutchman's music. She was seated with him in the Polo Grounds, enjoying his happiness even though the game baffled her and she knew nothing of the legend of John McGraw. They went together to Coney Island on a few summer Sundays. They took the ferry to and from New Jersey, with the cool salt spray dampening them both and the towers rising in the downtown city. They took the subway to the end of the line. They rode the Third Avenue El and the Ninth Avenue El to the same destinations, her eyes taking in everything, from the dark subway tunnels to the tenement living rooms where the human beings lived with the constant roar of trains, and then she tried to put all that she had seen into music. *I want to make this all into music,* she said. *American music. No: New York music. Full of car horns, not cattle; gangsters, not cowboys; poor women working street corners; thieves locked away in cells. All of that. . . .* He heard her arguing for socialism. He heard her saying that this was no democracy if women could not vote, more than 120 years after the Revolution. He heard her talking about Berlioz and Schoenberg and how her instructor in Vienna thought that all the past was now dead. He heard her tell him as they sat together near a cleared space on the North River that she was again pregnant, and how he hugged her in delight, and kissed her tearful face, and started to sing the song.

Molly, dear, now did you hear,
The news that's going 'round?

He heard her laughing at the silly words.

Molly, my Irish Molly,
my sweet acushla dear,
I'm almost off my trolley,
my lovely Irish Molly,
whenever you are near.

And thought: I do not believe in ghosts. But I know they exist, because I live with one.

He woke before seven and shadowboxed in the chilly room for five minutes with his hands open. Jab, left hook, right hand. Jab-jab, right hand. Hook, hook, double 'em up, step back, right hand. Jab, then bend, then the hook. The way he had been trained long ago in Packy Hanratty's gym upstairs from the saloon on Ninth Avenue. Except that now the right hand had no snap, would never again be a punch, was shoved into the air instead of tearing at space. The hand that once had painted, the hand that once punched. Long ago. Still, he could hear the roar from the packed smokers in Brooklyn and East Harlem, in those years when every other Irish kid wanted to be a fighter, even those kids who wanted to be doctors. Packy's motto was Above All, Do Some Harm. And he did.

Then he went into the bathroom, where he shaved at the sink and stepped under the shower, an ache in his right shoulder, some migrating sliver of shrapnel loosened by the shadowboxing, working its way to freedom. Or the shrapnel of worry. The shower was an ancient device, reminding him of the insane inventions of Rube Goldberg in the *Journal*. Knobs, pipes, the water sometimes scalding, sometimes tepid, always sputtering. He dried himself with a towel that was too small, thinking: I could get all this goddamned plumbing fixed, I could buy big towels, and fresh underwear. I could do all those things put off after the bank on Canal Street failed in '31 and took everything with it. I could . . .

As he dressed, the aroma of frying bacon penetrated the room and he could hear voices from below: the small voice of Carlito, the deeper, more plangent voice of Rose. Rose smiled as he entered the kitchen, spears of loose black hair falling over her brow, and the boy rose from his chair and embraced him. Both wore sweaters against the morning cold. Without a scarf, her neck looked more than an inch longer.

"Ga'paw! Look: baking!"

"Bay-*con*," Rose said. "Not *-ing*. Say it, boy, bay-*con*."

"Bay-*con*. Bay-*con*." He laughed and left Delaney and took his seat. "Bay-*con*."

Rose turned the bacon in the heavy black pan. "What a smart kid he is," she said, her back turned to both of them. "You're smart, Carlito."

Delaney faced the yard, while Rose removed the bacon to a sheet of newspaper, cracked eggs into the pan, and basted them with the hot fat. In the yard the snow was gone, except on the wrapping of Mr. Nobiletti's olive tree. The bushes seemed scrawny and barely alive. There were stains in the paint above the window, and paint was flaking on the wall behind the stove. *I could get a real paint job, not just a cat's lick. The whole kitchen, the bedrooms, everywhere, make it bright, make it alive. . . .* Rose poured coffee into his cup and returned to the stove. Her wrists were very thin, but they must be strong too. Cabled with tendons and muscle under the olive skin. Delaney sipped the dark sweet coffee and wondered about his heart. Coffee this dark and this strong can't be good for you, he thought. It tastes too good. Tastes like . . . hell, like Vienna. In the crowded coffeehouse that time with Molly, they were eating sweets, splurging on the bounty of scholarship money from Andrew Carnegie and Tammany Hall, and she saw Gustav Mahler come in with Alma, the pride and torment of his life. Molly trembled with excitement, wanting to go over to Mahler, to thank him, to embrace him, but didn't, because she didn't want to play the fool, didn't want to trigger Alma's jealousy either, and so she sent a note anyway in her imperfect German, and told Delaney that her heart would be pounding for a week.

Then suddenly the bacon and eggs were before them, and Rose turned off the stove and took her place at the table, her back to the yard. Five days had passed since Carlito arrived in his vestibule, four days since he met Rose Verga, and for the first time in many years, the feeling of family had entered James Finbar Delaney.

• • •

Rose gave him a list of things they needed for Carlito and for the house, written in a swift slanted hand in English: shoes and a sweater (spelled "swetter") and underclothes for Carlito; towels and sheets; food. He took forty dollars from the petty cash box in his desk but did not open the safe. "Oh, yeah, *toys,*" Rose said. "The boy needs something he can, how d'you say it? Play. He's got to play with something. He's a *boy.*" Her eyes were wide and serious and oddly comic. Delaney smiled as he handed her the money. Then he remembered Grace at three, going to bed each night with a stuffed monkey, and wondered if they made them anymore. He would find one himself. It was too cold still for a baseball, but he would get one for the boy's birthday in March. He told Rose that he was going to St. Vincent's, to do what they called rounds, and would be back around one. Monique knew all about it. He went into the kitchen to say good-bye to Carlito.

"Another thing," Rose said, furrowing her brow, a vertical line pointing down at her long nose.

"Yes?"

"That *suit.* You been wearing it five straight days."

He looked down at the suit, rumpled and lumpy, the trousers without a crease.

"I have another one," he said. "But it's too light for the winter."

She looked at him, amusement and pity mixed in her eyes.

"You're a *doctor.*"

"I know that, Rose, and —"

"You gotta dress good." She smiled, without showing her teeth. "You got those long underwears?" Delaney said yes, he had. "Then wear them, and you could put another suit on top of it."

"They itch," Delaney said.

"I wash them so hard there's nothing left to itch."

He smiled. "Whatever you say, Rose."

Carlito was now up on a chair, waving a spoon held in a small fist. He was trying with his free hand to take the lid off the sugar bowl.

"He's a real Irisher, this boy," Rose said, fully smiling now. "He wants sugar to put on top of butter on top of bread! That's why the Irish got the wors' teeth in New York!"

"I'll be right back," Delaney said.

He hurried up the stairs, chuckling as he went, and moved into the bedroom, closing the door behind him. He unlaced his shoes, then removed the rumpled suit and laid it on the bed. He rummaged in a bottom drawer and found a neatly folded flannel union suit. He was fastening the buttons on the seat when the door burst open and Carlito ran in, giggling, waving his spoon. Rose was in swift pursuit. Then she stopped abruptly, looked at Delaney, and laughed out loud.

"You better not go to no hospital like that!" she said.

"Get out of here."

Carlito ran behind Delaney, and Rose went after him, bending to scoop him up. As she rose, her left breast brushed against Delaney's arm. *Soft and full.* She paused, glanced at him with uncertain eyes, then hurried away with Carlito. A fresh scent hung in the air of the room. A suggestion of flowers.

Zimmerman was in the hall of the first floor when Delaney came down in his light suit, scratching where the union suit itched. Zimmerman was dressed for the river wind. The door was open, and he could see Monique bent over records at her desk.

"I've got to talk to you," Zimmerman said.

"Come in, but we've got to make it fast. I've got rounds today."

Delaney led the way into his office and closed the door behind them. Zimmerman took off his wool hat and scarf. His eyes moved around the crowded room.

"Well, he's gone," Zimmerman said.

"That's what I figured when I saw you."

"They came for him around five, three of them, carrying a stretcher with a heavy blanket, and went out a side door."

"What shape is he in?"

"Pretty good, considering."

"He always was a thick-headed son of a bitch."

"As we say down the Lower East Side, he's got the guts of a burglar."

They stood in silence for a few awkward seconds, while Zimmerman looked at the framed diplomas and certificates on the wall.

"You went to *Johns Hopkins?*"

"I did," Delaney said.

"Jesus Christ," Zimmerman said, looking at Delaney in a new way. "How'd you manage that?"

"I passed the exam," Delaney said. "The rest was luck, and the financial resources of Tammany Hall. My father was a leader and had a few bucks."

"I'll be goddamned. You never mentioned it before. Johns Hopkins . . ."

"You never asked."

"When was this anyway?"

"I finished in 1913. A long time ago. Before the war. You must have just been getting born."

"A couple years earlier. At 210 Allen Street. My father was a socialist, like everybody from Minsk, and hated Tammany."

"He wasn't alone."

Zimmerman stared at the diploma.

"Let me ask you a question. Don't answer if you don't want to."

"How'd I end up a GP on Horatio Street?"

"Yeah."

Delaney now looked at the framed diploma from Johns Hopkins.

"I wanted to be a surgeon, and for a while, a few years, I was. Then the war came. A few weeks before it ended, I got wounded." He turned to face Zimmerman and started flexing his right hand. "Everything got torn up and I lost my strength. The strength any surgeon must have. I've got feeling. I can examine a patient. I just don't have strength. So I decided to be a GP. As simple as that."

"That's terrible."

"No, it's not. A lot of guys I used to know wish they had my problem, but they're all dead. Here I can help a lot of people. And in a way, they're my own people. So —" He glanced at the clock. "Hey, Jake, I've got to go."

Zimmerman paused, then cleared his throat.

"I want to tell you something else," he said.

"I know," Delaney said. "So tell me."

"I'm keeping the money," Zimmerman said. "The money Eddie gave me."

"You earned it."

"It's not even for me. My parents, well, this goddamned Depression, it has them —"

"Don't explain, Jake."

"I could get in a shitpot of trouble if —"

"Stop. Let's walk to the hospital."

Zimmerman exhaled, the tension draining out of him.

"I can't. I've got to meet one of the other interns for a bite."

Delaney opened the door.

"I'll walk you to the corner."

After grand rounds at St. Vincent's, Delaney walked down the west side of Sixth Avenue, the El rising above him, the Jefferson Court House looming in the distance. At the corner of Tenth Street he saw the toy store. McNiff's Toys. Run by Billy McNiff, who had opened it in 1928, three weeks after leaving prison, with a grubstake from one of his friends who were in on the holdup for which Billy took the fall. The shop's windows were opaque with frost. Delaney went in. The small dark store was empty.

"Hello? Billy, you here?"

There was no answer, and he looked at the dusty toys in their bins. Tiny metal cars in bright colors, most of them Buicks. Bald, pink spaldeens, waiting for a stickball summer. Dolls with moving eyes, frozen into paralysis. Roller skates. A Flexible Flyer that nobody in the neighborhood could afford to race down a snowy hill. Surely stolen, Delaney thought. Somewhere uptown. Then, a dusty set of ice skates. A small red fire truck with a yellow ladder on top. Then he saw what he wanted: a bin full of teddy bears. He remembered an article in the *Times* where various pediatricians said that teddy bears gave young children a sense of security. There were no stuffed monkeys, and that was just as well. They would only remind him of the boy's mother. Ah, Grace, goddamn you. We should be in this dump together, looking at the toys, and you could pick out what the boy might like and I could pay. You could tell me what you know about him that I don't know. And then you could go, in pursuit of your goddamned husband, your last vision of utopia. You could give him a teddy bear too. I'll take care of the boy.

The door opened abruptly, with a draft of cold, and slammed shut as Billy McNiff walked in.

"Hello, Doc," he said, in a surprised way. "What the hell are you doin' here?"

"Looking for a few presents," Delaney said.

"We got 'em. At a good price too. Everything reduced ten pissent since Christmas. Who they for? Boy or girl?"

"Boy."

McNiff was a small wiry man who seemed to bounce while he was standing still. His face was pared down, fleshless, lipless, like a skull. His skin seemed sprayed on his bones. As he came closer to Delaney, the odor of rum rose from his mouth and his body. From the saloon across the street. McNiff produced a paddle with a ball attached by a stapled rubber band.

"This is a hot item," McNiff said. His eyes were glassy, and he started batting the ball with the paddle, missing three out of six times. "Kids love it."

"I'll take that, Billy," Delaney said. "And this teddy bear."

"What's he? A Teddy Roosevelt fan?"

Delaney didn't want a long talk, and said curtly: "Not at the moment."

McNiff started wrapping the toys in a copy of the *Daily News*.

"The kid is your grandson, I guess."

"You guess right."

"The mother on vacation?"

"Sort of."

"When's she get back?"

"Billy, just wrap the stuff. No interrogation, please."

McNiff laughed, his teeth brown and splintery.

"Sorry. It's a habit from my youth."

"What do I owe you?" Delaney said.

Out on the street, kids were everywhere, freed from the tenement flats.

Knocko Carmody came around a corner, in a gray fedora and long blue coat with a velvet collar. He grinned and embraced Delaney and asked how things were going and whether he needed anything.

"As a matter of fact . . ." Delaney paused. "As a matter of fact, I do need something. You know a steam heat guy?"

"Of course. My brother-in-law, Jimmy Spillane. Want me to send him over?"

"When he's free, Knocko," the doctor said. "I need an estimate."

"Done."

Knocko pulled out a pen and notebook and scribbled a reminder to himself. The way Big Jim did when he was doing his own form of grand rounds. Then Knocko stared for a moment at Delaney.

"You okay?" he said.

Delaney smiled. "Better than I thought I would be."

"That Rose Verga is a pisser, ain't she? Skinny as a rail, but she'd scare the shit out of a stevedore. A real hoodlum."

Hoodlum was high praise indeed from Knocko Carmody. Knocko glanced at his watch.

"I'll see you soon," Delaney said, picking up the message. "Maybe at Angela's. The boy likes bagetti."

"You blame him? You wouldn't want to give him *Irish* food, for Chrissakes." He paused, then said: "Well, I gotta go bribe a judge."

Knocko grinned, tapped Delaney on the shoulder, and went into a saloon called the Emerald Isle, walking the way Big Jim did, with an old-time West Side swagger, putting the weight on one foot and dragging the other.

Delaney got off the El at Twenty-third Street, hurrying down the rickety steps, Carlito's bundle under his good arm. He walked north. At Twenty-fifth Street, he turned left into the wind off the North River. There was an ambulance in front of Eddie Corso's brownstone, and a couple of cops inside a green-and-white cruiser, and a young gunsel in the uniform of gray fedora and long blue coat, leaning against the iron fence. The gate under the stoop opened and Bootsie stepped out. He gestured to Delaney with his head. Meaning "follow me."

"How is he?" Delaney said.

"I ain't the doctor," Bootsie said. "You are." He shook his head. "But he looks all right to me. Not great, but all right."

Bootsie led the way up a flight of stairs and into the bedroom. Eddie Corso was lying in bed, paler and leaner and subtly older. He smiled when he saw Delaney.

"Hey," he said, waving Bootsie out of the room. "You came." He sat up. "What's in the package? Cannoli?"

"Toys for the boy."

"None for me?"

"You're out for the season." Then: "I have to check you out, Eddie."

"I'm great. That kid you got me, Dr. Jake, he did a great job."

"Let me look."

Sighing, Eddie unbuttoned his nightshirt and with Delaney's help slipped it off his shoulders.

"I suppose you're leaving town," Delaney said, as he gently lifted a bandage to look at the wound. "I guess the cop car will escort you at least as far as the Holland Tunnel." Corso nodded, smiled, said nothing. Delaney said: "Let's see. . . ." Eddie Corso was right: the incision was clean, the stitches removed. Healing well. Zimmerman had done a fine job. Delaney started tamping down the adhesive of the bandages.

"Yeah, I'm going. Maybe Florida. I need a tan."

"You got a nurse to go with you in that ambulance? These things have to be changed twice a day."

"She's down in the kitchen. I stole her from St. Vincent's for six months."

"You're taking a nun to Florida?"

"She's not a nun. You think I'm nuts? Her name's Stella."

"Want me to talk to Stella before you go?"

"We'll call from the road we need advice." He smiled. "Maybe she's a plainclothes nun. She's definitely big on Hail Marys and Our Fathers."

"Maybe she'll save your soul, Eddie."

"Too late for that, I guess," he said, and laughed. Then winced. "Jesus, don't make me fuckin' laugh."

A pause. Then Delaney took Eddie Corso's hand.

"I wanted to thank you for . . . you know . . ."

"Shut up, you dumb Mick. Just use it for that kid. And if you need anything else, you know, like getting somebody killed, just call me. I'll be out by the pool."

• • •

Delaney took the El back downtown, looking around at the sparser crowd of passengers. He sometimes felt in trains the way he felt in emergency rooms. There were too many people to ever know them all. Every one had a story that he'd never hear, and he had heard more stories of human grief than most people. He met them in the present, but each of them had a past. Better to shut down, stop imagining, deal with all other human beings the way he dealt with patients. Cage the past. Deal with them, gently if necessary, and then seal them out of memory. They could vanish like the words of a song, recovered only in isolated fragments. Worry about your friends, he often thought, and the few people you love, and leave the rest to Providence and, as Big Jim used to sing, Paddy McGinty's goat. A song that always made Molly laugh. A song from the past.

From the moment he first saw her, he knew that Molly had a past. She was losing a child on a North River pier, and someone had helped place that child in her emptying womb. Someone from her very recent past. He knew that from the beginning, but never asked her about it. Not in St. Vincent's, as he tried to convince her to live, with soft words and gentle touches of her wrist. Not later. The nuns never asked either. They had seen too many humans move through those wards to judge any of them. So had Delaney. He never asked her about the past when she left the hospital, still full of sorrow and some form of muted anger. He didn't ask her when he saw her on Greenwich Street seven months later, healthy now, working at Wanamaker's as a salesgirl, living in a woman's boardinghouse. Nor did he pry in any way when they went together to Tony Pastor's on the following Saturday night. There he first saw her beautiful smile when the comedians started their routines, a smile full of release from sorrow, and later they walked across Union Square in the dim snowy night, and she took his arm and repeated three of the jokes and then laughed out loud, and they went into the restaurant, and still he did not ask. He knew that he must listen if she ever told her tale, but he could not ask. He did not ask when they were married. He did not ask in Baltimore, when they arrived to find the way to Johns Hopkins. He did not ask when they moved into Horatio Street, or in the years that followed. He did not ask in his letters from the war. He never asked, and she never told the tale. But he came to know something large and heavy about her: the tale lay within her, wordless, a wound unhealed.

Sitting alone at the end of the rattling elevated car, Delaney saw a young man at the other end, seventeen or eighteen, dressed in the sharp clothes of the apprentice hoodlum. He stood with his back to the door, hands before him like a prizefighter waiting to be introduced at the Garden, unwilling to sit and risk the ruin of his razored creases. And Delaney thought of Eddie Corso, and hoped he would be all right. He hoped Eddie would live many more years. He hoped the wound would not suddenly fester. He hoped there would be no stupid accident on the long road to Florida. He hoped no hired gunsel would hunt him down.

He got off at Fourteenth Street, glancing one final time at the apprentice hoodlum, who didn't move an inch. He walked past the Spanish church and the Spanish Benevolent Society and the Spanish grocery and turned left at the meat market and into Horatio Street. Kids were everywhere, defying the icy wind off the North River. Playing tag. Running after one another. Shuddering in doorways or vestibules, scheming, smoking cigarettes. He had treated most of them and would treat them again. The Rearden kid. The Caputo kid. The Corrigan twins. They moved in packs of six and seven, and he tried to imagine Carlito among them. They carried all the normal dangers: measles and scarlet fever and whooping cough. In summer there was polio, and all the filthy things they could contract while swimming off the North River piers. The normal diseases were just that: normal. Mayor La Guardia said a few days ago that he'd make vaccinations for kids mandatory, and maybe he'd be the rare politician who kept his word. Maybe.

The streets were full of other dangers. Knives and guns and the logic of the pack. He had treated people for such things too. Soon the boy gangsters would no longer swing aboard the Tenth Avenue trains, taking their percentage, not after the New York Central opened the elevated High Line above the street. Closer to the river, they were working on the Miller Highway too, that would carry automobiles above the cobblestones. But the High Line was something else, a commercial overpass that even cut through buildings above street level. But he could imagine the youth packs heaving ladders against walls and hopping the slow trains and hurling booty to the street. Children of the old Hudson Dusters, the vanished Whyos. Some of them learned too young to love trouble, and the more difficult the trouble, the better.

For most of a block, he was scared about Carlito. If the boy stayed here a long time, if he was to be here for years, he'd go to those streets on his own. The boy couldn't have Delaney with him every hour of the day. He couldn't have Rose Verga there either, for she could be gone in a month. Even if she stayed, the other kids would mock him if he used any woman as a bodyguard. Or a creaky, respectable grandfather. But he couldn't just move away. Couldn't afford another house. Couldn't just go. This was his place and he had made a vow. Promised himself in the mud and shit of France that if he lived he would serve his own people. For the rest of his fucking life. If he fled with Carlito to some leafy suburb, or to Brooklyn or the Bronx, the broken vow would eat his guts. He must find a way to stay.

But in spite of the vow, Delaney knew he must deal with practical matters. Where would the boy go to school? Sacred Heart was better than the public school. But there was trouble there too, and danger. Demented priests, seething with God's furies and their own tormenting desires. They planted the fear of Hell in their young charges along with hatred of the flesh. Carlito could be subjected to all those small mutilations that could leave scars for life. *God damn you, Grace.*

He went in under the stoop, and on the bench in the hall he saw a weeping young woman holding an infant. She rose when he entered, trying to speak. The child was silent and still. Behind her on the bench was Japs Brannigan, his high-cheekboned yellowed Asian face more like a wood sculpture than part of a living creature. He was there for the quinine. And there was old Sally Wilson, staring into the darkness at the far end of the waiting room. Delaney held up a hand, gesturing to them all.

"I need five minutes," he said. "Just give me that."

Monique was at her desk, her face flat and void of expression, her eyes tired. He closed the door behind him. He flashed on that morning, the first of May, 1909. Knocko was calling, a dock walloper then, not the president of the union. He said there was a woman on Pier 41 and she was in trouble. "She's a Mick," Knocko said. "I don't want the immigration idiots to send her out to the Island for lyin' or somethin'." Delaney pedaled the bike to the pier. In a dark corner Knocko had placed some longshoremen around the woman, holding blankets to shield her from the inspection of strangers. She was young, pale, beautiful, and semiconscious. She had just arrived alone in steerage from Ireland and was having a miscarriage. Molly.

"A guy named Jackie Spillane called," Monique said. "About steam heat."

Knocko had made the call. Again.

"I'll call him later," Delaney said. Then: "Where's the boy?"

"Rose took him with her, food shopping."

He held up the paper sack.

"I brought him a few things." He passed the sack to her, and Monique peered inside and smiled.

"Aw, that's great. He needs something to play with, that boy." She handed the sack back to him. "I found those American Express addresses for you too. Barcelona, Madrid, Paris."

"Just address the envelopes, and I'll mail them later. I still have to write the notes."

He paused again, then nodded toward the door to the waiting room.

"Is that child alive out there?" he whispered.

"I don't know," she said. "The baby started bleeding from the nose and mouth last night. I tried to get the mother to go to the hospital. She said, 'Absolutely not. I want this girl to live.' "

"Send her in first. Get the quinine ready for Brannigan, no charge. And what's ailing Princess Wilson?"

"She wants her husband back."

"I can't help her with that. He's been dead six years now."

"She thinks you can bring him back."

Delaney sighed. He noticed that Monique was chewing the inside of her mouth.

"You okay?"

"Yeah. No. Ah, hell, Doc, it's the usual. We got bills here, a slew of them, and when Rose gets back with the kid, they'll be worse."

"Hold on."

He went into his office and closed the door behind him. He turned the dial on the small safe, found the envelope, and removed a crisp hundred-dollar bill. He creased it and then went out and handed it to Monique.

"Change this somewhere. Not the bank. Pay some of the bills. And send in the woman with the baby."

Monique stared at the hundred-dollar bill.

"You rob a bank?"

"Sort of."

The woman's name was Bridget Smyth, "with a *y*." She was nineteen, unmarried, and her baby girl was seven weeks old. She was also dead. He looked at the dead girl on his examination table, and his eyes wandered to the browning photograph of John McGraw and Big Jim. The woman sobbed. *Touch her, for Chrissakes. Her baby is dead.*

He gently touched her bony forearm but didn't speak. She did.

"She's dead, isn't she?"

"Yes," Delaney said. "Pneumonia."

She lifted the dead infant and hugged her close and began to bawl. No words came from her, just the wracking wail of grief.

Delaney put an arm around her and held her tight and the door opened and Monique came in. He nodded at her, and Monique came over and eased him aside. She put an arm on her shoulder, whispering, trying to move her to the outer room.

Bridget Smyth snapped.

"Don't give me that effin' rubbish! She's dead! And there's no effin' food at me room and no effin' water, 'cause the pipes is froze, and no effin' heat, and her father is an effin' eejit, gone off some effin' place!" She bawled wordlessly, Monique holding her tight, Delaney caressing her bony arm. With his right hand.

"I'll call someone at Sacred Heart," Monique whispered. "Get a priest to help —"

"A *priest?* Never! I went to them and they turned me away. I *sinned,* I must *pay!*"

Her eyes were wide now, and mad. She looked at them and held the child fiercely and then rushed the door. Delaney moved in front of her.

"Out of me way!"

"I won't let you go this way," Delaney said, trying to sound both gentle and commanding. "We've got to arrange a proper burial. Wait. Just wait. We'll —"

"I know where to have the proper effin' burial! The two of us, together! In the effin' North River!"

Then she dissolved again, sobs mixing with wails, squatting with her back to the door and her unmoving child tight against her chest. Delaney whispered to Monique: "Get your coat. Stay with her, no matter where she tries to go." He mouthed the word Moriarty, which was the name of the undertaker on Ninth Avenue. She rubbed thumb and forefinger together, indicating the unspoken word "money," and raised her eyebrows.

"Use what I gave you," he said. "I'll get some more."

Together they raised Bridget Smyth from the floor and led her into the anteroom. She was silent now, and limp, as if her body was empty of the fuel of rage. The infant seemed like an extension of her own body, posed as a small Madonna awaiting some draftsman with a sepia stick.

Delaney closed his door now, breathing hard. The effing North River. . . . That summer evening, Molly walked toward the North River. There were still people on the streets, people she knew. Jackie Norris learned that in a few hours, with the help of his policeman's badge. She was alone, wearing a blue dress, saying to one old lady that she was going to the ruined pier to watch the sunset. No surprise. Delaney had gone there with her many times, finding the scorched but solid timbers that served as small bridges between more solid planks. Sitting with her in silence as the sky reddened over New Jersey. She would draw up her knees, her arms hugging them, staring at nothing. Now and then she'd mention some moment from the years before the war, some character, some song. She'd mention a play they'd seen. She'd mention a café in Vienna. But that summer evening, she went alone, wrapped in a shroud of her own hard solitude, for there were five patients waiting for Delaney. She never came back. O my Molly-O.

He rose slowly and went to the safe and took another hundred-dollar bill from the envelope, to cover expenses after Monique paid for the infant's funeral. And the woman's rent. And some food. Thinking: The North River is jammed with ice. Thank God.

Brannigan took his quinine and left, angling past Monique's empty desk. Then Sally Wilson came in. At twenty, she had been a star at Tony Pastor's, a lush princess of the Rialto. Delaney had never seen her perform, but she had once showed up at his old office on Jane Street carrying her scrapbook. As if to prove that she existed. There she was, in big bustles, or in tights, and the stories said that she had a wonderful contralto voice. Her hair was so blond it seemed white in the photographs. Now it truly was white, but she had added forty years and fifty pounds. Along the way, she'd had two sons and three husbands. The sons were gone, one now working in despair for the Republicans in Franklin Roosevelt's Washington, the other in California in the movie business. Or so she said. She only mourned the last husband.

"I can't sleep," she said abruptly. "I keep seeing Alfie, and when I turn over in bed, he's not there."

"Are you still drinking coffee?" Delaney asked gently.

"Of course."

"Stop," he said.

"You think it's just *coffee?*"

"Yes."

"But you didn't even *examine* me!"

"Well, do you have any physical symptoms?"

She always wanted him to examine her. She always had vague worries about her breasts, which were soft and heavy. She seldom said the word "cancer," but it must have been in her dreams.

"I have these flutters, especially at night, Dr. Delaney." She squeezed her left breast. "What do you call them flutters?"

"Palpitations."

"Right."

Delaney sighed. "Well, let's have a listen."

She stood up and unbuttoned her blouse, then turned her back and unfastened her white brassiere. Delaney had long ago trained himself to be objective when examining human beings, but Sally Wilson had not. Her breasts were large, fallen, blue-veined, but she lifted the left breast as if offering it to Delaney. The breast seemed to blush.

"They used to be beautiful," she said sadly.

"Breathe, please."

He listened. Then removed the stethoscope from his ears.

"The heartbeat is strong and regular, Miss Wilson."

She folded her arms under her breasts to form a shelf.

"I'm worried about lumps."

"There's a wonderful specialist at St. Vincent's, Miss Wilson. I can make an appointment if you want."

"I don't trust strangers. I need you to check."

He did, while she inhaled through clenched teeth, her eyes closed for almost a minute. Her body grew tauter.

"Everything seems fine," Delaney said. "No lumps, Miss Wilson. But I can make that appointment if . . ."

She relaxed, arms folded under breasts again.

"You can get dressed now, Miss Wilson."

He turned his back on her, heard her moving, a rustling of something silky. Her breathing was heavy.

"Every time I think of Alfie, I get the condition, the papulations."

He chuckled. "Maybe you should think about your second husband."

"*That* bastard."

"Well, I'll tell you what. Stop the coffee for a week and then come back. We'll see how you're doing."

When he turned she was wearing the brassiere but not the blouse.

"You'd have loved them," she said in a numb voice. "Everybody did."

He heard the gate clang and the outside door open and slam shut and Rose's voice and the laughing of Carlito. Bumping. Jumping. Shoes on wood. Blurred Italian. The boy's squealing laughter.

"Excuse me," he said to his patient, and went to greet them, smiling.

FIVE

LATER — AFTER THE BOY HAD PRACTICED WITH HIS PADDLEBALL until falling into a nap; after Delaney had written three notes to his daughter and folded them into the stamped envelopes; after he had hung his suit neatly in the bedroom closet and peeled off the union suit; after he had spoken with Jimmy Spillane about a Monday-morning visit to check out a system for steam heat; after reading the newspapers in a hot bath; after dressing again in warmer clothes — after all of that, he and Rose and the boy went to Angela's restaurant for an early dinner. He dropped the letters in a corner mailbox.

"This kid already grew half an inch in a week," Angela said, leading them to a corner table.

"The cooking," Rose said. "Whatta you expect?"

"He's gonna be bigger than the doc," Angela said.

"Bigger than the Statue of Liberty."

Carlito was indeed 33 inches tall and weighed 32 pounds. A big kid, from the genetic line that had given Delaney his six feet. They sat down and Angela suggested veal or a nice piece of fish and the boy said "bagetti" and then they ordered. Veal for Delaney. Sole for Rose. Carlito had already said what he wanted. Then Delaney asked for a glass of the house red, and Angela raised her eyebrows.

"That's the second glass a wine you had this year!"

"It might be the last."

"An' you, Rose — you on a diet or something?"

Rose blushed. "Just bring me the fish, Angela."

The place was half-empty. They talked and laughed and said hello to people they knew. Knocko Carmody came in with his camarilla, asked Delaney if Spillane had called, smiled when told he had. He kissed Rose on the cheek while murmuring, "Hey, you hoodlum, how are you?" Carlito squirmed in his high chair and Rose took him by the hand back past the kitchen to the bathroom. Delaney watched a fresh snowfall drifting softly on the street. The flakes were thick and there was no wind. Parked cars were now glistening from the melting snow. Some had not been moved since the New Year's storm. There was snow on the hats and shoulders of the new arrivals too. A few more people stopped to say hello to Delaney, exchanging small talk, giving him brief updates on the health of old patients. Nobody mentioned Eddie Corso. Or, for that matter, his daughter, Grace. He saw Rose emerge with Carlos by the hand. Angela threw her a conspiratorial glance. Then from the tables, a few men and more women reached for Carlito, touching him, talking baby talk, petting him as if he were a puppy.

They were silent through most of the meal, the food too delicious for chatter. The wine, alas, was too sweet, so Delaney sipped. Rose was very concentrated, lifting her food in a dainty way, as if remembering advice from the woman's page of the *Daily News*. She tamped down her shimmering vitality too. The restaurant was now crowded, and when Carlito finished, Angela came over.

"What about dessert?" Angela said.

Delaney ordered a cannoli, the boy wanted ice cream, Rose passed on both and asked for tea.

"You're gonna waste away, ragazza," Angela said, a thin smile on her face, as she touched Rose's shoulder. She glanced at Delaney and turned her back on Rose and hurried to another table. The mixed sound of men and women was higher now, a growly male baritone punctuated by shrill female whiskey laughter. The boy grinned every time someone laughed out loud.

They finished the desserts too quickly.

"This can't be good for us," Delaney said, "but I don't care."

"Once in while," Rose said, waving a hand in dismissal. "You eat dolces three times a day, you weigh four hundred pounds. But one cannoli? Faniente, nothing."

The boy rubbed his eyes, and Delaney called for the check and paid it. Dessert and the glass of wine were on the house. Rose buttoned up Carlito's jacket and then her own long coat, while Delaney pulled his hat tight on his brow. Angela hugged them all and said something in Italian to Rose, who smiled thinly and jutted her chin in a gesture of defiance. Delaney waved to the blur of crowded tables and they went out. The snow was emptying the streets and gathering on the fenders of the glistening cars. They turned left toward Horatio Street.

Then a car door opened. An angular, sallow man, with yellowing eyes under a wide-brimmed hat, stepped out of the backseat. He jammed his hands in his overcoat pockets, as if they contained something dangerous. There were three other men in the car and a lot of cigarette smoke. They had been waiting a while.

"Hey," the sallow man said.

Delaney looked at him, while Rose pulled Carlito closer.

"Me?" Delaney said.

"Yeah, you. I wanna talk to you."

"About what?"

"You know what."

"Tell me what."

"About Eddie."

"Eddie who?"

"Eddie Corso, that's who."

"What about him?"

"Where is he?"

Christ. Another punk gangster who's seen too many goddamned movies.

"I don't know."

"Of course you know. You saved his fuckin' life."

Rose stepped in, blurting in Italian: "Vai!" The sallow man looked as if he'd been slapped. Then she turned to Delaney, her tone shifting into deference. "Don't talk to this guy. Come on."

"Stay outta this, Rose," the sallow man said.

"Ah, bah fongool."

The man took out a pistol, letting his gun arm hang at his side.

"Put that away," Delaney said, stepping in front of Rose and the boy. Thinking: I can manage one left hook.

"There's three cops inside Angela's restaurant, pal," Delaney said calmly. "This is a very bad idea."

The sallow man glanced at the lights of Angela's and then at the car. An older man shook his head. No. The sallow man returned the gun to his pocket.

"You better remember where Eddie is," he said. "And let us know fast."

"Let's go," Delaney said, and took Rose by the arm and started for home through the falling snow. He felt himself breathing hard.

"Bah fongool," Carlito said.

They had gone half a block when the boy stopped and looked bleary. He couldn't move his feet. Delaney lifted him, carrying him home, feeling his puppy warmth through thick coats and falling snow. He remembered Eddie Corso's tutoring him in Italian that time in France. *Palle* were balls. A *cazzo* was a prick. *Fottere* meant fucking. But Eddie didn't know where *bah fongool* came from, although he did know what it meant. In search of precision, they went to see Lieutenant Rossetti, whose father was a writer for *Il Progresso* in New York. The lieutenant smiled. Yeah, he said, it comes from *va f'an culo,* which roughly means, Up your ass! Don't say it to anyone, unless you want to get shot. The next afternoon, Lieutenant Rossetti had the front of his brow blown off by a German sniper.

"I'm sorry I used a bad word back there," Rose said. "The boy, he remembers everything you say."

"Don't worry, Rose," Delaney said. "The guy deserved it. Just be careful. This is about me, not you."

"You didn't seem scared about the gun."

"Every gun is scary," he said. "But I've seen them before."

"In the war?"

"The war," he said. "And yes, around here too."

From long habit, he didn't elaborate. Rifles, mortars, grenades . . . and he'd seen gunshot wounds too. A lot of them. Too many of them. Way too many dead people too. But he hated talking like a tough guy.

"I know that guy," Rose said quietly. "The cafone with the gun."

"Who is he?"

"I'll tell you later," she said, glancing behind her at the empty sidewalk and the snowy stillness of the street. Her face was harder now.

When they reached the house, Rose opened the doors beneath the stoop, then gazed once again at the street. She locked the doors behind them, and Delaney carried the boy upstairs to the top-floor bedroom. Rose followed, removing her coat and hat, then draping them over the top-floor banister. In the light from the hallway, Delaney laid the boy on his bed, where the teddy bear was tucked under the covers. The ache was back in his right arm.

"Here, let me do this," Rose said, as if sensing that both arms were not the same now. She began to undress the boy. Delaney removed his coat and placed it on the banister beside hers. The boy's eyes opened.

He blinked, gazed at Rose, then at Delaney. He did not look frightened.

"Okay, come on now," Rose said, lifting the boy. "Brush your teeth, make pee pee."

She carried him into the bathroom. Delaney stood there, hearing flushing water, and Rose's murmuring voice. He glanced into her room. There was a notebook on top of the Italian-English dictionary. On the wall a calendar from *Il Progresso* showed Roman ruins. Delaney thought: I'm a sort of ruin too. And chuckled.

"Okay," Rose said, after flushing the toilet. "Now you go night-night, boy."

She pulled the covers aside and laid him down, and he hugged the teddy bear as she covered him. His eyes moved from Delaney to Rose. He turned his head to face the wall and whispered: "Mamá." He hugged the bear. Then he closed his eyes and fell into sleep. Rose glanced at Delaney, who saw unspoken emotion in her eyes. Pity. Or sorrow.

"Come on," she said. "I make you some tea."

He drank his tea in the Irish way, with milk and two sugars. Rose used a wedge of lemon and resisted the sugar. She folded her thin, sweatered arms and leaned on the table and talked about the man with the gun.

"They call him Gyp," she said. "Like one out of three gangsters. Once a week in the *Daily News,* they find some dead cafone in Brooklyn and his name is Gyp. Gyp Santucci . . . Gyp Ferraro . . . This guy, his name is Gyp Pavese. He lives with his mother up Spring Street. Thirty-fi' years old, he lives wit' his *mother.*"

"How do you know all this?" Delaney said, wanting to know about Gyp, wanting to know more about Rose.

"When I first come to America," she said, " I live in the same block as Gyp, across the street with a family from Genoa. I see him every day, dressed in clothes he can't afford, so I know he's a gangster. The people in my house say he's a knife guy. Couldn't fight Carlito and win, so he uses a knife on people." She turned her head as if embarrassed at what she was about to say. "One time, he comes to me, he says, 'Hey, baby, you gotta go out with me.' I say, 'No thanks.' Well, that makes him crazy, 'cause he thinks he's Rudolph Valentino. He asks me again, then again, until I say, 'Don't ask me again, Gyp.' " She smiled. "Or *else,* goddamn it."

About six strands of her hair had fallen loose, like brushstrokes. She sipped her tea, then went silent, as if she did not want to go on. She was like so many patients who had sat across from him and told only part of their story.

"But that wasn't the end of the story, was it?" he said.

"No."

"Tell me the rest."

She took a deep breath, then exhaled. "Well, the people from Genoa, my landlords, they worry all the time, they don't want trouble with gangsters. And so I move away, and live in Angela's house awhile." A muscle twitched in her cheek. "All this is, what? Five, six years ago . . ."

She drummed her nails on the tabletop. They were square and blocky and carefully trimmed. She seemed hesitant, as if afraid she was telling Delaney too much about herself.

"But Gyp didn't give up?" Delaney said.

She looked at him, then at the wall above the stove. "No. For a long time, I don't see him. Then I hear he's in jail. Good, I think, that's where he belongs, with his crazy mother too. I relax. Then I hear he's out of jail. Still, I'm okay. You know, it's New York: you move five blocks away, it's a different world. And I had lots of work. Cooking. Making hats. Sewing dresses. Stuff like that. Piecework, too, blouses . . ."

"And then Gyp came back."

"You got it, Dottore," she said. Nodding her head. "One morning I come out of the house, there's Gyp. Dressed all sharp, with a gray hat like tonight. He says he wants to see me, he's been in love with me for years, and then he says, 'If I can't have you, nobody else can have you.' "

She poked at the tea with a spoon. "What's the word? A threat?" Delaney nodded, encouraging her to go on. "Anyway, I think about going a long ways away, like California. Maybe China! I explain everything to Angela, and she says, 'Don't worry, I take care of this.' And she does. She talks to someone, and Mr. Someone talks to someone else, and Gyp stays away." She moved her head from side to side. "Until tonight."

Delaney sipped his tea, which was turning cold.

"He was there because of me, not you."

"Maybe," she said.

Delaney said, "Who were the guys in the car?"

"From the Frankie Botts mob. Up by Bleecker Street. The Naples boys."

"Frankie Botts?"

"Frankie Botticelli."

"Like the painter?"

"You know Sandro Botticelli?" she said, and smiled. "From Firenze? There's a painting he painted, you know, *very* famous. A naked lady with long hair, coming out of a clamshell. You know that painting? Venus! I used to look like that, except I'm never a blonde." Then she blushed, as if afraid the doctor might think she was flirting. She waved a hand in an airy way. "You know . . ."

For the first time, Delaney tried to imagine Rose naked. And stopped. And remembered buying a large framed print of *Birth of Venus* for Grace, on her fourteenth birthday. Her young eyes widened, and she stood before it, breathing deeply, flexing and unflexing her hands. Her hands then moved toward the tabouret, for paint and a brush. Poor Venus hung on the wall upstairs for a long time, and when Grace left with her man, the Botticelli went with her. Wherever that might be.

Rose broke the flash of reverie. "When Eddie Corso got shot, most people knew what happened. There's no secrets in Little Italy. They know he is shot by guys from Frankie Botts." A pause. "From Club 65, on Bleecker Street."

"Why?"

"Who knows? These people kill you for stepping on their shoes sometimes. But what I hear, it's about Eddie Corso saying no to shmeck."

"Heroin."

"I guess. Shmeck, shmeck . . . it's like a Jewish word, they use it all the time now."

Delaney finished the tea. He gazed out at the snow falling in the yard and remembered Eddie calling for morphine in a muddy field.

"Me? I think Gyp is the guy shot Eddie. Anybody else would of killed him." She got up. "You want more tea?"

"No. Thank you, Rose. No."

She took his cup and rinsed it.

"I hear four other guys got killed this week," Rose said flatly. "The *News* had some little story in the back about two of them, but it didn't mention Eddie Corso or Frankie Botts. Tonight? I guess they want to find Eddie and finish the job."

Delaney sighed.

"Jesus Christ," he said.

"Jesus Christ got nothing to do with it."

He couldn't sleep in the silent house. He glanced at the newspapers, reading about Roosevelt and the Import-Export Bank, and how La Guardia had ordered a big trash basket for his office, one he could use, he said, as his main filing cabinet. In the *Times* there was a story about the Nazis on page 23 and what Chancellor Hitler was planning, but there were few details. He lifted the books of poetry beside the bed: Yeats and Lord Byron and Walt Whitman. On some nights he tried to read at least one poem as if it were a prayer. But on this night his eyes glazed. He kept thinking about Gyp and the hoodlums and the danger that never goes away from the world.

He turned out the bedside lamp and lay in the dark, wishing he could pray. Not just mouth words. But pray as he did as a boy at Sacred Heart, in hope of divine intercession. He wanted to pray, above all, for Carlito, asking that he be kept safe to live a life. Safe from incurable disease. Safe from idiots with guns. Or knives. He wanted to pray for Grace too, for her to be safe wherever she was, on her way to the strange cities of the world. If he could pray, he would whisper something for Eddie Corso too, that he would be free of ambush or accident in his plunge along southbound roads. He would pray for Rose, that she stay alive through what was coming with the boy, that she could help him be for the boy what he had never been for Grace. That she could keep pushing her tough warmth into the house, and her street wisdom, and her decent heart. He hoped she would not fall in love with some man and vanish from their lives. He would pray for Rose, and pray for Angela too, and Knocko, and Zimmerman, and the nuns, and all the imperiled people of his daily passage.

But he had lost prayer somewhere along the way, along with faith. He had been educated to deal with the body, not the soul. In the Argonne, he lost what remained of the affairs of the soul, among the torn and broken bodies of the young, until the day came that he cursed God.

Now he lay without sleep. He knew all the magic potions that men and women used in order to sleep: pills and powders and whiskey and sex. But after his own wound, after the red mist that enclosed him for more than a week, after the hospital and the months of recovery and the return to New York, he had determined to live his life without anesthesia.

Who are you, mister? Grace said on the day he came home. She was just five years old.

I'm your father, Grace.

I don't believe you.

And Molly said: Yes, Grace, he's your father.

The girl burst into weeping and fled to the next room.

And Molly said: You see what you've done?

Yes, he could see what he had done. He saw it in Grace. He saw it in Molly. Over the weeks that followed, the little girl came around. She was cautious at first. Tentative. But she started hugging his good arm and sitting on his lap and giggling when he tickled her. But Molly never came around. He was certain that she had taken a lover while he was at the war. He did not confront her with his suspicion. She said nothing that would feed it. But if she had found someone else, at least for a while, he could not blame her. She was young, and handsome, and full of longings. Right here. In the world of aching flesh. But he was Quixote without a lance. Off to the war, to save human beings, a knight errant with a scalpel and a stethoscope. But the Illustrious Don of Cervantes had no children. And no wife. And he had Sancho Panza to ground him in the real world. And when the enchanters returned the Don for the final time to his home, there were no unspoken accusations. Before Delaney could strip away his ribbons and his medals and send his uniform to the army-navy store for sale to some fortunate young man who had skipped the war, he knew how much had changed. Delaney was standing in the dock, indicted by his wife's chilly scorn and his daughter's initial flight — even if that flight was only from one room to another. And it wasn't only Molly and little Grace. On the streets of the neighborhood he picked up the bitter glances of those who had lost sons in France while Delaney had survived. They would never forgive him for living. And there were other charges in the indictment. While he was at the war, his mother and father had died in a vile way, two days apart. So had others, of course, including many thousands of soldiers. No doctor could have saved any of them, surely not Delaney. But he could not ever be certain what might have happened had he stayed. Molly had sent him newspaper clippings saying that Big Jim and his wife had one of the largest funerals in the history of the West Village, on a day when no wind blew off the North River and the sun glared on the old cobblestones. On one clipping Molly had scrawled: "You should have been there. M." He could not tell whether she was scolding him or comforting him, or both. But some facts were beyond argument: his parents had died of the influenza, his wife and child were in danger, and Delaney wasn't there. He was in the hospital in France. And when he came home at last, he could not even pray for them.

Then he realized that in the list of people for whom he wished he could pray, he had left out Molly.

Yes, Molly: I would pray for you too, if I could.

At last, he slept.

The telephone rang in the morning dark. He reached for it and knocked some books off the night table.

"Hello?"

He heard breathing, but no words.

"Hello? This is Dr. Delaney."

"You better remember, Doc," the voice said. Low. Menacing. Burred by cigarettes.

Delaney sighed, reached over, and switched on the light. It was ten after six.

"Listen, pal," he said, in a tough voice that he tried to make reasonable. "Don't do this. I have nothing to remember. I don't know where Eddie Corso is or where he went. He could be in Staten Island. He could be in Utah. He could be in Russia. I don't have a clue. Don't call me again."

"We know where you live."

"The whole neighborhood knows where I live."

A pause, then: "We know where the kid lives."

Then Delaney felt the old West Side hardness rise in him for the first time in years, the fury of every street kid that came off the North River.

"You son of a bitch, Gyp," he said. "Don't you fucking dare."

"Remember fast."

Then a click and silence.

Delaney got up then, stepping on Yeats and Lord Byron, pulsing with fear and rage. He ripped off the nightshirt. He faced the mirror and threw savage punches at the air. Hook after hook after hook. His mouth was clamped shut and he snorted through his nose. He snarled. He shuddered. Touch that boy, he thought, and I'll fucking kill you.

Delaney washed quietly in the hour before daylight. He dressed in silence, before easing down the stairs to his office. As soon as it was light, he would call his friends on the cops: Danny Shapiro and Jackie Norris. He would call Knocko Carmody. One of them would find Gyp and lean on him a little. If they can't find him, he thought, I will.

He could smell the coffee before he saw Rose. The aroma moved under the door, through the cold morning air. Then there was a knock.

"Come in."

Rose entered, with a single cup on a tray, steam rising in the chill, a sugar bowl, a spoon. Her bathrobe was pulled tight.

"You want some toast, Dottore?" she said softly.

"Let's wait for the boy," he said. He stared at his desk. "I got a call a little while ago."

"I know," she said. "I hear it ringing."

"It was Gyp," he said.

"That bastid. Excuse me. What'd he say?"

He told her, and laid out plans for defending themselves. Defending the house. Defending Rose and Monique and the boy. She listened carefully.

Then the boy was there, squinting at them. He paused, then hurried to hug Rose's hips.

Later in the morning, he and Rose and Monique began building their fortress. Time moved quickly, although it seemed like only a few hours in a day busy with patients, here in the hall, out there in the tenements, off at the hospital. In fact, the work took four days. A locksmith arrived and added locks to the doors in front and back. An ornamental ironworker named Buscarelli took measurements for window guards, and they were in place two days later. Jimmy Spillane, wiry and dour, arrived with a short mustached carpenter named Mickey Mendoza, and Rose showed them into the basement with the boy tagging along. They went floor by floor, looking for places to install steam pipes and radiators. When they were finished, and Delaney left a patient to say good-bye, Mendoza said, in wonder:

"This kid speaks Spanish!"

"That's right," Delaney said.

"Sicilian too," Rose said.

"Where'd he learn Spanish like that? I'm from Puerto Rico and —"

"Mexico. He was there with his mother. He's a fast learner."

"I'm very impressed," Mendoza said, rubbing the boy's head as he moved to the door. "Hasta pronto, joven."

"Hasta pronto," the boy said. "Que le vaya bien!"

"I'll be goddamned," Mendoza said, and smiled as he and Jimmy Spillane went out. Spillane said glumly that they'd have an estimate the following morning. He said almost nothing else. When they were gone, Rose looked at Delaney.

"Why's this guy Spillane so unhappy?" she said.

Delaney sighed. "His mother came here one morning, maybe six years ago. I sent her to St. Vincent's. She died there."

Rose nodded but said nothing.

"Excuse me, but I have to work," Delaney said. He leaned down and hugged Carlito. "Be good, joven."

By afternoon there were new rules. The boy could no longer come to the area where the sick assembled. He couldn't come while they were there. He couldn't come when they were gone until after the place had been scoured of germs and microbes. Or at least most of them. The boy had to be kept safe from many things.

"I'll get someone to come in every day," Delaney said to Rose. "You'll never have time. Someone who can scrub the place down with disinfectant."

"I can do it."

"No, you can't. Help me find someone."

By the end of the week, Rose had found a black woman named Bessie. She was bone thin, and asked Delaney to examine her for tuberculosis before she started working around the boy. "My brother Roy, he got it," she explained. "You never know." Delaney examined her. She didn't have it. She began to arrive every afternoon for an hour, when the patients were gone. She wore gloves and a surgical mask, and was paid two dollars a week. The boy looked at her with curiosity, a woman with ebony skin, and resisted his banishment from the bottom hall, but Rose enforced the new rules.

"You can't get sick," she said to the boy. "You got too much to learn."

It wasn't only sickness that Delaney feared. Patients arrived without appointment. The door must be open. It could be open to some gunsel too. A punk like Gyp might fire shots at everyone. Or act on his implied threat and snatch the boy. On that first morning, Delaney explained to Rose and Monique about the phone call, and made his own calls to Danny Shapiro at the precinct, to Angela, to Knocko Carmody. They would watch the streets, listen for rumors, issue warnings. Shapiro was a tough young wiry detective, and said: "They won't get close enough to that kid to tell the color of his eyes."

And Rose blurted out fiercely: "They try to snatch Carlito, they gotta go through me."

Delaney said that wouldn't be necessary, but he was not truly sure. Once every hour or so, fear opened and closed in his stomach like a fist. He warded it off by focusing on the fear rising from his patients, but when the last patient was gone, the last house call made, he imagined gunmen in the shadows. Or the knife artist named Gyp.

"There's someone across the street in a car," Monique said on the second morning.

Delaney went upstairs to his bedroom window and peered out through the curtains. He smiled and came downstairs.

"It's two of Knocko's boys," he said. "Keeping an eye out."

"That didn't take long," she said.

"Make sure they get some coffee."

Later, Delaney rummaged deep into a bedroom closet and found the old Louisville Slugger that Big Jim had given to him in 1894, when he turned eight. Dried black tape was loose on the handle. He hefted the bat, feeling its weight, sensing its memory of doubles and groundouts, and then leaned it against the wall between the bed and the night table. After rounds, he stopped by Billy McNiff's and bought two more bats, each engraved with the signature of Mel Ott.

"A little cold for baseball," McNiff said.

"Spring is coming, Billy."

"That kid play ball?"

"He will."

"How old is he anyway?"

"Old enough."

On the way home, he began thinking of cutting a separate stairway into the back kitchen. To keep the boy away from patients and anyone else who might come in the door. He could not close the kitchen to Carlito, because the boy loved its Sicilian aura of plenitude, its position as a kind of warm center of the chilly house, and its entry into the garden. Delaney thought: I'll call Knocko to send over a carpenter to make an estimate. At home, Delaney placed one new bat beside Monique's desk and gave the second to Rose. She gripped the handle awkwardly, then smiled at Delaney.

"I don't know nothin' about baseball," she said.

"I'll teach you if you want. But this isn't for playing ball."

"It's for breaking a head, right?"

"Right."

She smiled in an odd way, then swung the bat sharply through the air, upper teeth clamped over her lower lip. He showed her how to hold the bat, and she swung again. This time something cold came into her eyes.

If Eddie Corso indirectly had created the sense of siege on Horatio Street, the bounty of Eddie Corso was providing solutions. Delaney thought with a chuckle: Maybe I can cut into the cornice on the roof and set up archers. To peer across the empty lot toward Jane Street. Aiming arrows. To pierce the hide of anyone they see with a mortar. Or a lance. Maybe we can take over the roof of the empty Logan house, the high ground. Maybe we can arrange snares that fall on a signal. Or string barbed wire all the way to the North River. Maybe . . .

The weather warmed on Thursday and the snow was gone on Friday. When Delaney went on house calls now, he noticed men standing in small groups at all corners of the block and on one of the rooftops across the street. The faces were not always the same. But he could pick out Knocko's boys, with their derby hats, and Danny Shapiro wandering from the precinct, and a few of the regulars from Angela's. All of them protecting their own, which, Delaney thought, in this case happens to be me. And the boy. And Monique. And Rose. I can never move now.

"It's like a block party around here," Rose said, and laughed. "How many of these guys — I mean *your* guys — you think have guns?" Delaney said he didn't want to know. In the places where he made house calls, neighbors nodded, and waited in the vestibules like guards. The word was out. This wasn't just a neighborhood. Delaney knew that it was a point of view, a way of looking at the world and living in it. They all believed in the unions, the longshoremen, the teamsters, the carpenters, the steamfitters, and so did their wives. Even out of work, the men were out of work as union men. In the twenties, more than a few of them had had their heads cracked in fights on picket lines, men like little Patty Rafferty, who sat now with vacant eyes in the dock wallopers' union hall. Some had cracked a few heads themselves. But they got the union, forever. They had voted for Roosevelt and said so, and some had voted for La Guardia and didn't say so, because they had never voted for a Republican in their lives. Now some of them were communists, vehement and certain, but Delaney was sure that wouldn't last. The communists did not easily forgive sin. On the West Side, sin and its forgiveness were part of the deal.

That's why he'd come back here. That's why he'd returned to make a second life with Molly and Grace after the war had destroyed so many things, including the certainties of that first life. These were his people. They needed him. They still did. And he needed them. They would fight if threatened, and he would fight for them, and with them. He would try to prolong their lives. Or save them. He would help them move their children through the ceaseless dangers of the streets. He would try as hard as he could to ease their pain. To bring them sleep. To give them another day, another week, another year. The reason was simple. Here all sins were forgiven. Even the sins of James Finbar Delaney.

On Sunday, the blessed day without patients, Rose was off work, wandering alone into the city. Delaney tried to convince her to stay home, but she only laughed. "Those bums can't fight when the sun is out. Don't worry. I'll be okay." And was gone.

Delaney took Carlito by the hand and walked down to Washington Street. The sun was bright and hard. They stood for a long time watching a lone freight train move on the High Line, testing the track, groaning, pulling loads of unseen cargo, bells ringing, steel wheels squealing, entering buildings from the north side and emerging on the south. He tried to see this wonder through the boy's eyes. Were these huge right-angled animals? Were they controlled monsters? Whatever he thought, the boy didn't want to leave.

"Tray," he said, pointing a mittened hand at a train. And adding, when it was gone, "More tray."

I will get him a picture book about trains, Delaney thought. And about animals. And the alphabet. He will learn to name the world. All of its plants and living creatures, its seas and ships, its cabbages and kings. In the spring, I will get him a book about baseball. And show him the photographs in the *Daily News,* of a man sliding into second base with the shortstop above him, firing to first for a double play.

Then they walked to the North River, empty on this cold day of rest. Only the train was moving behind them. He saw one of Knocko's boys watching from a discreet distance, hat pulled low, hands jammed in pockets. The boy stared in wonder at three huge ships tied to the few waterfront piers that were not emptied by the Depression. He saw a seagull descending in a diminishing circle and landing on a grimy piling. Then Delaney led him onto the abandoned pier where he and Molly had walked on summer evenings. He held the boy's small hand all the way, feeling the warmth. He wondered where Rose had gone on this empty Sunday. The North River was filled with broken boulders of ice, and Delaney explained the chunks to the boy, and how the river carried them away to the harbor to the left and then to the ocean, and the boy watched with great intensity. I will find a book about ships and rivers and the ocean sea.

Standing on the timbers of the pier, holding the boy's hand, Delaney realized that after a long frozen time, there was a fresh current in his own life too.

• • •

When he was in bed in the dark, longing for sleep, Delaney's patients vanished. The commandos of the neighborhood's self-defense corps had retired to quarters. Monique was off in her night place. Rose was upstairs with her dictionary and her *Daily News* beside her and a baseball bat in the corner. There were no sounds in the dark house. And yet he trembled. Afraid of sleep. For the boy now filled too many of his dreams.

One night he saw Carlito falling from the Brooklyn Bridge, calling, calling, his voice pathetic and pleading, vanishing into the black waters. On another night, the boy was running on Horatio Street toward the High Line and fell into an open sewer, into the place where cholera lived, and typhoid and polio. On a third night, the boy was at the rail of a freighter glazed with ice, carrying him away from a North River pier into the unseen Atlantic. And on another night, on the same icy ship, the boy started to climb the rail, as if to dive in and swim to shore, and his mother was suddenly there, Grace herself, pulling him back, the faces of both distorted with fear. That night he called to Grace to hold the boy, and then woke up at the sound of his own voice.

On this Sunday night, he huddled there in the dark, his heart thumping. Longing for sleep to come, in spite of dreams.

He woke abruptly from a dream of Carlito one night, the boy wedged in the gluey mud of a trench, wearing pajamas among helmeted men while explosions shook the earth. Jesus Christ. Jesus fucking Christ. Delaney lay there, heart pounding, his eyes blinking, and then saw a glow.

Against the far side of the room the glow was pale white, tinged with blue, as shimmery and pale as a watercolor. He stared. And then, like atoms coalescing, a figure formed, sitting in the wing chair.

It was Molly.

"Hello, James," she whispered.

He started to get up, to go to her.

"Don't move," she said. "Stay there."

He rose to his elbows, his heart now racing.

"Is it really you?" he said.

She didn't answer for a while.

"I want to tell you something," she said. She was wearing an overcoat and laced boots, but he could see her high cheekbones, the wide-spaced eyes, the lustrous hair, the long-fingered hands.

"I had to go away," she said. "It was the only way I could live."

"Where did you go?"

"Everywhere," she said. "To green fields. To soft rain. To music in mountains. Everywhere, James."

"But why?"

"To be free. And so you could be free too. Free of me."

"I didn't want to be free of you."

"But look at you. You have the boy. And you look happier than you ever were with me."

"Please, Molly, stay. Don't go away. Stay with me. And the boy, and we'll wait for Grace to return, and —"

He slipped out of bed now to go to her, to hold her, to embrace her, to weep into her hair.

"I must go," she said.

He took a few steps. And then she was gone. The glow faded into blackness.

Delaney turned to his pillow but did not weep.

SIX

THE MIDNIGHT VISION OF MOLLY WAS WITH HIM AT BREAKFAST, and stayed while he tended to the morning patients, and as he ate a sandwich with Rose on the lunch break in the kitchen, and while Carlito showed off his growing skill with the paddleball. Molly was with him later, as Delaney moved through the neighborhood on house calls, leaning into the wind, and while he examined a cancer case and a raving late stage of syphilis in a woman he knew as a child. An old longshoreman moaned with diabetes, all feeling gone from fingers and hands, and tried to hide his terror about amputation. A thirtyish daughter explained that her sixtyish mother had fallen into some valley of depression and would not come out. An infant wheezed with croup. He looked at each of them, focused on them tightly, touched them gently, recommended remedies in a voice he hoped was soothing and kind and knowing, and moved on, and Molly was still with him.

Goddamn it, Molly, give me some fucking peace. I have done enough penance.

He remembered that morning last April, after she'd disappeared the previous August, the whole empty winter gone by, when Jackie Norris from the Harbor Police showed up with a sheaf of papers filled with the names of floaters and jumpers, the grisly harvest of the spring harbor. "If she jumped," Norris said in a soft voice, "there's a small chance that she was carried out to the Narrows and then on to the Atlantic. That's pretty rare, Doc. Most times they end up around the horn in the East River, or they bump up against the shore in Brooklyn. Most times we find the bodies." He sighed. "But then again, maybe she didn't go in the North River at all."

"Maybe," Delaney said.

And yet he was filled with images of her swirling through the river waters, her long hair streaming as she floated free. Free of me. Free of the world. On some nights he saw her bumping against a roof of winter ice, separated from the air and the sky. On other nights, he saw her hand jutting from the water, desperate for rescue. All through the neighborhood that day, keeping his appointments with the sick and maimed, he saw her in her watery place, or remembered her sitting in the chair in the bedroom the night before, or heard her playing the piano in the sealed room on the top floor.

He returned at last to Horatio Street. Cottrell was walking from the subway, still dressed in the severe clothes of a banker, but he would not even glance at Delaney. Monique had gone home. On his desk he looked at the estimates on the steam heat system ($300, to start after April 1) and the cutting of new stairs directly into the kitchen ($100, to be started immediately), and checked phone messages at Monique's desk and the mail that looked personal. Nothing from Grace. There were two notes from patients who were now well, thanking him for his help. There was an invite to a Democratic Party Valentine's Day dance. There was a notice from the Metropolitan Museum about the opening of a show of art from the Renaissance. Among the artists was Botticelli. He should tell Rose. And then he thought about Frankie Botts, trying to imagine his face and his voice.

• • •

Delaney hurried upstairs to see Carlito and Rose. It was after seven now, and they already had eaten. Rose was seated on her bed, back against the wall, her legs extended, big downy slippers on her feet, reading the *Daily News* and marking it with a red pencil. She put the paper down and looked at him in an annoyed way. He went to the boy's bedroom. Carlito leaped from his bed and jumped at Delaney, who scooped him up and hugged him.

"Ga'paw! Ga'paw! Rose, Ga'paw home!"

She came in and the boy slithered out of Delaney's arms and grabbed the paddleball and started batting away.

"Dos, tres, quatro . . ."

He made it to nine and then missed.

"You okay?" Delaney said to Rose.

"Your dinner, it's cold," she said. Her face was stern, perhaps angry.

"I had all these patients, Rose . . ."

"Tell them you gotta eat."

"I'll eat it cold," he said. "Thank you, Rose. I'll just eat it cold."

Rose sighed and tightened the belt on her housecoat, which was covered with printed roses.

"Come on, I'll heat it up. I hope it's not too dry. Hey, boy. Put on your bathrobe."

In the warmth of the kitchen, the boy kept batting away, and counting in Spanish and English, while Rose fiddled at the stove, and the room filled with the garlicky aroma of simmering veal and tomatoes. Delaney watched the boy and glanced at Rose, her back to him, her waist more defined by the belt of the housecoat. She had hips, all right, and slender legs. Fat women must have called her skinny, but she would live a lot longer than they would. Her hair was brushed and gleaming. She placed a bread basket beside Delaney, then spread the veal and tomatoes on his plate and took it to him.

"Okay," she said. "Eat."

The boy sat down at his chair too, prepared to eat again.

"Not you, boy. Just your gran'pa. You ate already!"

The child sulked, a mixture of disappointment and confusion. He stretched an arm out on the table, his fingers fiddling with the sugar bowl, and then laid his head on his forearm. He was either exhausted or sulking. Probably both.

"I better take him up. You eat, Dottore. I'll come back and make tea."

The veal was still moist, and as he ate Delaney marveled at his good fortune. This woman was now essential to his life, and he knew almost nothing about her, except, perhaps, the most important things. Her ferocious passion for the child in her care. Her skills with food. Her intelligence. He knew the outlines of her life, as told to Monique on the first day that she arrived here. He knew about Gyp Pavese and the dangers of the streets that she had resisted. But little else. Who had scarred her face? Who were her lovers during the American years as a cook or a pieceworker? Perhaps he should not try to learn more. The potential for disaster, living in the same house, was too obvious. But if he knew nothing about her it was also possible that he would unwittingly insult her. He was sopping up sauce with the crisp Italian bread when she returned.

"This is great, Rose," he said. "Just great."

"It's even more great two hours ago."

He tried to explain how he couldn't always be sure how long a house call would last. She'd have to get used to his uncertain routines. Some patients need more time than others, he said. They're not machines. *That's what I told Molly too, but after a while she just didn't care.* In some way, he said to Rose, a house call was like baseball. There was no script. You didn't know who would win. Above all, there was no clock. It took as long as it needed.

"Don't say any more," she said. "I understand. You gotta go help people. It's not easy. I just want it, the food, to be *good* for you. You earn it. You work hard, I know that, and you got all these other things to worry about." She paused, slowing herself down. "So when you eat, it should be simple. You and the food. Besides, I told you: I don't know nothing about baseball."

She took his plate and laid it in the sink and ran the water. She grunted, flicked off the faucet. The kettle began to whistle on the stove. She lifted it and poured water into cups and laid a tea bag on each saucer. She placed his cup before him almost gently and he knew she was no longer angry.

"It must be hard, all them sick people," she said, taking a seat facing him, examining a wedge of lemon.

"Sometimes."

"I guess you dream about them?"

"When I was young, I did. I dreamed about them every night. Not so much now, except for the war."

"You were a doctor in the war, right?"

"Yes."

"You musta seen lots of terrible things."

"Yes," he said.

She squeezed lemon juice into her tea.

"My husband, he was in Caporetto."

"So he saw terrible things too."

"They made him crazy."

He waited for her to go on. She was very still, as if afraid of saying too much.

"Tell me about him," Delaney said, as if asking a patient how she was injured. Rose turned away.

"He wasn' my husband then, when he was at the war," she said, her voice wavery with recall. "I was thirteen when the war starts, and Caporetto was, I think, three years later." She cleared her throat. "Anyway, the war ends. He comes back, and there's a parade, and he's with the other soldiers, all with no legs or no arms, and his head is all bandages, and I notice him, because of the bandages. What I can see, he's very handsome. My father sees me looking and another year goes by, and then my father says I got to marry this man. That's when I hear his name the first time. Enrico Calvino. A beautiful name, no? But I don't know him, except for the bandages in the parade. So I say this to my father. I say, let this Enrico Calvino come and see me. And he does. He comes for three months, and takes me for to walk, and to the new cinema in Agrigento . . . He don't talk much. He has headaches, and he tells me, inside his head there's a, a —"

"Silver plate?"

"Sì, a plate inside. Made of silver. To hold his head together. Right that minute I should have left Agrigento. A man with metal in his head, he ain't ever gonna be normal. . . . But he's a hero of the war. How can I run away from a hero of the war?"

Most patients had a narrative that explained many things, and he had learned to be gentle in discovering it. But he wanted to stop now. To stop the process of knowing her. She was not a patient. She was not asking to be healed. He should leave her to tend the boy and cook and provide warmth to the house. But he wanted to know her too.

"And so?" he said.

"You want to know the whole story?"

"If you want to tell it."

"I didn't tell it to Monique. I didn't lie. But there's another story." A pause. "Maybe I better tell you, maybe you should know about me, if I'm gonna be here for the boy."

He waited, looking at her, and she began to talk.

Rose and her wounded husband got married and moved into a tiny house out where Agrigento ended and the olive groves began. A kitchen, a bedroom, that was all. Enrico Calvino was an old thirty-two and she was a very young nineteen. She discovered he was a fanatical Catholic and something of a mama's boy, but she tried. She offered no clinical details but implied that he was not a hero in bed.

She worked. He didn't. A year or two went by, and he started talking more and more about Benito Mussolini. "That was his job, talking about Mussolini," she said, and paused. "By then, I'm working in a fish house down by the water, because he can't work. I buy a used bicycle and go down in the morning, with big boots on my big feet, and back up the hills at night . . ."

Her face hardened and a sliver of bitterness came into her voice.

"But because I don't give him a baby boy, a nice little fascisti boy, he starts to hit me." Another pause. "A slap, then another, and after a while, punches."

Her chin jutted out, and she said, "Eh . . ." The sound of contempt. She stood up and poured more hot water in her cup and did the same for Delaney.

"Finally, I know I can't live with this Enrico no more. I can't live with him punching me no more. I can't take his sitting there, smoking cigarettes, not workin', not talking about anything except that goddamned Mussolini, and I start planning to get away."

She saved money, a few lire at a time. She checked boat schedules to Naples and trains to Torino and Genoa and Milano. She thought about La Merica. In the telling, the old buried rage blossomed. Her words came more quickly, her voice shifted to a higher pitch.

"One night, I come home late, and Enrico's there, drunk and pissed off. The big hero starts to yell. Where's my dinner? Where's my dinner and where's my baby boy? He calls me bad names, and I call him bad names, and then he comes for me with a knife, and I turn around and grab a stool, one of those small stools? With three legs?" She took a quick breath. "And I hit him in the head. The head with the, the, with the *plate*." Her voice fell. "And he goes down on the floor." A pause. "There's no blood, but I know he's dead."

She sipped the tea. She lowered her head, not looking at Delaney.

"I'm very scared," she said. "I mean, worse than scared. What's the word? *Panico*?"

"Panicked," Delaney said.

"Yeah, panicked. I think about burning the house down with Enrico inside. I think about going on the bike to the cliffs and jumping into the sea. I think: My life is over. I think: My parents, they'll be disgrace. I think a lot of things. Then I think: I want to live."

She looked up at Delaney as if trying to decode his face. Then turned away again.

"I wait a long time, till some clouds cover the moon. Then I drag Enrico out to the olive groves and leave him there. I go back to the house and make sure there's no blood, and I pack some clothes and get out the bike. I put Enrico down a dry well and drop big rocks on him, the rocks they use to mark the fields. Then I go. There's a midnight boat to Naples. I get on the boat with the bicycle and my bag of clothes, and I'm on my way. To America. To here. This house. This kitchen."

She looked exhausted and distraught now, shifting her body, clenching her hands. Delaney wanted to place his good hand on her and comfort her. He didn't move.

"I'm glad you told me all this, Rose," Delaney said quietly, and felt stupid for the clumsiness of his words.

"You not gonna fire me?"

"Of course not."

"I'm a murderer."

"In this country, self-defense is not murder."

She waved a hand as if dismissing the distinctions. She now seemed older, her thin face more drawn, as if debating the wisdom of saying anything at all. Delaney ended the silence, saying: "You'd better get some sleep, Rose."

Her eyes were full. She stood up and placed the cup in the sink. Then she turned on the faucet and watched running water quickly spill over the brim of the cup. She didn't say another word about her husband. She didn't mention Gyp Pavese. She said nothing at all about the boy she needed so much.

Instead, she said, "Buona notte, Dottore," and hurried to the hall.

He heard her footsteps rising heavily on the stairs. Her aroma lingered in the kitchen, roses melding with garlic. He had learned again that sometimes a kitchen was more intimate than a bedroom. Or even a doctor's office, where he had listened to so many confessions without any hope of granting absolution.

In the gray morning, wrapped in his bathrobe, he pushed aside the life within the house and glanced through the newspapers: 400,000 on relief in New York, Hitler ranting in Germany, fighting in China, a volcano erupting in Mexico. There was a photograph of the erupting mountain with a peasant in the foreground, dressed in white pajamas and sandals and holding a machete. You missed this, Grace. You missed the volcano. What paintings it might have inspired. I always thought that you had married Mexico even more than Santos. You were not a communist. You were an artist. Or so I thought. And never said.

Delaney sighed and skipped through the *Daily News*, where a story told about the glories of a new theater in Harlem called the Apollo, and he thought: I should go up there and see it. To listen. To see. Another story told about a woman in Brooklyn who had shot her husband dead. Delaney tried to imagine Rose on her final night in Agrigento. The husband with his knife. His eyes mad in the light of candles. Coming at her. Then Rose reaching for the three-legged stool. What have I done? She is here now. She is caring for the boy. And yet within her is a woman who killed. He imagined himself under oath in a court of law, explaining that yes, he had known about the death of her husband. But he could not imagine her ever killing again. Except to protect Carlito.

He dropped the newspapers on the carpet and got up to brush his teeth.

• • •

The boy played with his paddle and his teddy bear. Rose moved through the day without saying a word about her confession. Patients demanded help. The watchers kept watch on the street. That night, in a light trembling sleep, Delaney was on a melancholy strand of beach and something was behind him. An immense creature. He could not see it but heard the great weight of its body, feet smashing into sand, the foul gnashing of its breath, and he was running and running and running . . .

The ringing phone snapped him awake. He was still breathing in the darkness, still fleeing the unseen beast. He fumbled for the telephone. Something fell. From the sound, surely a book. Surely Lord Byron.

"Hello," he said softly.

He heard someone laughing. And then a man singing. Gyp Pavese.

Oh, you.

Forgot.

To re-mem-berrrrr . . .

"Listen to me, pal," Delaney said. "I want you to take a message to Frankie Botts."

There was silence, except for the man's breathing.

"Tell him I'm coming to see him today. Right after lunchtime. The Club 65."

Delaney hung up. The man, almost certainly Gyp Pavese, didn't call back. Delaney stretched out in the dark, taut and angry, flexing and unflexing his hands, his head teeming with scenarios.

In the morning, his guts were churning and his head ached. I can't live like this, he thought, but I can't die either. Too many people depend upon me. He imagined himself at Club 65, tape pasted over his mouth, punched in the stomach, bundled into a car. Racing away. And then told to get out an hour later, shot once, twice, six times, and dropped into a lime pit in Jersey. What if that happened? He descended to the kitchen, drawn by the sound of Caruso on the radio and bacon frying in a pan. He went in and Carlito came charging, to be lifted, hugged. "Ga'paw, g'mornin', Ga'paw! Buenos días!" The boy's warmth infused him with life. *They will not harm you, boy. I will hurt them first.* He glanced at Rose and remembered her saying the same words — they would have to go through her — and she gave him a troubled look and then a smile.

"Everything okay, Dottore?" Rose said.

"Nothing that can't be cured."

He whispered to Carlito. "You okay, big boy?"

The boy smiled in a cheeky way. "Okay." He pointed at his plate. "Bay-con an' egg!"

Delaney sat him back in his chair. Rose touched his plate.

"What's this?" she said, pointing at the plate.

"Play!" he said.

"Play-tuh."

"Play-t."

"And this?"

"Fook."

Rose laughed out loud, and Delaney grinned.

"No fook. That's a bad word. Faww-rrrrrr-kuh."

"Fork."

"And this?"

"Mesa!"

"No, no, in English!"

He paused, then blurted: "Table!"

He was naming the world, one glorious word at a time, but enough was enough. Time to eat. Carlito scooped up the scrambled eggs, dropping some of them off the fork, which he held firmly in his left hand. Rose came from the stove with Delaney's plate. The Italian station had a female soprano on the air now, but in his own skull he heard Jolson singing, in some lost year at the Winter Garden. *When there are gray skies, I don't mind gray skies, you make them blue, Sonny Boy . . .* And Molly scoffing at the sentimental rubbish, and then laughing when Delaney stood on a Broadway corner and sang the words, and promised her, in Jolie's voice, You ain't seen nuthin' yet . . .

He ate quickly, sipped the jolting dark coffee, kidded with the boy and with Rose. But the headache nagged. He would need an aspirin. There was one appointment he wished he could avoid. One that put fear in his guts and an ache in his head. Then he heard Monique come in, and she poked her head into the kitchen and smiled.

"Morning all," she said. "Looks like, uh, a busy day. They're already waiting outside, and it's thirteen degrees in the sun."

"Better bring them in, Monique." Then he raised an open palm. "Give me a bit of time first."

He hugged the boy a final time and thanked Rose and then went to his consulting room. He made some notes: Call Zimmerman. Call Knocko. Call Danny Shapiro at the station house. He took an aspirin, telling himself: Leave instructions, in case I'm killed. Then he sat there, guts churning again. What if Frankie Botts was a real animal, as Rose had called him? And then thought: After the war, I promised myself I'd never live again in fear. But now it's not just about me. It's the boy too . . . it's Rose.

He took a piece of stationery from his desk drawer and unscrewed his fountain pen. At the top he wrote the month, day, and year. Nineteen thirty-four. He addressed a note: *To Whom It May Concern.* He stated clearly that the bulk of his estate, his money, would go to the boy and his mother, Grace Delaney Santos. Monique and Rose would each receive ten percent. Mr. Carmody of the Longshoreman's Union would serve as executor. He wrote down the combination to the wall safe. Then he signed the note and sealed it in an envelope, which he marked *Just In Case.* Monique would know where to put it.

He took a deep breath, exhaled, and opened the door to the waiting area.

"Who's first?"

He was ready to vanish into their pain and not his own. The headache disappeared.

At ten-thirty, with no patients waiting and the room disinfected, Rose and Carlito came in. She was carrying a tray with a sandwich of prosciutto and mozzarella, and a glass of water. She seemed to know that there would be no more patients for a while. Carlito went to Delaney's leather bag.

"Ga'paw's bag," he said.

Rose placed the tray on Delaney's desk and said, "Eat something. You look terrible."

"No, I feel —"

"No back talk. Eat."

Carlito leaned an elbow on his thigh, and Delaney began to eat. Suddenly he was ravenously hungry. He gave the boy a crackling crust and he munched away.

"Pan bueno."

Rose said: "In English."

"Bread *good.*"

Was that his first adjective?

"The radio says good weather's on the way," Rose said. "Maybe two more days."

"I hope so. The sidewalk's like glass."

"Two more days, you use the bicycle."

"Pray for it, Rose."

"I don't pray, but it's gotta come. You gotta get sun. You don't have any color. You're gonna get sick. *You,* the dottore!" Then suddenly: "Carlito, don't eat your gran'father's sandwich."

"Samich."

They both laughed. Then Rose turned to Delaney.

"What are you worry about?" she said.

"The usual."

"Well, stop," she said. Then to the boy: "Come on, boy."

She took the tray and the plate with its crumbs and started for the door. She left the water.

"Rose?"

"Yeah?"

"That was the best damned sandwich I've had since I came home from the war."

She blushed slightly, then waved a dismissing hand at him.

"Baloney."

"No," Delaney said, and smiled. "Prosciut'."

"Puh-shoot," the boy said.

Around noon, when the last morning patient was gone, Delaney was still for a while and thought about Frankie Botts and how stupid it would be to die. Then he took a breath, exhaled slowly, lifted the envelope, and stepped into Monique's area. He handed it to her. "Just in case?" she said. He nodded. She told him that Rose had gone shopping with the boy, where various people would be watching.

"I have to go see a guy on Bleecker Street. Tell Rose I'll skip lunch."

"How long'll you be?"

"Two hours, most."

She looked at the schedule of house calls and the stack of bills. Delaney saw from the clock that it was twelve twenty-five.

"But if I'm not back by three, call Danny Shapiro, the detective, and Knocko Carmody. Tell them I went to Club 65. They'll know what to do."

She jotted a note on a pad. Then her eyes narrowed. "What's this all about?"

"I can't tell you till I get back."

He was donning his hat, scarf, and coat. She lifted the envelope again.

"Just in *case?* I don't like this even a *little* bit."

"Just in case I get hit by a car," he said, and forced a smile. "Just in case a flowerpot falls off a roof. Just in case a woman aims a gun at her husband and hits me. This is New York, Monique."

She started to say something, but he was gone, clanging the gate behind him.

He walked south and east, shivering on the corners when he stopped to let traffic pass. If it was thirteen degrees this morning, it must be twenty by now. The glaze of ice was melting in the noon sun, and as he walked more quickly, the movement warmed him. He was walking the long way, refusing train, trolley, or taxi, and he knew the true reason was fear. He was delaying his arrival at Club 65, like a patient facing surgery. Alone, he could feel his own trembling uncertainty. At Club 65 they might, after all, kill him. And he would be cursed as a goddamned fool.

On his walk the Depression was everywhere. Even on Broadway. Huge TO LET signs were taped inside the windows of abandoned stores. At every corner men in army greatcoats sold apples. When they first started to appear, three years earlier, all with VETERAN signs displayed in their racks, there were many photographs of them in the *Daily News.* Not anymore. Now they were almost as common as lampposts. He gave one hollow-eyed man a quarter and left the apples. "This," he explained, "is from Sergeant Corso." The man grunted something and stood there against the wall, out of the wind. Down the street, Delaney saw a woman, sagging with abandonment, trudging with two children, her gloveless hand outstretched. Her hair was wild and dirty. Her shoes flopped and she wore no socks. He gave her a dollar, and she looked astonished and burst into tears.

He turned east at West Third Street and saw more than a dozen grizzled men in a lot huddled around a fire in a battered garbage can, one of them roasting a potato on a stick. Maybe a baked or roasted potato would sop up the acids in his churning stomach. The lot was piled with anonymous rubble, strewn garbage, splintered timber, a dead dog picked apart by rats. The far wall was scorched by an old fire. One man took a swig from a wine bottle and passed it on. A half-block away he saw a line of men waiting for entrance to a government building. Most wore dirty overcoats, shirts with curling collars, neckties, old fedoras, as if trying to retain a lost respectability. Scattered among them were men with caps, union buttons, heavy boots. None talked, silenced by humiliation. A few read the meager listing of want ads in the *Times* or the *Herald-Tribune* or the *World. Come home and paint this, Grace. Come home.* And then he realized something large: He didn't really want her to come home. He wanted to be with the boy. He wanted to do what he was about to do, and live. And then he would make certain that the boy would live too.

The wind blew harder when he reached Bleecker Street. Up ahead he saw his destination. He shuddered in the wind.

Club 65 was a corner saloon, older than the century, with a triangular cement step at the main entrance. A side door opened into the back room, where long ago men could bring women. Once before the war, he'd even taken Molly here. Then it was called the Fenian Cove, and on Friday and Saturday nights they played the old music from Ireland. Not the Tin Pan Alley stuff of the Rialto on Fourteenth Street, with its sentimental delusions, its cheap stage-Irish jokes, but music made before anyone on the island spoke English. It was all flutes and drums and fiddles and pipes, and Molly loved it. Listen, she said, it's Smetana. Her face amazed. And he didn't know anything about Smetana, and she explained the way he used folk melodies from Czech villages in his music, and she was sure those villages had once been Celtic. "Just listen, James." A year later she took him to a concert of Smetana and said: Do you remember? The Fenian Cove? He didn't really remember clearly what was played there, but said of Smetana, Yes, I hear it, I hear Ireland.

Now he hesitated. Thinking: I don't need to do this. I can leave it for the police. For Danny Shapiro. For Jackie Norris. Leave it. Leave it. And then walked in as abruptly as he used to dive into the North River as a boy.

The bar was bright from the light of the street and was still laid out the way it had been in the years of Fenians and rumrunners. But there were far fewer drinkers now. Propped on stools at the bar, each forming a little triangle with one leg on the floor for balance, three men whispered inaudibly, as if their volume had been reduced by the sudden presence of a stranger. Another man was at the far end of the bar, near the window, hands in his pockets, gazing at the street. They all wore the gangster uniform: pearl-gray hat, dark unbuttoned overcoat, polished black shoes. The clothes said that not one of them was about to go to work, ever. As in memory, a passageway led to the back room. Delaney stepped to the bar. The bartender was a huge suety man with thinning hair and a pug's mashed nose. Delaney remembered Packy Hanratty's saying of such a face, If he could fight, he wouldn't have that nose. The bartender spread his large hands on the bar and leaned forward.

"Need directions?" he said.

"Just a beer," Delaney said, and laid a dollar on the bar. The man eased over to the tap and pulled a lager. He placed it in front of Delaney and lifted the dollar. He rang up ten cents on the register, brought the change back to him, and stared at Delaney.

"Is Frankie Botts around?" Delaney said.

"Who?"

"Frankie Botts."

"I don't know no Frankie Botts."

"Frankie Botticelli. Tell him Dr. Delaney is here. He should be expecting me."

The bartender stared harder at Delaney, then gestured with his head to one of the three men. They'd heard everything that was said. One of them slipped off his stool and strolled into the back room. He was back quickly, looking surprised.

"Hands up," he said.

Delaney raised his hands and was patted down.

"Back there," the man said.

Delaney left a nickel tip and carried the beer through the passageway. A window opened into a tiny kitchen, but there was no cook and no sign of food. In the corner of the large back room, four men were playing cards. There were booths along one wall, as in the old days, and about six tables, but nobody else except the card players. Delaney walked to them, taking off his hat, holding it in his bad right hand.

"Give me a minute, Doc," said the man who must have been Frankie Botts. "I wanna finish takin' these bastards' money."

The other players looked up in an amused way, and the game continued. The back room was warmer, radiators knocking with steam heat. The side door was closed. Each player had a pack of cigarettes in front of him: two Lucky Strikes, one Chesterfield, one Old Gold. They used a common ashtray. Three of the men each had a shot glass in hand, but Frankie Botts sipped from a cup of black American coffee, a distinction that made him look more sinister.

Delaney moved away from the table, sipping from his beer. Club 65 was the same kind of place where Eddie Corso had been shot on New Year's morning. The Good Men Club was Eddie's joint. Club 65 belonged to Frankie Botts. Neighborhood saloons that functioned as private clubs. All strangers were discouraged. There were framed photographs of prizefighters on one wall. Dempsey, of course, Mickey Walker, Tony Canzoneri, Jimmy McLarnin, others whose names he used to know, now vanished from memory. A framed cover of the *Police Gazette* showed Gene Tunney in his prime. One larger one was signed by Jimmy Braddock, who must have known the place well. The ballplayers were there too. Ruth and Gehrig and Crosetti. And high in the corner was Matty. From before the war, before Prohibition, before the Depression. Browning now, and dim. Christy Mathewson himself. And there were other photographs: soldiers in uniformed rows, all from the AEF, and he moved closer and peered at them. Looking for familiar faces, but seeing none. Two neighborhoods away from the North River, and the living and the dead were strangers. Every saloon south of Thirty-fourth Street used the same decorations.

Delaney turned at the sound of groans and saw that the game was over. Frankie Botts swept up the pot. He was a lean man in his early forties, elegantly dressed, hair slicked back like George Raft. His shirt was, as usual for a big-shot gangster, white on white, with linen threads in diamond patterns adding luxury to a cotton base. And as usual, he was wearing a pinkie ring. His eyes were black under trimmed brows. He remained seated while the others stood up and moved to the far side of the room, where they took a table out of earshot.

"Sit down," Botts said.

Delaney sat down, placed his beer beside him. It was going flat.

"You got some pair of balls, coming here," Botts said, his mouth a slit.

"Mr. Botticelli, I never did anything to you."

"Yeah? On the street, I hear you pissed off some people. On the street, I hear you saved Eddie Corso's miserable fuckin' life."

"He saved mine. Twice. In France."

Botts stared at him. His mouth got tighter.

"I don't want to hear no war stories."

Delaney shrugged. "Fine with me."

Botts moved a spoon through his coffee, sipped, then yelled across the room: "Charlie, I need a fresh coffee."

The one named Charlie hurried into the passage to the bar. Botts stared at Delaney.

"You was in France?"

"Yes."

"My brother Carmine was killed in France. That's him over there."

He turned to the wall and pointed at a photo of a handsome young man. He seemed to have been photographed by the same cameraman who had pointed his lens at the Fischetti boy now on the wall of Angela's restaurant. He remembered Packy Hanratty's old advice: Don't punch with a puncher. Box him.

"Where was he killed?" Delaney said politely.

"Château-Thierry."

"That was a horror. What outfit?"

"The Sixty-ninth. What else? He was there three days and bang! Good-bye, Carmine. He was just nineteen. A fuckin' waste." He paused. "They didn't just kill Carmine. They killed my mother too. She ain't been right ever since."

Delaney sighed, said: "I'm sorry for your trouble." The Irish cliché. Then added: "Eddie Corso was shot too. Twice."

"Yeah, but the prick lived."

"That wasn't Eddie's fault. The Germans did their best."

There was color now on the face of Frankie Botts. "Then, New Year's Day, *you* save him, *again*." His eyes sunk beneath his brows. They took on a metallic sheen. "And you cause nothing but trouble for me."

"Mr. Botticelli, I'm a doctor. It's what I do. I'd do it for you, too."

"Bullshit."

"Try me sometime. You know where I live. Unfortunately."

Charlie came in with a cup of coffee and placed it in front of Botts. His voice and manner were apologetic.

"Sorry, boss. Had to make a fresh pot . . ."

Frankie Botts waved him away. Without looking at Delaney, he sipped from the hot coffee, laid down the cup. The pinkie ring flashed.

Then looking up, the eyes still lurking below the brows, his body coiled as if to strike, he said: "So whatta you want from me?"

Delaney cleared his throat. "Tell your man Gyp Pavese to move to

Minnesota," he said. "He calls my house last night, two in the morning. He repeats a threat he made the other night. He's a clown, a knife artist, a gunsel, a prime jerk, and you must know it. But he's doing his act in your name."

"Why should I give a fuck?"

"First of all, if this clown Gyp kills me, there'll be open warfare. And you know it, Mr. Botts. I'm the only doctor they have over by the North River. They don't have much money anymore, but they do have guns. A lot of them. There'd be piles of corpses. Some pissed-off Mick will shoot at your guys and hit a little girl going to buy day-old bread. One of your guys will shoot out the window of a cab and kill a woman who lost a son at Château-Thierry. The war here would be more senseless than the war in France."

Thinking: Stop. You're making a speech. Get to the goddamned point.

"There's another thing," Delaney said, lowering his voice. "The most important thing of all." A pause. "I've got a kid living with me. He's three years old. My grandson. His mother's gone off. If anything happens to me, I don't know what will happen to that little boy." A beat. "And last night Gyp threatened to do something bad to the boy."

In the eyes of Botts, a shift. Irritation with Gyp? Annoyance? Certainly not sympathy.

"And I promise you, Mr. Botticelli, if Gyp puts the snatch on that boy, if Gyp *kills* him, I'll make sure Gyp dies. And a few other people too. That's not a threat. That's a promise."

"It sounds like a threat to me."

He tamped out the cigarette and stood up, scraping his chair on the tiled floor. The wall clock said one forty-five. Delaney tensed. A nod to the other gangsters could kill him.

"You wanna end this?" Botts said. "It's easy. Tell me where Eddie Corso is."

Delaney looked directly at him.

"I told you I don't know," he said. "I assume he's far away."

A pause.

"You better get outta here," Botts said. "While you can fuckin' walk."

Delaney went out the side door, pulling his hat tight against the bitter wind. He inhaled deeply, held his breath, then exhaled hard, making a small cloud of steam. His guts settled, as if he'd swallowed a gallon of vanilla ice cream. Nothing else was settled, but he had said his piece and was still alive. Frankie Botts knew better now what the stakes were. What could happen, if . . . He started walking west, glancing behind him. Nobody left Club 65. There were more people on Bleecker Street now, kids heading for school or home, women carrying groceries, men with slabs of lumber on their shoulders and others with toolboxes, hurrying along toward the Bowery or Broadway. He walked faster now, the sidewalk traffic thicker as he approached Broadway. And then he saw her, one hand inside the long blue coat, the other deep in a pocket, a dark wool hat pulled low over her ear, her men's boots large and clumsy. Rose.

He stopped and waited for her to reach him. Her face was tight and concentrated, all vertical lines, two of them above the long nose. Then, six feet away, she saw him. Her eyes glistened.

"You're here," she said. "Right here on Bleecker Street."

"Yes. And I still have a heartbeat."

"God damn you," she said, standing there, not taking her hands from the pockets of the coat. She looked smaller. Angry tears began coming.

"Why'd you go see Frankie Botts and not tell me? Why do I have to learn this from a note on Monique's desk, when she goes to the bathroom? About if you don't come back, call Knocko. Call Shapiro the cop. God damn you, Dottore!"

A few people turned their heads to look at them, and kept moving. Rose stepped back and wiped at her eyes with the sleeve of her coat. He hugged her, patting her back.

"Let's go home," he said quietly. "We can buy ice cream for Carlito."

SEVEN

When they turned into Horatio Street, the watchers were still there. Two of Knocko's boys. A plainclothes dick sent by Shapiro. One was facing the house from across the street, the others off to left and right, guarding the block, each with a view of the house. Delaney nodded to each of them. They nodded back, seeing Rose carrying the bag with the pint of ice cream. The shades were drawn in the Cottrell house, the boards still nailed shut in the house to the left, where so many Logans died in so few minutes.

They went into the front yard, and Delaney gave the watchers a little wave.

"We have to get these guys some coffee," he said.

"Of course."

The boy was in Monique's room, seated on a chair, his small legs dangling. The paddleball on the floor. He leaped up and ran to Rose. An odd emotion brushed across Monique's face: annoyance. Or relief. But she said nothing.

• • •

He called Knocko and then Shapiro and told them about his meeting with Frankie Botts. Each said the same thing: It ain't over, so watch your ass.

Rose brought coffee in a thermos to the watchers and handed each a cup. When she returned, her face was still ruddy from the cold. They had cheese sandwiches, each grilled into what she called a panino, and then they ate the ice cream. Delaney felt it move cleanly into his stomach, calming him. He was sure he felt even more creamy pleasure from the ice cream than the boy did himself. On the radio, Bing Crosby was singing "I Found a Million-Dollar Baby."

"You okay, Dottore?" Rose said.

"For now. What about you?"

"For now," she said. "For now."

Delaney hugged the boy and then dressed to go out on house calls. He returned at dusk. Kids were everywhere. He saw Mr. Cottrell step out of his daily taxi, locked in his permanent solitude. Knocko's men were still there. He dined with Rose and the boy on soup and bread, the boy delighted with both. Then the telephone rang in Delaney's office.

Rose gave him an ominous look. The phone kept ringing. Delaney hurried into his office and lifted the black receiver.

"Dr. Delaney here," he said.

"Hey, what's doing?"

Danny Shapiro, with a chuckle in his cop's voice.

"Hey, Danny," Delaney said, trying to smother the nerves in his voice. "Everything's normal here. Thanks to you and the rest of the neighborhood."

"Just checking," Shapiro said. "Hug that little boy."

"I will."

He stood there for a beat, then returned to the kitchen. Rose saw the relieved look on his face and smiled.

Alone in bed, Delaney saw again the metallic sunken eyes of Frankie Botts. Actors worked long hours in front of mirrors to master that look. But actors fired blanks. Botts had killed people, and would kill more. The offense didn't matter. Killing was a form of power. He imagined a ballpark. A river in flood. The olive tree in the garden, bursting into life. Anything but Frankie's eyes. He fell into a light sleep. There were no phone calls.

But in a dream, Delaney saw the boy in pajamas, walking the shoulder of a midnight highway. Trucks and cars roared by, while the boy kept saying, "Mamá . . . Mamá . . . Mamá." Over and over again. Then a Packard pulled over on the shoulder, behind the boy. A man in a fedora and long coat stepped out. Delaney started running to them, and then the snow came. No highway now. No trucks. No Packard. No coiled man in a long overcoat. No boy. Just the snow whining and blowing.

And Delaney woke up with his heart beating fast and the echo of a word in the dark room. He knew that the word must have been "Carlito."

In the morning, Rose smiled in a tentative way. The radio was on, with news from distant places. The boy walked into the kitchen, still bleary with sleep.

"Good morn', Rose. Good morn', Ga'paw."

Rose hugged him.

"Good morn*ing*, Carlos. You wash your hands?"

He nodded yes, then corrected himself.

"No," he said, and hurried off to the upstairs bathroom.

"First he tells a lie, like all kids," she said. "Then he changes his mind and tells the truth."

"That's a good habit to develop."

"He'll never be a politician," Rose said.

"You never know."

When the boy returned, his face was damp from washing. The room filled with the odor of frying bacon. He smiled.

"Goody," he said. "Bay-con!"

"You said it, boy," Rose said. "Very goody."

Delaney glanced at the *Daily News*. In Germany, the Nazis had rewritten the Psalms. In Vienna, there was talk of a socialist rising and Chancellor Dollfuss promised to smash it with all the power of the state. He remembered seeing Dollfuss at a street rally in Vienna: a small, vehement young man, lashing out at journalists who made fun of his size. Now he had power. And small men with guns were dangerous people.

He turned to the back page, where only sports mattered. There was a photo of Mel Ott after connecting with a ball during a spring training game in Miami Beach. Behind him in the box seats could be seen the blurred faces of exultant fans. Delaney was sure that a man in the third row, shaking a fist, was Eddie Corso. Out of focus. With a beard. And thought: Frankie Botts must read the *News* too.

He went on his house calls, charged with wary energy as he moved through the cold bright afternoon. He walked with energy, climbed stairs with energy, spoke energy into his patients. As he walked, he ignored the three feet of sidewalk directly in front of him and looked at everything. At men. At strange faces. At cars. It was dark when he came home. A lone guard sat in a parked car, a lone window open an inch to cut the steam on the windows. One of Knocko's muscle boys. They exchanged waves. Rose was humming some vagrant tune as she heated his meatballs and dropped pasta into boiling water. Carlito was upstairs in his bed.

"You look better," Rose said. "Color in your face . . ."

"It's the wind, not me, Rose."

"No phone calls today — I mean, from those guys."

"Don't worry about it."

"You're right. There's too much goddamn worry around here."

She ladled out the pasta and added the sauce, placed the food before him, and sat down to a cup of tea. The bread had been freshened in the oven.

"And Carlito?" Delaney said.

"Okay. He's a good boy. But I told him, no more ice cream till his birthday."

"Why not?"

"He'll get *fat,* that's why not. Get to look like a balloon in the Thanksgivin' Day parade."

Delaney laughed and so did Rose. He felt that this was now her domain, the room she ruled, as if she had been here for years.

After dinner he went into his office, the door open behind him. There were two new medical magazines, mail from St. Vincent's, and a large envelope from the alumni association at Johns Hopkins, surely soliciting money. He put aside the medical magazines. For a long time now, he only glanced at the journals of his trade, looking at them within the context of his patients. He wanted to read about a vaccine that would cure their ailments. Stop gangrene. End tuberculosis. Dry up gonorrhea. These breakthroughs never came. And he never read the articles on advances in surgery.

Underneath the newspapers was a sealed letter. Addressed to him in Grace's handwriting. With a Spanish stamp and postmark. He held it for a long moment. Then Rose was at the door, and he slipped it into his pocket.

"You better go read that upstairs," Rose said. Her eyes were full of some unsettled mixture of pity and resentment.

"I guess so," he said.

"Then go," she said. "I'll close up down here."

"See you in the morning," he said. Feeling all energy flee.

He laid the letter on the bed while he undressed. He washed and brushed his teeth, hearing Rose climbing the stairs, and then was alone in the silence. He donned pajamas and his robe and the old battered leather slippers. There was no sound from the street either, except the whine of the wind. He built a small fire to take the chill off the room. Then he was ready to sit down to read.

Dear Daddy,

I hope Carlito is well. I dream about him. I see his face when walking the streets or having a quick bite. I see a child his age and I fight back tears (most of the time). Sometimes I feel I've done the worst thing a mother can do to a child. Other times, I feel that I'm doing this all for Carlito. I hope that someday he will understand. Someday, when the world is more just, you will understand too, Daddy. Because I'm aware that I've done this to you too. You must be so angry with me, and so overwhelmed with things to do. Here in Barcelona, I see you too, walking the streets with your black bag.

I'll be back as soon as possible. I promise. But I have to find my husband first. I've reached out to people who might know him, and at least one was encouraging. I can't say more.

I'm writing this from a table in the Plaza Real, a beautiful square down near the bottom of the Ramblas, the great street of Barcelona. It's early morning. Later it will be crowded. I'm learning the map of the tables in the plaza. The table of the communists. The table of the left Republicans. The table of the anarchists. The table of the socialists. There is no table for the conservatives, or the monarchists, or the fascists. At least I don't know if there is. I doubt it, not here in red Barcelona, where the bishops now keep the doors of all churches locked against the rabble. At the Plaza Real, everybody reads newspapers and smokes cigarettes and drinks the tallest glasses of beer this side of Yorkville. There is much talk of armed struggle, which I've picked up from scraps of conversation. I've bought a sketchbook and charcoal and sketch at the table, as attentive as a spy. I'm staying at a small pension a few blocks away from the Plaza, cheap and clean, but noisy at night. By the time you read this, I might be at another place, so keep using American Express. Try to send me a photograph of Carlito.

One other thing, Daddy. It's hard for me to say this, but Momma is not coming back. You must face that reality. She is almost certainly dead. It's time for you to get on with your life. I know that I'm not a very good person to be telling you how to live your life. In my own foolish way, I've done what Momma did to you: disappeared. But I know I'll be back. Momma will not come back. You should find a good woman who will love you in the way you deserve.

With all my love, and please hug my little boy, who is also yours,
Grace

This time he did not weep. He read Grace's letter again, and looked for his fountain pen to write a reply. Full of anger. The pen was not in his jacket. He must have left it on his desk. And now, a sense of relief brought on drowsiness, and he did not want to go back down the stairs. He knew where Grace was. At least he had that. He knew that five days earlier she was safe enough to sit at a café table and write to him. His reply could wait until morning. Perhaps by then his fury would be gone, like the end of a fever. He moved to the bed and picked up Byron, but he did not read. He thought: Tomorrow I must buy a camera.

• • •

Dearest Grace,

I was so happy to hear from you, to know (more or less) where you are, and that you are safe. Please don't worry. What is done is done, and I suppose you must finish your task before coming home again. It has been bitter cold here, and the casualties of the Depression are everywhere. But we are getting by, better than most.

Carlito is a delight. He is now a champion with the paddleball. He is also a southpaw. He has grown about half an inch since he got here, and is a huge fan of bacon and eggs, Italian bread, and bagetti with meatballs. He seems to add between seven and ten words of English every day. I've hired a housekeeper, an Italian immigrant woman who speaks English. She is in your old studio, and Carlito is next door. Between her and Monique, I can still do my work.

Send me messages as often as possible. Later today I'll buy a Brownie and make some photos. Thank you for what you said about your mother, though I haven't yet accepted that final reality. Here, too, is a little bit of money. Above all, do not vanish.

With much love,
Dad

He slipped a hundred-dollar bill inside the envelope, and a second sheet of blank paper to hide it better, then addressed the envelope and sealed it. He sat there for a long moment. He had erased his anger. He hoped his words were not too cold or pompous. Then he heard the boy jumping down the stairs. "Ga'paw!" the boy shouted. "Ga'paw!"

They came in a steady line: two men who needed quinine; a sixteen-year-old girl with permanent headaches; a haggard man who had been coughing for seven weeks; a man suffering from what was surely leukemia; a fat wheezing woman whose swollen legs refused to take her across a room; a woman with tuberculosis who could never afford the pampered exile of Saranac Lake. He did what he could.

Monique went off to mail the letter to Barcelona and to buy a cheap camera and some film. Her annoyed look was still in place. *I have to talk to her, find out . . .* Then the last patient was gone, and Delaney sat there looking at old mail. He tore some of it in half and dropped it in his wastebasket. He riffled through the *Daily News*. The phone kept ringing, but Delaney ignored it. Then an aggravated Rose came through from the kitchen and lifted the receiver.

"Dr. Delaney's office," she said, the way Monique always answered the phone. She listened, then picked up a pencil.

"What's the address, you know, where you live?"

She wrote down the details. "Thank you," she said. "I'll tell the doctor. No, I don't know what time he can come. Fast as he can. But in the afternoon, after he eats."

She started for the kitchen, and the telephone rang again. She sat down in Monique's chair and picked it up.

"Dr. Delaney's office. Okay, what's the problem? You got stabbed? Where? No, I don't mean your house, I mean what part of your body? The *knee?* Where was your boyfriend — on the *floor?* Lady, listen to me, listen to me, okay? The doctor don't do house calls for *stabbings!* That's for the cops. You call the cops right now, okay?"

Now Carlito was there too, trying to understand what was keeping Rose from the kitchen, and Delaney was standing in the open doorway to his office, looking down at Rose and smiling.

"You're doing great, Rose."

"These people, your patients, they're all a little crazy, ain't they?"

She looked at him in a blank way.

Delaney smiled again and said: "They have good reason, some of them."

Monique came in near the end of lunch, her face ruddy from the cold, carrying a small bag. She sat at her desk, saw the notes made by Rose. Delaney came to her.

"Someone's been sitting at *my* desk," she said in an arch way, as if telling a child a story about bears.

"Yeah, the phone kept ringing, and Rose —"

"It's my desk, Jim," she said in a clipped way.

"Of course it is."

"You want her to do my job, send me home."

She was more than annoyed now; she was angry.

"Ah, Monique, for God's sake —"

"She's taking over this house. I don't like it."

Delaney sighed. "I'll talk to her."

"Better you than me."

"I need you, Monique."

"Yeah."

She took a new Brownie from the bag and explained it in a crisp way to Delaney, the two of them examining the apparatus and reading the instructions and inserting a roll of film.

"You can figure out the rest," Monique said, and sat down at her desk. Delaney thought: Maybe her boyfriend has moved to Alaska.

On Sunday morning, puttering in the kitchen with Carlito, Delaney saw Rose as she was leaving. She had light makeup on her cheeks and a faint trace of lipstick on her mouth. Her long blue coat was brushed clean, and the wide shoes were polished. She did not say where she was going, and he did not ask. It was Sunday. Her day. And it would be foolish to worry about her. She smiled as she handed him the camera. Carlito hugged her hips.

"You remember how you do this?" she said.

"I think so."

"Maybe you better get more film, Dottore."

She said "film" the way the Irish said it. Two syllables.

"Maybe you could get a shoeshine too." She smiled. "You deserve it."

"Okay, Rose."

Then she was gone. He thought: Maybe she goes to church. Maybe she has relatives here that she's never mentioned. Maybe she has a lover.

• • •

Delaney and Carlito walked under a cold sun to Astor Place, to pick up the Lexington Avenue local. The boy's mittened hand was warm, and he gazed at everything he saw. Delaney helped him in the naming of the world. Newsstand. Garbage can. Bus. Taxi. Car. Lamppost. Sidewalk. Street. All nouns. He was still too young for most verbs.

"This is the subway," Delaney explained, as they entered the kiosk at Fourth Avenue. He glanced left at the many used-book stores that stretched to Union Square. A woman carried a heavy bag of books into one of them, perhaps to raise the cash to eat for three days.

"Ubway," Carlito said.

"S-s-s-subway," Delaney said.

"S-s-s-subway," Carlito said.

"Good!"

"Sssssubway!"

They passed through the turnstile to the crowded platform. Fewer trains were running on Sundays, to save money, but nobody seemed irritated by the long wait. It was Sunday. Delaney held the boy's hand more tightly. Many people were reading the *Daily News*, starting with the sports section in the back of the paper and moving forward. Others were absorbed by Dick Tracy or Orphan Annie in the Sunday color comics. In the distance, they could all hear a train deep in the tunnel, and they shifted, stepped back from the edge of the platform, tucked the newspapers under their arms. Carlito's eyes widened as the train rolled into the station, its wheels squealing, the air shoved aside, and lurched to a sudden halt.

"Tray!" the boy said. "Big tray!"

They stepped inside the car, the boy absorbing everything: the many people, their woolen odor. Every seat was taken on the long straw-covered benches, and Delaney grabbed an overhead handle and held on to Carlito with his free hand, after checking the bulk of the camera in his pocket. He did not explain to the boy about pickpockets. Carlito was standing directly in front of a heavy light-skinned black woman with a flowered hat. She was reading a Bible. No doubt heading uptown to church. He looked down and realized that Carlito was staring at the woman. She was not as dark as Bessie, the woman who came to clean. Her skin was more golden than black. The boy looked up at Delaney, and mouthed the word "Mamá" with a puzzled look on his face. Delaney squeezed his hand, thinking: Perhaps he's thinking of the bronze skins of Mexico. Perhaps this woman reminds him of what was left behind, and thus of his mother. The woman could feel the boy's stare. She looked at him, smiled, and returned to the Old Testament. Carlito smiled too.

They made all the stops, Union Square, Twenty-third Street, Twenty-eighth Street, Thirty-third Street, and finally came into Grand Central. They turned to leave with almost all the other passengers, but the black woman sat there, determined to go on to a place where she could worship her God among her own people. Carlito smiled at her and said, "Bye." She smiled back and said, "Bye-bye, little boy."

Delaney took the boy's hand to climb the stairs out of the subway. They were halfway to the top when the boy paused and looked behind him, as if memorizing the route. It was as if his eyes were also shutters. Delaney reached down and started to lift him, but the boy resisted: he did not want to be carried. They came to the top, and the boy stopped to watch a man in a business suit getting his shoes polished. What was this?

"Shoeshine," Delaney said.

"Hoo-shy," the boy said.

Delaney pointed at his own scuffed shoes and repeated the word, and remembered Rose in her wide men's shoes.

"Hoo-shine," the boy said, and they moved on. They saw a small crowd gathered around a bone-thin banjo player who was singing "Swanee" for the New Yorkers. Carlito stared at the man's hand, strumming the banjo. He stood blinking, remembering something. *Does he hear the guitars of Mexico? Is some memory of his father making a move?* The boy turned to Delaney and pointed at the banjo player's rat-colored boots, worn without socks.

"Hoo-shine," the boy said.

"Yes, Carlito. He needs a shoeshine. But then, so do I."

They walked on and passed under a wide arch, and then they were in the main concourse, and Delaney felt again as astonished as the boy must feel. He and Carlito just stood there, as some people hurried past them to departing trains while others stared at announcement boards, listening to an amplified voice barking about tracks and times. The voice caromed off such an immense plenitude of marble that it was almost unintelligible, and many people turned to one another, as if saying, "What track?"

Delaney could tell from their clothes and movement which people had jobs. The best-dressed people walked with a sense of destination. The others were in a permanent waiting room. The boy gazed around him, seeing beams of light pushing down from high arched windows to the station floor, and a ceiling that was blue and flecked with stars, and a wide marble staircase rising as if in a palace.

"Grand Central," Delaney said, waving his arms in an encompassing way, holding the Brownie in his left hand. The boy did not try to say the two words. It was as if the place was so filled with grandeur and complexity that it could not have a name.

Then they walked around the great wide spaces, Delaney wishing there were enough light to make photographs, deciding there wasn't. Then he saw another shine parlor, with three tall chairs for customers. And thought: Rose was right, I need a shoeshine. I might even deserve it. He led Carlito into the parlor and climbed onto a chair, placing his feet on the polished steel footrests. A small Italian man in his forties started brushing away the stains of winter.

"How's business?" Delaney said.

"Lousy. Nobody got money for shoeshines."

"They say it's getting better."

"Yeah? I don't believe dem." He was applying black polish to the shoes now. The skin of his hands was blacker than the polish.

Standing below him, Carlito was fixed on the process of the shoeshine. A fat man in a velvet-collared overcoat climbed into the empty chair beside Delaney.

"Christ, that's the best exercise I had in months," the man said, wheezing. "Climbin' into this chair, it's like going to the fifth floor somewhere."

Delaney glanced at him. The face was familiar, from Big Jim's club in the old days. And once in a while, at Angela's. Pink face, veiny nose. He couldn't remember the name. Delaney nodded a hello.

"Carmine," the man said, "you gotta make *one* chair close to the ground. A chair for fat guys."

"Den where am I gonna work, Judge?" Carmine said. "On my knees?"

They all laughed, and now Carmine was working on the final stage of Delaney's shine, using saliva to help bring each shoe to a high glistening polish. The boy looked as if he'd seen a magic act. In a way, Delaney thought, given the state of my shoes, that's what it was.

Delaney smiled in thanks at Carmine and started climbing down from the chair. The fat man paused. He squinted down at Delaney, who passed fifty cents to Carmine's blackened hand.

"I *thought* that was you," the man said. "You're Big Jim Delaney's kid, right?"

"That's right."

"Harry Flanagan," the man said, offering a pudgy hand to be shaken. "Please' to meet ya. I seen you box, before the war, some smoker down Baxter Street. You had a good right hand, I remember that."

"Thanks."

"Fast. Right on the button."

"It's a long time ago."

A pause. "It was terrible what happened to your folks."

"It was."

"Your father took care of my mother one winter, when we didn't have what to eat."

"He took care of a lot of people."

"You keep boxing in the army?"

"No, I hurt my arm in the war."

"That goddamned war . . ."

Carmine was working hard now, while Carlito ignored the talk, staring at Delaney's shoes.

"Just last night, at the club, I heard you had some trouble, downtown," Flanagan said, speaking out of an unmoving mouth like an old Whyo, or a Hudson Duster, the baddest of the West Side Irish gangsters.

"We're working on it," Delaney said.

Flanagan sighed and shook his head. "These new guys," he said. "They gotta work it out." He took a wallet from his jacket pocket and removed a business card.

"I'm a judge now," he said, handing Delaney the card. "Thanks to your dad." He smiled at Delaney. "You need anything, call me."

Then he nodded down at Carlito. "Who's this guy?"

"My grandson."

"How are ya, kid?" the judge said. "Don't let your grandfather make you into a doctor. Get a job that *pays.*"

"Take care, Judge," Delaney said, with a laugh. The boy squatted down and touched the gleaming surface of Delaney's shoes.

"Hoo-shine, Ga'paw," he said. "Hoo-shine."

Delaney took the boy by the hand and walked out into the marble grandeur of the station.

They came out onto Lexington Avenue, easing past a man selling the remains of the Sunday newspapers, and two silent men peddling apples, and a woman beggar. They walked to the corner of Forty-second Street. Taxis arrived in a steady line at the station entrance halfway up the block. A heavyset cop in a long coat sipped from a cardboard cup of tea. Horns blared.

"Look up," Delaney said to Carlito, gesturing above him with the camera.

The boy looked up and released a whoosh of astonished air.

Rising above the sidewalk across the street, glaring white in the hard sun, going higher and higher and higher, aimed into the sky, was the Chrysler Building. Neither Delaney nor the boy could see the top of the spire. They could not see the gargoyles on the sixty-first floor, designed like hood ornaments on Mr. Chrysler's automobiles. The boy would see them in some future year. But now, on this cold Sunday, he was seeing the largest thing he had ever seen in his life. Delaney named it for him. Then he peered into the viewfinder and framed Carlito as the boy was looking up. He snapped that photograph. Then he snapped another, of the boy pointing, and then a third, squatting low, trying to get the Chrysler into the frame. He was sure he had failed, that the building would be out of focus. Carlito was still gazing into the sky.

They walked now to Forty-third Street, for another view of the immense building. Delaney snapped a few more pictures. They moved toward Third Avenue, where so many little restaurants were clustered under the El. There was a long line of men on the south side of the street, waiting to enter the basement of St. Agnes Roman Catholic Church. To Delaney they looked like prisoners of war. Carlito was puzzled about the mass of men, looking up at their faces, unshaven, gaunt, bleary. Delaney did not try to explain about a soup kitchen. Up a wide slate stoop, the doors of the red-brick church opened and parishioners streamed out, most with pink Irish faces, hats pulled low, scarves around necks. They did not look toward the men waiting for soup. Bells began to ring, calling parishioners to the noon mass. A few arriving men and women saw friends coming out while they went in. They smiled, shook hands, and kept moving. The line of defeated men now reached all the way to Lexington Avenue.

"Let's eat," Delaney said to the boy.

Carlito smiled: “Eat! Sí!”

At Third Avenue, they stopped on the corner as an elevated train pulled into the station. Delaney made a picture of Carlito with the El behind him, something that Grace would recognize. He had taken her on the El when she was a little girl, after the war.

“Subway!” the boy said in an excited way.

Delaney pointed at the ground. “No, the subway is down below. This is the El.”

“El?”

“Yes, and we’ll go up those stairs later and ride the El home. Let’s eat first.”

The odor of frying frankfurters drew him into a small place with stools at the counter and three small tables against the wall. The stools and table were full, a sure sign that the food was good. He saw some faces from the stoop of St. Agnes, all chewing, and leaned over the counter and ordered two franks and two orange drinks.

“Hot dogs,” Delaney said.

“Hot dog-sss,” the boy said, perfectly.

“This is mustard,” Delaney said, slathering his own frankfurter with the bright yellow sauce. “You might not like the taste, so first try mine . . .”

The boy examined Delaney’s hot dog with suspicious eyes. He pushed a tentative finger into the mustard and then tasted it. He made a face. No. He didn’t like mustard. Delaney handed him the plain frankfurter. With his small bare hand, Carlito had some trouble handling the roll and the hot dog together, and after the first bite, which he chewed earnestly, even thoughtfully, he took the frankfurter out of the roll and chewed it with increasing energy, alternating with bites of the roll. Delaney finished his own hot dog.

“That was *good,*” Delaney said.

“Mmmm. Hmmmm,” the boy said, working on the last succulent inch of his frankfurter.

"Want more?"

Carlito shook his head up and down, smiling with his mouth full. He swallowed and said, "Yes, please, Ga'paw."

Please? It was the first time he'd heard the boy use the word. Did he teach him to say it, or did Rose? Delaney waved at the counterman and held up two fingers.

They climbed the stairs to the El, both a bit drowsy, their stomachs full. Delaney made a final photograph as the downtown train came into the station. There were plenty of seats, and the boy sat beside him and then turned and gazed out the window at the passing tenements. A light snow was falling. Across the aisle, a young Italian woman sat primly, purse on her lap, avoiding all eye contact. High cheekbones. High unlined brow. Long nose, a trace of down on her upper lip. She wore rouge and lipstick too. *Where does Rose go on Sundays? Is there a relative, friends? Is there a lover?* The woman got off at Fourteenth Street.

"Next stop," Delaney said.

The boy turned from the window. Delaney squeezed his hand. Soon they would be home.

EIGHT

MONDAY MORNING WAS NOISY WITH HAMMERING AND SAWING and the voices of workmen building the new passage from upstairs into the kitchen. When they were finished, Carlito would no longer be exposed to the germs of the patients on his way to lunch. It was noisy too with patients, during what Delaney called the Monday Morning Rush Hour. A man with an infected black eye. A six-year-old girl with raging fever and diarrhea. A fat woman with boils under each arm, screaming as he lanced them and cleaned them and covered them with wads of cotton. They came in one after another, gripped by the narcissism of pain. *Take me first, Doc. I'm hurtin', Jesus, I'm hurtin'* . . . Again, he did what he could. After the last patient left at ten minutes to one, Monique slipped into his office, with a grim look on her face.

"There's a guy here to see you," she said. "He showed me a badge. He says he's from the FBI."

"What does he want?"

"To talk to you."

"Give me a couple of minutes."

She closed the door behind her, and Delaney stood at his desk, his eyes moving across the walls but seeing nothing. Any cheap hoodlum could have a fake badge. They all had them during Prohibition. At least Rose and Carlito were out, off to a shoe store on Fourteenth Street, so neither would be touched by a new sense of alarm. But he didn't like visits from people who claimed to be the FBI. An agent wasn't here to get something for a migraine. He thought of Eddie Corso, and the secret admission to St. Vincent's. But that was a local matter, not the concern of the Feds, unless he failed to declare the money on his income tax returns. But that would be next year. No matter what, he would never discuss Eddie Corso. But then, the visit might be about something else. Someone from the Frankie Botts mob might have called in a tip about Rose. That she was a Wop — without papers. Someone might know that she had killed her husband in the old country.

Or it could be about someone else, a patient, an acquaintance, a politician. He had no obligation to talk about what happened with patients. He was, in that sense, like a priest. He had been taught long ago that many secrets were passed in the office of a doctor, and none of them must leave. Still: the FBI? He must warn Zimmerman. And then had a sudden thought: *It must be about Grace.* He opened his door.

"Yes?" he said.

A young man stood up, holding his hat in his hands, and his coat draped over his forearm. His dark blond hair was cut short. He had pale eyebrows, pale blue eyes. About thirty. The young man moved past Monique.

"Dr. Delaney?" he said.

"That's me."

He flashed a badge.

"Edward Callahan," he said. "FBI."

Delaney gestured for Callahan to pass into his office, then closed the door behind them.

"Have a seat," Delaney said, moving into his own chair. "What's this all about?"

"Excuse me for intruding on your busy day," the agent said, sitting with a kind of performed ease in the chair reserved for patients. He placed a notebook on his knee and took a pen from his breast pocket. "Let me get straight to the point: I'm looking for your daughter."

So that was it. I was right. Not Eddie Corso. Nor Rose. Grace.

"I don't know where she is," Delaney said.

"We think you do," Callahan said, smiling in a knowing way, his voice dropping into a deeper tone. "You received a letter a few days ago. We think it was from her. From Grace Delaney Santos. It was postmarked Barcelona, Spain."

"I assume you have a court order to snoop through my mail," Delaney said.

"The letter wasn't opened," he said, trying to sound reassuring. Delaney noticed that his fingernails were perfectly trimmed and polished. His dark blue suit was well cut, almost as severely as the clothes worn by Mr. Cottrell. "Besides, we're not specifically looking for your daughter. We're looking for her husband."

"I don't know where he is either," Delaney said. "I've never even met the man." Callahan scribbled on a pad, taking notes. "I do know he's a Mexican citizen. Beyond that —" He shrugged. "Why is the FBI interested?"

"We've had inquiries from the Mexican government," Callahan said. "Mr. Santos is a member of the PCM — the Mexican Communist Party."

"And?" Delaney said. "Is that a crime?"

"No, but bombing is. The Mexican government believes Santos was responsible for bombing two government office buildings in Guadalajara." His tone was level. "They want to locate him before he bombs anything else." He gestured as if he believed this was a bit of a stretch, but went on gravely: "They have reports he went to Spain, where all sorts of unrest is in the air. Or maybe even to Moscow. And that gets us back to your daughter, Grace. If anyone knows where Santos is, she should." He smiled. "For all we know, he could be in the Bronx."

"Or Brooklyn."

Callahan laughed. "Worse — New Jersey!"

He stared at Delaney, as if hoping he would fill the void with words. Delaney stared back.

"So?" Callahan said.

"I've told you all I know. Which is virtually nothing."

Callahan took his coat off his lap and laid it on the floor.

"Dr. Delaney, we might be able to help you with something. If you help us." Delaney looked at him blankly. "We know you have your grandson here. We know you are, what's the best way to say this? Under siege. From the Frankie Botts mob. We can do something about that."

Delaney stood up. He noted Callahan's dark brown brogans and their high polished sheen.

"Thanks for stopping by, Mr. Callahan."

Callahan didn't move. He stared at Delaney, absorbing his own dismissal. Then he closed his notebook and reached down for his coat.

"Think about it," Callahan said, and stood up to face Delaney. He smiled in a practiced way. Then handed Delaney a card. "Think about it."

He went out, thanking Monique as he left. Delaney looked at the card, then placed it under his blotter beside the card of Harry Flanagan, the judge. Yeah, he thought: I'll think about it, you son of a bitch.

• • •

Twenty minutes after Callahan left, Carlito rushed into the office and climbed onto his lap.

"Hot dog!" he said. There were still no verbs. "Hot dog, Gran'pa."

Another advance: Ga'paw was now Gran'pa!

"You want hot dogs?"

"Hot dog."

"Say: 'I want hot dogs.' "

"I wan' hot dogsss."

His first verb. The verb "to want." Everybody's first verb.

Rose came to the door, smiling, her hair loose across her brow, cheeks still flushed from the February cold. She told him lunch was ready. He thought: *Where does she go on Sunday?*

Rose lifted the boy and took him past the planks of the carpenters, the sawhorse, the toolboxes, toward the kitchen. There was an odor of cut wood in the air. The worker named Mendoza laughed and said, "Buenas tardes, niño," and Carlos answered, "Bey-nas tardes." The other workmen were gone, but Mendoza was eating a sandwich, sitting on the stairs. "Hello, Doctor," he said. "Pretty busy here today." Delaney told him it was always busy on Monday. Thinking: *We even had a visit from the G-men.* He asked Monique to try to find Zimmerman at St. Vincent's and then walked into the kitchen.

"This kid wants hot dogs!" Rose said. "I gotta nice sandwich for him, un panino, and he keeps saying he wants a hot dog. He did the same up Fourteen' Street. Hot dog, hot dog . . ."

Delaney smiled. She put the sandwiches before them, along with glasses of lemonade. Carlito's sandwich was cut into quarters.

"I want hot dog," the boy said. The verb. *That* verb. Rose ignored him.

Delaney thought the panino was delicious, and so did the boy; he held each piece in two hands and took small, methodical bites. The memory of hot dogs fled the kitchen. Monique poked her head into the room.

"I got Zimmerman for you."

Delaney excused himself and took the call in his office.

"Everything okay?" Zimmerman said.

"Yes, but —"

"But what?"

"A guy from the FBI was here a little while ago. In case he comes poking around the hospital, you don't know anything about my personal life, especially my daughter. I'll be at rounds tomorrow and explain everything."

"You just did," Zimmerman said. "I only know you from the halls of St. Vincent's."

"How's it going there?"

"I want a vacation. Just one hour. Or two hours, go see a movie. I hear they've got sound now."

"We'll talk tomorrow."

Back at the table, Delaney finished his sandwich and sipped the lemonade. Thinking: How did Rose find lemons in February? Then she pointed at Carlito's feet.

"Look at what I got. On sale, one dollar, off a pushcart. Buster Browns!"

Carlito held up his left foot and pointed at the shoe.

"Hoo-shine!"

Delaney wrote a quick note to Grace, telling her about the visit from Callahan. His tone was flat and cold. *Don't mail any important letters to the house. I'll send you an address that's safe. You can blather away about simple stuff, the cathedrals, Goya. Just nothing that you don't want to share with the FBI.* He asked Monique to mail the letter, but not from here in the neighborhood. She gave him a knowing look. It wasn't necessary to mention the FBI. Then Delaney went off on house calls, and his rage began to build.

• • •

As always on Monday, his last stop would be on Mott Street, in Chinatown. From a pay phone on Canal Street, he called a lawyer named O'Dwyer, who confirmed that he didn't need formal paperwork to have Carlito living with him. If the boy stayed six months, Delaney could apply to become the legal guardian. So he knew that the FBI could not use Carlos to force him to take the king's shilling, as Big Jim used to call it. Later, at Angela's, he would arrange an alternate address. He called Rose too, said he would be a little late, but that they would all go to Angela's. "Good," Rose said. "I'll make the boy take a nap. And hope he don't dream about hot dogs."

Now he was turning right off Canal Street, into Mott Street and a flood of Chinese faces, most of them male. Even under Roosevelt, there had been no change in the laws against Chinese immigration. But Chinese seamen could jump ship, slipping into the water off Coney Island, or just walking down the gangplank in Red Hook, and make their way to Mott Street or Pell. They could come down the Hudson Valley from Canada. It wasn't as easy for women. Still, there were a few women in Chinatown, and that was why he was here.

He crossed the street at Transfiguration Church, which in the nineteenth century had consoled the Irish poor from the Five Points and now served the Italians from Little Italy. He glanced at the church. A few older women moved in and out of the front door, dressed in black. Maybe this is where she goes on Sundays, Delaney thought. Maybe she comes here and listens to mass. Maybe she meets people from the old country. People she can talk with in Italian. Even a few people who knew Enrico Calvino in Agrigento, and knew that God would forgive her for breaking the man's head.

At 26 Mott Street, he pressed the bell for the top floor and casually looked around to see if anyone had followed him. Nobody had. Or at least no Caucasians. The door clicked and he climbed the stairs, carrying his black leather bag. On the top floor, Tommy Chin was waiting for him, smiling broadly. He was dressed sharply, wearing a suit with razor creases that broke cleanly over polished leather shoes.

"Hey, Doc, how are you?"

Tommy Chin was second generation, and talked like Cagney. He shook Delaney's hand and smiled broadly.

"I'm okay," Delaney said. "Just a little beat."

"You want coffee?"

"That'd be good."

Delaney followed Chin into his office, with its two windows opening into the yard, its desk, its framed photographs of Chin with various politicians and police captains. There was a second door, and Chin cracked it open and said something in Chinese. He waved Delaney to a chair and then sat behind his desk.

"How's it going?" Delaney said.

"Lousy. Everything's slow. Nobody's got much money, this goddamn Depression, and the first thing these guys do is cut down on ginch. All the wives must be happy."

"Or deeply *un*happy."

Chin laughed. A Chinese woman came in, about fifty years old, her glossy black hair pulled back in a severe way, carrying a tray of coffee and sweets. She nodded at him in a wordless, intimate way. Delaney had known her since before the war, before Molly, before everything. Liann. He had treated her for gonorrhea three times, but she never gave it to him. She smiled, nodded, vanished.

"Where are the ladies?" Delaney said.

"One flight down, waiting for you," Chin said. "The usual place. You know, Monday is Monday, the day we're closed. They go and shop. They eat somewhere, usually some American place. They listen to the radio. Maybe they dream about some rich guy that'll take them away for good. The usual stuff broads think about."

As they filled cups with coffee, Delaney wondered if Tommy Chin was now selling cocaine and heroin out of the building, in addition to women. Or supplying shmeck to Frankie Botts. To keep tradition alive. Long ago, ten years before the war, when Tommy Chin was just a tough teenager, this was a famous opium den. Society ladies came every day to smoke a pipe and maybe get fucked by young Chinese guys, including Tommy Chin. The place wasn't exactly a pleasure dome, but it did offer pleasure.

"I'd better go do the exams," Delaney said. "I've got a dinner date with my grandson."

"First, sit back and finish your coffee," Tommy Chin said.

They sipped the last of the coffee and then rose together and went out the door. They could hear music coming from the third floor, then stepped into the parlor, with its couches and bar and chandeliers and odor of perfume. Tommy walked over to the cathedral-shaped Philco and lowered the volume, saying something in Chinese. There were five women, all in heavy bathrobes and slippers, like people waiting for a steam room. They smiled at Delaney. His arrival always told them that they had finished another week in America. Then Liann entered from the door to a smaller room, and gestured for Delaney to follow her. She pointed at one of the women, who stood up in a bored way.

"See you later," Tommy Chin said. "Do the work of the Lord."

The first woman went straight to a hard narrow bed and sat on the edge, kicking off her slippers. Liann took a corner chair, an expressionless chaperone. Beside her was a sink. When Delaney had first told Tommy Chin that he wanted someone there, Tommy was surprised and then pleased. A witness. A translator.

The woman was about thirty, and she laid back, closed her eyes, and opened her legs. Like every woman in the house, she had shaved her pubic hair. Delaney donned rubber gloves and went methodically through the examination, peering into all of her openings. The first girl was clean. He nodded, and she smiled and got up, pulling the robe around her. He went out, and a second girl came in, and then a third. All clean. No sign of bumps or lesions, no chancres, nothing running and glistening. They all smelled of soap. They all had smooth ivory skin. After each woman departed, he washed his gloved hands in the hot water of the sink.

The fourth woman was really a girl. Perhaps sixteen, but who knew? And she was shy and trembling. She stretched on the hard bed but did not open her shift. Liann said something in Chinese. The girl turned on her side, facing Delaney, and opened her shift. There was a bandage over her right nipple. He lifted it and saw that her nipple was almost severed. She lifted a leg. The flesh around her vulva was red. He gently turned her over. Her anus was worse, sore and torn. Her buttocks were purple from punches. There were bite marks on her back.

"What happened to her?" Delaney said. He glanced at the girl and her eyes were filled with tears.

"Some big Irishman," Liann said. "Last night."

"Jesus Christ."

He reached in the bag and took out iodine and cleaned her wounded nipple. The girl winced, then sobbed. He bandaged the nipple. Then he handed her a jar of unguent.

"Tell her to use this for a week. Front and back."

Liann explained in Chinese, and the girl took the jar. She said something.

"She want to know, she have a disease?"

"I don't think so."

"What about baby? The guy threw away condom."

"Next week I'll bring some things for a test."

Liann explained, but the girl was not consoled. It must have been a savage night.

"Take her off the line," Delaney said. "At least until I can see her next Monday. And the guy that did this? Don't let him in the door again."

The last girl was clean too, and he closed his bag, took an envelope from Liann. and went down to the street.

The night had arrived, dark and windy. An elderly Italian woman stepped out of Transfiguration, steam leaking from her mouth, a lumpy black pyramid. She stood there for a long moment, enclosed in Sicilian solitude.

I want.

That verb.

I want too.

I want. I want.

NINE

THE BOY TOOK HIS TEDDY BEAR WITH HIM TO DINNER, AND REvealed his name. Osito.

"It means 'little bear' in Spanish," Rose said, grinning. "I asked Mendoza, the carpenter. Now the bear has a name, Carlito takes him everyplace. Osito this, Osito that . . . even bed at night." A pause. "Someone to hold on to, I guess."

Delaney thought there was a faint wistful note in her voice, but he did not respond as they walked through the cold evening to Angela's restaurant. Rose held the boy's free hand, while the boy hugged Osito.

The restaurant was half-empty, as it was on every Monday night, and a smiling Angela came to greet them. She led them to a table against a wall, out of the cold drafts of the opening door. Italian ballads played on the radio in the kitchen, with many mandolins. Angela waved and a waiter brought the high chair for Carlito. She pinched Rose's cheek and whispered in Italian, then pushed her breasts against Delaney. She leaned down to Carlito.

"Okay. Wha's this guy's name?" she said, pointing at the bear.

"Osito!" the boy blurted.

"An' what's he gonna eat?"

"Hot dog!"

"We don't have no hot dogs in here, boy. This is a *good* restaurant. So no hot dog!"

"Okay, I want bagetti!"

"*That* we got!"

Carlito climbed into the high chair and squashed the bear beside him, with its paws on the tray. Delaney and Rose told Angela what they wanted, and she went off to the kitchen. Delaney gazed casually around at the other diners. One stranger, sitting alone, was facing the door and reading the *World*. He was wearing a badly cut suit but seemed too old to be working for the FBI and too out of style to be a gangster. Others nodded hello to Delaney, and he smiled back. Rose played nervously with a fork, tapping the tines on the tablecloth.

"The guy readin' the paper," she said quietly. "I don't like his look."

"He's too old to be a bad guy, Rose," Delaney said.

"Don't be so sure."

"I'm not," Delaney said. And he wasn't. There were many kinds of bad guys, and their badness could be as real as blood.

He got up to walk toward the men's room, casually looking again at the stranger, and near the kitchen he stopped to talk with Angela. They were out of the view of the man reading the newspaper.

"I need something," he said.

"Like what?"

"A safe address," he said. "For mail. Nothing else. Where my daughter can write me without getting her letters opened."

"I'll give it to you with the check."

"Also: The guy with the newspaper, alone. You ever see him before?"

"A couple'a days ago."

"Keep an eye on him for me. Okay?"

"Okay."

Later, drowsy with food and exhausted by the long day, Delaney read Byron for a while in bed, and then turned off the light. Sleep did not come. Images of the day moved through his mind, glimpses of ivory skin, a flash of the absolute certainty in Callahan's eyes, the metallic look of a man who judged others. But Delaney could never judge the women in Tommy Chin's house on Mott Street. They did what they must. In some ways, their lives were now better than what they'd left behind. It was true of them. As it was true of some Irish women not long ago, and some Jews and Italians, and all the others who had found their various ways to the indifferent city between two rivers. Some, but not all.

He heard water running in the bath upstairs. Rose. Her heavy peasant tread. To the room. Back to the bath. The boy surely asleep, hugging Osito. Then silence. The water taps closed. Rose in the bath. His mind filled with images. How many nights did I spend in that tub with Molly? She murmurous with pleasure. Leading me wet to the music room, to stretch upon a yellow beach towel, to scream. Laughing once and saying: That was a C over G. But more often silent. More often humming some vagrant tune.

Delaney dozed then, hugging a pillow. After a while, he was snapped into clarity. The door had cracked open. A dim figure in the dark. He could smell the soap before he saw her. Rose. She said nothing. The door closed behind her. He heard her remove her robe. By the time she slipped in beside him, he was already hard.

He reached for her, to touch her flesh.

Rose was not there. The only flesh was his own.

For days, as the winter gave way to the first rumors of spring, he maintained a formal distance from her, afraid of making a mistake.

Rose went shopping with Carlito and his teddy bear. She bathed the boy, and cleaned his clothes, and prepared lunch and supper for the three of them. In small awkward ways, Rose showed Delaney that she knew something had shifted in him, but she gave him no obvious signs of her unspoken knowledge. She never used the language of affection, except to the boy. She did not touch Delaney, even in the most casual way, nor did he touch her. He was always Dottore. Not Jim. Everything was as before, and at the same time, it was not.

But across the days of other people's illness and damage and painful unhappiness, the days of endless casualties, he carried Rose with him now. She and the boy had formed a current in his life, like a secret stream flowing south through the North River, all the way from the distant mountains. It was a stream that was always in the present, not in the past, nor the future.

Then as February drew to an end, the past came rushing back. Delaney came down into the kitchen for breakfast on Monday morning and Rose and Carlito smiled at him. The boy's mouth was full of bread. The teddy bear dozed. The radio played at low volume.

"Some baseball guy died," Rose said. "It was on the radio."

"What was his name?"

"I don't know," she said. "I don't know from baseball."

He turned up the volume, while Rose busied herself at the stove. He moved around the dial. Finally he heard the name McGraw.

"John McGraw," he said. "It was John McGraw."

He tried to explain to Rose that John McGraw was the manager of the New York Giants, the manager for as long as anyone could remember, from before the Great War right up until two years ago, when Bill Terry took over.

"You knew this McGraw?" Rose said.

"Not really," Delaney said. "He was a friend of my father's. But I met him many times."

"I'm sorry he died," she said in a soft voice.

"So am I," Delaney said.

The morning patients were all sorry too, even the women. Delaney listened to the patients, and examined them, and spoke banalities, and wrote prescriptions for them. He wished he could go to the Polo Grounds and say a proper farewell. When the last morning patient left, Monique handed him a letter.

"For you," she said.

He took the letter, addressed in Grace's handwriting to a Harry Miller on West Nineteenth Street, and slipped it under his desk blotter. Then he called in one of the malarial vets for his quinine. The letter would wait. It had spent days crossing the Atlantic. A few hours would make no difference now.

On every house call, the talk was of McGraw. Do I have that thing that killed John McGraw? said one flabby man, gray from the long winter. Sure, he was a grand tough fellow, wasn't he? said another.

"You've got a ruptured appendix, Eddie," he said to a heavy longshoreman named Doyle on Jane Street. "You'll have to go to the hospital."

"Not me."

"There's no choice. You stay here, Eddie, you die."

"Shit," Eddie Doyle said, as if he'd been sentenced to the electric chair. After a while, he reached for his trousers, hanging on the bedpost. Delaney would have to make still another call to St. Vincent's for still another ambulance to pick up still another man who lived alone with the sour odor of age and isolation. His wife was dead of "the con," tuberculosis, which Eddie still called consumption. A man whose three daughters were gone off to the distant Bronx with their husbands and kids. A man left alone with Jimmy Walker on the wall.

"I hear McGraw is dead," Doyle said softly.

"True. They'll have a mass for him at St. Patrick's."

"Uptown St. Patrick's or downtown?"

"The one with the most seats."

"Your father woulda been there for sure," Eddie Doyle said.

"For sure."

"They were real good friends, wunt they?"

"They were."

"Help me on with this, Doc, will ya? I'm hurtin' too bad to move."

Delaney called for the ambulance from the corner candy store, where everybody was talking about McGraw. Almost all working men, with nowhere to go, least of all home.

Before dinner that night, he sat by the bedroom fire and read the letter from Grace.

Dear Daddy,

I got your note. It's hard to believe that you have been visited by the FBI. There is great hope here for Roosevelt, that he will change things in America, that he will recognize how many people have been hurt by the Depression. Not just in America, but in Spain too, and in all of Europe. But how can there be true hope if people with badges come to your office? You, who have never done anything except try to help people?

That's why there are many Spaniards who believe there is no hope unless the people take up arms. The communists sneer at Roosevelt as a tool of Wall Street, and maybe they're right. I don't know. I'm not a true part of it. But do not be surprised if there is a rising. Or a civil war. The fascists have their supporters here too. They love Mussolini. They are happy about Hitler. Who knows what might happen?

I met a man yesterday who saw my husband a few months ago. He said he will try to get a message to him. I will let you know.

I miss Carlito with all my heart. Send me news. Send me photos. I am at the same place. But American Express is best. Use the name Leonora Córdoba. I miss you too, Daddy.

Saludos, y mucho cariño, G.

He wrote a brief note and enclosed snapshots of Carlito on the streets of New York, and one with Rose and Monique. He hoped they would fill her with longing, not only for her son, but for Grand Central and the Chrysler Building and the Third Avenue El. Her city. Home. Where she lived with Molly while he was away at the war, where she did not know him when he returned. The place where she made ten thousand drawings on the way to the future. Where she was determined to find her own way in the world even if it meant leaving. Even, indeed, if it meant leaving her son in a vestibule. To pursue a man who blew up buildings in the name of utopia. And maybe blew up people. For a moment, he felt a treasonous flutter around the heart. One part of the truth was that he didn't want Grace to return. He wanted the boy for himself. And so did Rose. For Rose, it was even worse. She needed him.

He told Rose that he had to go to the Wednesday funeral of John McGraw at St. Patrick's Cathedral.

"Why?" Rose said.

"He was a friend of my father's," he said in a cool way. "I never made it to my father's funeral. Or my mother's." She looked at him and waited for the reason. "They died in the flu epidemic. I was in a hospital in France." A pause. "So that's why I have to go to St. Patrick's, Rose."

She touched his shoulder, then quickly removed her hand.

"Do you want to go to the funeral, Rose?" Delaney said.

"Alone?"

"Of course not. With me. With Carlito."

She furrowed her brow in a thoughtful way.

"I don't think so," she said.

"Why not?"

"I don't believe all this church stuff."

"Neither do I."

"So why you want to go?"

"It's about a man. McGraw. It's not about God."

She looked at the boy, then into the yard. The snow was now all gone, and she leaned forward at the window and squinted at the sight of a yellow bird in one of the skeletal trees. Abruptly the hardy scout flew off into the sunny cold.

"The truth?" Rose said. "I want to go, jus' to see for myself. But I *won't* go. First, I don't have clothes. All the fancy people, the big shots, politicians, and actors and all that? With them, I can't wear what I got. Not and walk in the door with you."

"Don't be silly," he said.

"Silly to you. Not to me. I don't want to shame you, Dottore."

"You couldn't shame me if you showed up in overalls."

But he knew what she meant. Even now, even in the Depression, the codes of class prevailed in certain parts of New York. The schools you went to and the accents of speech and the clothes you wore. Delaney was a doctor, with degrees on the wall from fine schools. He was the son of a politician who was a friend of John McGraw's. He owned a house. He was surviving the worst times. And Rose? She was a housekeeper, a kind of governess, who went to the fourth grade in Sicily. There were women like her still, in Gramercy Park, on Lower Fifth Avenue, on the Upper East Side. Her clothes were what she could afford. She carried a bloody secret about her husband. She must be certain, Delaney thought, that the observers in the pews of St. Patrick's would know her. They would sneer, more at Delaney than at her.

He saw that her eyes were moist, and she was gnawing at the inside of her cheek. The same cheek that carried the fine scar.

"Well," she said, and breathed out. "Maybe." A pause. "Okay."

She gazed into the yard. "That's an olive tree, right?" she said. "All wrapped up."

"Yes."

"Soon we gotta take its coat off," she said. "An olive tree, it needs the sun. Us too."

When Monique arrived, Delaney gave her fifty dollars to buy a dress and boots for Rose to wear to the McGraw funeral. He asked her to go with Rose and prop up her confidence. Monique gave him an insulted look.

"What am I now?" she said. "A fashion consultant?"

"No, but if we go to the funeral, I don't want her to feel, you know . . ."

"Like a maid? A cook? A governess? That's what she is, Jim."

"That's not very kind, Monique," he said, thinking: She's jealous, for Christ's sake. No, she's also right. She's saying what everyone at St. Patrick's might say. Or enough of them who cared to watch closely. And he thought: Maybe I should just tell Rose that I've had second thoughts. That I want to relieve her of any feelings of pressure or obligation. I should tell her that, well, anyway, the crowd will be too immense. That I can tell her all about it when I get home. And then he thought: No, I might wound her even more deeply. She might think I'm ashamed of her. That I believe she is just what Monique thinks she is: a servant, and nothing more. And I will inflict another scar.

The phone rang. Monique murmured, took down information, and hung up. Then she sat there, in a sullen little pool.

Delaney went into his office. Through the door, he could hear the voices of Monique and Rose. The door opened, and the boy walked in, smiling.

• • •

On Wednesday morning, Delaney placed the milk beside the cornflakes and crisped the Italian bread, and Carlito kept glancing at the door, looking for Rose. So did Delaney. The funeral was at ten, which meant they'd have to leave before nine if they were to have any hopes of getting into the cathedral. It was now after eight. Knocko Carmody had told him the night before: "Keep an eye out for Danny Shapiro. He's working the funeral. The main door, Fifth Avenue. And look for me too. Don't worry. We'll get you in." A pause, and a chuckle. "I can't guarantee how good the seats'll be."

Carlito suddenly raised his head over his cereal. He could hear sounds upstairs, then harder steps on the stairs, then a pause. The door opened.

Delaney sucked in some breath. Carlito froze, as if he had been expecting someone else, not this stranger.

Rose had pulled a wide-brimmed black hat low over her brow, like Greta Garbo. Her conservative black dress fit loosely, the hem below the knee. The twenties were long gone, and Rose was certainly never a flapper. She wore a black scarf, no lipstick, light rouge. The color in her cheeks deepened as she smiled shyly. The scar was covered with powder.

"Hoo-shine, Rose!" the boy said, pointing at her feet. They were encased in high laced black boots, brought to a brilliant polish. The boy hurried over and lightly touched the polished leather. "Gran'pa! Look!"

Delaney said: "You look beautiful."

"Ah, shoosh," Rose said.

And blushed even more deeply. She moved around the kitchen in a tentative way, like a girl wearing her mother's shoes.

Before they reached the subway, Rose had begun to totter awkwardly on her high-heeled boots.

"Ooof," Rose said. "It was easier walking in these at the shoe store."

"We can get a cab," Delaney said. "Or we can go home."

"No. A cab costs too much. Let's go."

They moved on to the subway.

Her hobbling was worse as they walked toward the crowd around the cathedral on Fifth Avenue, with the RCA Building rising across the street, high above its incomplete neighbors in Rockefeller Center. Under her hat, Rose was now wide-eyed, seeing actresses in mink stepping out of limousines, their skin tanned from Florida or California, and the Tammany pols moving somberly up the steps of the cathedral wearing black armbands, and some of the old ballplayers moving among them, big and wide-shouldered in camel's hair coats. Carlito was between Delaney and Rose, each of his hands held tightly in the thickening human swarm. He seemed awed, perhaps even frightened, by the size of the ballplayers and the sight of more human beings than he'd ever seen in one place, even Grand Central. Suddenly Delaney was nervous too. In this crowd, a knife would be better than a gun. Silently jammed into belly or back. Some random hoodlum, maybe even Gyp Pavese himself. Spotting them in the crowd, striking, then hurrying to Club 65 for a payday. He gripped the boy's hand and glanced around. Rose squinted at him, as if sensing his thoughts.

"Don't worry," she said, using a shoulder to force a way through the gawkers.

Reporters and photographers were everywhere, scribbling notes or aiming Speed Graphics, attending the arrivals of saloon royalty. Delaney recognized old bootleggers and stagedoor Johnnies and Ziegfeld girls and at least one woman who was a famous madam. There were men in shabby clothes among them, brothers of those human ruins that Delaney had seen so often on breadlines or on house calls. Some were wiping at tears with their coat sleeves. Weeping for McGraw. Perhaps for themselves when young.

Rose took Delaney's ruined arm as they came closer to the steps, her hand holding him tight, and she lifted the boy and whispered to him, calming him with her soothing tone. On the top steps, Delaney saw Danny Shapiro, pressed back into uniformed duty for the day, his lean face alert, his dark eyes scanning the crowd. Shapiro pointed at Delaney and gestured to himself, and they nudged their way to him, and Shapiro got them into the cathedral.

"You're on your own now, Doc," Shapiro said, and laughed. "I'm a Dodger fan and a Jew. I can't help with anything else in this ballpark."

They stood with others against the back wall, Delaney gazing down the empty center aisle, which awaited the pallbearers and the coffin. As they arrived, each man removed his hat, some holding them to their chests, others letting them dangle from their hands. Delaney placed his fedora over his heart. There were many bald heads in the cathedral now and women with white gloves. To the right Delaney spotted Knocko Carmody flashing a thumbs-up and gesturing toward the aisle on the right. They went that way.

The boy was pointing at the soaring ceiling, the chapels, the paintings of men in robes, and the many other things he could not name. A man nailed to a cross, bleeding from his hands and head. A grieving woman in thick robes. Rose removed the boy's gloves and shoved them in her pocket, and then she too gazed around her. Everything was luminous with electric lights, a thousand candles, stained-glass windows, an unseen organist playing Handel. They went down the side aisle, slowed by two veterans on crutches, and followed the turning of a thousand heads as John McCormack walked down the center aisle with his wife, guided by an usher. The great tenor was pudgier now than he had been before the war. The McCormacks were led to the front pews where McGraw's family would sit. Against the far wall, on the left, Delaney saw Izzy the Atheist standing alone, wearing a necktie. Delaney knew that he was not there because the funeral of John McGraw was a religious event. For Izzy the Atheist this must be extra innings.

As he, Rose, and Carlito inched forward, he saw Harry Flanagan, the Tammany judge who got his shoes shined in Grand Central. He gestured to Delaney to take the tight space in his own row. He and Rose started easing into the pew, the boy held by Rose, and others moved to the side. There were hard oaken kneelers on the floor before them and little room for feet. Delaney sat next to Flanagan with Rose beside him and the boy on her lap. She sighed as weight came off her feet. Delaney smiled at Flanagan.

"Hello, Judge," Delaney said. "Thanks for making room."

"I liked church better when I was smaller," Flanagan said. His coat was folded high off his lap, a derby on top. His suit jacket was open to allow for his stomach. Flanagan shook hands with Delaney and nodded amiably at Rose.

"This is Rose Verga," Delaney said. "And you've already met my grandson, Carlos."

"Can he pitch a few innings of relief?"

"Soon. He's a southpaw."

"That's the only kinda relief pitcher."

Delaney smiled and turned to Rose, who seemed puzzled at men talking baseball when a corpse was about to enter the center aisle.

She whispered: "The Irish are all crazy."

Now there was a greater stir, and heads turned to see Will Rogers coming down the aisle alone, tanned, lean, dressed in a dark business suit. His rolling gait said that he was a star, but there was no expression on his face and no vanity. Up front an usher was signaling him to come forward, and Rogers slipped into the same pew that had welcomed McCormack.

"That's that cowboy guy," Rose whispered. "The guy with the rope."

"That's him."

The boy didn't look at Rogers. He was growing drowsy with the odor of burnt wax and the heat rising from many bodies, most of all from Rose. He put his head on her shoulder. Then came George M.

Cohan, short and pugnacious, in the McGraw mold. He tried to walk with the solemnity required by the occasion, but still slipped into his old Broadway bounce. Delaney remembered that day in the first months of the war in France when the New Yorkers were marching toward the fighting and someone started singing "Give My Regards to Broadway." And then they all were singing, slowly, like a dirge. Asking someone, anyone, to remember them to Herald Square, and to tell all the gang at Forty-second Street that they would soon be there. Some of them were still in France, forever.

As he turned to look at Cohan, Delaney saw others looking at him, and at Rose. People who knew his father. Downtown people. Two women whispered, then averted their eyes. He saw another vaguely familiar face three rows behind them. Then the McGraw family entered the main aisle, but Delaney glanced again at the man three rows back. Long ago, before the war, before Johns Hopkins, before Vienna, the man was a regular at Big Jim's club and had gone often to the Polo Grounds with the Tammany braves. With them, but not one of them. He looked exactly the same now as he did then. What was his name? Where had he been? Cormac. Cormac something. A face unmarked by time. Some kind of newspaper guy. Cormac . . .

The pallbearers were suddenly at the entrance, the coffin on their shoulders. Incense thickened the air. The organ boomed its announcement of requiem. Everybody stood. Rose glanced at Delaney with sad, distracted eyes. A few more women looked at Delaney and Rose, and she must have seen the disdain in their eyes. She held the awakened Carlito, one hand on his small back. And John McGraw was carried toward the altar.

Through the ceremony, Rose seemed to shrink away from Delaney, slumping in her tight seat while the tones of Latin made Carlito doze. Delaney stared at his hands, as always unable to pray. Carlito's eyes closed. Delaney squeezed Rose's arm, cradling the warmth moving into his fingers. She looked at him from under the black brim of her hat, surprised, her eyes wary and glistening. Then, on the altar, the mass was over. *Ita missa est.* They all stood, Flanagan wheezing, the boy stirring. The oaken kneelers were tight and unforgiving against the arches of their feet, as they inhaled the scented air. The pallbearers again lifted the coffin and slowly carried it down the center aisle, with the McGraw family and his closest friends trailing behind. McCormack. Cohan. Rogers. The organist played a muted farewell. Through the open doors, they could hear bagpipes skirling, voices of vanished Celtic kings. Carlito opened his eyes in a sleepy way. It had been a long morning.

"Let them all go out," Delaney whispered to Rose. "Then we'll find a taxi."

"No. no. It costs too much."

"We'll take a cab."

A woman in the row behind them touched Delaney's arm. She was about fifty, wearing a suitably discreet hat and a coat with a fur collar.

"You're Jim Delaney, am I right?"

Delaney smiled thinly. "That's me."

"I met you at your father's club, a long time ago, when we still lived downtown. I'm Janet Bradford. I was a Muldoon then. Before the war."

"Of course," Delaney said, not remembering her at all. He offered a hand and she shook it. "Nice to see you again," he said.

She turned to Rose: "And who is this, may I ask?"

"This is Rose Verga, and that's my grandson," he said.

Rose nodded. The woman looked at her with the eyes of a prosecutor.

"Buon giorno," the woman said.

"Good morning to you too," Rose said, and turned to look at the empty altar.

Flanagan was pulling on his coat and smiled at Delaney as he edged toward the aisle from the emptying pew. Delaney was relieved to turn his back on Janet Bradford, the former Muldoon.

"Good to see you again," Flanagan said.

"Good to see you too," Delaney said. "Thanks for making room for us."

"Hey, the room was there. We just hadda scrunch up a little. Try to come around the club sometime."

"I will," Delaney said. "When I get some time. You know, the patients await me. Right now we're gonna wait for the crowd to leave."

"I don't blame you," Flanagan said, and shook hands. Carlito began making squirming sounds. Delaney hugged the boy. "We'll go home soon," he said.

"Home," the boy said.

A soft rain was falling as the taxi carried them down Fifth Avenue. It was a spring rain, falling straight from the grayness of sky, with no wind driving it from the North River. Rose had pushed herself against the window, holding the boy's hand. She did not look at the streets.

"How do they feel?" Delaney said, nodding at her boots.

"Not so bad," Rose said.

Carlito looked at her, as if trying to unravel the meaning of her tone. She did not move, and the boy watched the unreeling streets: the rain, the trolley cars, the other taxis and cars, the few pedestrians. Delaney realized that this was Carlito's first ride in a car since coming to New York. Perhaps his first ride ever. Occasionally the boy looked hard at the driver, the graying back of his head, the wheel he held in his hands.

Rose looked at nothing, her jaw slack.

"Is there something bothering you beyond your feet?" Delaney said.

"No."

"Tell me the truth."

"Ah, you know . . ."

"No, I don't."

She was silent and still for a long moment.

"They look at you," she said. "Then they look at me. Then they look at you."

"So?"

"They thinking, What's *he* doing with *her*? . . ."

She seemed about to weep. He squeezed her hand, then released it. *Just affection here. Nothing else.*

Delaney said: "Maybe they're thinking, What's she doing with *him?* A beautiful young woman with a scrawny old Mick."

She turned to him, returning his grin. Then wiped at tears with her bare wrist. Carlito looked confused.

Rose said, "I'm sorry." Then to the boy: "Hey, Carlito, what d'you want for lunch?"

"Bagetti."

"Always bagetti. Bagetti, bagetti, bagetti." Then to Delaney: "You sure he's not half Italian?"

She looked at him, hugging Carlito. Then she gazed out past the taxi window and its little rivers of rain. In this place a long way from Agrigento. There was a faint smile on her face. She had wiped so hard at her tears he could now see the scar.

They came in under the stoop, and Rose was hurting. Delaney sat her on the empty patients' bench and knelt to unlace her boots, widening the leather tongues, while Carlito watched. Delaney widened the opening still more and tried to ease the right boot off. Rose grimaced, tightening her mouth. When the first boot was off, and on the floor, Rose moaned. *Oh,* she said. *Oh oh oh.* They did the same with the left boot. Her thick black stockings were soaked.

"Rose," Delaney said. "Listen to me. Go upstairs to your room. Slowly. Get undressed and into bed, and peel off the socks. Very gently. As gently as you can. Leave the socks on for now, I don't want you getting any splinters. Your feet will hurt going up the stairs, but I'll be up in a few minutes and do something for the pain. Okay?"

"Okay," she whispered.

"Carlito, you stay here with me."

Rose stood up, bit her lip against the pain caused by her weight, and without a word started up the stairs, holding the banister. Delaney went to his office, Carlito beside him. He checked the contents of his bag. Then he went out to the mailbox on the gate. A few notes, in childish writing, asking for help. *Please come when you can. My mother can't move her legs. My father's hand is broke.* Patients who had found the door mysteriously locked on Horatio Street and could not read the sign saying the office was closed for the day and had their American children write out their pleas for help. Delaney gazed around him. The street was awash with the rain. He thought: I have to work on the olive tree.

He climbed the stairs, two at a time, with the boy lagging behind him. Delaney walked through the open door of Rose's room. Her black dress was hung neatly on a hanger, the hat slung over the hook. Rose was on her back in bed, wearing her flowered bathrobe, her feet exposed. She did not look at him.

Her feet were swollen. A yellowing blister the size of a quarter had started forming on the sole of her right foot, and the big and little toes of her left foot were rubbed raw. A crevice of skin had opened on the arch of her right foot. Delaney opened his bag as Carlito reached the open door. The boy paused, eyes wide with concern.

"Oh, oh, oh: Rosa, oh!"

He went directly to her and gently touched her face with his small fingers.

"*Oh,* Rosa. *Oh,* Rosa!"

She started to bawl. Without looking at Delaney, she took the boy's hands and kissed them and said his name and bawled.

Then: "Don't worry, Carlito. The doctor, he's going to fix me. Don't worry, this is nothing. I love you, boy, don't you worry. . . ."

Delaney cleaned the arch with alcohol, massaging the foot with his good hand. Some blood seeped out. He wiped it, then cleaned the wound again. Gently, easily. She winced when he applied iodine with a glass dropper. Her toenails were trim and clean. He could feel the warmth of her body. Then he wrapped gauze around the arch of her foot and made it firm with adhesive tape, and then he was done.

"Okay, now just rest," Delaney said. "I'll bring some ice in a cloth to stop the swelling."

She took a breath and slowly exhaled, as if calming herself, and then whispered, "I can't rest. I gotta feed this boy. You too."

Delaney went past her and drew the window shade.

"We'll manage, Rose. Today, *we* feed *you.*"

She turned her head. The boy touched her face, wiping at tears. His own face was confused and sad. Rose was hurting and he didn't know what to do about it.

They managed. Delaney used his best physician's tone to tell Rose to stay off her feet. Angela sent over sandwiches from the restaurant, along with copies of the *Daily News* and *Il Progresso.* Rose read the newspapers and applied ice to her feet and dozed. In dreams, she mumbled in Italian. The boy kept watch. The rain slowed and then stopped.

That first evening, Delaney placed a water jug and a glass beside her bed, talked with her for an hour about what they had seen in the morning in the great cathedral. He said he was sorry for putting her through the ordeal of the trip to St. Patrick's.

"We could have listened to it on the radio," he said.

"No. It was like a *show.*"

"That's exactly what it was."

"Except for those goddamned women. And my shoes."

Now the boots were wasted, she said. They cost money and they were a waste. He said there was a shoe repair store on Ninth Avenue that specialized in stretching shoes and boots. Run by Mr. Nobiletti, the shoemaker.

"He gave me the olive tree," he said. "I was going to call him anyway."

She said she didn't want to see the boots again for the rest of her life. She waved a dismissive hand and cursed in Sicilian. Delaney smiled, and then she did too. He changed the dressing again, caressing her wounded feet. Both were awkward in the intimacy of the small room. Several times, Rose began to say something then stopped herself. Delaney realized he was doing the same, but was smoothing the silence with his practiced bedside manner. He felt that Rose was afraid to go past certain boundaries. And so was he. Then he went into the bathroom to run water for Carlito's bath. By the time the boy was clean and dressed, Rose had fallen into sleep.

While she slept, Delaney moved the radio to the hall outside Rose's room. Around seven, he heated one of Angela's sandwiches in the oven and poured a glass of water, and then he and the boy went to the top floor. When they arrived, she reached over and switched on the bedside lamp.

"Dinnertime," Delaney said.

"Hey, come on, I can't —"

"Eat," Delaney said.

"A samich for you, Rosa," the boy said.

She sighed and sat up with the tray on her lap and her feet hidden beneath the blankets. He laid the radio against a wall and plugged it in. Verdi played on the Italian station, and he turned down the volume.

"God damn you, Dottore," she whispered. And bit into the sandwich and smiled.

Over the next few days, a new routine took over. Delaney and Carlito brought Rose her food. Delaney explained certain mysterious words that she had found in the *Daily News*. Carlito entertained her with paddleball and conversations with Osito. When Delaney moved through the warming parish, attending to patients, Angela came by to visit with Rose, and Monique swallowed her resentment or irritation and visited for a while too. Bessie, the cleaning woman, told jokes and made Rose laugh. They all somehow ate, although the house had lost the aroma of garlic and oil. Each night Delaney changed the bandages and told tales of some of the patients.

Alone in his bedroom, he read the newspapers, all about La Guardia and what Roosevelt was planning and what Hitler was doing. The numbers of the unemployed were beginning to stall, and that was mild good news. Maybe the goddamned Depression would be over soon. He leafed through the stack of medical journals. He filled in the records of patients. He heard opera descending from the upstairs rooms and the sounds of Carlito running and bursts of his laughter. The boy was taking care of Rose too. Delaney wrote to Grace, saying little about Rose, and a lot about Carlito's presence at McGraw's funeral. He addressed an envelope to Leonora Córdoba at American Express in Barcelona and enclosed the letter and five ten-dollar bills. And spoke in his mind to Grace the words he could not write on paper.

Find your goddamned husband. But don't worry. We are fine here without you. Just be careful. I don't like what I'm reading. About tensions in Spain, about rumors of revolt. Stay away from barricades, those new castles in Spain. Your barricades are here, daughter. Your son is here. Rose is hugging him in your place. And the sentence he could never write: *Don't come home.*

Have no fear, Delaney told himself. Spring is almost here.

TEN

SPRING CAME ON SUNDAY, BUT NOT IN THE MORNING HOURS. IN the gray chilly darkness of morning, Delaney prepared coffee, found a tray, and carried a cup to the top floor, with a plate of crisped Italian bread and a slab of butter. Rose laughed, sat up, and slammed the pillow. "Breakfast in bed," she whispered, savoring the words. "Just like the movies." There was no sound from Carlito's room.

"You can get out of bed now," he said. "Just don't wear the new boots until we get them stretched."

She swung around on the bed and placed her feet on the floor. She moved her toes up and down then slid her feet into the slippers.

"The truth? I been up already. I go to the bathroom, of course. I look in the boy's room. I sneak downstairs if nobody's here and see if everything is okay." She smiled. "Otherwise it's like jail."

She reached for a piece of bread and held the plate under her chin while she bit into it. She flipped off the slippers, then sat up in bed, still moving her toes. She looked up at him. Delaney smiled.

• • •

She joined him in the kitchen, carrying the tray, with its still full coffee cup and empty plate. The belt of her bathrobe was pulled tight. She was walking easily now, and he could see that the bandage was gone.

"Everything's normal again," she said. "I hope."

"And a normal Sunday for you is a day off," Delaney said.

"No, no," she said. "I miss a couple days, I gotta make them up. I owe you, Dottore."

"Rose, I already made plans," he said. "So make this really normal with a normal Sunday."

She looked relieved. "Okay," she said.

Delaney told Rose that he planned to take the boy on a long walk. He would tire him out, and then they could all sleep a long time. Then he realized that her cup remained full. He made a sour face.

"You're right," he said. "That's pretty lousy coffee."

She glanced at the clock. "Want me to make a fresh pot?"

"It's your *day off,* Rose."

She smiled and then Carlito entered in his pajamas, holding the bear and grinning in a sleepy way. He hugged Rose's hips. Then he walked into the light that was now streaming through the backyard windows and hugged Delaney, who hugged him back.

"Good morning, big fella."

He remembered Big Jim calling him big fella from the time he was the size of this boy. This boy that Big Jim didn't live to see.

" 'Lo, Gran'pa."

"Let's eat."

Rose started to place the warm loaf of Italian bread on the table, but Delaney took her elbow, moved her aside, and said: "It's Sunday."

"Okay," she said. "I better get dressed. Carlito? When you finish come up and get dressed."

"Okay, Rosa."

And she was gone. Delaney watched her go, then took cornflakes from the closet and milk from the icebox. Normal. It was Sunday. She was never here on Sunday.

Then the telephone rang. Twice. A third time. He was suddenly rheumy with dread. But then thought: It could be news. From Knocko. Or Danny Shapiro. Or Grace. He went through to the office and lifted the receiver.

"Hello," he said.

Someone was breathing on the other end. But no words were said.

Carlito dressed warmly, and they went walking east, with church bells ding-donging everywhere. Delaney could not tell Catholic church bells from Protestant church bells. Some were joyful. Some were somber. All were a form of summons, calling the faithful to services, as they had for centuries. He loved the sound but ignored the summons. Delaney felt warmer, holding the boy's hand.

As they reached Broadway, Delaney squatted down and showed Carlito how to tuck the bear inside his coat, with its head sticking out, leaving the boy's hands free. He could swing both gloved hands now, Delaney explained, or he could jam them in his pockets. And he could still talk to Osito. When Delaney stood up, a woman was smiling at him. She was about fifty, wearing a Sunday hat bedecked with artificial spring flowers. There was no makeup on her fleshy features. She wasn't flirting. She didn't seem amused. She just seemed happy to see a grown man, no longer young, caring for a small boy.

"What a handsome lad," she said.

"That he is," said Delaney. "Thank you."

She nodded and moved on, walking downtown. He noticed that her long dress stopped above large feet. The feet of Connemara, not Agrigento. She merged with the crowd.

They turned west on Eighth Street, heading to Fifth Avenue. As they came closer, the boy stopped again. Up ahead was the Sixth Avenue Elevated, turning into Greenwich Street. For a moment, Delaney froze. Against the window of a saloon, he saw the bartender from Club 65, dressed in a camel's hair coat and brown fedora. He was watching Delaney and the boy. Then he turned abruptly and walked away.

"Gran'pa, look!" the boy said excitedly, pointing to the distant sight of iron pillars rising from the street. "The El!"

"Yes, that's the El all right. But it's not the one we saw before. It's a different El."

The boy's brow furrowed, and he whispered something to the bear. There was no train visible on the El. Delaney looked in the other direction and saw a man in a gray belted coat peering into a store window. The man who was alone in Angela's that night. *Goddamn. I'm being followed. By two different guys!*

"Let's go up onna El, Gran'pa."

"Not now. Maybe later."

The boy mumbled to the bear in a disappointed way. Delaney was sure that the bear was disappointed too. When he looked back, the man in the gray coat was gone. A G-man? Watching the same target as the bartender from the gangster joint? Maybe it was just an accident, Delaney thought. Maybe the bartender was out for a Sunday-morning stroll. Just like us. And saw me. Maybe the G-man, if he was a G-man, just needed a rest after sitting through mass. Maybe, but not likely. And who called this morning? Who was breathing into the telephone? Delaney noticed a hot dog shop on the other side of the street and, sensing danger, steered the boy left into a used-book store. From behind the streaky window, he looked back into the street and did not see the man in the gray coat or the bartender. Why would they follow me around? They must know I'm not part of the great communist plot. And Frankie Botts knows I'm not that hard to find. Killing me would be simple.

The boy was gazing around him at walls of books, and at tables piled with larger volumes. At the far end of the room, a man with a thick red beard and heavy horn-rimmed glasses sat at a desk. He wore a bulky gray sweater and a loose red scarf in the chill of the room. He looked up and then went back to reading his own book. Classical music played from a radio. There were a few other men in the store, examining books, locked in solitude. There were no women. Delaney turned to Carlito and gestured at the walls and table.

"Books," Delaney said. "These are all books."

"Books."

They drifted around the store, the boy touching the books as if they were polished shoes. They came to a table of children's books. Delaney searched them for a book about trains or the great oceans. Nothing. But there were some treasures. *A Child's Garden of Verses. Peter Rabbit. Treasure Island. The Story of Babar.* Delaney wondered what the boy could comprehend. It was too soon for Long John Silver. But maybe I could read him the lovely Stevenson verses and put poetry in his head to stay. I could start him up the road to Byron and Whitman and Yeats. He picked up the copy. It was worn, but unmarked by scribblings in pencils or crayons. Then he opened the Babar book. The illustrations were bright with primary colors, as innocent as Matisse, with all those gray elephants in green suits, exploring the world.

"Look at this," Delaney said to the boy, who took the large book in his small hands. He sat on the floor and peered at the images of elephants and ponds and jungle and a city that was surely Paris. He turned the pages with growing anticipation. He pointed at a bear's face on one page.

"You like that book?" Delaney said.

"Yes, Gran'pa. I like it."

"Give me a buck for da two of dem," the owner said, in the tones of Brooklyn. His fingers and teeth were yellow from tobacco.

"Thanks."

"Dat Stevenson book, da pomes are pretty nice," he said, sliding the books into a paper bag. "But y' know, dat Babar is pure colonialist propaganda."

Delaney wanted to laugh and didn't. The man was so serious he didn't want to hurt his feelings. "Could be," Delaney said. "But I like the pictures, and so does the boy."

The owner shrugged. "Just warnin' you."

"Thanks."

They turned into lower Fifth Avenue, with its stately Georgian houses and the Brevoort Hotel, and up ahead was the Washington Arch and the green swath of the park beyond. The boy stopped and gazed up at the arch, as if he'd seen it before somewhere. He pointed and looked up at Delaney with a questioning face.

"The arch," Delaney said.

"Arch."

In six or seven years, he would tell the boy about Stanford White, who designed the arch, and how Big Jim was at the opening with all the other boys from Tammany Hall. He would explain Tammany Hall soon enough. After a long while, he would tell the boy how Stanford White died. Shot down by the crazy husband of a discarded young mistress. He could explain the meaning of all this carved stone. For now, it was enough to take the boy's hand and cross the street. A uniformed cop in a long uniform overcoat stood before the arch, shifting his weight from foot to foot, tapping his club into the bare palm of his left hand.

"Good morning, Officer," Delaney said.

"Good morning," the cop said, a bit startled.

"Morning," the boy said.

They walked under the arch and back around, with Delaney pointing at the bas-reliefs and George Washington and details the boy would learn about later. All the time, he was scanning the square for the man in the gray coat or the bartender from Club 65. No sign of either of them. Then he and the boy faced the six acres of Washington Square. Under the grass and the walkways, the bones of thousands of human beings were buried. For a long time, it was the city's Potter's Field, where the bodies of the lonesome poor were dropped in ditches and covered with dirt. Here the victims of smallpox lay wrapped in yellow shrouds. Murderers were dropped after being hung from the gallows on the northwest corner. On foggy nights, the residents always insisted, the ghosts of the unhappy dead rose to walk the world again. That too must wait. The boy was still too young for ghost stories. He was still learning the names of the visible world.

They walked into the park, the boy swinging his arms freely. Under the brightening gray sky, students from New York University walked in groups across the park, talking intensely. Professors crossed their paths, overcoats open to the warming day. Carlito stared at a boy his own age who was pedaling a yellow tricycle under the watchful gaze of a red-haired Irish governess. There were battered men here too, as there were everywhere, sitting alone on benches. And on one bench, he saw the man in the gray coat, reading a *Daily News*. I should just confront him, Delaney thought. Go over there and . . .

Then Delaney was distracted by a man in a velvet-collared overcoat and modest gray fedora, walking in a jerky way from the Minetta Lane end of the park. It was Mr. Cottrell. Alone and far from Horatio Street. He staggered, then fell facedown, the fedora rolling a few feet. People stopped to look. Delaney ran to him, dragging Carlito. He squatted beside Mr. Cottrell and gently turned him over. His eyes were open, but he did not seem to be seeing anything. He certainly showed no sign of recognizing Delaney. Two students paused about ten feet away. Delaney called to them as he squatted beside the fallen man.

"*Hey!* There's a cop just past the arch. Tell him to call an ambulance. *Right now!* This man's having a heart attack."

The students hurried away to the arch. Carlito was looking down at the man, his face tense, holding the bag of books to his chest. Delaney leaned close to the stricken man's ear.

"Don't worry, Mr. Cottrell," he said. "The ambulance is coming. Don't worry. Try to breathe. Slow, yes, like that. Breathe . . ."

The cop arrived as Delaney placed Cottrell's hat on his chest.

"They're on their way," he said. "This guy gonna make it?"

"Maybe."

Delaney and the boy watched as the ambulance pulled away to the east with its siren wailing. About fifteen other people watched too, including the governess and the boy with the tricycle. The man in the gray coat was gone. Delaney thought about Mr. Cottrell, locked within his bitter cell, and what he would think if he learned who had tried to help him. I couldn't save his son, Delaney thought, but maybe I've helped save him. He wondered what Cottrell was doing here. Down beyond Minetta Lane there were whorehouses that had been there since the Civil War. There were also churches. Maybe he just was out for a walk. Maybe alone, in an anonymous crowd, with the winter easing, he could find some consolation. Maybe.

Delaney gripped the boy's mittened hand. He took a deep cleansing breath, then exhaled. Then saw people looking into the brightening sky. Some of them were smiling. The boy looked up too, and pointed.

"Gran'pa, look! El sol!"

"Yes," Delaney said, smiling too. "El sol. The sun."

"The sun!"

Delaney could feel winter seeping out of him. He fought against tears.

They stopped to celebrate in a hot dog place on Sheridan Square. First they scrubbed their hands in the men's room and dried them with sheets of the *New York Times* stacked above the bowl. They went to the counter, and Delaney lifted Carlito onto a stool, and the counterman asked what they wanted. Two hot dogs, Delaney said. Mustard in a bowl. Sure thing, the man said. This time Carlito insisted on trying mustard on his hot dog, instead of his fingertip, as if it were a sign of manhood. The counterman placed a bowl of mustard before him, with a wooden stick to be used for dipping. Delaney tried to help the boy, but Carlito insisted on doing it himself. He splashed mustard on the bear and on his own coat.

"Don't worry, boy," Delaney said, wiping at the mustard with a handkerchief. The boy looked embarrassed. "I mean it, boy: Don't worry."

Carlito made a face at the first taste of mustard, but was able to chew and make a face at the same time. As he worked his way along the length of the hot dog, the boy seemed to enjoy it more. He looked slyly at Delaney, who was consuming his own hot dog, as if they were engaged in a conspiracy. To hell with Rose.

Then a man was beside him. The bartender from Club 65. The man who had vanished from Washington Square.

"Hello, Doc," he said.

"Hello. What's your name again?"

"It don't matter. Whatta ya hear from Eddie Corso?"

"Not a word."

"Mr. Botts, the boss, well, he's still very interested."

"Let me ask you something, mister. You been following me?"

"Nah, I was just passin' by. It's a nice day. The sun is shining. A good day for a walk."

"That's what we're going to do too. Just walk in the sun. Give my regards to Mr. Botts."

He nodded to the man, took the boy by the hand, and walked out. He didn't look back. They walked west toward the North River. The sun followed them, brightening every street, casting long sharp black shadows under the El as they crossed, bringing vivid color from the bricks of the buildings. *These fuckers are everywhere. Feds and gangsters. Jesus Christ . . .* More tenement windows were being opened, welcoming the breeze, letting it scour the sour winter air of the flats. Kids were arriving in noisy battalions. Running, leaping, playing tag, throwing balls and catching them. One kid burst out of the door with what was called a pusho, a scooter made of a milk box nailed to a two-by-four, with a dismembered roller skate serving as wheels. Carlito watched them all. They were offering him lessons in what it was to be a boy.

Delaney looked at the Cottrell house, but there were no signs of life. He thought about ringing the bell and explaining what had happened to Cottrell and how the ambulance had taken him to Bellevue. He didn't. They were probably at the hospital now, on watch. Like hundreds of others all over the city on this day when the sun had returned from exile.

They entered under the stoop, the boy whipping off his coat. He called Rose's name in the hallway, but there was no answer. He wanted to show her his books.

"Later," Delaney said. "Now we take a nap."

"Okay. I like a nap."

He woke abruptly from a formless dream and saw the clock: four forty-five. Still Sunday. He remembered the man in the gray suit, and the bartender from Club 65. His breath kept coming in short panicky gasps. He remembered Mr. Cottrell and wondered if he was alive or dead. He rose and went to the bathroom and stepped into the shower and scrubbed himself. He dried, then dressed quickly, in rough clothes. When he opened the door, he could hear Carlito talking below to Rose. She was back from wherever she went on Sundays. The aroma of garlic and oil rose through the house. He hurried down to the kitchen.

She looked at him and held up Carlito's coat.

"Mustard on his coat!" she said with a laugh. "I know what that means!"

He laughed too.

"*Hot* dogs!" she said, and now Carlito was giggling in a delighted way. The bear was seated on the fourth chair. Rose draped the coat on the empty chair.

"Rosa," the boy said. "We see the sun."

With that, she put her hands up, palms out.

"The sun, it's beautiful," she said. "It makes everything grow."

They ate veal and pasta and bread, Delaney joking about how the hot dogs rose off the grill and flew into their mouths. Veal, he said, was definitely better. There was good color in Rose's cheeks. She moved more easily now on her feet, and never mentioned the killer boots or murderous women at the funeral of John McGraw. Delaney cleared the table and washed the dishes while Rose helped Carlito feed imaginary food to the bear. When they finished eating, Delaney sat back in his chair. He said nothing about the man from Club 65. Or the man in the gray suit. He didn't even mention what had happened to Mr. Cottrell.

"Okay," Delaney said. "Some work to do."

She looked at him in an apprehensive way, as he moved into the shed that led to the yard. He lifted the old Arrow bicycle and carried it through the kitchen into the hall where patients sat in the mornings. Rose and Carlito followed.

"We'll need some newspapers, so we don't dirty the floor," he said. "And I have to find the oil in the shed . . ."

Rose produced some old newspapers while Delaney found the oil and then started tearing away tape and covering from the bicycle. Carlito ripped at the wrappings too. Then the naked bicycle stood there, as if shrinking into shyness. For twenty minutes, the three of them wiped away the dust of winter and spots of rust, using sandpaper and oil, and Delaney then oiled the gears.

"What a beauty," Rose whispered. "Che bello."

"Can you ride?"

"Of course. I can't drive a car or a bus, but a bicycle, sì!"

"Hold this steady."

Delaney lifted Carlito into the wide basket fastened to the front handlebars. It usually held his bag when he went on house calls. The boy looked uncertain and then smiled broadly when he fit perfectly, with his small legs draped over the front.

"He can be the chief!" Rose said. "Like on a fire engine."

"The navigator," Delaney said. "He can hold my bag in his lap."

"Yeah, a navigator like Cristoforo Colombo."

Delaney thought: Sailing without charts, right into the future.

That night he slept without dreams and awoke before six to a new sound.

Birds.

Unseen, but out there for sure. Their chatter celebrating the coming day with calls and whistles. Some must have worried about the presence of bullying seagulls. But mainly they issued songs of joy. Away off he heard the baritone horn of a liner, coming into the North River to one of the Midtown piers. Delaney felt the way he did every morning when he was twenty.

He shaved and showered and dressed. At Sacred Heart when he was a boy, they celebrated the first Friday of each month. But the central figure was always a dead man on a cross. They should have celebrated Mondays. They should have celebrated birdsong. They should have sung in Latin about foghorns.

Rose still slept, but the boy was up, and Delaney told him to dress.

"We're going for a ride," he said.

Fifteen minutes later, Delaney wheeled the bicycle into the areaway at the front of the house, with the bundled-up boy beside him. To the east in Brooklyn, the sun was struggling ro rise. Most snow was gone, and he saw that the yard was carpeted with dead leaves and litter and needed sweeping. That would have to wait. He placed clamps on his trouser bottoms and opened the front gate and wheeled the bicycle to the sidewalk. He lifted Carlito into the seat.

"Hold on, big fella," he said.

And began to pedal. Slowly at first, with the back of the boy's head before and below his own. Struggling for balance, finding it, then pedaling harder. He saw some silhouetted men waving as he passed, and he waved back. Then he saw the light burning in Mr. Nobiletti's shoe repair store. Getting an early start. He pulled over and went in with the boy.

Mr. Nobiletti nodded, his balding head shiny from exertion, his lips clamped upon nails, which he removed one at a time to hammer into the fresh sole of a boot on his steel last.

"Good morning, Mr. N."

The old man nodded.

"This is my grandson, Carlos."

Mr. Nobiletti looked down and smiled, still hammering. Then the final nail was driven. He smiled. He had hard white teeth.

"Buon giorno, Dottore."

"Good morning to you too, Mr. N. Listen, when you have a chance, can you come over? I want to undress the olive tree."

The shoemaker looked out, and smiled.

"T'morrow, hokay?"

"Tomorrow."

Back in the street, there was still no automobile traffic, and Delaney felt his blood beginning to move. From his heart, through his legs, making a round-trip back to his heart. He felt young. He could not see the boy's face, but saw his small hands holding the rim of the basket and his head turning as new things appeared. He could smell the bakery before he saw it. The wonderful bakery of Mr. Ferraro, from Napoli, even older now than Delaney. Delaney remembered walking these streets as an altar boy, heading for the six-thirty mass at Sacred Heart, struggling with the demands of his fast when the odor of fresh bread and rolls filled the dark air and tempted him to sin. On this fresh morning, he turned right and saw the light spilling from the bakery, with Reilly's newsstand beside it, and he could see Mr. Lanzano's ice wagon pulled up in front, with nobody on the seat. He was making a delivery to the store. Oil for the boiler. Or ice for the icebox. And almost surely he was buying a fresh roll and a thick coffee at the counter.

"Stay here, Carlito," he said, pushing down the kickstand. "I'll be right back."

Mr. Lanzano smiled as he entered, and said buon giorno, and sipped his tiny cup of the darkest coffee on the West Side. Even darker than the coffee of Rose Verga. Delaney returned the greeting in Italian, and the image of Rose scribbled through him. The dark glossy hair. The fine scar. Mr. Ferraro came from the back room, where the ovens were, sweaty and balding, with a towellike sash across his brow. The scent of fresh bread was like a delirious floury perfume, the best aroma in the city. Delaney held up two fingers, and Ferraro smiled and slid two fresh loaves into a bag and handed them over. Delaney paid and went out, wishing both men a lovely day.

He handed the loaves to Carlito, who laid them across his lap. Then he went next door to the newsstand and took the newspapers off the stand, waved at Reilly in the dark interior so that the delivery boy would be saved a trip. Then he mounted the bicycle and they were off.

All the way back to the house on Horatio Street, Carlito was silent, hugging the warm bread with one hand, holding on with the other, newspapers stuffed against his back. He was looking at the world that was arriving after the long winter. So was Delaney. Winter was the worst time, for patients, for people trapped in the dirty air of tenements, for coughs and colds and worse problems, and for boys. But they were moving into a better place together. To hell with the Depression, and Hitler, and the troubles in Spain. To hell with Frankie Botts and the man in the gray coat. To hell with Grace. To hell with Molly. He would forget about things he could not cure. It was spring.

Delaney lifted Carlito from the basket and leaned the bike against the wall in the waiting area. He handed Carlito the fresh bread. But when they went into the kitchen, Rose was there in her flowered bathrobe, leaning with her back to the sink. She was angry.

"You don't leave a note!" she said. "You don't wake me up! I think maybe Carlito is sick and you take him to the hospital. Worse: I think you are kidnapped by some gangster!"

"We wanted to surprise you, Rose."

"Some surprise!"

He thought: Please don't be a pain in the ass, Rose. Carlito handed her the bread, looking troubled, and she took the loaves and calmed him by rubbing his head.

"Thank you, Carlito," she said. "What a good boy."

"Eat, Rosa!" the boy said. "We all eat!"

The boy smiled, and so did Rose.

"Eat!" Delaney said. He laid the newspapers on the table. "And later, *read*."

The day moved quickly, with fewer patients in the morning and house calls made easier by the bicycle. He used a chain and lock to secure the bicycle to the fences of the tenements, and noticed the odor of garbage rising from the dented metal cans. Patients were more cheerful. From Reilly's candy store, he called a friend at Bellevue to check the condition of Mr. Cottrell. The doctor came back after a few minutes. "Critical, but stable. He should live." He called St. Vincent's too, to check on some patients and to tell Zimmerman that he would start grand rounds again in a few days and they could have lunch when everything was done. Delaney felt as he did when he was an intern himself: filled with endless energy, ready to help anyone feel better.

He made it to Tommy Chin's around four, when it was still light. The wounded girl had healed. The others were clean. Liann looked unhappy, as usual, and Tommy Chin said business was picking up.

"It must be the weather," he said. "It fills them with romance."

He rode home on the bicycle, through the thickening traffic, wary of trucks. When he turned into Horatio Street he saw Callahan, the FBI agent, talking to an older man in a tweed coat and hat. The man who wore the gray coat to Washington Square. Delaney stopped, lifted the bicycle to the sidewalk, and walked to them.

"Are you guys looking for the unemployment office?" Delaney said.

"Hello, Doctor," Callahan said. He looked uneasy. "You're home early."

"Maybe you're here for the view?"

"Come on, Doctor," Callahan said in an amiable way. "You know why we're here." The man in the tweed coat glanced around at the street, which was lively now with kids and unemployed men, with women staring down from open windows in the tenements.

Callahan squinted and said: "You heard from your daughter?"

"No. Have you?"

Callahan sighed, took the other man by the elbow, and walked away.

He talked awhile in his office with Monique, telling her that he thought Rose should get a raise. She made a face and said, "It's a little early for that, isn't it?" Delaney said that Rose put in a lot of hours and the boy loved her and he didn't want her to walk away for another job that paid more. Monique sighed. "I'd like you to tell her, Monique. Not me."

"You just gotta add some rules to the deal," Monique said. "She's too goddamn bossy, Jim. She thinks she knows you better than I do, and what's good for you, and all that. Sometimes it pisses me off."

Delaney looked at her in an annoyed way, then pulled a chair beside her desk and sat down. She wouldn't look at him, her fingers busy with papers.

"Monique?"

"Yeah?"

"Listen to me, Monique." She looked up at him. "You are very, very important to this house. And to me. I truthfully could not do what I do if you weren't here. I want you here for as long as I do this work." He paused. "But goddamn it, the boy has changed things. And Rose has to be here too. For as long as the boy needs her."

Monique looked unhappy. "I guess," she said.

"I promise I'll talk to her about the bossy stuff. For now, don't get in a fight with her."

She sulked for a long moment. And then exhaled hard, as if saying it was time to move on.

"Speaking of the boy, what about his birthday?" she said. "It's St. Patrick's Day, right? It'll be here before you know it."

"I know, Monique," Delaney said, pushing the chair back and then standing.

"My advice?" Monique said. "Don't take him to the parade. He'll think it's for him, and that could ruin his life."

"You're right, of course. Even if you do sound bossy."

She smiled in a thin way. "And don't get him a dog. Rose'll have to walk him — or it'll be left to me."

"Okay, no dog. Any mail?"

"Nothing important," she said. "An' by the way, some guy called three times but wouldn't leave a name. I told him you couldn't call back if he didn't leave a name. But he hung up each time."

"Maybe it was Hoover," he said. "Always on the job."

"He sounded more hoodlum than Hoover, you ask me."

He peeled the wrappers off two medical journals and signed some checks, and then he could hear Rose and Carlito coming down the stairs.

After they ate together, and after they walked together down to the North River and Carlito stared a long time at a passing liner, and after they returned in the chilly night air, they went back to the kitchen for tea. Rose had bought some biscotti from the bakery, and music played quietly from the Italian station, and they talked about why there was no such thing as Irish food while there were hundreds of kinds of Italian foods, all delicious. Delaney said that the bad luck of the Irish was the problem.

"Sicily was conquered by the Arabs, and they knew how to cook," he said. "But the poor luckless Irish were conquered by the English, and they didn't even know how to eat. For them, food was fuel, like coal. Pleasure of any kind was a sin."

"So how'd they get so many babies?"

"They could do something about the food," Delaney said, "but they couldn't do anything about human beings in bed."

Rose laughed. Carlito looked preoccupied. He waited for a break in the talk, and then he went to Delaney and pointed upstairs.

"I want my book, Ga'paw," he said.

"Damn, I forgot," Delaney said. "Where'd I leave his books, Rose?"

"Upstairs. I know where."

Delaney rinsed the cups and saucers, and Rose put away the cream and the rest of the biscotti, and they went upstairs together.

Rose found the books on top of the armoire, still in their bag.

"You read to him," Rose said. "I'm goin' to run a bath."

Delaney and the boy went into his room and took off their shoes, and he stretched out on the small bed with the boy curled beside him. They could hear the water running in the tub. Rose leaned on the doorframe, arms folded across her breasts. Delaney held up the two books. "Which one?" The boy pointed to *The Story of Babar.* Delaney opened the book, and the first page showed a gray baby elephant being swung in a hammock by an older elephant. They were surrounded by green jungle. Rose came in and sat at the foot of the bed, while the water ran slowly.

Delaney read the text, running a finger over the words, and pointing at the things they named: *"In the great forest a little elephant was born. His name was Babar. His mother loved him very much. She rocked him to sleep with her trunk while singing softly to him."*

"Babar," Carlito said. "He's an evvafent." Rose smiled as Delaney turned the page.

"Babar grew bigger. Soon he played with the other little elephants. He was a very good little elephant. See him digging in the sand with his shell?"

Delaney pointed at elephants swimming in a pond and elephants playing football and elephants parading, holding other elephants' tails in their trunks, and elephants snacking on oranges and bananas, with the jungle in the background and pink mountains in the distance. The little elephant named Babar had a seashell in his snout and was carving away at a small pile of sand.

"Let me see that," Rose said, grinning, and Delaney turned the book. "Wow! That's a great spot!"

Then Delaney went to the next spread. On the left page the little elephant was riding on his mother's back, while a monkey and a red bird watched from a bush. To the side, behind another bush, a man with a helmet was firing a gun.

"One day, Babar was riding happily on his mother's back when a wicked hunter, hidden behind some bushes, shot at them."

Delaney glanced at the boy, whose eyes were suddenly wide. He thought he should stop. But he went on.

"The hunter's shot killed Babar's mother! The monkey hid, the birds flew away. And Babar cried."

Tears began seeping from Carlito's eyes.

"I want Mamá," he whispered.

He wasn't speaking to Delaney. Or to Rose.

"I want Mamá!"

Rose stood up abruptly and hurried into the bathroom. She closed the door. The running water stopped. Delaney hugged the boy and laid down the book.

"Carlito, boy, Carlito, big fella, don't worry," he said. "It's a story, that's all."

"Mamá," the boy whispered, his voice charged with anguish.

"Your mama's not dead, boy. Your mama's coming back."

The boy sobbed in a small way, and Delaney consoled him, using soothing tones, and then decided he should continue the story. If it was, as he had told the boy, a story, then he should finish the story. He opened the book and showed the boy the drawing of Babar running away to safety, and finding his way to a town. *"He hardly knew what to make of it because this was the first time he had seen so many houses. So many things were new to him! The broad streets! The automobiles and buses!"* To Delaney, the town was Paris. It could have been New York.

He was near the middle of the story when Rose came out of the bathroom in her robe, to the sound of draining water. She didn't look at them. She walked heavily to her own room, and Delaney could hear the door click shut.

He resumed the story, with Babar walking on two legs like a human and wearing a bright green suit, which made Carlito smile. And after a while, Carlito fell asleep. Delaney was still for a long time and then slowly detached himself from the sleeping boy, closed the book, and turned off the light. He slipped the Babar book under the mattress and left the door open a crack as Rose always did. Then he looked at Rose's door. He knocked, turned the knob, and went in.

Rose was awake in the dark. He went to her and sat beside her, inhaling the aroma of soap laced with hurt.

"He didn't mean anything," he said quietly.

"Oh, I know. Come on . . ."

Her voice was choked. He slid an open hand under her head, and felt the pillow damp across his knuckles.

"Please don't cry, Rose," he said.

She was silent then for almost a minute. Then she cleared her throat.

"I gotta leave here," she said. "This ain't right. I'm not his mother, and he knows it and you know it. My heart is killing me. I gotta go."

He held her tight now, pulling her to him.

"I won't let you," he said.

ELEVEN

Rose did not leave. Nor did she speak to him the next morning about what had happened. Perhaps nothing had happened, except that he had held her until she fell asleep. A moment of intimacy, one lonesome human consoling another. Nothing big, nothing major. But Delaney knew it was a lot more than nothing.

At seven-thirty, Mr. Nobiletti arrived carrying shears, and smiling when Rose greeted him in Italian. Both were from Sicily, although the towns were far apart. Both must have dreamed on certain nights about olive groves. They went into the yard together, with Delaney and Carlito after them, and Mr. Nobiletti stared at the wrapped tree.

"It should be okay," he said to Delaney.

"A tough New York tree," Delaney said.

The older man began cutting through the cords and tar paper, dropping strips on the earth, which was softening into grassy mud. He said nothing. Carlito lifted each strip as it fell, carried it to the back door, and made a neat pile. Then the last strips fell away and the tree stood before them. To Delaney it was as scrawny as a girl of twelve, each branch curving and seeming to reach for the distant sun.

Rose clapped her hands and then whispered: "Che bello! Che bello!"

Tears were brimming in her eyes as she caressed the branches. Here was Sicily in a yard near the North River. She hugged Mr. Nobiletti. She squeezed Carlos. She smiled in an embarrassed, teary way at Delaney. Sicily was here.

Later in the morning, after Nobiletti had gone off with her punishing boots, Delaney gave her the Babar book to read, so that she would see that it was not about the mother, really, but about having a life, no matter what. It was a story. That's all. A story for kids. It was also a story about the consolations of cities. She carried the book to her room, but she did not speak about it. Across the morning, in abrupt moments between patients, Delaney remembered the beating of her heart.

Around the house, Rose moved with purpose, in and out of the yard as if expecting instant life from the olive tree, showering the boy with affection. She thanked Delaney for the raise and said, with deadpan irony, that she was thinking of investing in the stock market. She showed the boy how the sun was falling on the tree and the other growing things in the yard, and how soon they would be full of life. "You'll see," she told him. "Life is green."

Three days later, she tried on her widened shoes and wore them in the house for a few hours at a time, always with white cotton socks. "Black socks are for cops," she said. She listened to the Italian radio station, and hummed arias to herself. If Rose had been frightened that things would fall apart, the moment seemed to have passed.

In the warming evenings, they began to take walks after an early dinner. They went down to the North River piers, and Delaney sometimes thought about the many evenings when he had grieved here for

Molly. One night in the second week after his return from the war, he told her: "I'll never go away again, Molly. I promise you that." She looked at him with such angry suspicion in her eyes that it struck him as permanent hostility. But as months slipped into years, Delaney kept his word. He did not go away again, not even for a night. But their lives were not the same. To be sure, there was surface civility. They would talk in a cool way about Grace, and her schooling, and her affection for painters and for the game of baseball, and Molly kept reminding Delaney that he was spoiling the girl. He would mumble something about lost time and shrug, and Molly would seethe. They sometimes discussed politics. They talked about what might be coming to the world after the stock market collapsed in October 1929. But Delaney often felt as if he could be talking to a neighbor. Her anger was always there beneath the civility. It wasn't simply about the war. It was about him, about his being a doctor, about his obligation to help others, about many things. He taught himself to live with it, telling himself that Molly, after all, was Irish. Everything could be forgotten, except the grudge. Their bed became a place almost exclusively devoted to sleeping. Molly would turn her back to him, sending a familiar signal that another day was over. He would sometimes long for flesh and intimacy. For hair and teeth and wetness. Or a simple night of dancing. Until she finally turned her back on him for the final time and walked to the river.

But he did not, of course, mention any of this to Rose. On their walks, the boy was between them, a link, a bond, a kind of gift. And Delaney made no moves that could be seen by Rose, or by strangers, as expressions of intimacy. The boy was all. He loved to see a liner moving at dusk on the river, with the sun vanishing into New Jersey. He loved seeing a train grind slowly south on the High Line.

Then one evening as the sun began to fade, they went to Jane Street to show the boy the firehouse. The doors had been closed through the hard winter days, but now they were open, and the engine was gleaming and redder than the vanishing sun. Two mustached firemen were smoking cigarettes and nodded to Delaney, right out of the days when the fire companies supplied the infantry to Tammany Hall. Then suddenly bells began to ring loudly, metallically, and the cigarettes were flipped into the street and other men were thumping down stairs and sliding down the fire pole, pulling on rubbery raincoats and boots and reaching for axes stacked against the wall. The boy backed away from the fierceness of the sight, and then the lights of the engine came on, and a siren screamed, and the engine pulled out, making a slow turn toward the city, with men hanging off the sides, and then, all power and controlled passion, it roared away.

The boy was frozen in astonishment. Rose lifted him and hurried him to the middle of the street so he could watch the engine on its way to work.

"Fire engine," she said. "That's a fire engine, ragazzo."

The boy's jaw was slack with awe. And Delaney knew what he must do in the next few days.

St. Patrick's Day fell on Saturday, and in the morning they stood three feet apart in the areaway watching the neighborhood empty. The boy peered through the grillwork of the fence while Irish music came from everywhere, out of open tenement windows, from the old streets of the Five Points, from Tin Pan Alley, from distant Kerry and Antrim and Mayo. They watched the entire student body of Sacred Heart, garbed in maroon uniforms, march east to the subway. They saw men in green ties, long coats, and a few vaudeville green derbies, coming from the saloons beyond the High Line, and clusters of women following the men. Some wore green buttons that said ENGLAND, OUT OF IRELAND. Most of the men nodded to Delaney as they passed. They were all going uptown to the parade.

"They must wonder why you're not going to the parade, Dottore."

"They know I've got patients," he said.

Rose sat on the second step of the stoop, and Carlito climbed up behind her, to see better.

"Some of these guys," Rose said, "they're gonna need you tonight. After they beat the hell out of each other."

Delaney laughed. "Let's hope whatever they do, they do it uptown."

He had taken part in many of these parades before the war, starting in the ranks of Sacred Heart, and later marching with his father, and he hated them and loved them too. Above all, he loved the defiant pride of the marchers. When he was twelve he asked Big Jim why the parade was on Fifth Avenue, where all the rich lived and the only Irish were doormen and maids. And his father said, Big fella, it's simple: to show those bastards that they got the money but we got the votes. Delaney loved that part, the Tammany tale, and the sense among all of them that they too owned a piece of New York, they had purchased it with sweat and will, they were New Yorkers forever. He hated other things, starting with the clergy, plump and sleek, and how they insisted that the parade was a Catholic event, not just an Irish event. That meant they had no room for Jonathan Swift or Wolfe Tone, for Oscar Wilde or William Butler Yeats. He hated the drunkenness too, men embracing the stereotype and careening around the Irish joints on Third Avenue after they had marched. Hated above all what would happen to them in the night, or to their wives. He had treated too many of them. He knew all the reasons: the way the British refused to give them power of any kind, except to get drunk and assault their women. Drunks were no threat to power. Knew the reasons, but hated seeing their leftovers on the streets of New York. Still, in other ways, the Irish tale was a noble one, all about people who kept getting knocked down and kept getting up. He would tell that tale to Carlito too. Eventually.

"I went to the parade, five, six years ago," Rose said. "Lots of guys throwing up on their shoes."

Delaney said: "Were they at least nice to you?"

"Falling all over me," she said, and grinned, and turned her attention to the last stragglers heading east, three old women of the type who used to be called shawlies, widows who stayed in church for hours each day. They wore shawls now too, and long dresses and warm coats.

Rose said: "I should walk wit' these women. Look at them feet."

They indeed had huge feet. Larger, by far, than Rose's, but from similar histories. They had worked the stony fields of Connemara or Donegal, before embarking forever for New York. He knew one of them. The one in the center, with blue eyes like ice water. Dunn. Bridey Dunn. He remembered her fury when he told her that her son had polio and there was nothing to be done. There was no cure. The boy would live all of his life with a maimed leg. Bridey stopped and gazed from Delaney to Rose.

"So here you are with your whore," Bridey said. The word was pronounced "who-uh." The New York style. Rose tensed, as if preparing for combat.

"Good morning, Mrs. Dunn. Happy St. Patrick's Day."

"Bad cess to you and your good wishes, Dr. Delaney."

The two other shawlies were at her elbows, trying to move her along, but Mrs. Dunn shook them off.

"You're a bloody disgrace," she said. "Living in sin with this trollop."

"Hey, you," Rose said, with heat in her voice. "Shut up and go to the parade."

Delaney stepped in front of Rose, his back to Mrs. Dunn. "Ignore this fool," he said. "I'll explain later." But Rose stepped to the side and hissed at Mrs. Dunn. "Go on, get the hell outta here!"

"I'll sic the coppers on the pair of yiz. I'll get the priest over here! Yiz are a disgrace to all of us!"

"Bah fongool!" Rose shouted. And then her friends led Mrs. Dunn away to the east, snarling and sputtering all the way. Carlito ran to Rose and embraced her hips.

• • •

Delaney explained to Rose about Mrs. Dunn's son, who probably picked up polio swimming in the North River and was now almost twenty, with a permanently maimed leg. He explained how Mrs. Dunn was like many other people: she had to blame someone for misfortune, and the doctor was the easiest target. In cases of incurable disease, a doctor was only a messenger, but they chose to blame the messenger.

"But she was after me too," Rose said. "Not just you. But me! And she doesn't even know me!"

"She knows you a little better now."

Rose looked away, with some shame in her face.

"I'm sorry I used bad words," she said.

"I don't blame you," Delaney said. "But it wasn't you she wanted to hurt, it was me."

"You feel hurt?"

"A little," he said. "I should have defended you better."

"Hey, I can take care of myself."

"I know you can," he said, remembering the affectionate way that Knocko Carmody called her a hoodlum. To him the word was a compliment.

"I just don't like it when there's some secret going on and I don't know what it is." She was silent for a beat. "Know what I mean?"

Then he told her about the single phone call with the breathing sound but no voice. He told her about seeing the bartender from Club 65 on the Sunday walk, and about Callahan and his friend in the tweed coat.

"Thanks for telling me," she said. "I gotta watch even better now."

And then went upstairs to work.

At one-thirty that afternoon, after dealing with a scattered lot of Saturday-morning patients, Delaney sat down at the kitchen table.

There would be no house calls on this day of celebration. It was as if the entire neighborhood had gone up to Fifth Avenue to sing and march. In the warmth of the kitchen, he felt almost dizzy from the aroma of olive oil, basil, garlic, and simmering beef. Osito was on the chair to Delaney's left, Carlito to his right. As always, Italian music was playing very low. Then Rose turned from the stove, grinning, to present the meal.

"Okay, something special, somethin' new!"

"What is, Rosa?" the boy said.

"Braciol'," she answered. "With pasta in oil!"

She laid plates in front of Delaney and Carlito and then one for herself. Carlito stared in a suspicious way at the mysterious new food. A rolled tube of beef, covered with dark red sauce.

"Watch," she said to the boy, and reached over to cut his rolled beef in pieces.

"You see? Beef, with cheese inside, and *sauce!*"

He stared at the braciole, not moving. Delaney took a piece and started chewing.

"This is great," he said. Carlito lifted a piece with his left hand and took a tentative bite. His face was dubious and then subtly relaxed. He began to chew. Rose looked relieved.

"This great!" the boy said.

The boy lifted another piece on his fork. Now he was eating, not merely chewing, and began splashing sauce to his left and right, spearing pasta with his fork, making sounds but no words. *Mmmm, uh. Mmm, mmm, mmm.* Rose winked at Delaney, who answered with sounds too.

"Mmmm, mmmmm, mmmmm, uh!"

The boy shared another piece of braciole with Delaney, and chewed away on the pasta, and then his plate was empty and he sat back and belched.

"*Hey,* don't do that, boy! That's bad manners. They think you a mameluke!"

"A what?" Delaney said.

"A mook! It's like some kind of Arab. You know, they eat, they like it, they make a sound like —" She groped for the word, gesturing at her throat with a little wave of the hand. "Uh —"

"A belch," Delaney said. "Or a burp."

"Burp!" the boy said.

Rose got up, and so did Delaney, and they laid the plates on the side of the sink. Rose took four smaller plates and placed them on the table. One was for the bear. Then she smiled and said to the boy: "I gotta go burp."

She went out to the hall, closing the door behind her.

"You liked the braciol', didn't you?" Delaney said.

The boy shook his head up and down, with much energy: "Good! Very good. Ba-zhoal . . . very, very good, Gran'pa."

Then the door opened and Rose was there with a vanilla cake on a platter and three green candles burning brightly and a huge grin on her face. She began to sing.

"Happy birthday to you, Happy birthday to you —"

Delaney was up now and into the song:

"Happy birthday, Carlito — Happy birthday to yoooooooou!"

Rose placed the cake on the table and took a large flat knife from a drawer, while Delaney hugged the boy. The boy looked as if some memory was forcing its way into his mind, a memory of another birthday in another country. Delaney knew that at three, the events of turning two could be a long time ago. A third of a lifetime.

"It's your birthday, boy! You, *today*" — she touched his chest — "you are *three!*"

She held up three fingers, then pointed at the cake and the three burning candles and said: "Now, you blow them out!" She turned her head and started blowing. "Just blow out the candles!"

The boy didn't move. Delaney now demonstrated the minor art of blowing.

"Blow them out, big fella," he said. "You're three years old!"

Carlito stood up on the chair and braced himself with his hands on the table and looked at the candles and took a deep breath and started to blow. One candle went out, and then he pounced on the other two, blowing wetly and hard, and then all three were out, with little tendrils of smoke rising from the wicks. Rose hugged him hard and he grinned widely. "Three," the boy said, and Rose lifted the candles out of the cake and laid them carefully on the table and cut a slice for each of them, including Osito, the bear. She placed two cups of black Italian coffee on the table and filled a small glass of milk for Carlito. The boy loved the cake and then stole Osito's portion, and smeared his cheeks with cream, and licked his fingers. He got up and pushed a small lump of cake into the bear's mouth, and then Rose was standing again.

"I gotta burp another time," she said. In ten seconds she was back with two brightly wrapped packages. One was very bulky, and she placed it on the floor. The other was a book. That was from her to Carlito, and Delaney didn't know what it was.

"This is for you, Carlito, for your birthday . . ."

He took it and felt its shape.

"It's a book!" he said.

"Yeah," Rose said, "but *what* book?"

"Take the paper off, Carlito," Delaney said.

The boy began to remove the paper, tentatively, cautiously, and then more quickly. He burst into a squeal.

"Babar!"

He held the book and stared at the cover. *The Travels of Babar.* He started turning the pages quickly. Delaney looked at Rose, who was smiling while tears welled in her eyes. God, she is tough, he thought. Lovely and tough. And he hoped the boy would not call for his mother.

"Open the other one, ragazzo," she said in a softer voice.

The boy was standing on the floor now. He put the book on Osito's chair and turned to the much bulkier package and began to attack it.

The paper seemed to fly away. And there it was, red and gleaming and beautiful: a fire engine.

"Fi' engine, Gran'pa, it's a *fi' engine!*"

Rose whooped and clapped her hands. The boy jumped up and down. The fire engine was low and strong with a seat for a driver to sit upon, so that he could propel himself with his legs, and a wheel for steering. Delaney showed the boy how to slide onto the seat and how to use his legs, and then Carlito was propelling himself all around the kitchen, as Rose jumped out of his way in mock horror and Delaney stood up on a chair, feeling young, exuberant, full of delight and something like joy.

"Happy birthday, Carlito, happy birthday to yoooouuuuuuu."

After an hour, the boy started fading. He pedaled more slowly. He sagged in his seat, leaning on the steering wheel. His eyes, which had been so bright with excitement, began to close. The telephone rang in the office. Delaney went to answer it, gesturing upstairs. Rose nodded agreement and lifted the boy. Delaney paused as he picked up the black telephone receiver, wondering if this would be another heavy breather. It was Zimmerman.

"Your neighbor?" Zimmerman said. "I just heard from one of the guys at Bellevue. And that Mr. Cottrell, he'll be discharged tomorrow."

"Great!"

"He a friend of yours?"

"No, but I'm glad he'll live. How's it going there, Jake, on this day of Irish days?"

"It's a little like what the Somme must've been. The casualties are rolling in."

"Stay alert," Delaney said, "and make sure there's plenty of iodine for the wounded."

He put the fire truck in the shed leading to the yard and straightened out the dish towels and chairs and then went to the top floor. He could hear water running. He could hear Rose speaking softly, telling the boy he shouldn't worry: the fire truck would be there later. Delaney turned and went down the stairs. He could hear Rose humming an aria.

In the office, he wrote a note to Grace, describing the boy's birthday and how they had avoided the parade, afraid of spoiling him, and how he was sure the boy now wanted to grow up to be a fireman. He enclosed fifty dollars and sealed and addressed the envelope to Leonora Córdoba and slipped it under the blotter. Then he went to his bedroom. He undressed and donned his robe and stretched out above the covers in the gray light. From a long way off, he could hear a raw tenor singing about the mountains of Mourne, his voice full of longing and melancholy along the early evening streets. What was his name? The writer of the song? French. Of course. Percy French. Before the war, before Vienna, he and Molly had gone to see the famous Mr. French at a recital in Steinway Hall. Delaney thought the man's songs would make Molly smile. Instead they provoked her anger. He never took her to another Irish evening or even to the parade. On this day, the Irish laughter and the Irish brawling and the rowdy Irish songs were all uptown. Down here in the West Village, there was only this lone tenor. Singing Percy French. It was as if the unseen singer was standing on the High Line flinging the words down the North River to the harbor and then through the Narrows and across the Atlantic to some Irish village that was forever lost.

Delaney slipped under the covers, seeking warmth, and was awake a long time. He thought about Grace, off in Barcelona, and realized that his anger at her had ebbed. In his mind now, when he faced his daughter, he had stopped shouting. And he was thinking in a cooler way about Molly. Soon he must open her locked room and put her things in cartons and store them in the basement, on new shelves, high and dry. He would wrap her framed photographs too, the silvery faces of her heroes, separating them with the musical scores, and seal them with tape. The piano would stay. Perhaps when the boy gives up his fire engine he will play piano. Here, or somewhere else. But Delaney now felt that Grace was almost surely right about her mother. That top-floor room contained Molly's ghost. It reeked with death. He must open the door, and leave it open, and give it over to life.

Delaney dozed then, hearing nothing, free of all images.

He was woken by the telephone.

"Doc?" a growly voice said.

"Yes. Who's this?"

"Brick O'Loughlin."

"Hello, Brick, what's the problem?"

"I think I hoit my wife. Bad."

Ah, Christ.

"I oney hit her once. She gave me lip, and I bopped her, and now she's on the floor, and she ain't movin'."

Delaney sighed. "You better call the coppers, Brick."

"I can't, Doc. I gotta be sure. I wanna help her, I don't want her dead."

Delaney switched on the lamp and glanced at the clock: seven thirty-five. What day? Or what night? St. Patrick's Day. Then thought: O'Loughlin's two blocks away.

"I'll be there as soon as I can. Don't move her."

He removed the robe, pulled on clothes and shoes, went upstairs. The boy was asleep, snuggled against Rose's breasts.

"I have an emergency," he whispered. She nodded sleepily. And he was gone.

Brick answered his knock, reeking of whiskey but looking sober.

"Where is she?"

Brick led him to the kitchen. Poor thin middle-aged Maisie O'Loughlin was flat on the worn linoleum floor. Her eyes were open and sightless. The left side of her face was swollen. Delaney squatted and took her pulse.

"I oney hit her one shot, Doc, I swear."

"That's all you needed, Brick. She's dead."

Brick sobbed. "Aw, *fuck.* Aw, shit." He began weeping. "Oh, Maisie, I'm so fuckin' sorry. Why'd you make me do it? Why'd you hafta fuckin' die on me?"

He started to lift her by the shoulders, and Delaney told him to stop, that the cops wouldn't want her moved, and the man laid her down gently and kept whispering her name, Maisie, Maisie, and Delaney said he would go to the corner and call the cops.

"I'll be right back," he said. "Don't do anything, Brick. Don't do anything at all."

Brick was still weeping twenty minutes later when two sour, chubby detectives arrived, dressed in plain clothes. They also smelled vaguely of whiskey. Delaney thought: It's a great day for the Irish.

The dark streets were full of drunks as he walked home. Some were singing. Some were alone and staggering, holding the fences of the areaways to stay erect. None of them were with women. A hard wind was now blowing off the North River, and he heard a foghorn blowing and some muted Irish music from an unseen place. The song was called "Never Take the Horseshoe from the Door." Harrigan and Hart. Every door in the neighborhood needs a horseshoe, he thought, starting with mine. Delaney's mind wandered. He wished he could go somewhere else. He needed sun and laughter and the colors of the earth. He needed a sky streaked with orange. He needed always, day after day, the aroma of basil and tomatoes, of garlic and oil. He needed Titian and Tintoretto and Botticelli. And a horseshoe on the door. He needed laughter. He needed flesh.

In the kitchen, the boy was awake again, wearing blue pajamas and knitted blue slippers and pushing himself hard on the fire truck, making the sound of sirens, while Rose sat in a kitchen chair and watched.

"This guy makes me tired just watchin'," she said, and smiled.

"We going to a *fire*, Gran'pa!"

Death and pain and longing went away, like smoke rising from a ruin.

Later, after eating the last bits of the braciole, and some pieces of birthday cake, they all went upstairs. Rose sat on the foot of the boy's bed, and Delaney started reading the new Babar book to Carlito. The elephant was now the king, floating in a balloon through the sky with his bride, Queen Celeste. They find their way to the shores of the Mediterranean, above a tiny ship on blue water, and a curving harbor town, a golden vision far from the North River. But then they are blown far out to sea and crash on a desert island. They ride on a whale. They explore the island. Then a massive black ship appears . . .

"Wow, look at that! A ship, Gran'pa!"

A lifeboat arrives and an animal trainer takes over, and then they are in a circus. A king and queen turned into performers! They escape and find the Old Lady from the first book, and then they are among snowcapped mountains, and they are skiing. But they are homesick for their own country, and the Old Lady arranges an airplane to take them home and goes with them.

But when they arrive home, the country of the elephants is destroyed. There has been a war with the rhinoceroses . . .

Delaney thought: Only a Frenchman could have written this book. Someone from a country wrecked by war, soaked with blood, for nothing. Someone who knew about Verdun. Rose came around and stared at the pages about the war, but said nothing, perhaps locked into memory of what happens when wars end. Delaney and the boy got to the scene where Babar and the others painted giant eyes on each other's asses and frightened the rhinos away, and where everything started to be the way it used to be. Carlito laughed at the scene with the elephants' butts, and this time he did not say that he wanted his mama. Rose hugged him as Delaney closed the book.

"Okay," she said. "Time for to sleep."

"I want Babar again, Rosa!"

"Tomorrow," she said, and then, as if remembering the next day was Sunday, added, "or Monday."

The boy slammed the pillow with a fist, and his brows furrowed and his face reddened. A tantrum. At last.

"I want *Babar*!" he screamed, and held the book to his chest and turned on his stomach. He screamed into the pillow. Rose looked alarmed.

"Stop that! Stop it *now*, Carlito!"

He screamed and twisted.

"Stop!" Rose shouted. Delaney reached for her arm and squeezed it gently.

"Let him get it out," he said softly. "It's his birthday, Rose. And he's crying for a *book*."

She looked ashamed and stepped back.

"I'm sorry," she whispered, and turned away.

"For God's sake, don't be *sorry*, Rose. I know what you're doing."

"I never seen him like this."

"Nor have I."

"Maybe he wants his . . . you know."

"No, he just wants Babar."

The screaming had stopped. They sat on different sides of the boy's bed. He was very still, but not asleep. Rose put a hand on his shoulders.

"Okay, boy. You got Babar."

He turned, his eyes red, his face distraught. Both arms were wrapped around his book. He said nothing.

"But no more screaming, okay?"

"Okay."

"Let me read it to you," she said.

"Okay."

Delaney hugged the boy. "Happy birthday, big fella," he said.

He went down to the kitchen and filled a cup with the last of the coffee. He felt oddly better. Have we spoiled him by giving in? Okay, we spoiled him. It was for a book. For a book.

He sat there for a while, thinking about the end of poor Maisie O'Loughlin, and the fate of her poor stupid husband Brick, and wondered how many similar events he had been a part of in that neighborhood, as a bit player at other people's tragedies. Faces and bodies flashed before him in fragments: beaten faces, bloodied and swollen, not all of them female. What was the man's name who had his head split open with a ballpeen hammer? Houlihan? Or was it Harrigan? They didn't always save the mayhem for St. Patrick's Day. And none of them meant to kill anyone. Just hurt them very badly. He remembered someone at Big Jim's club giving him advice when he was sixteen or seventeen: "Never marry a girl you can't knock out with one punch." And the guy laughed, and the other men laughed, and Delaney laughed too. But it wasn't funny, and the people were not always Irish. They had no monopoly on kitchen or bedroom violence. Some of the Italians were pretty good at it too. And a few of the Jews. And he tried to imagine Rose when she lifted the three-legged chair and broke her husband's skull. An act of pure clarity, one that sent her into exile. Sending her here. He wondered if she had regrets.

Then she was there, coming into the kitchen.

"That boy's gonna sleep for two days," she said. "You want fresh coffee?"

"Sure," he said. "I bet he gets up tomorrow while it's dark."

She started pouring water in a pot, her hands busy in an effortless way.

"Let me ask you something," Delaney said. "You don't have to answer if you don't want to."

She looked at him warily. "Sure."

"Where do you go on Sundays?"

She didn't turn to face him.

"Here and there," she said.

"I see."

"Why d'you want to know?"

"There's a show — I mentioned it to you — up at the Metropolitan. Botticelli. I thought maybe tomorrow we could go to see it. You and me and Carlito." He paused. "And tomorrow is Sunday."

She looked at him in a tentative way.

"The guy from Firenze? He's pretty good. . . ." She smiled. "The problem is he got the same name as that shadrool Frankie Botts."

"What's a shadrool?" he said, and smiled.

"Like a — never mind. It's a bad word, that's all you need to know."

He laughed. "I think I know a lot of shadrools."

"It really means a kind of a, in English, you call it a squish."

"A squash."

"Yeah. That's it, a squash. A vegetable. But, ah, never mind."

The aroma of fresh coffee started filling the room. She took his cup.

"What time you want to go see this show?"

"Around one o'clock."

She chewed the inside of her mouth as she placed the cup before him.

"Maybe I could do that," she said. "I got to do something first, in the morning. But hey, Carlito can't bring the fire engine to a museum."

He didn't ask her where she went on Sunday mornings.

• • •

She came back that Sunday at twelve-thirty. Carlito hugged her and said, "Hurry, hurry, hurry, Rosa." She excused herself and went upstairs. When she returned she was wearing the boots that had caused her so much grief. Stretched and widened by Mr. Nobiletti. Carlito pointed at them. "Shoes, Rosa, *your* shoes." His English getting better every day. She smiled at Delaney in a confident way and said: "Let's go."

When they came up from the Lexington Avenue subway at Eighty-sixth Street, the neighborhood was still filthy from the parade, with garbage rising in pyramids from corner cans. The sanitation men did not work on Sunday. And the street was still carpeted with discarded paper flags, all of them Irish, sandwich wrappings, beer bottles, scattered newspapers, at least two crushed hats, and things without names. One older man in a frayed coat was examining the trash, pocketing some objects, moving on. Delaney took them left on Park Avenue, then right on Eighty-fourth Street, and here it was cleaner, with the old haughty mansions peering down at them in limestone disdain. And up ahead was the museum, a palace fit for Versailles.

"That's it," Delaney said. "Right there across Fifth Avenue."

"It looks like kings live there," Rose said.

"They do," he said.

They went up the wide stairs, and Delaney turned to look at the far side of the avenue, remembering the years before the Great War, when some of the mansions, built to last forever, were being torn down after thirty years of life to make room for apartment houses, and how one St. Patrick's Day there were rumors of impending violence and plywood boards covered many of the windows. Not even a stone was thrown, but the rumors themselves made the morning papers. Most of the Irish just laughed. After all, they had the votes, and the votes were not rumors.

They entered the museum's great hall, and the boy took a breath and stared around him at the stone columns and arches and the sense of invincible power. To Delaney it was always like something out of the drawings of Piranesi. To the boy, it was something else.

"A church!" he said.

"In a way," Delaney said. "But not for any god. It's a church of art, boy."

Rose looked around uneasily, seeing women in pairs, with clothes that fit exactly and fancy hats and small feet. The sort of women who had sniffed at her from the pews of St. Patrick's Cathedral. There were men too, of course, men who seemed to be surviving the Depression without pain, wearing the long well-cut coats you saw on Wall Street, making remarks to each other and laughing, or looking at lone women with special interest. A few paused to examine Rose, but she stared at them until they looked away. Delaney thought: Say nothing rude, fellas, or she'll bite your fucking noses off.

"You come here a lot?" she said to Delaney.

"Not often enough," he said. "When I was young, I used to come every week."

He remembered coming here for the first time when he was twelve, in a year when he dreamed about becoming an artist. He was alone. He made it to the door but not through it. A guard stopped him and said, This is no place for you, sonny. Looking at his downtown clothes, his soiled knickers, his rough street-scuffed shoes. The Delaneys weren't poor, but there was no dress code downtown on the West Side. Young Delaney just wanted to see Rubens and Caravaggio and Vermeer, the painters he'd seen in black-and-white in the only art book at school. He wanted the real thing. But he just wasn't dressed for them. He left in tears, and that night he told Big Jim. The next day his father went to see the Tammany bosses, and they started a campaign to open the Metropolitan to all New Yorkers. A few months later, all the Irish and all the Italians, all the poor Jews and all the black kids, all the Chinese, all the poorest of the poor, all started coming to the great museum. They were coming still. God bless Tammany.

Then Carlito made an excited sound and pulled Rose along and into a room full of medieval armor. All visors and polished metal and swords, rising above him. Mysterious. Malignant. Scary.

"You see, Carlito," Rose said, "in olden times, these dopes always had wars. They would fight about God. Fight about land. But most of all, they would fight to get swag."

"You better explain swag," Delaney said.

"Swag is stuff you steal," she said. "You go into some castle, the guy has paintings, silver, nice chairs, beds, fancy stuff. You kill all the people in the castle, then you take the swag home."

The boy pointed at two glassed-in shields encrusted with jewels.

"Swag!" he said.

"You see," Rose said. "This kid understands *everything!*"

The boy wanted to stay all day, but Rose told him they had to go upstairs and see something else. They would come back later. He took her hand with a grudging look on his face. He clearly wanted to stay with the swag.

They climbed the wide central stairs to the second floor and followed signs to the Botticelli show. Then it was Delaney's turn to suck in his breath. The gallery was more crowded than he expected, murmurous with talk, and he understood why. There on one wall was the *Primavera* and on another *The Birth of Venus.* On loan from the Uffizi, as a gesture of international goodwill by Benito Mussolini. Delaney lost his awareness of Rose and of Carlito. There were Botticelli drawings too, and smaller Botticelli paintings, but he stood in front of the *Primavera* like a predator. The painting was food. He wanted to caress it, hold it in his hands, lick its glazed surface, plunge into it, dive into the Florentine light. Years vanished, decades were erased, and he was again the boy who had come here to the feast of art.

Thinking: Great paintings made me want to be an artist. They made me want to be Mantegna or Verrocchio, Rembrandt or Vermeer. Made me want to put brush on canvas or boards, to make marks that would last forever. Thinking: I was so young that I thought it was possible, that I could actually do it. And the great paintings sent me into art classes on Saturdays and on two evenings a week. Aged sixteen. They made me want to see. To see everything in the world around me, really see it, the buildings and the streets and the many colors of the sky.

He wasn't conscious of turning, of moving through knots of other people, but he was being pulled, pushed, lifted toward Venus. His heart was beating fast. There were the delicate hands, the thick dark blond hair, the sinuous outlines, the frank, intimate eyes. More powerful than any reproduction in an art book. Thinking: Rose said she used to look like this, except she was never a blonde. Here there were no bleeding Christs, no kings or dukes, no transported martyrs. Botticelli loved pagan flesh. Pagan eyes. A pagan landscape, washed by the sea.

"You okay?" Rose whispered.

"Oh, yes, sure, I'm okay," Delaney said.

"You got tears in your eyes."

He smiled, and wiped his eyes with a handkerchief.

"Aaah, it's okay. It's just — they're beautiful."

"I better take Carlito back to the guys with the iron masks."

"Why?"

"I don't know, he's like, you know, look at him —"

Carlito was standing alone, staring at Venus rising from her shell. Some of the adults were amused at his presence before her, and his intensity.

"Your daughter — his mother — she is a blonde?"

"As a matter of fact, yes."

"Well . . ."

An older man turned to Delaney, a smile on his face, his eyes twinkling.

"That boy is either going to be an artist or a critic," he said. "Look at that concentration!" He peered at Rose through rimless glasses. "He is certainly a beautiful boy, and you, I take it, are his mother."

"Well, I —"

"He certainly has his father's hair," the man said, glancing at Delaney. "Congratulations, sir and madam."

The man walked away, and Delaney thought: With his mannered style, he has to be an actor. And remembered the old line: I'll never forget what's-his-name. Rose was lost in thought. He took Carlito's hand and said to Rose: "Let's see the other things."

They looked at many elegant drawings, and a sketchbook in a glass box, and then paused before Botticelli's portrait of Dante Alighieri: hawk-faced, oddly dangerous for a poet.

"I don't want to look at this," she said.

"Why?"

"Don't you see it? The face, I mean. Don't you see who it looks like?"

Then he saw it: Frankie Botts.

"Let's go back to the swag."

"No," Delaney said. "Let's go home."

On the way out, Carlito turned a final time to look at the blond Venus rising from the sea.

On the subway downtown, his mind was full of questions. How does Rose know what Frankie Botts looks like? Then answered himself: Because she knew Gyp Pavese and must have seen him with his boss, with Frankie Botts. She definitely knew that he ran things out of Club 65. But that didn't explain her deep silence, sitting now on one side of Carlito, with the boy dozing against her as the packed train squealed through tunnels. It had to be the actor. The older man thought they were married, and that the boy was theirs. That must be it. And she must be thinking about how impossible that would be. How impossible all of it would be. That Grace would surely come home. Rising from the sea. She would take away what was hers. This boy. And then Rose would go too.

Delaney retreated into his own silence.

• • •

A frail rain was falling when they came up from the subway, and the skies were as gray and leaky as their mood. He lifted Carlito, and they began walking quickly to the west. When they reached Ninth Avenue, the wind was blowing hard from the North River. Then Rose took Carlito from him, and he realized that his right arm was aching again. They turned into the areaway on Horatio Street, and while Delaney fumbled with his keys, the door opened at the top of the stoop next door. A stout woman in an overcoat came out on the wide top step. He hadn't seen her for a long time but knew it was Mrs. Cottrell.

"Dr. Delaney," she said, brushing a hand against the rain. "Wait, Doctor, wait!" She stepped into the vestibule and emerged with an umbrella. A gust of wind flopped it into uselessness. She dropped the umbrella and came clumsily down the steps.

"Come on," Rose said, opening Delaney's gate with her own keys. "You'll get pneumonia out there."

"Yes, but —"

Mrs. Cottrell had reached their areaway. Her ruined umbrella was careening on her stoop, rising, falling. Delaney tensed for a blow.

"I just want to thank you, Doctor," she said. "You saved my husband's life. The doctor at Bellevue told me about it, all about it. Another ten minutes, he'd have been gone. I know we've been mean to you, no, *nasty.* That was my fault. But I was so — Anyway, thank you, thank you."

She took his good hand in both of hers.

"Get inside, Mrs. Cottrell. Take care of your husband."

"Thank you," she said. "Thank you."

"You're welcome," Delaney said, and hurried into his own house.

Rose was inside the second door and helped him off with his coat and hung it on the coat tree. She opened the door again and shook the rain off his hat. Carlito came racing from the kitchen on the fire engine. Delaney shuddered.

"That hypocrite," she said, her use of the word rhyming with "light."

"Ah, it's only human," Delaney said.

"She doesn't talk to you, for what? Four years? And then she's sorry."

"Well —"

"Go upstairs and get dry clothes," she said. "I'll make something to eat."

The boy made the sound of a siren.

Delaney was in bed that night, reading Byron's very funny poem about George III while the rain drummed steadily on Horatio Street. Rose and the boy were sleeping, and he craved sleep himself, but it would not come. The words blurred on the page. He tried to imagine Mrs. Cottrell on the day her son was killed and Delaney could not save him. She was thinner then, even pretty, but rage is always ugly. She must have raged at the driver of the car and at her husband and at God. She certainly raged at Delaney. Standing by the ambulance, pointing a long finger. "It was you! You could have saved him! You could have saved him! You! You!"

And he knew he hadn't saved her husband. Anybody in Washington Square would have found the cop, and the cop would have called Bellevue, and there the interns and nurses would have done everything possible. As they had done. But maybe now it would at least be better. Nothing could be done about 97 Horatio, with its colony of ghosts. But maybe Mrs. Cottrell would come to the back garden of 93 and talk across the fence with Rose, about the weather and the birds and the olive tree. But no: she would have to look at Carlito and think of her son, and —

The telephone rang. At ten forty-seven. Again. Then again. He lifted the receiver.

"Hello?" Delaney said.

"It's me. The guy from Bleecker Street."

"Hello, Mr. Botts."

"I been trying to fine you."

"You didn't leave a message."

"I don't leave messages." He could picture Botts smiling in the movie gangster style. "I deliver them."

Ah, Christ, Delaney thought, then said: "What's the problem?"

"My mother's sick."

"Is she in pain?"

"Some. But you know these people from the old country: they never admit nothin'."

"If she's hurting, Mr. Botts, go to a hospital."

"Somethin's the matter, but she won't tell me."

"Can it wait until tomorrow afternoon?"

"I guess."

"Give me the address," Delaney said, lifting the pencil from the bedside table, moving the pad. He wrote down the address on Grand Street, and Botts told him it was upstairs from Di Palo's cheese store.

"There's one other thing," Frankie Botts said. "She don't speak much English."

"And I don't speak Italian."

"I thought maybe you could bring that hoodlum that takes care of the kid. So she could translate, know what I mean?"

"I'll ask," Delaney said.

"Don't worry," Botts said. "You'll be safe." A pause. Then: "I hear you got the G-men on your ass."

"They came by," Delaney said.

"Looking for Eddie Corso too?"

"His name never came up. If it did, I couldn't tell them anything anyway, because I don't know where he is."

Botts sighed. Then: "Tomorrow at two-thirty? Before you start your house calls."

"You know my hours pretty good, Mr. Botts."

"I know a lot of things."

Botts hung up, and Delaney sat on the edge of the bed, staring at the carpet. It could be a setup, he thought, a way to get me out of this neighborhood, and the men who guard me, and then do what he wants to do. But that made little sense. Botts was no fool. He knows the Feds are watching me. He knows I'll probably tell everyone where I'm going. Monique. My friends. The cops.

No, Botts might be telling me the truth. His mother is sick. And every gangster Delaney had ever known was sick in the head about his mother. Irish gangsters most of all. But the Jews too, and the Italians. They all insisted they had accepted a bitter cup in order to make life better for Mama. Maybe that's all it is. Again.

TWELVE

In the morning, in his bedroom, fresh from a shower, a bathrobe loose across his shoulders, Delaney glanced at the newspapers. There was a huge taxi strike, with twenty-five thousand hackies out on the street. La Guardia, speaking as a New Yorker and an American and not as a Republican, said in a speech that everybody must support President Roosevelt. The Giants were working their way east and north, playing exhibition games. John Dillinger was spotted in Santa Fe and in Oregon on the same weekend, but did not rob any banks. There was no news from Spain. And no sound from the top floor.

He removed the robe and sat on the edge of the bed. He felt stronger, younger, after only a week on the bicycle. I'll have to work even harder now, pedal more furiously, or the Italian food will smother my Celtic bones. His eyes fell on the books beside the bed, and the third volume from the top was a selection of the work of Dante Alighieri. He slipped it out. The frontispiece was a small black-and-white version of the portrait at the Met that looked like Frankie Botts. He started dressing for the day, and wondered what would happen in the afternoon on Grand Street.

That afternoon they walked to Grand and Mott from the subway, and Rose was sullen most of the way. Carlito was now in the care of Monique, and Rose wasn't pleased to be drafted into Delaney's service. She wore her old shoes and walked quickly, as if wanting to rush back to Horatio Street. The streets here were crowded, the last of the pushcarts parked beside the curbs. In the newspapers, La Guardia was saying that he would get all the pushcarts off the streets because they were unsanitary, but suggesting that they were part of the stereotype of Italians and thus had to go. Most were still on the streets, but because of the strike, the taxis were not. Rose moved through the neighborhood as if it was at once familiar and alien.

"I don't like doing this," Rose said when they were a block away.

"It's not for him," Delaney said. "It's for his mother."

"You know she's Sicilian, right?"

"I thought Frankie was a Neapolitan."

"No, it was a — how do you say it? Mix marriage?"

Delaney wanted to laugh but didn't. "That's why Frankie must have asked for you."

She shrugged and looked ahead in a dark wary way. "Maybe."

She paused to examine the window of Di Palo's cheese store. Little signs were pinned into the cheeses: ragusana, romano, mozzarella. Her lips moved, as if saying the names, but no words emerged.

"I could make some great stuff out of that window," she said, repressing a smile.

"We'll stop on the way home."

Delaney looked at the bells on the doorframe in front of the vestibule. One was marked B, nothing more, and he pressed it. A buzzer rang, and as he pushed on the door something clicked and the door opened. Ah, the rewards of crime. Only gangsters could afford electrically controlled locks in the tenements of New York. Delaney led the way up the narrow stairs, with low-wattage lights above them. Each step and landing was covered with brownish linoleum. The banister smelled of lemon juice. Cooking odors filled the air, along with the aromas of cheese from the store, all mixed with music from the Italian radio stations. Frankie Botts was alone on the third-floor landing.

"Up here," he said, leaning over the banister. "Right here."

On the landing, Botts had assumed a pose of command, hands jammed in the pockets of a dark suit, a lightbulb above him emphasizing his shadowed eyes and high cheekbones. Delaney thought: Christ, he looks like a painting by Caravaggio. A single light and the deepest darkness. The sense of menace was palpable. He shook hands with Botts, but Rose stood with her arms folded across her breasts. She was wearing a dark blue sweater, and her eyes were examining the place, never looking directly at Frankie Botts. Down the steps was the safety of the streets. Up one final flight was the roof. In some houses in New York, the roof was for hurling people into the yards.

They passed into the kitchen, and Frankie closed the door behind them and turned two locks. There were no bodyguards in sight. The kitchen was like a thousand others: stove, refrigerator, table, chairs, a sink. The bare table had the texture of bone from many scrubbings. A framed lithograph of the Bay of Naples was on one wall, a young man in an army uniform on another. That was Carmine, killed in Château-Thierry, the same photograph that was hanging in Club 65. The one whose death had so hurt Frankie's mother. She was obviously a woman who would not surrender her hurt.

"Where's the patient?"

"In here," Botts said.

He led the way through the flat, passing more photographs of Carmine, and several of a young woman and a young Italian man, made in a studio in some city in the old country. Delaney was sure the woman was Frankie's mother, with her vehement Sicilian eyes, and the man with her was surely Frankie's father. His face was amused. The apartment was immaculately clean.

"Right here," Frankie said.

He opened a door to a back bedroom. The shade was drawn. An old woman in blue pajamas was lying under the covers of a bed with a dark carved wooden headboard. She still resembled the young woman in the framed photograph. Her hair now was almost white, pulled back in a bun, but it was the same woman. She had handsome lined features, and was breathing in a shallow way. Her eyes were closed. A votive candle flickered on a bureau, but there was no other light. The top of the bureau was cluttered with more framed photographs, one showing the entire family with a New York river in the background, and separate ones of Frankie in a baseball uniform and Carmine in a summer shirt and long pants. In one, Frankie stood with his kid brother, both smiling, Frankie taller and more muscular. Delaney had seen many bureaus like this one. He laid his bag on the floor.

"Momma?" Frankie said.

Her eyes came open, the irises a washy blue, and she blinked at the strange faces of Delaney and Rose. She seemed as wary as Rose was. Frankie went around to the side of the bed and turned on a lamp.

"Momma, this is the doctor," Botts said in Italian. "He's here to see you."

She answered, "I don't want to go to the hospital."

Frankie said: "He knows that, Momma. But he gotta examine you, see what's the problem."

"I don't want nobody looking at me," she said in English. "It's too ugly."

Then she saw Rose.

"Who's she?"

"I'm like a nurse, signora," Rose said in Sicilian. "I'm here to help the doctor."

"That's right, Momma," Frankie said in English.

The woman sighed in an accepting way and said, "You get outta here, Frankie. Okay?"

Frankie shrugged, backed out of the room, and left Rose and Delaney with his mother.

"You have to show me the problem, Mrs. Botticelli," Delaney said, and to be sure, Rose translated. The old woman seemed reassured and began to unbutton the top of her pajamas. Her scrawny chest and belly were covered with sores, some erupting into blisters. Delaney leaned forward to see them better, and touched them gently.

"You see?" the old woman said. "Disgusting!"

"The doctor's going to fix it," Rose said in Sicilian. "Don't worry. He's the best."

"It's so awful," the old woman said. "I want to die."

When Delaney came out ten minutes later, Frankie was leaning against a window, staring at the street.

"Jesus, that was fast," he said.

"The problem is called herpes zoster," Delaney said. "It comes from nerves, worry, any kind of stress. The common name is shingles."

"Shingles? Like on a fuckin' roof?"

"That's the word. Don't ask me why. They can be very painful for a while, and they itch. They come late in life to people who had chicken pox when they were kids. Somehow the chicken pox virus stays alive, buried in the body, waiting to make a move. She gets full of worry and then, *pow:* shingles. But they're nothing to worry about. I mean, you don't die from shingles."

"So whatta we do?"

Delaney was already writing a prescription.

"First get this cream. She has to apply it four times a day. If she can't do it, have someone come in and do it for her. I had a small jar in my bag, and Rose is applying it now." Delaney filled out another prescription. "This is for some pills. To ease the pain. One after every meal."

"She ain't eatin'."

"Make sure she eats something, Frankie. Three times a day. For strength. Otherwise, she's okay. No fever, strong heartbeat. How old is she?"

"How should I know? She'd never tell us. You know these people from the old country. They think they're always in front of the grand jury. . . . I figure sixty-five, seventy, something like that."

Rose came out of the bedroom, then stepped into a hall bathroom. They could hear water running as she washed her hands.

"I'll come back same time next Monday," Delaney said. "And see how she's doing."

Botts took an envelope from his jacket pocket and handed it to Delaney. "For you," he said. Delaney brushed it away.

"You know what I want," Delaney said.

"I do?"

"Call off your boys, Frankie. Let us all live in peace down on Horatio Street."

The sleet returned to the gangster's eyes. His body tensed and coiled, and he turned away. "There's a lot of things involved," Botts said. "I gotta talk to my people." Rose emerged from the bathroom, and Botts returned the envelope to his pocket. Rose nodded a cool good-bye to Frankie Botts, opened the two locks of the door, and stepped into the hall.

"Let me think about it," Botts said. "Like I said, there's lots of things involved."

"Starting with my grandson."

"No, starting wit' that fucking Eddie Corso."

Delaney lifted his bag and followed Rose into the hall. He did not shake hands or say good-bye. Going down the stairs, she looked at him, as if saying: What was that all about?

"We'll talk later," he said.

On the crowded street in front of the building, Rose looked straight at Delaney.

"That was nice with the mother," she said. "What you did, the way you talked to her. She's scared to death, and you made her feel safe. Very nice."

"You helped too, Rose. You helped a lot."

"I know," she said. "She wouldn't let a man put the cream on her. And it made me feel better. But I can't stand that comorrista Frankie."

"I wasn't there just for her," Delaney said. "I want Frankie to leave us all alone."

"Then you better not cure the old lady," she said. "As soon as she gets better, they come looking for you." She laughed. "Faster if she dies."

He grinned and said, "I thought about both possibilities."

She looked serious now. "What's the matter with her?"

He explained about shingles and its roots in chicken pox and how it can be triggered by worry. Her brow furrowed.

"Can we give it to Carlito?" she said.

"Probably not," he said. "But we'd better wash again when we get home."

She nodded and went into the cheese store, and Delaney stood there watching the ceaseless movement of the street. Now he spotted two men from Club 65, sitting in a parked car, watching him. They had pulled guard duty on Grand Street. Frankie Botts said there were other people involved. But he wouldn't have to consult with these neckless gunsels. They were just enlisted men from the infantry of the Mob. Then he was sure that Frankie Botts did not need to consult with anybody else. He wanted Delaney to care for his mother, to cure her, and he would not lift the threat until the task was done. But at least for now, they were safe. He felt lighter, and watched the schoolkids running around the pushcarts.

After a while, Rose stepped out of the store with a smile on her face and a brown paper bag in her hand. Delaney reached for the bag, and she pulled it away from him.

"Hey, you got a bad arm. Just carry your doctor bag. This doesn't weigh much, so don't even try."

She was issuing orders, and her tone pleased him. It meant that she was more comfortable with him now, that she believed he would see the joke in what she was saying, that she wasn't just a person who worked for him. She had made sergeant.

"Whatever you say, Rose."

They moved west through the crowds, while Puccini's music played from several open windows. He glanced at her, and she seemed thoughtful.

"Maybe I could be a nurse."

Delaney said: "You already are."

In the following weeks, they lived by the certainties of routine. The ache in his arm went away. The bad dreams ended. In the mornings, he took Carlito on the bicycle to buy bread and newspapers. On days of spring rain, he covered him with a poncho that Rose had found on Fourteenth Street. He took Rose with him to visit Frankie's mother, and the blisters healed, but the dark stains remained on her itching skin. He showed Rose how to take the woman's pulse and temperature, and back in the office he explained how to enter the information on the woman's record sheet. Monique was not happy about any of this.

"I got two things to tell you," she said one afternoon. "One, I'm not a babysitter. I can't handle all this and the boy too. He's adorable, but I just can't do it." She took a deep breath, exhaled. "And Rose? She's not a nurse. She does the records, she goes on a house call, what the hell is that?"

"It's just for one patient, Monique."

"I know, but it's the way she does it. Going in the file cabinet, taking the patient record sheet, writing stuff that isn't spelled right. I just don't like it."

"Maybe you could do it together."

"No, *I'm* the nurse."

Delaney sighed.

"Give me a few more weeks."

"I'm serious, Jim. I just might quit."

He looked at her hard. "Don't do that, Monique. Don't even say it. For God's sake. The patient speaks Sicilian, and I need Rose there. The way I need you here. Capisce?"

She looked away.

"I hope you capisce where you're going with all this," she said. He did not answer, and went into his office.

Days passed. He noticed that Rose's diction while speaking English was becoming crisper, and she told him to correct her when she said the words wrong, the way he corrected Carlito. Most mornings she took the boy grocery shopping, while Delaney handled patients and while Bessie cleaned, and in the afternoons he pedaled hard from one house call to another. Rose went with him to see Mrs. Botticelli. He did not bring Rose with him to examine the Chinese women on Mott Street.

More and more people were on the streets now, exulting in the good weather, and he waved to Mr. Lanzano, the oil and ice man, and Fierro, the sign painter, and Mr. Nobiletti, the shoemaker. He explained to Danny Shapiro that a medical truce was under way and there was no need for cops on the block. He had a cup of coffee with Knocko Carmody and explained the truce. Knocko was pleased and promised him two ducats for opening day at the Polo Grounds. "Make it the first Sunday *after* opening day," Delaney said. "You got it," Knocko said. One morning Delaney stopped at a shipping company on Fourteenth Street and ordered twelve book cartons and some tape and three lithographic crayons, and later told Monique that when the goods arrived, she should have them stacked in Molly's room. He lunched with Jake Zimmerman. He examined the window of Billy McNiff's toy store. He went on grand rounds at St. Vincent's. He read the newspapers. There was a story deep inside the *Times* about growing tension in Spain, and mergers of the left-wing parties, and talk of the coming struggle. But there was no real news, and no letter from Grace. He wondered if the FBI had intercepted all of them.

Rose took over the records of Carlito, weighing him, measuring him, exclaiming one evening to Delaney that his legs were already harder from pedaling the fire engine and maybe even longer. This made Delaney laugh. Rose said: "I'm not kiddin' around! Take a look!" Looking at the boy's legs, he thought: Maybe she's right. She took the boy's temperature every morning. She examined him carefully after each evening's bath, searching for signs of chicken pox, saying, "I don't want this kid getting shingles when he's sixty!" She never did say where she went on Sundays.

One Saturday evening, Rose said: "You want to come with me tomorrow?"

"Where?" Delaney said.

"Where I go on Sunday morning," she said. "You asked me about it."

"Sure," he said. "We'll go together. The three of us."

The next morning they walked west and then north. The boy was excited, pointing out new churches and new stores and another firehouse. Then they turned toward the North River. Ahead a crowd of men waited before a church called St. Brendan's. Rose said: "Hey, Jimmy, how are you?"

A small dirty man smiled at her. "Just great, Rose," he said. "Just great, now that you're here."

He had hollow colorless eyes, white hair growing in tufts from his ears, a heavy rat-colored coat. He smelled like shit. Delaney edged away from him, lifting the boy, thinking: I should have brought surgical masks. If I'd known we were coming here. Rose pushed forward, past the shit-smelling man, took the boy from Delaney, and led the way to a side entrance. The men here all knew her name too. *Mornin', Rose . . . God bless ya, Rose . . . Hey, Rose, get that sauce goin', Rose.* She waved to them and kept moving, burying the boy's face against her shoulder.

The path to the old lower church was down three steps into a gloomy alley. In the old days, the overflow crowds heard mass down here, but times had changed, for the worse. Here and everywhere. The downstairs space was no longer a church. There were more than fifty long tables, each occupied by men having Sunday breakfast. At the front of the low-ceilinged lower church, there was a kitchen where the altar once stood. A few men were on line with metal trays, stragglers scooping up watery scrambled eggs and mashed potatoes and coffee. A growling mesh of talk provided the basic sound, punctuated by occasional bursts of laughter and the clatter of metal trays. They were all men. Some ignored breakfast. They were waiting for lunch. Waiting for Rose.

"I work here Sunday mornings," Rose said, "getting lunch ready for these guys." She returned the boy to Delaney, told them to wait, and walked to the side of the steam tables into a back room. The way altar boys once walked to the sacristy. Carlito's eyes were full of questions, but he said nothing. Rising off the men was an odor of dried sweat, dirty clothes, unwashed feet, and despair.

Rose reappeared behind the counter with a pale green cotton uniform over her street clothes and a dark green apron looped around her neck. She had tied a handkerchief across her mouth and was nodding, gesturing, ladling out the last remnants of breakfast to newcomers. They came in more slowly now, a few volunteers waiting until other men left spaces at the tables before admitting new ones. Breakfast was almost over. Rose turned to the kitchen and began pouring water into a huge pot for soup. The early-afternoon meal was next, and she was clearly the boss. She began chopping vegetables and slicing chicken and gesturing with her hands to some of the others. A young black man helped her lay all the pieces on platters, covering them with dish towels against the flies. Then she started preparing the sauce. The black man opened can after can of tomato sauce, sliding them to her along a counter, and Rose emptied each into a huge pot. Then she added freshly diced tomatoes. Her hands moved as quickly as they did in the kitchen on Horatio Street. She never once looked at Delaney and the boy.

The boy kept pointing at Rose and saying her name and smiling. But Delaney thought: I must get him away from here. The place is a germ farm. Everything might be in the air. From tuberculosis on down. He waved at Rose and caught her attention and gestured toward the exit and then at the boy. She stopped what she was doing and came around from behind the counter and down the aisle. She lowered the handkerchief, smiling broadly.

"So you see what I do on Sundays," she said.

"I do," he said. "It's beautiful."

"I make the sauce, and they have a big meal of ziti and chicken at two o'clock. When I'm already gone. It's the best they get all week. They come from all over."

"This is great work, Rose."

He meant it.

"Hey," she said. "See you later."

She turned, lifted her handkerchief to her nose, and hurried back to the kitchen. Delaney took the boy's hand and they went out into the hard city, heading for the park. When they reached the corner, the sun was shining. Delaney inhaled deeply, breathing in the morning air. Breathing the spring.

That night she came home looking drained, but now Delaney understood. Her Sundays were for the casualties of peace. For all those sad, fucked-up, beaten-up, or beaten-down men who had survived the Great War, who had made marriages and fathered children and roared in speakeasies and danced until dawn and then blew it all. She didn't judge them. She tried to comfort them, to put a little good sauce into their lives, at least once a week. Delaney started to boil water for coffee, and when she tried to move him away from the stove, he stood in front of her, his hands up, his palms out. Carlito came to Delaney's side, grinned, and put up his hands too.

"You've had a long day, Rose. Now it's our turn."

"Come on, no jokes, please."

He opened the refrigerator and lifted out the flat box from Angela's and placed it on the table. The boy blurted: "For *you,* Rosa!" She blushed, turned away, squeezed the boy's right hand. Delaney opened the box to the tightly wrapped sandwiches, the container of soup, the bread, the cannoli.

"Just sit," Delaney said. "We know where the oil is, and the butter, and the pot to heat up the soup. Just sit."

"Sit, Rosa," said the boy, patting the seat of her chair. She eased into the chair, hugging the boy, looking at Delaney.

While they ate, she explained how St. Brendan's worked, using leftover food from grocery chains and restaurants (including Angela's), and how the priests raised money with bingo games and raffles, and how it was never enough. Delaney wished he had taken Frankie's money and given it to Rose for the Sunday kitchen. She finished her half sandwich and sipped her coffee. The boy slipped off the chair, mounted the fire engine, and banged it into the door to the yard. Rose laughed out loud.

"Hey! Ragazzo! You gonna *hurt* yourself!"

He laughed. "No, Rosa. No."

Rose turned to Delaney, arms folded on the tabletop.

"I guess you want to know where I go after we feed the men," she said.

"I wonder sometimes, sure," Delaney said, thinking: She reads minds too.

"It's pretty simple," she said, looking at him in a new way, as if suspecting he might be jealous. She smiled sweetly. "I don't have a boyfriend, if that's what you think."

"You have the right."

"I know better."

"So?"

"I go to the movies," she said.

"That's *it?*" Delaney said, feeling something like relief. He smiled. "You go to the movies?"

"Every Sunday," she said. "They are so — what's the word? — wonderful."

She said the word with a hair of pride in her voice for saying it exactly.

"What's your favorite?"

"Last week I saw *Flying Down to Rio.* It's got that actress Dolores Del Rio, who's the most beautiful girl in the world. Dark hair, a long neck, long legs, a face, *ooof.* And she dances with that skinny guy, he can't do nothing wrong. Every step he's perfect, and relaxed, and like one hundred percent *American.* That Fred Astaire. I wanted to stay and see it twice, but then I'd have to sit through a gangster movie. I hate gangster movies." A pause. "You know why." Another pause. "I hate gangsters."

"And today? What did you see?"

"The truth?" She chuckled. "I like to go over the East Side, a place called the Palestine, that everybody there calls the Itch, and I see *King Kong* again. The fifth time since it come out last year." Now she was smiling broadly. "It's just so wonderful. The greatest love story ever!" Her face darkened slightly. "That poor monkey, he falls in love with Fay Wray and what happens? He dies! Because he loves her! I cry every time."

"Imagine if he met Dolores Del Rio."

She laughed out loud. "And tried to dance like Fred Astaire."

She leaned against Delaney, and he put his good hand on her shoulder and pulled her closer.

On the following Sunday morning, the city was drowning under a heavy spring rain. In his office, Delaney opened the safe and took a hundred-dollar bill out of Eddie Corso's envelope. He addressed a new envelope, to St. Brendan's, slipped in the bill, sealed the envelope, and gave it to Rose.

"A contribution to your Sunday work," he said. "Don't tell them where it came from. They might ask if I'm in a state of grace."

She looked at him in a confused, dubious way.

"You don't have to do this," she said.

"I know," he said. "But I want to."

Then he handed her a manila envelope.

"There are face masks in here," he said. "The kind we use at the hospital. They tie at the back of your head. Wear one. You never know what's floating around in the air of St. Brendan's beautiful restaurant." He smiled. "And if you get a cold or something, you won't pass it to the food." A beat. "Or Carlito."

She took the pale blue masks from the envelope and looked at them.

"They might think I'm some kind of a bank robber. Lady Dillinger feeds the poor!"

"Rose, I doubt that very much."

She shrugged, slipped the envelopes into her pocketbook, donned her own poncho and winter boots, and went out to feed the poor. For a while, Delaney and the boy watched the rain pelting the backyard, where flowers were bending under the assault. The thirsty limbs of the olive tree reached for the sky. Then he turned to the boy.

"Come on, big fella," Delaney said. "We have work to do."

They climbed together to the top floor, and Delaney took out his keys and opened the door to Molly's room. He switched on some lamps and raised the window shades. The boy gazed around.

"That's a *piano!*" he said, as if suddenly retrieving the word in Spanish.

"You can play if you like," Delaney said, and raised the top. He plunked one key. There was no echo of the past. "You see," he said, "each key has a different sound." He plinked another key, and another. Then he lifted the boy onto the stool. "Play, Carlito. Make music."

He turned to the flattened boxes leaning against the bookcase, and to the roll of tape and pair of scissors. A stack of old newspapers was lying on the floor. Thank you, Monique. He unfolded one box. The boy plinked a key, then another, each one tentative. Delaney taped the bottom of the box, and placed it on the floor, and started to stack Molly's scores. Schoenberg. Mahler. Bach. He remembered how Molly would come home from the Steinway store on Union Square with her face flushed and happy and a new score in her hand, and how she would go directly to this room. Here, she vanished into the music, forgetting the world, the house, Grace, me. Some passages were repeated over and over again, and he could hear the Ringstrasse in some of them, that year before the war. Now the boy was pounding the keys with two hands, a prodigy of atonality and dissonance, or just a kid making noise, and Delaney thought: Molly would have winced over this, and loved it too.

By the time Delaney was on the second box, Carlito came off the stool, bored with playing at the piano, and stood beside Delaney. He asked the boy to put a finger on the tape while he cut it with the scissors. He flipped the box to its taped bottom, and Carlito began to bring books from a lower shelf. Some belonged to Grace when she was not yet ten years old.

"Let's keep these," Delaney said. "Make a pile right there."

"Okay, Gran'pa," the boy said, and sat on the rug, looking at the books, turning the pages, seeing visions of Oz and Sherwood Forest.

Delaney remembered buying the Oz book on Fourth Avenue, just before leaving for the war. *The Wonderful Wizard of Oz.* By L. Frank Baum. The fourth edition. Molly said in one letter that she was reading it to Grace, who loved the illustrations, but never said that she had finished it. He handed *Oz* to the boy and told him to hold on to it. Robin Hood could wait. He put a Matisse book aside for himself, with tipped-in illustrations in splashy color. He filled two more boxes, sealed and marked them, and then Carlito looked up. He was looking at an illustration from *Oz.*

"Gran'pa, what is this?"

"That's the Tin Man," he said. "And that's the Cowardly Lion. They're going to the Emerald City. Later I'll read it to you."

"Read it *now!*" the boy said. "Come on, Gran'pa."

"In about an hour, Carlito. We just have to finish the job." Understanding that the boy didn't know an hour from a month. "We'll work fast, okay?"

And so they did. Certain shelves were emptied, others remained full, and a dozen boxes were taped and marked and sealed. He locked the door behind him. On Monday, Monique was bringing someone to carry the packed cartons to the shelves in the basement, far from the heat or the hazards of weather. As they went downstairs, the boy carried *The Wonderful Wizard of Oz* and Delaney clutched the Matisse book. Thinking: Maybe I can start painting again, with my left hand. When he was sixteen he lasted three months at the Art Students League, where the drawing instructor first showed him *Gray's Anatomy,* that fat masterpiece of bones and muscles and the hidden terrain of the body. Later the teacher told him sadly that he didn't really have what it took for art. But *Gray's Anatomy* led him to the alternative dream of becoming a surgeon. He no longer had what it took for that, he thought, but maybe he could make paintings now that didn't have to be art. That were just color and form and filled with emotion. Like a spring day. And Carlito could do the same. Up there in the room they were reclaiming from ghosts.

• • •

Delaney and the boy heated up the minestrone that Rose had left in the refrigerator for their lunch, and ate it with bread and a saucer of olive oil. The boy squinted at Delaney.

"Gran'pa? Why you have white hair?"

"Well, it's not completely white, is it?" Delaney said, brushing a hand through his hair. "I mean, there's brown hair there too."

"Yes, but Rosa has no white hair."

"She's young, big fella. I'm old."

He gazed at Delaney. "What is old?"

"It's when . . ." He hesitated. What the hell was it? "It's when you have a lot of birthdays and you live a long time."

The boy tried to understand but gave it up and turned his attention to the stuffed bear. Delaney thought: You'll know soon enough.

Later they went upstairs and stretched out on the boy's bed, and Delaney read to him the beginning of the tale of Dorothy and her magic slippers, and after a while both were asleep.

In the evening, when the rain had eased, they went to Angela's. Rose was not home yet, and Delaney wished that she was with them. Angela gave them a table for two along the wall. One large table was presided over by Harry Flanagan, the Tammany guy. He waved hello and Delaney waved back. The others at the table turned their heads and nodded too.

They were almost finished with dinner when Billy McNiff stepped in the door. He went directly to Delaney.

"Hey, Doc? I just passed your house. There's two cop cars there, and an ambulance just pulled up."

Delaney stood up and waved at Angela, who sensed an emergency and told him: "Go, go."

He lifted the boy and hurried out, and as he turned into Horatio

Street he saw the two squad cars with red dome lights turning. An ambulance was backed up to the curb, its back doors open. *Don't let it be Rose.* A small crowd was forming, with excited kids running around, and women with folded arms, and many men. When he reached the house, Danny Shapiro was outside, his badge pinned to his zipper jacket, smoking a cigarette and talking to a uniformed cop. He stepped on the butt when he saw Delaney.

"What's up?" Delaney said.

"Come on in," Shapiro said. "See for y'self."

Delaney put Carlito down and said: "Wait here, Carlito."

"I want Rosa," the boy said. He looked about to break into tears.

The uniformed cop said: "I'll take care of him. Don't worry, Doc."

The cop lifted the boy and started talking to him in a low voice, but the boy's anxiety did not go away. Delaney stepped into the vestibule. A man was stretched out on the floor of the waiting area, while two ambulance medics worked on him, wiping blood off his face. One medic was thin, the other beefy. Both said hello to Delaney. He recognized them from St. Vincent's.

"You know this guy?" Shapiro said.

"Yeah," Delaney said. "His name is Callahan. He's an FBI man."

"Jesus Christ," Shapiro said. "Then the ID is real. I figured he's some gonif with a phony ID."

"Where's Rose?"

"In your office," Shapiro said. "She says she heard a noise and tiptoed down the stairs and sees this guy picking the lock on your office."

"And then?"

"She hits him with a fuckin' baseball bat."

Delaney's eyes widened. "Is he alive?"

"Barely." He looked down at the stricken man. "Take a look, Doctor."

Delaney squatted beside the medics, found a pulse, then pictured Rose with her Louisville Slugger parked each night beside her bed. The man's eyes were still closed.

"There's a seven-inch gash in his head, which is why there's so much blood," the thin medic said. "It looks to be just a scalp wound, but inside, who knows?"

"An inch lower, she hits the temple? He's a corpse," the beefy medic said.

"You need to get him X-rayed," Delaney said. "See if his skull is broken."

"Yeah," the thin medic said. "There's a concussion for sure."

"What are you waiting for? Shouldn't he be —"

"His boss is on the way, from the FBI. We were told, do nothing."

Delaney stood up and said to Shapiro, "Where's the weapon?"

"Over there," Shapiro said.

The bat was leaning in a corner against the wall.

"When you searched this guy," Delaney said, "was he carrying a search warrant?"

"Not unless it's in his shoe," Shapiro said. "He *was* packing a thirty-eight."

Delaney pushed into his office, without touching the door handle. Rose was in his chair, her elbows on his desk, her hands cradling her head. Her face was flushed, her eyes glittery.

"I'm sorry to cause all this trouble," she said softly.

"You didn't cause it. The guy on the floor out there — he caused it. He broke into our house. You defended yourself and the house."

"Who is he?"

"His name's Callahan. He's an FBI man, trying to track down my daughter, Grace."

Rose groaned. "Ah, hell. I'm doomed. I gotta get out of here. If I killed a G-man, then —"

"Calm down. He's alive. And he might be in more trouble than you. It looks like he has no warrant. That's a piece of paper from a judge allowing him to go into someone's house."

"But I broke his head. Just like my goddam husband."

She stood up, anxiously balling and relaxing her fingers, her words speeding now. "No matter what. They're sure to investigate me. And I'm a — I don't have *papers.*" She inhaled deeply, then exhaled almost desperately. "They could throw me outta the country! Away from Carlito! Away from *you.*"

Rose turned her back to him and choked off a sob. Delaney went to her and hugged her.

"Never," he said. "Never."

When Delaney stepped back into the waiting area, Callahan was sitting up, with his back to the wall. His eyes were open, but he was still somewhere else, like a fighter who'd been knocked out. A rough bandage was wrapped around his head to stop the bleeding from the scalp. Another casualty. And he suspected that Callahan's pain was compounded by humiliation. The man did not look at him. Delaney could not repress a sense of pity.

"Where'd the medics go?" Delaney said.

"They got another run," Shapiro said. "The Feds are coming themselves to pick this guy up."

"What? This dope has to go to a hospital *now!*"

"Yeah, but the G-men say they'll handle it."

"Fuck the G-men." He went back into his office and picked up the telephone. Shapiro grabbed his wrist.

"Leave it alone, Jim."

Delaney sighed and placed the receiver back on the hook. In a corner, Rose was staring at him. He went to her and squeezed her hand in a gentle way. Then he went back to the hall, Shapiro behind him.

"Will they charge Rose with anything?" Delaney said.

"They might, but I doubt it, if they don't have a warrant. I mean, the newspapers would kill them. No warrant and it's breakin' and entering." He sighed. "But who knows, with these fucking amateurs. Some people actually think those G-men movies are true. Cops and newspapermen know they are bullshit. So do ninety-two percent of the people who lived through Prohibition."

Delaney said: "I'll be right back."

He stepped outside, and Carlito was sobbing in the arms of the big cop and reaching with his left hand for Delaney. The crowd was larger in the street.

"I'll take him off your hands, officer. "

"Sure thing," the cop said, passing the boy to Delaney. Carlito kept whispering *granpagranpagranpa* and holding him with both hands around the neck. Delaney carried him back inside, talking quietly to the boy. He eased past Shapiro and another cop and the stricken Callahan into his office. Rose came to them with tears in her eyes. The boy spoke her name and reached for her, and she took him in her arms and murmured softly in English and Sicilian, making a sound that was more music than language. Then Delaney heard the gate open and slam, followed by the slamming of the vestibule door.

"Stay here," he said, and went out to the waiting area.

A short barrel-chested man in a gray fedora and an open overcoat was standing with fists on his hips. Delaney thought: Another movie version of J. Edgar Hoover. Another bullshit tough guy. Two more men in fedoras and open overcoats stood behind him, dressed like Callahan. One of them was holding a furled upright stretcher.

"Who's in charge here?" the short guy said.

"I am," said Shapiro, flashing his detective's badge. "Danny Shapiro, New York Police Department. Who are you?"

"Tillman," the short guy said in an annoyed voice. "FBI."

"I showed you my tin," Shapiro said. "Where's yours?"

Tillman said, "Christ," reached inside his coat, and removed a wallet displaying a card with his face on it.

"Welcome to Horatio Street," Shapiro said.

"All right," Tillman said. "What happened here?"

"Simple," Shapiro said, glancing at Delaney. "This guy on the floor broke in here — you can see the open window on the second floor.

He's an FBI agent, but it looks like he's got no warrant. And he starts picking the lock to Dr. Delaney's office."

"That you?"

"That's me," Delaney said.

"Where were you?"

"Having dinner with my grandson at Angela's restaurant. Right around the corner."

"And then?" Tillman said.

Shapiro continued: "The woman who takes care of the boy, Rose Verga, was upstairs in her room — she's off Sundays. She's taking a nap. Then she hears something. She picks up a baseball bat and comes down the stairs. Very quiet. She sees this guy, he turns, like he's reaching for a rod in his belt, and she hits him in the head. That's all."

Tillman shook his head, his eyes moving from Shapiro to Callahan to Delaney and back to Shapiro.

"All right," Tillman said, indicating Callahan. "The special ambulance is outside, it'll take this guy away." He nodded at the two men, and they unfurled the stretcher and went to Callahan. Then he said to Shapiro: "Where's the woman?"

Delaney showed him into the office. Rose looked oddly defiant now, holding the boy close to her. He identified himself and asked her name. She told him.

"All right, Miss Verga, here's what I want you to do," Tillman said. "I want you to stay right here tonight, in this house. I could put you in a cell tonight, but that wouldn't help anything. I want you down at federal court tomorrow morning, got that? You know where it is?"

"I do," Delaney said.

"Don't try to run away," Tillman said to Rose. "You'll be in big trouble."

"Okay," Rose said. Carlito was squirming.

"At federal court, you go to room 110. I'll be there. We'll take a statement. You can have a lawyer with you if you think that's necessary. Depending on what happens, you might face criminal charges. You understand me?"

"You mean if something bad happens to Callahan?" Delaney said.

"Something bad already did," Tillman said.

He stepped into the hall. Callahan and the stretcher bearers were out of the house. "Good night, gentlemen," Tillman said. And he was gone.

Delaney faced Shapiro. "New York one," Shapiro said, "Feds nothing."

Then he was gone too. Delaney locked the door behind him.

At the sound of the gate slamming, the office door opened and Carlito ran out, with Rose behind him. Rose still seemed alarmed, as if prepared for sudden flight.

"That's it?" she said.

"Until tomorrow morning at the courthouse," Delaney said. He noticed that her face had hardened and her eyes were full of fright. "I'll go with you."

She came to him, and he put his arms around her. If fear had an odor, it was rising from her. She felt smaller and oddly younger.

"Don't cry, Rosa," the boy said.

For the first time in years, Delaney wanted to dance.

"Now . . . ," Rose said.

"Now everybody needs a good night's sleep."

Rose and the boy started up the stairs. Delaney went first to his office, looking for a business card.

The vast sea was empty and scarlet. The immense wave rose and rose and rose, carrying Delaney with its surging power, and then crested, held, seemed frozen, and then fell, dropping straight down into a darker crimson trough, and the trough was not empty. Tinpot helmets bobbed everywhere, going under then rising, faces contorted under the helmets, all mouths open, dozens of them, hundreds, drowning in the blood-red tide. He could see Eddie Corso without a helmet, his eyes glittery with fear, close enough to see and hear but too far to reach. There were dozens of soldiers whose faces he knew, but the only name he could remember was Eddie Corso's. He began to see others: Knocko and Zimmerman and Mr. Lanzano. Packy Hanratty. Angela. All wearing helmets. All except Eddie and the boy. He was in the crimson water too, his eyes wide, full of terror, and Delaney tried to swim to him, calling *Carlito! Carlito! Carlito!* Delaney's legs seemed to weigh three hundred pounds, and his right arm was useless, and he could not reach the boy. *Carlito! Carlito! Carlito!*

And then he was awake, and Rose was sitting beside him on the bed, caressing his sweaty face. Rose. This time not an illusion, not a scribble of dream or desire. Real. With her odor of flowers. In a bathrobe in the dark.

"You okay?" she whispered hoarsely.

"Yes," he said, feeling a tremble in his voice. "Yes. Sure. Just a bad dream."

"You were calling the boy."

"Did I wake you up?"

"No, I wasn't asleep."

"I'm okay," Delaney said.

"No, you're not."

She stretched out on top of the covers and pulled him close, her right arm across his chest. He could hear her breathing, cool and steady. A vague aroma of basil was now mixed with the smell of flowers.

"It wasn't just Carlito," she said. "I know. I couldn't sleep with worrying. About going away. About living somewhere without the boy." A beat; then, in a reluctant voice: "Without you."

"Don't go away," he said.

He wanted to hold her face, to kiss her cheeks and brow and lips and neck. But he was afraid. If I cross this street, he thought, if I open this door, where will it lead? Will I ruin something? Everything? Will I *force* her to choose flight?

Thinking: Don't play with her.

Thinking: Don't take advantage of her goodness, her sense of unworthiness, her confusion.

Thinking: She came to me. Full of her own needs. Perhaps even acting out a farewell.

"It's cold here tonight," she said, and lifted her arm from his chest, and touched his face, and sat up.

Thinking: Don't go. Please don't go.

She folded back the blanket and sheet on her side of the bed and slipped in beside him. She bent her leg and slid it over his thigh, infusing him with warmth, while her hands moved to his face and neck. Her breathing was thicker. He realized in the dark that her bathrobe was open, and he could feel her breasts, pliant and full, and her hard nipples. And then it was hair and flesh and tongue, then it was sounds without words, then it was belly and bottom, and hands moving, and legs, and softness and hardness, and muscles taut, then it was wetness and then entry into deep endless warmth.

"Dottore," she whispered.

"Rosa."

THIRTEEN

Just before eight-thirty in the morning, they boarded the local train going downtown to Chambers Street. Rose was dressed in the same black clothes and stretched boots she wore to St. Patrick's, but her face was bare of powder. She was hatless, her hair held tight with oyster-colored clasps. Walking beside her to the station, Delaney absorbed her tense silence. Monique had arrived early, after Delaney's call. The patients would have to wait. But the tension was surely not about the boy. It was about everything else.

On the crowded train, the knuckles of her hand were white as she gripped the long bar above the packed seats. Delaney saw a film of sweat on her upper lip. She nodded when he said, "Just two stops and we're there." He stared at the reflection of her distracted face in the window glass as they moved through the black tunnel. She was looking at nothing. Or at things stirring vividly within her head. The blood seeping from Callahan's scalp. Tillman's badge. And perhaps most important: the visit later to Delaney's bed. Delaney himself was still full of what had happened between them in the dark. They had crossed a line together. In the morning, everything had been the same, and utterly changed.

He glanced at the reflections in the windows: shopgirls anxious to be on time, Wall Street clerks in linty double-breasted suits, a uniformed cop with a drained face, heading to Brooklyn. Many read newspapers. All seemed gripped by the seediness of the Depression. None could have imagined what was filling Rose's mind, or Delaney's.

They came up onto Chambers Street, in the bright morning river light, slanting to the west from Brooklyn. They started walking to Broadway, and at the corner a small ice truck made a sudden turn, angrily blaring its horn. Rose jumped in alarm, shouted in Sicilian, and took Delaney's arm. He squeezed it closer.

"Easy, Rose," he said, and smiled. "Usually guys like that just run you over."

She threw him a dark glance but said nothing. They walked uptown two blocks to Duane Street, and he could feel her gathering her strength for what awaited them. Her face was harder, her brow furrowed, her eyes focused on the sidewalk directly in front of them. Her grip on his arm grew tighter. They turned east on Duane Street, and saw up ahead the vast brightness of Foley Square. It was named for Tom Foley, who ran a saloon and was a chieftain in Tammany Hall and a good friend of Big Jim's. Long ago, Foley gave a job to a kid named Al Smith, who had never finished the eighth grade, and Smith went on to become governor of New York and the Democratic candidate for president in 1928. Smith didn't forget that Foley had given him his life, and pushed hard to name the square after him, as it was constructed on the site of the old Collect Pond and the Five Points slum. On the far side of the square, Delaney could see the new federal courthouse, its steel frame rising more than thirty stories into the sky, to be finished in another year. The FBI office was a block to the north. He mentioned none of this to Rose. She was rehearsing her secret script. Questions. Answers.

They turned into an office building on Duane Street and took an elevator to the sixth floor. She released her grip on his arm. They stepped out of the elevator into a small reception area, with a woman behind a sliding glass window.

"Dr. Delaney to see Judge Flanagan, please," he said.

"One moment, sir."

She hit a button, whispered into the phone, then turned to Delaney and motioned to an oaken door.

"Go right in, sir."

Across the carpeted room, Harry Flanagan rose from a swivel chair behind a cluttered desk, a wide smile on his face. He was not wearing a jacket, and the many curves of his body were emphasized by his wilting white shirt.

"Good morning, Dr. Delaney," he said, extending a hand for Delaney to shake. "And this must be, Miss, uh —"

"Verga," Rose said. "Rose Verga."

"Nice to meet you, Miss Verga," he said.

"Likewise," she said.

"Have a seat," he said, and Rose sat in one of the two chairs facing the judge's desk. Then Flanagan gestured with his head to Delaney and walked to a wall covered with framed photographs. Delaney followed. There were pictures of ballplayers and prizefighters, soldiers and politicians. Al Smith was there and Jimmy Walker, who was away now in European exile. And there were many group photographs from political dinners and chowder outings and trips to Saratoga and the Polo Grounds. Flanagan pointed a finger at one group shot.

"I noticed this when I came in this morning," he said. "It's gotta be, what? Nineteen thirteen? Anyway, before the war. Right there in the middle is Tom Foley, that they named the square after. Look who's next to him. That's your father, Doctor. That's Big Jim." Delaney squinted. It was Big Jim all right. "And next to him? That's *me*. I musta been seventy-five pounds lighter!" He laughed. "But look at this runt, over here on the left? That kid. Know who that is?"

Delaney shrugged. He didn't know.

"That's your man Tillman," he said. "He came out of St. Brigid's, his father dead, and Tom Foley, bless his heart, helped put him through law school. He ended up at the Justice Department during the war, and Hoover made him part of the Palmer Raids. When they started the FBI, he was right there."

"I'll be damned," Delaney said.

Flanagan wheezed and returned to the swivel chair. Rose was trying hard to decode this conversation and sat very still, her face empty of emotion. Delaney took the other chair.

"Anyway, I called Mr. Tillman this morning," Flanagan said, in a dry tone. "I reminded him who your father was, I reminded him that this fella Callahan didn't have a search warrant. I reminded him what the papers would do with all this. He was very nice."

Then he paused for a beat. He focused on Rose.

"Go home," he said. "It's all over."

Rose went loose, with sounds coming from her, but no words. *Uh.* Just *uh* and *uh* and *uh.* Her hands moved without purpose. Delaney stood up. He felt as if his own tension was leaking out on the carpet.

"Thanks, Judge," he said, shaking Flanagan's hand with both of his own. "Thanks very much."

"Yes," Rose said. "Many, many thanks."

Flanagan glanced at his wristwatch and stood up too.

"What is it the great Boss Tweed once said?" he said, and grinned. "It's better to know the judge than to know the law."

Back on Duane Street, she put a hand on a scrawny tree and started to laugh. Bent over. Released. Men and women hurrying past looked at her, and the women smiled and the men seemed baffled. All kept moving. Then Delaney saw that she was sobbing through the laughter. He handed her a handkerchief, and she wiped at her face and giggled like a youngster.

"Oh, Dottore. Oh, thank you. Oh, you crazy Irish. Oh."

He put an arm around her waist and guided her to Broadway. Across the street was a large cafeteria called the Broadway Café, and they went in. She had not eaten breakfast, and he had only sipped from a cup of coffee. The place was loud with talk and the clatter of dishes and silverware. Many tables were filled: lawyers and defendants, reporters from the *Sun*, which was a block away, groups of three or four middle-aged uptown women preparing for a day of shopping for downtown bargains. Delaney and Rose paused inside the door, then saw two men get up from a table. One was clearly a lawyer, the other clearly a mug. The mug was dressed in a chalk-striped suit and looked nervous. Delaney nodded as they went to meet their fate, and Delaney and Rose sat down. There were empty coffee cups and some plates on the table, and a cigarette burning in an ashtray. A young man cleared the table, stubbing out the cigarette, and then a waitress in a green uniform came to them and faced Delaney, a pencil poised above her pad.

"What's yours, sweetheart?" she said.

He explained to Rose: "No menus here."

"Uh, let me see," Rose said. "How about a roll with butter, a fried egg, and a jelly doughnut."

"You want the fried egg on the jelly doughnut?" the waitress said. Then giggled. "Just kiddin'," she said. She was about forty, with a tough Irish face. Rose said separate plates would be fine. Delaney said, "Just the buttered roll, and coffee, please. Black coffee."

The waitress hurried away. He looked at Rose across the table.

"I want to dance," she said.

"Like Dolores Del Rio?"

"Yeah," she said, and squeezed his wrist. "On the wings of an airplane."

Across the day, she did not speak about what had happened in the night. In early afternoon, they went to see Mrs. Botticelli, who made jokes in Sicilian and said she was feeling much better. Rose bought cheese in Di Palo's and some oranges from a pushcart. She showed deference to Monique, and played in the garden with the boy, and Delaney went on house calls. That night she returned to Delaney's bed. And the night after that. And the night after that.

Delaney did not say anything either. He was happy that she did not affect a girlish shyness, or a giggling modesty. She wasn't a girl. She was in her middle thirties, not her teens. Through the days, she was as she was before, with only subtle changes. She flashed him intimate smiles, she touched a casual hand to his face, but she did not talk about what they now shared. On their walks with Carlito in the evenings, she showed nothing in the street, did not take his arm, did not hold his hand. She never used the word "love."

In the luminous dark of Delaney's bedroom, she was not shy either. They did many things with each other, like humans finding water after drought. One night she straddled him on the armchair. On another, she joined him in the shower, the lights out, and she soaped him and he soaped her until neither could wait another second and they moved barefoot, hair wild and wet, to the bed. Sometimes, in full passion, she covered her face with the pillow, fearful of waking the boy with her screams.

Carlito never woke. He was exhausted from pedaling his fire truck, often now on the sidewalk outside the house. Or he was full of the sly silent contentment of pasta. Or both. Each night, after the boy fell into sleep, Rose slipped beside Delaney, bringing warmth, changing the air and making it more humid, the two of them erasing loneliness. He never heard her leave, but she was always gone in the morning. Her presence now was larger in the house. She walked with greater confidence, exuding a sense that it was her house too. She was more comfortable than ever, and so was Delaney.

• • •

They began to talk in the dark before sleep would come to Delaney.

She said: "Is your wife alive?"

"I don't know. She disappeared and was never seen again. Dead or alive."

"You miss her?"

"Sometimes."

"You dream about her sometimes?"

"Sometimes."

Silence.

"I dream about my husband sometimes too. Calvino, with the plate in his head. Sometimes he's even that handsome guy I saw after the war. Most times he's a goddamn monster."

She was silent then.

"I dream about the boy too. I dream about Carlito."

"Me too."

"They scare me, those Carlito dreams."

He remembered the scarlet sea.

"Me too," he said.

And laughed.

There was no fresh letter from Grace, and very little news in the papers about Spain. He thought of calling Tillman, asking if the mail from Leonora Córdoba was being stopped by some new young FBI zealot who had discovered the secret address. Then thought Tillman would be embarrassed or angry or both if he asked. Let it alone, he told himself. As he made his house calls, Delaney heard much talk about the Giants, with opening day coming on fast, and how this would be another immense year for the Giants after the great World Series win over the Senators of Washington. McGraw would not see it, of course, but Bill Terry was a great manager, along with being a splendid hitter, and Mel Ott was sure to have a big year at bat, and the pitching was strong, even if Adolfo Luque, the ancient Cuban, was another year older. One afternoon Delaney spent twenty minutes with an old man in Hudson Street, his wife dead, his children gone off to their own lives, his lungs choked by a million cigarettes, and they talked baseball, and how Gus Mancuso was still not able to play, on account of getting typhoid during the off-season. Delaney went to see the mother of Frankie Botts, with Rose beside him, and the old woman said she wanted to know about the Giants. "I just want to go one more time to the Polo Grounds," she said in Sicilian. Delaney said, "You'll see a lot more Giant games. Later in the summer." Tears appeared in her eyes, and later, out on Grand Street, where the two hoodlums remained on guard duty in their car, Rose said: "I don't understand this. How come one old lady from Sicily cares about this baseball?"

"Because she's an American now," Delaney said.

Then it was the Sunday after opening day, and over breakfast he and the boy talked about baseball. The boy still didn't know what Delaney meant, but he listened intently, looking at the photographs on the back page of the *Daily News*. Then Rose came into the kitchen, dressed for Sunday, smiling broadly.

"You guys got a big day today," she said. "The Polo Grounds!"

"Bay-ball," Carlito said with a grin.

"*Base*-ball."

"Bayz-ball."

"Good, Carlito," Delaney said. "Baseball!"

"Have a great time," Rose said, and went off to feed the men who would not be making it to the Polo Grounds anytime soon.

It was dark when Rose came home, and Carlito ran to her and started talking about what he had seen in the Polo Grounds. The words came in an excited rush. The boy was describing the world now, not simply naming it.

"Rosa, they have bats like you! Big bats, all bats in their hands, and they hit a ball, and they run. They run very fast, and they jump into the base. There's grass all over, and lots of people. They all, they —" He paused, groping for the word, raising his hands in the air.

"Cheer," Delaney said.

"Sí, they cheer, Rosa. All of them. Many, many people. Then they come with the bat again and they throw the ball and they hit the ball in the air, Rosa! Up high in the air!"

"You got to take me there someday, Carlito," Rose said. "And explain to me how they play."

"Yeah! And Osito too! But we can play in, in, the bagyard too."

"Not when it's dark, boy!"

"No, in the sun, Rosa."

Later, they all went up to bed. Later, Rose opened Delaney's door and entered the intimate darkness.

The next day, there were three letters from Grace, all with different postmarks, Nothing told him that they had been opened, but he was sure that Tillman had sent them on. Delaney couldn't read them, because the Monday-morning rush was on outside his door.

Later, he thought. Always later. Now the quinine men were there, yellow with malaria. A few strangers. A woman with what was surely leukemia. One lunger. A hernia. A broken nose. And Sally Wilson, hoping again to have her breasts gripped in a man's hands.

"I'm sure it's a lump," she said.

Delaney sighed and said: "Let's see."

When they were all gone, he sat heavily at the desk and opened the letters from Grace. Each was brief. Her husband was back in Spain but she hadn't made contact yet. Somebody would try to bring her to him, or him to her. She was making drawings of Barcelona and its people. She missed Carlito and hoped to see him soon. But the husband, Santos, was essential. "I just have to resolve this," she wrote, "and then try to get on with my life." She thanked him for everything and apologized again for leaving the boy on his doorstep. Delaney put the letters back in their envelopes and slipped them under the desk blotter.

Then he filled out records. Sally Wilson: That was wrong. I can't have her here anymore. The coldness of examination is in me, but not in her, and I'm servicing her. And I can't go to the Chinese women anymore. I know I'm just providing medical services. But to Rose it would be like an act of infidelity. He thought about Grace. About her possible return. And what it might do to all of them. To him. To the boy. To Rose.

At lunch Rose talked about the Bing Crosby movie she'd seen the day before on Fourteenth Street, and how Crosby was a wonderful singer, and so relaxed, and how she always heard him now on the radio. Mentioning him, she smiled widely. The boy wandered in and out of the back door, which was open to the garden and the olive tree. Rose did not bring him a baseball bat.

Delaney looked at Rose and saw that her face was smoother now, her skin rosier, her smile oddly wider. Some of it must have been from the sun. But maybe it was also from what they did in the night. He wanted now to hold her and kiss her and feel her pressing against him. Then he thought of Grace's letters, and felt each minute ticking away. He wished for clarity, but it did not come.

That afternoon, at Billy McNiff's, he bought a baseball and a small child's glove. At the art supply store near Cooper Union, he picked up three brushes, watercolors, crayons, two pads of paper, some charcoal, and pencils. In Molly's room, he and Rose set up two facing chairs for Carlito, and a table for Delaney.

"This is great," Rose said, as she gazed around the room that had always been closed and was now wide-open. She was beaming as Delaney showed the boy how to use the crayons. Now they were both southpaws, and Delaney drew a crude head of a man wearing a baseball cap, with big eyes and a wide grin, then handed the crayons to Carlito.

"You try it now, big fella," he said.

The boy chose a red crayon and began with his left hand to make a head. Rose went downstairs, but Delaney and Carlito stayed in the room for more than an hour. The boy did little more than scribble, while Delaney tried putting watercolor on paper with his own left hand. He painted a crude house, and a cruder bicycle in a front yard, and the sun shining in the sky. Carlito watched and then tried doing the same with his crayons. When they went downstairs to eat, they left the door open.

That night she held him tightly, as if trying to calm him. Or herself.

"You okay?" she whispered.

"Yes."

"Something happened," she said.

"There were some letters from Grace."

A pause. Then: "She's coming home?"

"Maybe."

He could feel her deflate. Now he held her tight. He touched her damp face. He could feel the faint ridge of the scar.

"Who did this to you?"

"I told you. Some guy."

"Want to tell me about it?"

She was quiet for a long time.

"I was here almost a year," she said. "Living in a rooming house.

My own room. With a lock." A pause. "I didn't know much English. I was lonesome. And I met this guy."

Her breathing was shallow now.

"An old story . . . I start going out with him. Here and there, mostly speakeasies, you know. . . . He's very handsome, thin, a good dancer. His Italian is very bad, all mixed up with American, but so is my English, and anyway . . . that wasn't what it was all about." Another pause. "He had a wife too. I saw her a few times. Everything on her was big, top and bottom. Some kind of an American. I know this could be bad trouble, and I want to break up with this guy, but he won't let me. Another jealous guinea." A final pause. "Then one night I'm packin' to leave and he catches me in the hall and starts yelling and I curse him and his whole family and *whoosh:* the knife comes out and he cuts my face. Then he says, Okay, *go.*"

Silence.

"You went."

"To Jersey City. When I come back, I know he's around someplace, but it was over. Around this time, I start having my trouble with Gyp, another guinea gangster that used a knife. That's why I hate these gangster movies."

He touched the scar again, up now on one elbow.

"What was his name — the guy that cut you?"

"It doesn't matter. He put a mark on me." A pause. "Now it's the past. Nothing can be done."

He felt her emptying beside him, at once ashamed of her confession and relieved to get it said. He held her closer and kissed the scar.

FOURTEEN

For days Rose was her old self. He did not mention the scar. She was cheerful, busy, focused, intimate, while routine established its discipline. She did not mention Grace again, nor the possibility of her return. Without words, she made Delaney believe that the present was everything, a kind of joy, even if the future might contain dread. Perhaps, he thought, this is an illusion. I think it's true because I want it to be true. But as he and the boy tossed a ball around in the backyard, both using left hands, or when they made pictures in the room they now called the studio, or when they sat down for dinner in the golden aroma of oil and basil, and when Rose slipped into his dark room at night, Delaney allowed himself to feel happy. No matter what might happen, he would have these moments as long as he lived.

One afternoon he passed a music store on Broome Street, where old hand-wound Victrolas were for sale, and many 78 rpm records. He tried several machines, testing them with an old Brunswick record of Crosby singing "I Surrender Dear." The records were ten cents each, and he bought ten: Crosby, Russ Columbo, Rudy Vallee. The records and the bulky Victrola were piled into the basket on his bicycle and lashed safely with cord by the man from the music store. Then Delaney slipped the handle of his leather bag inside his belt and pedaled home.

Delaney arrived with his secondhand treasures, to whoops from Rose and scrutiny from the boy, and they went to the top floor and through the open doors of the studio. He placed the Victrola on top of the piano and tried to wind it with his good left hand. His movements were clumsy, and Rose edged him aside.

"Let me do that," she said. And wound it taut, while Delaney lifted Russ Columbo's version of "I Surrender Dear," holding it on the edges, and placed it on the turntable. Rose gazed at the needle, which was new, then cocked the arm and laid it on the record. The voice of Russ Columbo filled the room.

"Moo-zick!" the boy exclaimed, as if seeing a magic act. "Moo-zick!"

He sat at the piano and plunked various keys, and Rose clapped her hands in delight. When the song ended, she put the needle back at the beginning of the record and they did it again, Delaney keeping time with his feet, Rose singing along. Here. Now.

In the night, she did not talk about the boy. It was as if she had already accepted the possibility of his departure. She merged with Delaney, flesh to flesh, her body excited in the now, while forging images that would last for another day, or a month, or always. But above all, now and now and now and now. One night he reached for baby oil on the night table and began to knead the pliant flesh of her back, and her buttocks, and the back of her legs. Her breathing was deep, hoarse, rhythmic. Then he turned her and rubbed the oil into her feet, into the wide hard soles, softening them, into and between toes, into arches and ankles. Her breathing grew more rapid, second after second, deep in the now, until she reached for the pillow and screamed into its dense softness.

During breakfast on a Saturday, the telephone began ringing. Delaney wanted to ignore it, to hold off still another demand for relief. Then he sighed and went into his office.

"Hello?"

And heard a familiar voice.

"I need morphine, fast."

Eddie Corso.

"Where are you?"

"In New York. I need to see you."

"Where and when?"

"You're off tomorrow?"

"Yeah, but so is the woman. I have the boy."

"Bring him."

"Bring him? Eddie, last time I looked there were four platoons of wiseguys looking for you. All with guns."

"I'm a long way from Bleecker Street. It's safe here or I wouldn't be talking to you." A pause. "Besides, I got my own guys."

"That's what I need: a crossfire. Jesus Christ, Eddie, the boy is three years old."

A sigh. "I need to see you, Doc."

Delaney answered with a heavier sigh, fluttering his lips. "Where are you?"

After he hung up, Delaney stared at the telephone. At the scribbled directions. Then at the safe. The treasure of Eddie Corso was dwindling, eroded by the costs of the steam heat system. The house next winter would be warm. But here came the past.

• • •

On Sunday morning, he told Rose that he was taking the boy to Coney Island and would be back in the afternoon.

"Hey, I want to go to Coney Island too," she said, smiling a wide grin. Her skin was already darker from early summer. And Carlito was browner too.

"We'll all go together on the Fourth of July," he said. "Lots of fireworks."

"That's a month from now."

He gambled that she could not change her schedule.

"So come with us," he said.

She sighed. "Too late. They expect me at St. Brendan's."

"Next week," Delaney said, relieved. "Make sure you get a bathing suit."

"No! I can't go around in a bathing suit, and all those young guys watching, all those dirty old guys."

She laughed harder.

"Okay," he said, "I'll go in my long underwear!"

She shoved him hard, the good shoulder. "You do that and I get back on the train."

Rose dressed and hurried off to perform her corporal works of mercy. Carlito played on his fire engine, shouting, *Fire in Coney Isling, fire in Coney Isling*. Delaney went into his office. He stared at the telephone, then dialed the number for Frankie Botts.

"Yeah?"

"It's Dr. Delaney, Mr. Botticelli."

"Hey, howaya?" he said, the tone friendly.

"I've been going over records this morning, and I don't think I have to see your mother anymore."

"What?"

"She's got no pain. She's walking. All the blisters have healed. She's got spots on her skin that might take a while to fade. But she's okay, Frankie."

Silence. Then: "You sure?"

"I'm sure. She can still use the salve, once a day. But she's okay. Any problems, call me."

"Let me ass you somethin'. Can she go to a ballgame?"

"Sure. As long as you're with her."

Botts exhaled. "That is great fuckin' news. Thanks. Thanks for everything."

"What about our understanding, Frankie?"

"What understanding?"

"I take care of your mother and everything is over down here," Delaney said. "We don't have to walk around looking over our shoulders."

Botts grunted. "I'll call you back."

He hung up. Delaney sat there for a while, thinking: You son of a bitch.

They caught the Sea Beach Express at Union Square. The train was packed with men and women and kids, many wearing straw hats, or carrying blankets and lunch baskets, all full of a glad anticipation. He held Carlito's hand tightly as the laughing crowds parted to allow still more people to board the train. The air was dense. The overhead fans had been shut off long ago, to save money. Many people were sweating heavily. Delaney was sure he could smell tenements.

The train plunged under the river, racing to Brooklyn, racing to the sea. It was as if they all had the same slogan: To hell with the Depression, the sea is free. At the end of the car, the door was open to catch a breeze from the cool tunnel, and four young men started to sing "Toot, Toot, Tootsie." Almost all the others joined them. When they came to the line *If you don't get a letter, then you'll know I'm in jail,* they were shouting the words. How many of them had been in jail? More than a few. How many had friends in jail, or relatives, or children? Even more. *Toot, Toot, Tootsie, don't cry, Toot, Toot, Tootsie, good-bye . . .*

Then they were up out of tunnels, and the Brooklyn sky was above them, with the Brooklyn light glancing off the unseen harbor, just like in a Vermeer. Nobody got off, and nobody new could get on. The singing continued. "That Old Gang of Mine." Then "My Buddy." Carlito was planted strongly on the floor, holding a pole, and his visible world was all elbows and hips and knees, the bottoms of baskets, hands dangling or clenched together, and, when he looked up, all chins and nostrils.

Then there was a brightening and then they started coming into the terminal, and the whole car roared. Last stop. Everybody off. Carlito's eyes were wide with excitement. The train stopped. The doors opened. And some of the passengers began to run toward the ocean and the sand.

Delaney and Carlito walked more slowly. He looked behind him, but it was impossible to know if they had been followed. Certainly nobody on the Sea Beach Express was wearing a pearl-gray fedora. There was a carousel ahead of them, going around and around, up and down, with slum kids mounted on brightly painted plaster horses while music from Tin Pan Alley or the circus played loudly. The crowds milled and men blinked and mothers called to children, and they all went out to Surf Avenue.

This was his too, and he knew the geography of Coney the way he knew the West Village. He and Carlito stood on the sidewalk, and he pointed out the swirling towers of Luna Park to the left, as if conjured by Scheherazade, and then at Feltman's across the street. He had brought Molly here once to listen to the Bavarian music in the beer garden, while Grace ran around, a year younger than Carlito, and when he asked Molly what she thought of Coney, she said, I don't have the skin for this place. On this day, the boy was blinking again, closing his personal shutters as if taking photographs, while the crowds swirled around them. A clock told Delaney he was fifteen minutes early.

He and the boy crossed the street where lines were forming to enter Steeplechase the Funny Place, with its huge grinning face. The boy watched a train inching slowly to the apex of the roller coaster, poising, then dropping while people screamed.

"What is?" the boy said.

"A roller coaster," Delaney said. "It's scary."

"Can we go too?"

"Not today, Carlito. Someday."

He remembered being here with Grace when she was seven, and how she insisted that he take her on the roller coaster, and how he sat beside her as it climbed, and how terrified she was when it dropped so hard and fast. She screamed and screamed as he held her with his good left hand. Later she continued sobbing and said she never wanted to see Coney Island again, and for three years she didn't. On this day, as on that day long ago, the vendors were selling hot corn and ice cream and lemon ices and watermelon. Off on the side, a burly man raised a huge hammer and brought it down, and a hard rubber disk rose high on a cable and hit a bell and everybody cheered. Another man was aiming a rifle at a moving tin rabbit, fired, missed, fired again, missed again. In the next booth, a young man wound up like a pitcher and threw a baseball at a target with a hole in the center. The ball bounced away.

"He need a bat, Gran'pa," the boy said. "And a glove."

"He sure does."

It was time to go see Eddie Corso. Delaney took Carlito's hand and started walking back across Surf Avenue. The boy stopped and looked back at the baseball range.

"I want to see more! I want to f'wow a ball, Gran'pa. Please!"

"We have to meet someone, boy. Come on."

The boy stood still, refusing to budge. Delaney spoke the boy's name. The boy did not move. Delaney went over to him and tried to take his hand. The boy half turned and folded his arms across his chest. His lower lip protruded now, his brow furrowed.

A heavy woman in her fifties paused and looked from Carlito to Delaney.

"You better give him a good whack, mister," she said. " 'Cause that kid ain't goin' nowheres."

"I ain't goin' no ways," Carlito said.

The heavy woman said, "Whad I tell ya?"

Delaney thought: Fuck off, lady.

But squatted down beside Carlito.

"Listen to me, Carlito." The boy looked at him. "I know you want to stay. But first we have to go somewhere else. All of this, the bats and balls and guns, they'll still be here. But I have to meet a friend, and then we can come back."

The boy looked at Delaney with doubt in his eyes. Then he sighed, a form of surrender. Delaney stood and took his hand, and they walked across the wide avenue.

Then a man in a straw boater and sunglasses and a thick mustache emerged from the eddying crowds.

"Hey, Doc, glad you could make it. Come on."

It was Bootsie.

His plain black Ford was parked on a side street and they got into it. The boy was still resisting. He wanted loud music, guns, baseball, watermelon. He clearly didn't want to get into a car. Delaney placed him on his lap. Bootsie turned into the two-way traffic on Surf Avenue and inched along, with Steeplechase across the street on the beach side. Delaney could see Scoville's, the saloon where for years his father and the other Tammany guys celebrated the birthday of John McKane, the nineteenth-century Tammany prince of Coney Island. The ritual started when McKane came home from Sing Sing in 1898. The old Coney boss died a year later, but the ritual went on, ending only with the double calamity of the influenza epidemic and Prohibition. And here was Scoville's open again, and he wondered how many people were left alive who remembered McKane in his heyday.

Then Bootsie turned right into a side street and pulled into a driveway beside an old-fashioned bungalow on a street of identical bungalows. Kids played in the sandy front yards. Men walked home with the Sunday papers.

"This is it," Bootsie announced, opening his door. The boy looked surprised. A house? Where is the sea?

"Thanks, pal."

The door opened on the porch and there was Eddie Corso. In white slacks, sandals, and a sport shirt. His skin was dark and oiled and he had grown a white beard, neatly trimmed. He and Delaney embraced. There were no stale morphine jokes. Delaney stepped back and held Eddie's shoulders.

"You look good, Sergeant. Where'd you get the tan?"

"Out west." He waved a hand around at the neighborhood. "Here too."

"And the beard?"

"Out west too. Do I look like a rabbi?"

"One full of wisdom and years."

"This is the boy, huh?"

"This is the boy, all right." Delaney moved the boy a few inches closer. "Carlito, this is my friend."

" 'Lo," the boy said, offering his hand. Corso shook it. Delaney never said Corso's name. In the age of the holy G-men, you never knew when they might drag a three-year-old before a grand jury. A breeze off the sea made a porch rocker move slightly.

Corso said, "Come on in, get a cold drink."

When he led the way back inside, bells jangled on the outside door, and then he pushed through an inside screen door. Delaney looked around. There was a wide room inside the doors, with a couch and two chairs and a low table. There was a small kitchen with an icebox and a counter. The back of the house was dark, with two closed doors sealing off the bedrooms. It felt like what it was: a place for transients. There was a pistol on the counter. Another pistol was on the low table. Corso opened the icebox.

"Le's see. I got Cokes, some beers. . . . You don't drink, but what about the kid?"

"He's off the beer for now, Sergeant."

Delaney noticed the boy staring at the gun on the low table. Corso popped open three Coca-Colas.

"One small favor. Carlito has his eye on that gun."

"Oh, shit, I forgot." He turned to Bootsie. "Stick that rod somewheres. Then go work on your tan while I talk to the good doctor."

"Sure thing, boss."

Bootsie placed the pistol on a shelf above the sink, then went outside. He left the outside door open and the breeze came through the screen door. Delaney could hear the sound of the rocker moving heavily, as Bootsie watched the street.

"How do you feel?" he said to Corso.

"Pretty good." Corso opened his shirt. His body was tanned but the scar remained a livid white. Delaney ran his fingers over it. It would fade. The way Rose's scar had faded.

"He did a good job, that fella at the hospital," Corso said.

"He sure did."

"So why are you back?" Delaney said quietly.

"You know why."

"No, I don't. Last I heard, you were getting out of the rackets."

"I am," Corso said, and sipped from the Coke bottle. "But first I got some unfinished business."

Carlito stood up from the couch and stared through the screen door at some kids playing in the street.

"Forget about it," Delaney said. "Just leave it alone."

"You know I can't do that."

Delaney sighed, and stared at the Coke bottle in his bad hand.

"I gotta ask you a few things," Corso said.

"You mean about Frankie Botts and me?"

"Yeah."

"I was treating his mother. She had a bad case of shingles."

Corso smiled. "A case of what?"

Delaney explained, and noticed Carlito at the screen door, staring past Bootsie at the street.

"And you brought that woman, what's her name? She's taking care of the kid?"

"Rose. To translate for the old lady." A pause. "I told Frankie I would treat his mother if he would call off his boys. Somehow Frankie blamed me for saving your life on New Year's Day. He wanted me to tell him where you were. I told the truth. I didn't know. Even if I knew, I wouldn't tell. But some guys came around, a guy named Gyp. There were phone calls. I *was* afraid. For Rose. For the boy."

Corso stared hard at Delaney, then exhaled and leaned back in his chair.

"Stay away from Frankie Botts," he said. "It could be dangerous."

"The treatment's over. His mother's okay."

"Good. Stay the fuck away."

There was a silence. Delaney knew what he was talking about. The rules of the brutal trade said that if you hit me, I'll hit you back. If it takes a lifetime.

"When it's over, my friend, what'll you do?"

"Go far away. Where they'll never think of findin' me."

"You'd live in the Bronx?" Delaney said, and smiled.

Corso laughed. "Nah, I'd keep runnin' into them goddamn Yankee fans. Arrogant bastids. I'd be sure to get locked up for attempted homicide."

He stood up and stretched. Carlito came over and sat beside Delaney. There was a bowl of change on the table before him, nickels, dimes, quarters. No pennies. He began stacking them by denomination.

"That woman, that Rose," Corso said. "Everything I hear, she's good people. A hoodlum, but good people."

"She is."

"Don't fuck her over, Doc."

"I won't."

Delaney stood up. The boy started dropping the coins back in their bowl. Two at a time. Then a few single coins. Then three and four. All the while making the sighing sounds of boredom.

"I'd better take this fella to the beach," Delaney said.

"And the hot dogs at Feltman's."

They embraced by the screen door. Corso stepped back.

"You know where I'm thinkin' of goin'?" He paused. "Back to France."

"Jesus, pal."

"I want to see that Paris. Sit at a table on some boulevard and have a cognac and watch the broads go by." Another pause. "Then get me a car and drive down to where we were. To the place where all the guys died. To where all the rain was and all the fuckin' mud. Just go and say good-bye the right way.

"Then," Corso said, brightening. "Then I go down the south of France. Get the sun. Get laid once a week. Look at the sea."

"Send me your address," Delaney said. "Under another name, please."

Corso laughed.

Delaney and the boy strolled to the boardwalk and looked at the sea and the hundreds of thousands of people on blankets, drinking beer and Coke and wine, heating up food, devouring sandwiches. He tried to imagine Eddie Corso on the Riviera and smiled. He and the boy took off their shoes and held them tight, rolled up their trousers, and moved down wooden stairs and through the spaces between sandy blankets, the sand itself very hot, and into the surf. The boy ran out, then retreated as a fresh wave broke, then ran again. He saw some boys splashing girls, and turned and splashed with his left hand at Delaney, who splashed back. A black Lab shook off an immense amount of water, soaking Delaney and the squealing boy, then crashed again into the surf after a tossed ball. Delaney wished he could stay there forever.

On Thursday morning, he took Carlito on the old Arrow bicycle and pedaled off for the bread and newspapers. At Reilly's he saw the tabloids shouting from the newsstand.

MOB BOSS
RUB OUT

He didn't need to read them to know who had been killed. But he bought all the papers and took them home with the bread. Rose had already heard the news on the radio. How one Frank Botticelli was in a car with two others when they were cut off by a bread truck on West Eighteenth Street and the car was riddled by machine-gun fire. More than one hundred shots were fired. All three were dead.

"How come I don't feel bad?" she said, her arms folded tightly across her breasts.

"It must be sad for the mother," Delaney said.

"Maybe it's a relief."

He hugged her.

FIFTEEN

He gazed out at the olive tree, its fresh leaves a silvery green in the morning sun. He hoped that Eddie Corso was riding the Atlantic, bound for Le Havre. He knew he shouldn't feel that way. He knew he might have headed off the murder with one call to Danny Shapiro. He couldn't do that. Not in this neighborhood. Not in a place where the informer was the lowest form of human. Besides, his friendship with Eddie Corso was forever. It was part of the war. For Eddie, the quarrel with Frankie Botts was complete, according to the rules of his world. They were not Delaney's rules. But he understood them. Now, he hoped, it was over. Rose knew that it was not.

"They're sure to come looking for you," she said. "You know that, right? And maybe for me."

"Why? It's over."

"These guys, it's never over."

She placed fried eggs before Delaney and the boy. She prepared nothing for herself except coffee.

"Look," she said. "They know you've been going to see Frankie's mother. You know something about him, how he lives. They know you are a friend of Eddie Corso. They know you saved his life on New Year's." She turned her gaze to the olive tree, while the boy ate greedily. "They're sure to figure you helped set up Frankie." She looked directly at Delaney now. "They know I've been going there too, to see Frankie's mother, to be the nurse. So to them, maybe I'm part of the setup too."

"We'll deal with it," Delaney said.

"So will they," Rose said.

She looked again at the olive tree.

"Some of those olive trees," she said, "they live five hundred years. That one will be there after we're all dead and gone."

She sipped her coffee, swallowing her dread.

"Let's deal with the next couple of weeks," Delaney said.

In his office, he called Danny Shapiro, who was out on his own house calls. This was a busy morning for detectives. Delaney left a message. Then he called Knocko Carmody. He didn't have to explain.

"Yeah, I read the papers," Knocko said. "Don't worry."

"I'll try."

"How's the steam heat comin'?" Knocko said.

"They should be finished this week."

"Just in time for July."

"It should be great," Delaney said.

Knocko hung up, and Delaney knew that men would soon be watching the street again. He told Rose, and she looked unconvinced. He heard Monique come in, and talked to her too. She would keep the inside door locked and only allow regular patients in to see him. She nodded toward the kitchen.

"She better be very careful," Monique said. "Neapolitans like shooting Sicilians, male or female."

"Rose didn't cause this, Monique."

"No, but to them she's part of it, for sure."

On house calls after lunch, pedaling steadily on the old Arrow, he watched every passing car, every unfamiliar face. Thinking: It would be stupid to die in this cheap Mob melodrama. Stupid to be a one-day story in the *Daily News*, three paragraphs maybe, or maybe page one if nothing else happened that day. The tabloids wanted to keep this story alive. The Mob sold many things, including newspapers. On a newsstand, he saw the headline in the *Journal*: COPS FEAR GANG WAR. How many times had he read that headline since the days of Prohibition? I don't even need to read it. I know more about it than the reporter. So did Rose, who never went to gangster movies.

Delaney's calls took him past the Good Men Social and Athletic Club, where Eddie Corso had been shot among the funny hats and noisemakers of New Year's Eve. There was a TO LET sign in the window. On the corner, a few men stared at him, and one of them nodded. He looked up and saw another man peering down from the rooftop. Scouts of a defending army, awaiting the counterattack.

In late afternoon, he came down tenement stairs after treating a woman named O'Toole, whose body was being eaten by cancer. She didn't care about Frankie Botts or Eddie Corso or the Giants. She just wanted to live a little longer. "I want to see my granddaughter graduate from grammar school," she said. "Down at Sacred Heart." That is, she wanted to live for two more weeks. He would try his best. That's all he ever could do.

Delaney stepped into the fading sunlight at the top of Mrs. O'Toole's stoop, took a breath, saw a few men talking on the corner. He went down to unlock his bicycle, chained to the iron fence. He heard leathery footsteps and looked up. A movie gangster was walking hard, wearing his gray fedora and a pin-striped suit, pulling his face tightly over his teeth.

"Hey, you," he said.

"Me?"

The man stood over him now. "Yeah, get into the car."

Two houses down, the door of a car opened onto the sidewalk.

"Why?"

" 'Cause I said so, that's why," the man said, putting a hand inside his jacket.

Delaney smiled, still squatting, thinking: All shoulder, all my weight, everything on it.

And stood up abruptly, took a step, and whipped the left hook with everything behind it, grunting as he threw it, and hit the man on the side of the jaw. He heard something crack. The man went down hard on his back, one leg bent awkwardly beneath him, the other leg shaking. His eyes were rolled up under his brow. Then a fat man came out of the parked car, holding a gun, waddling and cursing.

And here came Knocko's boys: six of them, big and burly, hefting bats and axe handles. Two bounced their wooden bats off the skull of the fat guy, who went down, his pistol rattling on the sidewalk. They kicked his face into bleeding meat. Another two men dragged the driver out of the car, while a third man drove an ice pick into the wheels. A skinny young red-haired man hit the driver with a hook, and he went down. Then a pale green van came around the corner. The back doors opened, and Knocko's boys lifted the three unconscious gangsters, heaved them into the interior, and drove off. It was all over in a few brutal minutes.

Delaney trembled. *Could've died. Could have been dead right now.* His left hand hurt, but he flexed it and was sure nothing had been broken. The skin of his middle knuckle was torn, but nothing else. He finished unlocking the bicycle and placed his bag in the basket. The skinny red-haired kid came over.

"I'm Liam Hanratty," he said. "My grandfather was Packy. You know, that trained you a long time ago? He told me about you. Now I know he wasn't bullshitting."

"Looks like he taught you pretty good himself," Delaney said. "I saw that hook."

"He said you had a terrific *double* hook. Body, then head."

Delaney shrugged, then shook hands gently with the young man.

"Where'd they take those guys?" Delaney said.

"Where else? The North River, I guess."

He laughed.

"Teach them somethin'," he said. "Don't fuck wit' the neighborhood."

Delaney left before the police arrived.

Danny Shapiro arrived after dinner, while Carlito slept in his room. Rose gave the detective a plate of ravioli and a beer. They sat at the kitchen table.

"We rounded up as many guys as we could find," Shapiro said. "Corso's old mob. Frankie's mob. We locked them in separate jails. But this could go on awhile."

Rose said, "I don't know when it ends."

"When they start marryin' each other," Shapiro said.

"Ha! Never."

"Maybe that's best," Shapiro said. "They ever get together, we're all in trouble."

"Maybe they should all see *Romeo and Juliet* sometime," Delaney said.

"Yeah, they get together too, Romeo and his Juliet," Shapiro said. "Except they're dead."

Shapiro laughed with Delaney. Rose only smiled. She had mastered the *Daily News*, Delaney thought, but Shakespeare would take a little longer. Shapiro finished his ravioli, wiping the plate clean. He sipped his beer.

"Well, what should we do?" Delaney said. "Right here."

"Stay in the house. Keep the doors locked."

"Impossible," Rose said. "That boy has to walk, I have to buy food."

"And I've got house calls every afternoon."

"Just for a few days," Shapiro said. "Give them time to cool off. Racket guys need peace and quiet to do business. They'll calm down. But it might get worse before it gets better."

He got up to leave.

"The food was great, Rose," he said.

"Thanks," she said.

They walked to the door. Shapiro looked at Delaney.

"Did you know this was coming?"

"Put it this way, Danny. I wasn't surprised."

Shapiro looked down.

"What happened to your left hand, Doc?" he said.

"Nothing much."

"That ain't what I heard," Shapiro said, and smiled.

"Don't believe everything you hear."

"If I did, half the city would be in the can."

He tapped Delaney on the left shoulder and then he was gone. Rose locked the gate and the inside door. Then she folded her arms and stared at Delaney.

"Okay, tell me," she said. "What happen to your left hand?"

"Let me brush my teeth first."

He told her in the dark, and she laughed and then went silent. He could hear her breathing harder.

"I told you it wasn't over," she said.

Then she started kissing him. His face and his neck and his skinned left hand.

In the morning, they learned from the newspapers and the radio that Shapiro was right. It got worse. Two fully clothed bodies were fished from the North River and identified as members of the Frankie Botts mob. There was no sign of their hats. Around midnight a group of masked men kicked in the locked door of Club 65, heaved gasoline bombs into the empty interior, and left. The firemen came and poured water into the empty store and left it a wet smoking mess. The families that lived in the apartments above the bar all got to the street safely and would live with the stench of smoke for a few weeks. No deaths. Just a strategic bombing. A show.

There were six more killings, scattered from Mulberry Street to Times Square, where a Corso man died in a movie house with an ice pick in his ear. But there was no sign of hoodlums in the neighborhood. Delaney went on working. He saw patients every morning. He made house calls. He stared at the olive tree. He painted bad paintings alongside Carlito. He made love to Rose at night. The papers said that the funeral of Frankie Botts would take place on Monday morning at Our Lady of Pompeii R.C. Church. There was even a photograph of Frankie's mother leaving a funeral parlor on Second Avenue, frail, dressed in black, her face stern, a few stray hoodlums in the background, and two uniformed cops. On Saturday morning, Rose and the boy went shopping. Monique was uneasy.

"I don't like her taking the boy out there," Monique said, gesturing toward the street.

"He needs larger sneakers, and socks too," he said. "She knows all the cheap places up on Fourteenth Street."

"Still . . ."

"Rose says gangsters don't get up this early."

"Well, she should know."

He ignored the edge in her voice.

"Any mail from Spain?" he said.

"No, just bills. I'll have them ready later."

He turned to the door of his office.

"Send in the first patient."

And so he spent the morning dealing with other people's pain and fear. A woman with a spreading rash. An old longshoreman whose feet were red and swollen with diabetes. A young mother who was runny with gonorrhea and shame, both driven into her by a drunken husband. A man in his forties, shuddering and half-mad from the DTs, accompanied by a frightened teenaged daughter. A woman whose sputum and cough revealed the consumption. Two vets who needed quinine, and one who was losing feeling in a leg that had been lacerated at Château-Thierry. A black eye. A swollen jaw. A runny ear that gave off a vile odor. Pain. Fear. The need for relief or hope. None of them mentioned the gang war. In his office, Delaney fiddled with his pen.

He wrote a single word on his pad.

Rose.

That Saturday night, he was sipping tea after dinner, thinking of taking Carlito back to Coney Island, to ride with him on the mechanical horses in Steeplechase. Or among the turrets and minarets of Luna Park. Rose was upstairs with the boy. The phone rang. And rang. He picked it up. It was Jackie Norris, from the Harbor Police.

"Hey, Doc," he said. "Can you come over here to Brooklyn tomorrow? The Kings County morgue."

"Why?"

"I think we found something."

They dropped off Carlito with Angela, and Rose said she would pick him up as soon as she finished at St. Brendan's. Her face was apprehensive, because Delaney had told her in the night where he was going and why he could not take the boy. She said nothing, but her face told him that she was imagining many scenarios. Angela seemed delighted, and the boy was smiling and carrying his teddy bear. Delaney and Rose each told the boy that they would return soon and kissed his cheek. Then turned to Angela. She smiled at them in a knowing way. The harpies might not know. Mr. and Mrs. Cottrell might not know. Angela knew what they did in the night.

They said good-bye, and Delaney walked Rose part of the way to St. Brendan's. Few words were spoken.

"If it's her," Rose said at the corner of Fourteenth Street and Eighth, "what are you going to do?"

"Bury her," he said. "What else can I do?"

"And your daughter? She comes for the funeral?"

"Maybe." He hugged Rose. "First I have to see if it's Molly."

Rose walked quickly toward St. Brendan's. Delaney watched her for a few minutes. She turned and waved but did not smile. He waved back, and then headed for the subway.

On the train out to Brooklyn, many Sunday-morning riders pored over the *Daily News.* The headline shouted: 2 MORE SLAIN. But he didn't buy a paper, even from a kid hawking them in the subway cars. He wasn't keeping score. On this morning, he didn't even care who won the Giants game.

Jackie Norris was waiting at the main entrance to Kings County Hospital, smoking a cigarette. His suit was rumpled, and he had the *Daily News* tucked under one arm. He saw Delaney and flipped his cigarette into the grass.

"Doc," he said. And nodded.

"How'd you find her?"

"If it's her."

They walked inside, and Norris led the way to a long corridor, flashing his badge.

"Some black guy pulls outta Red Hook in a little putt-putt," Norris said. "He's headin' for Sheepshead Bay to do a little crabbin'. You know, grab free lunch for the family. It's a little windy, a little chop in the water, so he stays near shore." Norris nodded at a beefy nurse with an Irish face. "Then he looks down in the rocks near the Narrows, *this* side of the Narrows, the New York side, and he sees, maybe eight, ten feet down — he sees a skull."

They followed signs to the morgue.

"When he gets to Sheepshead Bay, he calls the cops," Norris said. "They call the Harbor Police, and next thing you know, I'm here."

They passed the corridor leading to the emergency room, and Delaney could hear a woman moaning in pain. A sound he had been hearing all of his life. They went through the door of the morgue. A fat balding clerk looked up from his desk just inside the door. He was reading the sports section of the *Daily News.*

"Yeah?" he said.

Norris showed his badge. "We're here to make a possible ID. Unidentified woman fished out of the Narrows yesterday."

The man opened a ledger book in an annoyed way and ran a plump finger down a list of entries.

"Try F-11," he said. "And sign in here."

They walked down aisles of cabinets containing the dead. Six closed trays above each other, like floors in a tenement. For Delaney, all morgues were the same: the same bleak lighting, the same damp concrete floors, the same odors of pine and formaldehyde. They stopped at F-11.

"This ain't gonna be easy," Norris said.

"I know," Delaney said. "But I've got no choice, Jackie."

Norris slid out the tray. The skull was closest to them, the other bones arranged into the deepest part of the tray. One femur was missing, and other bones as well. Delaney stepped to the side to look down upon the skull. It was grinning, like every other skull he had ever seen. Grinning in mockery of the living. Grinning with secret knowledge. He reached down and used his right hand to move the lower mandible. There on the right was the molar filled with gold by that dentist just off the Ringstrasse. *It's my damned Irish teeth, Molly said. They make contact with Viennese chocolate and they rot.* To the right of her head were the folded remnants of her blue dress, faded and shredded by tides and time. *Oh, Molly.*

"It's her," he said. "I recognize the filling. That's part of the dress she was wearing, the last time anyone saw her alive. . . . Thank you, Jackie."

"When I heard there were a few pieces of blue dress, I thought, Maybe this is her. It's what you told me."

"The filling, that's the right tooth."

"You can see we don't have all the bones," Norris said. "The guys will look again Monday morning, weather permittin'." A pause. "There's no sign of damage. No bones broke by bullets, no cracks in her head from a blackjack or anything."

Delaney took a last look, then slid the tray back into its cabinet.

"I'll ask the coroner to make the cause of death 'accident,' " Norris said. "That way you can bury her in a Catholic cemetery if you want."

"Thanks, Jackie," Delaney said, ignoring the suggestion of suicide, and started walking through the clammy dampness toward the exit, with Norris behind him. He knew the routine. The bureaucracy of death. He would sign a few papers. A clerk would stamp them. Norris would add them to his files and go off to his office the next day and talk to the coroner and later stamp the entire folder Case Closed. Then life would go on. There were dozens of people every year who ended up as corpses in the harbor. Delaney did what must be done, shook hands with Norris, and then walked toward the sun of Sunday morning.

All the way back to Manhattan, images of Molly in life kept rising from memory. On that North River pier the first time he saw her, incoherent with pain and loss. Laughing at Tony Pastor's. Walking through downtown Baltimore. Sneering at Al Jolson and baseball and the Irish songs from Tin Pan Alley. Then laughing as Delaney began to sing the songs. Walking across Union Square at dusk. Molly hugging the infant Grace in a hospital bed, her face fierce and protective. Her face and body lost in music, enraged music, and Brahms too. They had danced. He could always say that. They had danced at Tammany rackets and neighborhood weddings. They had danced in Vienna. And to an oompah band at Feltman's on Coney Island. Always a waltz. Never anything else. A waltz always brought them to their feet, to grasp each other's hands, and she could be carried out of her angers. Sitting on the train, he realized something else: It was the past. As distant now as all those browning photographs scattered around bars and offices and homes all over New York.

Still, he began to hum Strauss on the subway, the tune rising from him without thought, and a woman looked at him from her seat across the car and smiled. Gray-haired, missing a bicuspid. Here, in the real world. He stopped humming. She reminded him that the world was for the living. The train pulled into Fourteenth Street.

"That was nice," she said as Delaney got up. "A waltz on a Sunday morning. Thank you."

"You're welcome," he said, and smiled as he got off. He did not try to explain that he was thinking of a woman he once loved with all of himself, and loved no more.

At the house on Horatio Street, Rose and Carlito were waiting. She had skipped the movie to pick up the boy, and when Delaney came in she folded her arms and set her face, as if expecting a blow.

"Well?" she said.

"It was her," he said.

She breathed out hard, then unfolded her arms and let them hang loosely.

"Well, that's that," she said.

Delaney looked toward the door.

"I'm going to take a little walk, Rose. Just collect my thoughts."

"Sure," she said, and touched his face.

"A half hour," he said. "No more."

"We'll be here."

They walked to the gate together.

"Okay, Carlos, come on," she said. "We'll change your clothes."

"I want to go with Gran'pa."

"No, he has to do something. He'll be right back."

"Please, Rosa."

"You heard me. No."

Delaney walked toward the river. He saw familiar faces and nodded hello. About a dozen kids were playing stickball beyond the High Line. The other kids were not yet back from the beach. A young woman pushed a child in a stroller. A drunken older man held on to a lamppost like a figure in a temperance poster, speaking steadily to himself. At water's edge, Delaney walked to the pier where he'd gone so many times with Molly, long ago.

I hope you knew how much I loved you, Molly, when you chose the river over life.

He stood alone, watching the current move south to the Narrows and the sea beyond. On the next pier to the north, some kids took turns leaping into the river, riding the current to the pier beyond his own. A tugboat grunted north, a seagoing club fighter, fearless, tough.

I want to tell you something, Molly. I'm very sorry for all the things that I did and didn't do. But you chose the river, and the rocks at its gate. I am alive. I will live. I have found the aroma of life, and it's full of garlic and basil and oil.

SIXTEEN

Delaney woke up alone at five in the morning and knew he could not return to sleep. He sat on the edge of the bed, his mind full of Molly's bones. In some way, they were beautiful. A watercolor made of earth colors. Something Thomas Eakins could have painted. He wondered how they had been streaked, what chemicals had flowed around them, making such subtle marks. They had been scoured and bleached and stained. Now they would be returned to the earth.

He stood up and went into the bathroom to shower. The bones stayed with him. He had lived for many months with an image of Molly moving through the current, her hair streaming out behind her, and he wondered which part of her flesh went first and which went last. He imagined her scalp and hair were last, but he could never be sure. Perhaps she had hit her head on a piling when she fell, and gashed that part of her flesh, and the current started to lift it, to peel it away. That scalp he had grasped in ecstasy. That hair that he had curled in his fingers. Ah, Molly.

He dressed in the dark and went out at the top of the stoop, his ring of keys twined in his fingers. He stood there, in the place where Carlito had come into his life, and looked toward the North River. Then he turned back into the house.

On Monday morning, he took the bicycle and rode with Carlito to get the bread and the newspapers. The *Daily News* headline said, in a disappointed way: MOB TRUCE? The *News* did have the best police reporters in the city, and they said that leaders of the Corso and Botticelli clans had a "sitdown" on Saturday night. Not in Little Italy. In the Bronx. Delaney smiled. If Eddie had been asked, he would have insisted on New Jersey. Never the Bronx. The *News* reporters added that one test of the cease-fire would take place Monday at the funeral of Frankie Botts, expected to be one of the biggest in Mob history. The cops were mobilizing more than eight hundred men to help keep the peace. Mayor La Guardia urged all decent citizens to stay home or go to work. But the *News* underlined a simple fact: as of early Monday morning, when they went to press, there had been no reported deaths for twenty-four hours.

There was nothing in any of the newspapers about Molly. Jackie Norris had made certain of that. So Delaney sat down at his desk and wrote a telegram to Grace. SAD NEWS STOP MOTHER'S REMAINS FOUND STOP CAN YOU COME FOR BURIAL QUERY ADVISE SOONEST DAD. He clipped a note to the text for Monique, telling her to send it to the address on the Plaza Real and to American Express in Barcelona and Madrid.

Then Carlito ran in with his teddy bear. Smiling and happy. Rose brought Delaney a fried egg sandwich and lifted Carlito. The smudges under her eyes were darker. She seemed desperately in need of sleep, and he was sure he knew what was keeping her awake.

Monique arrived, and he handed her the telegram message. She glanced at it, then turned to him.

"Oh, Jim," she said. "I'm so sorry."

"At least we know," he said.

She glanced toward the kitchen.

"What's gonna happen?" she said.

"I don't know."

Then he went to work, nodding toward the door at the unseen patients. More than ever he understood that he needed their pain to keep from thinking about his own.

That afternoon Monique asked Delaney about arrangements. "How are you gonna do this?" she said. He told her there would be no wake and no funeral mass, and that Molly's bones might be buried in the same plot occupied by Big Jim and his wife out at Green-Wood Cemetery in Brooklyn. "I have to call the cemetery," he said. "Or maybe you could." Monique looked at him in a dubious way. "You sure?" she said. "No mass?" He reminded her that Molly had left no will and no instructions, not even about the music, and had never mentioned any relatives in Ireland.

"I do know that she hated the church," he said. Then shrugged. "Well, maybe just a ceremony at the funeral home. Or at the grave. Family and friends. I have to ask Grace. If she comes home."

"That could be a long time. Maybe never."

"True."

"You've got to have *something*."

He was deliberately vague. "Well, we have a little time . . ."

Monique shook her head. And Delaney wondered why Monique was reacting this way. She had never much liked Molly, and Molly had never much liked Monique. They tolerated each other, with crisp efficiency. Perhaps it was about Rose. Perhaps Monique wanted to be in charge, with no role for the bossy new interloper. No: that was probably not it. Monique was suggesting that he wasn't reacting with sufficient ceremonial grief. That he was not gilding himself in platitude. It was like so much of life now: she wanted him to perform grief, and she would perform sympathy, even if she did not feel it.

"Let's talk later," he said, and retreated to his office. He called Casey the undertaker and asked him to take custody of Molly's remains from the hospital and hold them until a date was chosen for the burial. "The date's not set yet, Mr. Casey." And Casey said he understood. He did not explain that the date depended upon Grace. Burial would take place soon if Grace did not want to return. Molly would be buried without the presence of her daughter. The date would be later if Grace found a ship for New York. He began to imagine a small ceremony in Green-Wood. When it was over, they could walk up the slope to the peak of the hill and look down upon the Narrows.

He didn't eat much that evening and began to doze at the table. Rose touched him gently.

"You go up to bed," she said. "You need sleep. You need to clear your head."

"I do," he said. "We have to talk about all this."

"Not tonight," she said, turning to the drowsy Carlito. "You look worse than he does."

"But —"

"I won't come down tonight," she said, a slight chill in her voice. "I can't. It's not right."

"I got over Molly a long time ago, Rose."

"Yeah," she said, "but this, it's all still alive."

That night Delaney did not sleep a real sleep. It was not Molly who kept him awake. It was Grace. She would determine the future. How would she react to Rose? With snooty contempt? With the cold eyes of the women in St. Patrick's that morning? In spite of all her glib talk about socialism and class equality, Grace could be haughty too. She was, after all, Molly's daughter. He wondered what Grace would do.

She might plan to move back into 95 Horatio, to reclaim her room as she reclaimed her son. Or she might go somewhere else, up to the Village, back to the West, or even Mexico, taking her son with her. I could not stop her, but if she tries to take him to Spain, I would try.

He tossed in the darkness, but could not find a position that eased the ache in his bad arm. His mind teemed with questions that had no answers. How would Rose react to Grace? She had done what Rose could not imagine doing: she had left her child to the tender mercies of others. He imagined Rose staring at Grace, arms folded, full of Sicilian vehemence. And, of course, all of this might never happen. Rose might simply pack and go.

He changed positions again, and pulled a pillow over his face, and smelled Rose on it, and moved to his left, pushing the pillow to the right. That hot night, he finally slept and dreamed once more about the snow.

In the morning, Delaney did not want to read the newspapers, but Rose pointed out the photograph on the front page of the *Daily News*. The gleaming coffin of Frankie Botts was being carried into Our Lady of Pompeii by six burly pallbearers. Behind them were the other mourners, all properly dressed in black, most of them male, except for Frankie's mother. She was directly behind the coffin. Three rows behind her was Bootsie.

"You see this?" Rose said.

"I see it now."

"It's like a, uh, un simbolo?"

"A symbol of what?" Delaney said.

"That it's over, at least for now. Bootsie, they all know he's from the Corso gang, and here he is, dressed in black, showing some kind of respect. Right behind the mother. Even the cops know. And those guys beside him? They are Corso guys too."

"What do you think?"

She placed the newspaper on a chair. "I think, wait and see."

Delaney laughed and told her what Danny Shapiro had told him, that if the Sicilians and the Neapolitans ever got together, we'd all be in trouble. Rose smiled, but her eyes remained wary. She looked around the kitchen with focused eyes, as if forcing every detail into memory. He touched her arm.

"A day at a time," he said, ashamed of his own banality. "A day at a time."

Later, when the hour of house calls arrived, he wheeled the Arrow through the areaway under the hot sun and saw Izzy the Atheist sitting on the stoop. He was wearing a sweat-stained denim shirt, dungarees, and sneakers. He stood up, came to Delaney, and put a hand on his shoulder.

"I'm so sorry, Doc," he said. "I heard about Molly."

"Thanks, Iz. At least the mystery is over. Or most of it."

"There anything I can do?"

"Just stay healthy, Izzy."

Izzy lit a Camel with a wooden match he scraped into flame on the back of the dungarees.

"You having any kind of ceremony?" Izzy said.

"Something small. Private. No mass."

"Good. And Grace? She comin' to it?"

"I'm waiting to hear."

Izzy exhaled a small cloud of smoke.

"Ah, well," he said. "You and me, Doc, we come from a long line of dead people."

"That we do, Iz. That we do."

Then he was off to the emergency wards of the neighborhood.

There was no word that day from Grace, and that night Rose returned to his bed. In the hot dark, they made love almost desperately. It was as if both knew that time was running out. In bed, after all, they could erupt into the certainties of flesh. Afterward they lay together, holding hands. The room was thick with her various aromas, including sex.

"You know what I feel bad about?" she said quietly. "There were some things I wanted to do." Her voice had fatalism in it, but no self-pity. "For Carlo. With you."

"What do you mean?" he said. "What are you driving at, Rose?"

"If your daughter comes back," she said in a cool way, "it means I have to leave."

"No, it doesn't."

"Come on, Dottore. How do you say? Face the facts."

He held her tightly, inhaling her aromas.

"We can work it out," he said. "I'm sure of that, Rose."

She turned her head, but he could feel her breathing on his hand. They were quiet a long time.

"These things you wanted to do," Delaney said. "What are they?"

"It doesn't matter now," she said, in a tone that implied: It's too late.

"Like what, Rose?"

"Like going to Coney Island." A pause. "The three of us." Another pause. "Just like the people I see in the *Daily News* on Mondays. With a blanket, and food, and Carlito with a pail and a shovel." She exhaled. "The merry-go-round. Steeplechase the Funny Place. I been there before, you know, been to Coney Island. But never on the sand. Never with you and the boy."

"And never in a bathing suit," he said. "What else?"

"I want to go to a bookstore on Fourth Avenue and get that boy a book about trains."

"That's on my list too."

"That boy is crazy about trains and boats and fire engines."

"He sure is."

They were both quiet for a long while.

"And I want to go dancing with you," she whispered. "Get dressed up, get Angela to mind the boy, and just go dance."

"Fred Astaire I'm not."

"So what? I'm no Dolores Del Rio either."

She inhaled, held her breath, exhaled.

"I just want to do that," she whispered. "To remember it. That's all."

Delaney felt his own tears welling, then fought them off.

"Let's try to do them all," he said.

There was still no word from Grace on Wednesday, and he plodded through the day as if it were any other day in a hot June. Some patients were talking again about the Giants. They were playing good ball. Terry was hitting, and so was Ott, and Hubbell was still the best pitcher in the National League. Delaney started reading the sports pages again and only glanced at the news pages.

"Terrible stuff is coming," Zimmerman said over a hurried lunch near St. Vincent's. "Look at Bulgaria: a fascist dictatorship. Look at Lithuania: a coup that failed, but more coming. Look at Austria: Dollfuss is a dictator, a fascist, and they just made a deal giving the Catholic church control of all state education. Fuck the Jews, or the Protestants, or the atheists. Look at Latvia: another fascist dictatorship. Look at Estonia —"

"Look at the Phillies. They keep winning."

"Come on, Dr. D., this is fucking serious." His face was tense and grim. "Hitler's meeting for the first time with Mussolini *tomorrow!* All the people down the East Side, they read the *Forvetz* and figure the Nazis are getting ready to land in Staten Island."

"Forgive me, Jake," Delaney said. He squeezed Zimmerman's bony forearm. "I was trying to cheer you up and made things worse."

Zimmerman looked suddenly alarmed. "Hey, Doctor, please," he said, his voice rising. "I could never get mad at *you*. It's just that — these Nazi fucks are killing Jews *because they are Jews!* Not because they're murderers or rapists or perverts, or anything else. Because they're *Jews!*"

Two men at an opposite table looked at Zimmerman and Delaney. One of them seethed with anger. The other sneered. Delaney counted out some change and motioned to the waiter.

"Let's go," he said.

"Sorry," Zimmerman said.

"It's me that's sorry, Jake."

They walked to the door. As it closed behind them, they could hear the words "fuckin' kikes . . ." Zimmerman stopped and reached for the door handle to go back inside. Delaney locked his left hand on the younger man's wrist.

"Not now," he said. "Not yet."

The telegram arrived Thursday morning, delivered by a Western Union messenger. He handed it to Monique, who gave him a dime tip. Delaney was consoling an agonized woman named Margaret Devlin, who had permanent migraines, when Monique entered.

"Excuse me," she said. "This is what you've been waiting for, Doctor."

He excused himself to his patient and opened the telegram.

ARRIVING JUNE 23 SS ANDALUSIA SPANISH LINE STOP WAIT FOR ME STOP MUCH LOVE GRACE.

Delaney thought: I'll tell Rose tonight.

And so he did. First they made love until she covered her face with the pillow and held it with both hands and screamed as if wounded. They were quiet for a long time, except for their breathing. Then he spoke.

"The telegram came today," he said. "She gets home on the twenty-third."

Rose was quiet, as if figuring out a calendar. Today was the fourteenth.

Then: "That's nine days from now."

"Right."

She was quiet again, then spoke in a soft, controlled voice.

"I knew she would come," she said. "It's her mother. It's you. And she has to get back what is hers. Her room. Her son."

Her voice cracked slightly on the last word, a chord of desolation.

"One thing I learned in this world? Things don't last. People say they do. They don't. Your friends, they die. The wars go on and on and on, then they end. People say they will love each other for the rest of their lives, and they don't."

There was nothing bitter in her voice. Only acceptance. Or a kind of rough wisdom. He pulled her close to him. He wanted to tell her that everything would turn out all right. He couldn't. He simply didn't know, and he could not harm her with a cheap lie. Too many lies were told in bed. He did not want to add to them.

He dozed for a time, and then she reached for him with her hand, and they made love again, erasing dread for a little while.

The boy remained unaware of what was coming. The arrival of his mother was never mentioned. At night, Delaney read to him about Oz. Across the days, he played with Osito, and pushed his fire engine around, and went to the garden and batted the small ball with his paddle under the branches of the olive tree. Rose introduced him to a new passion: watermelon.

"Don't spit the seeds on the floor, boy," she told him. "Put them on this little plate. Later we'll plant them in the garden."

He looked at her uncertainly, and then at Delaney, as if not sure what seeds did, or why they would be taken to the garden. But he loved the chilled watermelon, taking big bites from his slice, the juice wetting his cheeks and running down to his chin. He removed each glistening black seed and placed it carefully on the plate and then took another bite.

"Good, Rosa," he said. "This is good!"

"You bet," she said. "And good *for* you."

"Wahtuh-melon," he said. "I like it!"

Delaney was busy all Monday morning with people scorched, scalded, and blistered by the weekend's sun. One man showed up shirtless, the touch of any fabric causing agony. Another was white with Noxzema, and still hurting. It was so predictable that Delaney laughed when one casualty of the sun god left, and was grinning when the next arrived. In between there were the normal cases: a man with a fractured jaw, a woman with a TB cough, a child with a fever. All the hurt and harm that made up the dailiness of his life.

That night in the dark, he told Rose that they would go dancing on Friday night. He did not have to remind her that Grace would arrive on Saturday.

"You're kidding, right?" she said.

"No. Monique found me someone to watch Carlito."

"Not some crazy person?"

"Her sister."

"Monique's got a sister?"

"She works at Metropolitan Life."

"For me, it's hard to think Monique even has a mother."

"Hey, she's not *that* bad."

"Not to you. To me, it's another story."

They were quiet for a long while.

"Friday night," she said. She did not mention that it might be their last night together, and neither did he. "Dancing."

She kissed him on the forehead.

Monique's sister Yvette arrived just before seven. She was a plumper, more cheerful version of Monique, and a few years older. She wore a business suit that was wrinkled by the heat. Monique was waiting for her, and they talked in a sketchy way with Delaney about their childhood and Yvette's three sons and their father and mother. Rose was upstairs getting ready. Carlito looked apprehensive.

"He sure is a handsome boy, all right," Yvette said. "You're right about that, Sis."

"With a great tan too," Monique said. "And it's only June. Wait till August."

"By August he's gonna look like a movie star."

Monique said good-bye and left. She had made her point: she was not a babysitter. Then the hall door opened and Rose was there. She was wearing a white summer dress and flat white shoes, and the whiteness set off the rich gold of her skin. A small white purse dangled from her wrist. A plump rose from the front garden was pinned to the dress. She wore no jewelry. Her lipstick was pale and pink, and she needed no rouge. Delaney thought: God damn, she is beautiful.

"Oh, Rosa," the boy blurted out, as if thinking the same thing, without words. He rushed to her. She smiled and hugged him.

"Don't get watermelon juice on the dress, boy," she said. He smiled and touched his face.

"Gran'pa make me wash," he said, holding out his hands with the palms up.

"You see? Gran'pa thinks of everything."

Rose and Yvette shook hands and then talked in a corner of the room about the yellow box in the upstairs bathroom, the boy's toothbrush, and his books. There was a piece of cake in the icebox and some milk. Rose smiled and turned to Carlito.

"Okay, Carlito, we're going out. So you be a good boy and do what Yvette says, and we'll see you later."

The boy looked uneasy, as if he wanted to go with them. But Rose kissed him on the cheek and went out first, as if to avoid inspection by neighbors while holding the arm of Delaney. Yvette took Carlito's hand and said, "Let's look at the kitchen." Delaney left three minutes after Rose. They would meet on Ninth Avenue and take the subway into the night. He imagined the arrival of the *Andalusia* in the morning and then drove the image away. What will be, will be. Tonight we dance.

Times Square was bright, noisy, packed. It was not New Year's Eve, but the crowds moved and eddied in the same way. Rose took his arm, holding her purse close to her breasts, gazing around at the gaud and the glitter, or watching the sidewalk in front of her so that she would not stumble. They paused to listen to a street band that featured a black boy tap-dancing for coins, then slowly continued uptown. Delaney remembered when it was all called Longacre Square, and was here in 1904 when the *Times* opened its new headquarters, extorting the name change from the Tammany boys downtown. It was at first a place for swells, for men in tuxedos and women in ball gowns, for midnight places like Rector's and Shanley's and Churchill's, Healy's and Bustanoby's. They came with chorus girls and mistresses and even, occasionally, with their wives, for steaks and chops and champagne and dancing to stringed orchestras. Delaney had often been among them, inhaling perfumed shoulders on dance floors. He had even believed that the great lesson of Times Square was a simple one: sin could be elegant. A long time ago. When he was young.

But the swells were all gone now, along with their watering holes, driven out by Prohibition and now the goddamned Depression. Hypocrisy and bad times had served as the great social levelers. He looked up at the hotels and wondered if Larry Dorsey was working again in one of them, after his terrible New Year's Eve. He hoped so. And vowed to call him. On every street he saw patrols of hard boys from Hell's Kitchen, lean and furtive and angry, moving through the crowds after walking east from the tenements on the North River. A few were shining shoes. Most searched for careless marks, with their wallets plump in back pockets. Some women were offering swift joy in side street hotels, and never mentioned gonorrhea. Where was the building that he visited that time with Big Jim, where they sat for an hour with George M. Cohan? And what was the name of that dancer from Earl Carroll's Vanities, the one with the creamy skin and the long legs? For weeks he had danced with her every night. Now it had been seven years since he had danced with anyone.

He and Rose moved slowly through packed streets, bumping into other people, laughing at the sights. A fat old woman in a shawl sang "Mother Machree" and offered apples for two cents. A tenor proclaimed his passion for Madame Butterfly in a cloud of frying hot dogs. Another man put a dancing cocker spaniel through his routine, in which the dog always did the opposite of what he was ordered and made people laugh. Rose and Delaney didn't laugh at the veterans they saw on almost every corner. One held a scrawled sign on cardboard. LOST LEG IN FRANCE NEED HELP. Delaney slipped him a quarter and moved on with Rose. They paused to look at the tall beefy cops planted on their big Morgan horses, easy and laughing, but ready for trouble. "Carlito would love these guys!" Rose said. Delaney squeezed her arm in agreement. Above them, the lights of huge signs blinked in crazy syncopation, sending out fragments of nouns, and no verbs. RUPPERT WRIGLEY BABY RUTH BARS. Others were pieces of movies. CRIME DOCTOR. STINGAREE. WITCHING HOUR. Behind them, the electric ribbon on the Times Tower said something about Albania and kept moving. Another message said: GIANTS LOSE TO CUBS 5–4. They passed more hot dog places and skee-ball parlors and a place called the Pokerino. Every movie house lobby was guarded by sour uniformed young men, who served as bouncers and barkers. Newsstands waited for the bulldog editions of the *News* and *Mirror.* Inside every restaurant, above the counter, there were framed photographs of Franklin D. Roosevelt. Delaney and Rose could hear music everywhere. Moving through the great crowd, Delaney felt his own kind of relief. Here nobody could ever care about his problems. Your daughter arrives tomorrow? Fine, let her sleep on the couch. But don't bother me right now, sport.

Then they reached Fifty-first Street.

"Here we are," Delaney said, and looked up at the sign.

She followed his look, and moved a hand gently to his neck.

"Goddamn you," she whispered in a hoarse voice. "You should of told me."

They paused while she wiped her cheeks dry with a small frilly handkerchief. Then they walked together into Roseland.

There were no empty tables or chairs and the bar was packed, so they went directly to the crowded dance floor. There must have been eight hundred people in the place, old people and kids, many red from the sun, most sweating, some pressed hard against each other. The lights were muted. The band was playing "You Made Me Love You." He put his right hand on her waist and took her right hand in his left, and they began to move. A fox trot. He could feel her tension, her fear of clumsiness, and he was careful not to step on her feet. She was smaller in his arms than she seemed in bed. At first Rose maintained a formal distance between them, and then as she relaxed, she pressed against him. Everybody seemed to know the words of the tune.

I didn't want to do it,
I didn't want to do it . . .

Rose whispered the words too, and then Delaney followed. A mustached young trumpet player played a solo without changing the beat, and when the tune ended, there was loud applause. The dancers were making clear that they wanted nothing complicated, nothing sweaty. They wanted romance. So did Delaney and Rose. Here they could be in the real world and still be intimate. Here, for a few hours, they could believe that they would be together forever.

And so they danced and danced, Rose growing more skillful as she went along, more relaxed, following his body and the slight pressure of his hands, then trying small moves of her own. "You know how to do this," she said. "You must've done it with a lot of women."

"But never with you," he said. "And not for a long, long time."

In the midst of the intimate crowd, and the music, and the sound of sliding shoes, he realized that strangers probably saw them as an older man with a handsome younger woman. Which was true. Or as a boss with his secretary. Or even as husband and wife, as the man believed at the museum. And why not? His hair was whitening and hers was a lustrous black. She will outlive me, if she has any luck at all. She will not outlive the boy. If the boy's luck holds too. Then the set ended, many dancers applauded, the band stood up, and a four-piece combo replaced them. They started playing Dixieland. Rose took Delaney's good hand and moved off the floor.

"Wait here for me," she said. "I got to go to the ladies' room."

He stood next to a pole and watched her walk away. So did some men and a few women. Then she was gone, and he watched a dozen older couples doing the Charleston, crossing hands from knee to knee, laughing, happy, indomitable. They were his age, at least. For these precious moments they could forget the bad times. They could forget defeat. Once they were young. Once they had danced. They were doing it again.

From the packed bar he heard trills of bright female laughter, and male growls, and more laughter. Maybe the whiskey was laughing. But maybe it was just people having a good time, making loss into triumph, sorrow into life. Tonight was last night's tomorrow. Tomorrow is another day. Or night.

The Dixieland band departed, and the house band of Larry Ellis returned. The oldest player was hauling a bass fiddle. He was about thirty. They started to play "Stormy Weather" just as Rose returned.

"More women in there than at S. Klein," she said. "Powdering their nose, spraying themselves. Talking about men. Nothing else! Men and men and men."

Delaney laughed. "As long as they weren't talking about baseball."

"Come on, Fred. Let's dance."

"Whatever you say, Miss Del Rio."

They danced along with hundreds of others, and eased without effort into "The Devil and the Deep Blue Sea." Long extended versions, not the clipped three minutes of phonograph records, with each of four musicians taking a solo, on trumpet, clarinet, trombone, and tenor sax. Delaney thought: I have lived too long in the country of numbness. I won't live there again. I want to become a citizen of Roseland.

"Compared to you, that Fred Astaire is a show-off," she murmured.

"Compared to you, Dolores Del Rio is ugly."

"You are a liar."

Then a singer came onstage, skinny, in a jacket a size bigger than he was, black hair, high cheekbones. He was holding a microphone. Without introduction he began to sing in a thin intense voice.

Life is just a bowl of cherries
Don't take it serious —

Some of the dancers took up the lyrics.

— it's too mysterious.
You work, you save, you worry so —

Now the dancers were louder.

But you can't take your dough
When you go, go, go!

They all knew the next verse, even Delaney, and all of Roseland was singing it, except Rose. She didn't know the words.

So keep repeating it's the berries,
The strongest oak must fall,
The sweet things in life
To you were just loaned,
So how can you lose
What you've never owned?
Life is just a bowl of cherries
So LIVE and LAUGH at it all . . .

They roared the final lines, living tough and laughing at the whole goddamned world.

"Who *is* this Wop?" Rose said.

"I doubt he's without papers. The voice is pure New York."

"His mother should be ashamed. That kid needs to *eat!*"

The young singer began a version of "Melancholy Baby," somehow making the words romantic without being sentimental. The voice was urban, pure, new. Not Crosby. Not Russ Columbo. Definitely not Jolson. Delaney was sure his father was a fireman or worked three days a week in a factory. And thought: *The strongest oak must fall.* He pushed his face into Rose's hair, inhaling the aroma of soap and oil. One ballad led to another for more than fifteen minutes. Then the singer said into the microphone: "Ladies and gentlemen, the national anthem."

Without missing a beat, he began to sing, while the band supported him with a kind of Times Square dirge.

They used to tell me I was building a dream,
And so I followed the mob.
When there was earth to plow, or guns to bear,
I was always right there on the job.

Some of the older men, the men Delaney's age, stopped dancing. They knew this song too. They knew every word because in a big way, it was about them.

They used to tell me I was building a dream,
With peace and glory ahead,
Why should I be standing in line —
Just waiting for a piece of bread?

The singer was crooning the song, making it into a kind of blues, and more and more people stopped dancing and started singing.

Once I built a railroad, I made it run,
Made it race against time.
Once I built a railroad, now it's done —
Brother, can you spare a dime?

Delaney and Rose were not dancing now either, and as they looked around and the verses continued he could see the anger in the men and some of the women. Many men punched out each word with a clenched fist. Some of them surely had been shot at. Some of them surely had been hit. Delaney thought: This singer must have been four when the war ended. Same as Grace. And yet he is making it his song too.

Once in khaki suits, gee, we looked swell
Full of that Yankee Doodle dee dum,
Half a million boots went slogging through Hell —
And I was the kid with the drum —

The drummer added a rim shot and someone in the reed section yelled *Hey!* Then the singer lowered his voice, almost speaking the final lines of the anthem.

Say, don't you remember?
They called me Al.
It was "Al" all of the time.

Why don't you remember,
I'm your pal?

They all roared the final line, Delaney among them.

Say Buddy, can you spare a dime?

Then the young singer was gone, and Rose leaned into Delaney and held him tight, one hand pressed into the back of his neck. The band began to play "Stardust" in the packed intimacy of Roseland. He took her hand.

SEVENTEEN

THE PIER WAS A LONG HIGH UGLY BARN MADE OF CORRUGATED iron and splintery timbers, rusting with time and the Depression. He walked its length, his footsteps echoing in the dim light, and remembered the piers of Europe before the war, with their crowded bars and restaurants, their glad sense of imminent arrival, and the din and bustle of the New York piers, loud with the moneyed celebrations of departure. *How did Rose get here? Where did she make landfall in this great strange scary city, with nothing but guts to get her through?* A few couples passed along the pier, pausing to look out at the river through the open doors, joined in solitude. The slip was still empty, awaiting the arrival of the *Andalusia,* but Delaney could see the gulls watching from the next pier. Orange peels were floating in the water. Small waves slapped against timber. An unseen whistler was offering the melody of a song, off in the rusting silence. "It Had to Be You." And lyrics rose in Delaney.

I wandered around
And finally found
Somebody who . . .

He walked back to the stevedores' office, where Knocko had promised a chair. One of the stevedores stood up, smiling. There were two others waiting to go to work, and a phone on a scarred table.

"Have some coffee, Doc," he said. "And, oh, Knocko called. The *Andalusia*? It's out at quarantine, jus' past da Narrows. Should be pretty soon now."

"Thanks, Mr. McGinty," Delaney said, and poured some coffee. It tasted like aluminum. The men started talking about the Giants and the goddamned Yankees. McGinty lit a thin Italian cigar. Delaney eased over to the door, trying to evade the smoke. The unseen whistler was now offering "Life Is Just a Bowl of Cherries." Was he at Roseland too? Did he also believe that even the strongest oak must fall? *Oh, Rose . . .* He couldn't remember what he had written to Grace about Rose. He didn't remember whether he had even told Grace her name. He did tell her that he had found a woman to help with Carlito. He did remember that. But in her own letters she was not very curious about the details. He remembered telling Molly when Grace was small: I will spoil her? All right, I will spoil her. And he had, and had paid a price. Grace had sent one final letter before leaving Spain, brief and elliptical, that arrived three days before the *Andalusia* was due. The big news was personal: it was over with Rafael, her husband, the boy's father. *In Moscow he fell in love with a Bulgarian woman! Can you believe it? When he told me I burst out laughing! A Bulgarian! And I thought he was in love with Lenin!!!* So she would arrive with hopes of curing her own solitude. Almost certainly with Carlito. Who had cured the solitude of Rose. *And mine too.*

Knocko called in a bulletin. The *Andalusia* was being lashed to a tug and the pilot was on board, to guide her in to safety. A bookmaker called and McGinty mentioned Likely Lad in the sixth at Belmont.

Then Knocko again. The ship was coming into the Narrows. *How many times had this ship passed Molly's bones, going and coming? How many other ships had done the same?* Another bookmaker called. The whistling stopped.

Delaney filled with images of Rose and what she might be doing at this very moment. Each image drove into him a stab of impending loss. Rose, fixing a last lunch for the boy. Rose, packing her bags. Rose alone, lugging her bags down Horatio Street. Bending under their weight. Pausing to gather strength, her eyes wild. Looking for a taxi that would take her away from Horatio Street before Delaney arrived with his daughter.

He stepped back, staring down at the rough planks of the pier, silently addressing himself. And Rose. I wouldn't blame you, Rose, if you went away forever. You don't need any of this. My daughter, Molly's ghost, the boy. Why should you want any of this? That's why I've never mentioned anything permanent to you. Never said those big little words that come at the end of every movie romance. They make movies about *getting* married, but not about *being* married. That's why I've never even whispered certain words to you, Rose. Maybe I just lack guts. Maybe I'm afraid that I'll let myself believe again in permanence and then wake up one morning and find that you're gone too. And, of course, maybe you fear the same about me. But I'm too old now for such fears. I just don't want to hurt you, woman. Now, or ever. Or to see you hurt because of me. By uptown snobs or downtown shawlies. The world has taught me that not a goddamned thing is ever certain.

That morning, he had treated patients until eleven-thirty, his right shoulder aching from tension. The long night's dancing had been joy. Waking was not. He wished he could relax into something like peace. When the last patient left, Rose came in to see him alone in the office.

"All my life," she said in a husky voice, "I'm going to remember all those people singing about the guy that just needed a dime." She paused. "All my life, I'm going to remember dancing with you too, Jim. All my life." She touched his face fondly. She had never called him Jim before. "No matter what happens."

He knew that she had pondered these words, had even privately rehearsed them. He felt himself tremble. But she didn't wait for a reply. She hurried out, without collapsing into self-pity. She has pride, he thought, but no vanity, and the pride will keep her from saying anything that would sound like begging. She did not want a dime's worth of Delaney.

She and the boy were out again when he left for the pier. Delaney wore a white sport shirt and decided to walk. The humidity was rising off the North River, and he felt as if he needed shears to pass through the dense air. And the sun was climbing. The heat would get worse. And now on the pier hours had passed, and he was drinking coffee with the stevedores as they argued the comparative merits of Bill Terry and John McGraw as a manager. The phone rang. This time it was for Delaney.

"It'll be docked in twenty minutes," Knocko said. "I'll see you there."

They were standing together about thirty feet from the gangplank when the first passengers began descending. Knocko had already sent three longshoremen into the ship for the luggage. He had talked to the customs people too. An old couple walked unsteadily down to the pier, where the man did a little jig. A refugee, for sure. From what was coming in Spain. Or Germany. Now they were both safe. They walked away holding hands, into America. Three young men followed, rich kids coming back from a time in Europe that they did not pay for themselves, laughing and grab-assing all the way. A man in a chauffeur's uniform went to greet them with a bow. Two old women, dressed in clothes from the time before the war, moved down the gangplank, clutching the railing. They might never see the Prado again or the palaces of Venice or walk together along the Ringstrasse. None seemed surprised by the rusting, unpainted condition of the pier. The *Andalusia* was not a luxury liner.

Then he saw Grace. She was at the top of the gangway, wearing dark slacks, a patterned blouse, a black beret. She squinted into the darkness of the giant shed. Delaney waved and she leaned forward, then smiled and moved faster, and hit the pier running. She went straight to Delaney and made a little leap and they embraced and hugged.

"Oh, Daddy, oh, Daddy, oh," she said. Then dropped her voice. "Oh, Daddy. I'm so sorry. For everything."

"Welcome home, Grace."

Then she saw Knocko.

"Oh, Mr. Carmody! How *are* you! Thank you for coming!"

"You play any softball over there?" he said, and grinned.

"Not an inning," she said. "How about tomorrow?"

They walked together toward the street side of the shed, and the longshoremen came up behind them with one large bag and two smaller ones, and they passed into the sunlight and the sparsely crowded avenue that ran along the piers. Before the Depression, Delaney thought, the crowds were so thick here you couldn't cross without a rifle. Grace took off her beret and stuffed it in her belt. Her blond hair was darker and coarser, from too many years of hard water. Her smile was still lovely, her eyes remained a lustrous brown. But Delaney thought: She is twenty and looks thirty. Lines were scratched into her brow. Her mouth was more severe.

"I can't wait to see Carlito," she said.

"He doesn't know you're coming," Delaney said. "I didn't want him getting nervous." He looked directly at her. "But first we have to talk, Grace."

"Oh, there'll be plenty of time to talk, Dad."

"Now, Grace."

The longshoremen were loading her bags into the trunk of

Knocko's Packard. He could see several canvases tied with cord. He went over to the car, but Knocko wasn't there. The driver was standing at the door, smoking.

"Listen, could you go over to my house and wait for me?" Delaney said. "You know where it is. My daughter and I will walk home."

"Sure thing, Doc," he said. He got into the loaded car. Delaney turned to the longshoremen and tried to pass them a tip. "It's okay, Doc," the heavier one said. "It's taken care of."

Delaney turned to Grace. She was staring out at the river.

"The waterfront looks bad from the ship," she said. "It looks worse up close, doesn't it?"

"The Depression did it," he said. "Not just to the waterfront."

"Even Barcelona looks better," she said.

She glanced at him as they started walking downtown beside the piers and the gaps.

"You're angry, aren't you, Daddy?"

"Yes."

She jammed her hands in her pockets. "I don't blame you."

"You were selfish and careless, goddamn it," he said, trying to wring the anger out of his voice. "That boy's whole world was ripped up. He was crying for you, Mamá, Mamá, for days. Goddamn it."

She looked as if she'd been slapped. A longshoreman passed, hook in his belt, lost in thought. She touched Delaney's arm, and he could smell the sea rising from her clothes.

"We have to talk about *now*," Delaney said. "What you're going to do *now*."

"Okay. First, we have to take care of what I came for," she said, bristling slightly. "We have to get my mother buried. My mother. Your wife. *Now*."

"It's all arranged," he said. "There'll be no mass, but we'll go with her to the cemetery. The Green-Wood in Brooklyn. That's where we can say good-bye . . ."

She asked for details, and he provided them in a low, clinical voice, blocking the current of anger. They saw a small crowd of men around the entrance to a pier and a black freighter docking, like the ship in the Babar book. A hot dog cart with an umbrella was feeding the men. He thought of Carlos. And then Rose.

"I wonder what happened to her," Grace said. "Did she just give up? Did she slip and fall?"

"There was no note," he said. "We'll never know."

And told himself: Get to it. Get to *now.*

"Can I see her?" Grace said.

"I don't think that's a good idea, Grace. Remember her in life. The good and the bad."

"Do *you* remember her?"

"Of course."

Get to it.

"What else are you going to do, Grace? What are you going to do *today?*"

She seemed startled by the question, and stopped walking. Her eyes reminded him of Carlito's when he was scolded.

"I'm going home," she said.

"To stay?"

"I don't know."

"You don't know," he said in a flat voice.

"You said *today.* You said *now.*" Her eyes flashed, her mouth seemed harder. "Can't we talk about this later?"

"No."

They were at Christopher Street now, with its pedestrian path under the highway, and a stoplight. He took her hand as he so often did when she was a child, and they hurried across. They waited for one lone truck as it groaned and turned, carrying heavy crates into the city. When they reached the opposite side, he released her hand. She stood there and faced him.

"Daddy, listen to me, Daddy," she said with some heat. "Please listen. I did what I did because I *had* to. It wasn't forever. It was for what

I thought would be a month, at most. I had to find my *husband.* I had to know if he was alive or dead. If I didn't know, I couldn't get on with my life." She paused for breath. "I thought I couldn't be a decent mother to Carlito if I didn't resolve the thing with Rafael."

Delaney wondered: From what movie did she take this scenario? From what novel? Oh, how young she is.

"And so I went. I —"

Across the street, a few vagrants stood together, passing a pint of wine from one mouth to another. Some kids with a basket and a blanket were walking east to the subway. Delaney saw none of them. He stared into his daughter's face.

"Goddamn it, Grace. You could have called me and said you were coming and why. You could have brought the boy into the house and introduced him to me and explained who I was. You could have slept in your own bed. You could have stayed a few days, taken another ship —"

"It was the last ship to Spain until the spring!"

"Then you could have figured it out better, goddamn it. You could have come a week early. Not the night before! Instead —"

She turned her back on him and began to sob.

"Stop!" he said, hating his own prosecutorial vehemence but unable to cage it. "You've got to face what you've done!" His voice lowered. "Now there are other people involved. Not just you."

She turned to him. Her eyes were wet and she was sniffling, but she had stopped crying.

"And you have to face what you did when I was small."

"I *have* faced it. I did what this whole neighborhood did, when the young men went off to the war. But yes, I didn't have to go. And yes, I was sorry. But I tried and I tried and I tried to make it up to you. I spoiled you. I forgave everything, even if I could not forgive myself. But Carlos is *also* three years old. How could you do to him what I did to you?"

She seemed to be shrinking. He took her elbow and walked east, then took a left, heading for Horatio Street. His heart was drumming.

"I'm sorry," he said. "I don't want to make this worse." She didn't reply. "And it turned out —" He groped for the right words. "It turned out that Carlos was a gift. His innocence was a gift. His way of looking at the world, and naming it, and showing it to me fresh: that was a gift, Grace." Say it, he thought. Now. "And because of him, I received another gift. A woman."

She slowed down as they walked on Washington Street. Away off they heard the elevated train squealing against its tracks.

"The woman who came to help you with him?" she said. "In one of your letters, you mentioned —"

"Rose," he said. "Her name is Rose Verga." She said nothing, taking this in. "She's Sicilian. In her thirties. Speaks very good English." He paused. "When she and Carlos arrived, I was numb. I'm not numb anymore."

She took his good arm above the elbow and leaned into him.

"Oh, Daddy, I'm so happy for you," she said in a croaking voice, and Delaney thought: Save me please, O Lord, from the banality of the young.

They walked faster and his mind became a jumble. What if Rose goes? She can't go. But what if she does? I'll look for her and bring her back. But where will I look? No. She can't go. She can't. But if she goes, what then happens to Grace and Carlito? What happens to them if Rose stays? She can't go. But what if she does?

So much else remained unsaid. He wanted to talk to Grace. She had uttered only a few sentences about Molly and not a word about Rafael Santos. Was he staying in Spain with his Bulgarian woman? Would he come to New York too? Would he choose his wife and child instead of his new woman? And then where would they go? To utopia? Where exactly was that glorious place?

They turned into Horatio Street, and he could see Grace looking at all the familiar places. The tenements on the corner. The house of the Cottrells and the boarded-up facade of the ghost house. This was the fragment of the world that she knew better than any other. She stared at the stoop of 95 Horatio.

"The last time I was here," she said in a drained voice, "it was covered with snow, and so was I."

He said nothing. The Packard was parked in front, the windows open, cigarette smoke oozing from the interior. He walked over and leaned in.

"Okay, boys," Delaney said, "I'll go up and open the doors at the top of the stoop. Just leave the bags in the hall." He had his keys out. "Is this stuff heavy?"

"Not bad, Doc," the bulkiest man said, climbing out of the car and going to the trunk. "No problem."

Delaney went to the stoop.

"Wait here," he said to Grace. She had put the beret back on her head and was standing in the areaway, her back to the fence. She was gazing at the irises, planted by Rose. Her face was slack and tired and uncertain.

Delaney hurried up the stoop and opened both sets of doors and waved to the men. There was nobody in the hall of the parlor floor. Was Rose already gone? The men came up the steps, the bulky man lugging the large suitcase, the other man the two smaller bags, the driver holding the wrapped paintings. They placed them on the parquet floors of the hall. This time Delaney insisted that they take a tip, and sent his best wishes and thanks to Mr. Carmody. Then they went back down the stoop. Delaney waited, listening, heard nothing. No voices. No music. Maybe she's gone.

He locked the doors behind, and paused on the stoop. Grace seemed ready, as if she had sealed away the spoiled little girl that still lived within. Now she had to deal with Carlito and the mysterious woman named Rose. And they would have to deal with her. Delaney longed for the consolation of numbness. And he went down the steps.

• • •

Monique came to the door as they walked in under the stoop.

"Well, look at *you,* girl," she said, and hugged Grace, then stepped back and looked again. "Prettier than ever."

"Hello, Monique. You look *exactly* the same."

"And you, girl, you're a grown woman. I'll be damned."

Delaney was behind Grace, and they all stood for an awkward moment.

"Where is he?" Grace said softly.

"In the yard," Monique said. Adding a deadpan message to Delaney: "With Rose."

She was here. For now. She had not fled. Delaney led Grace through the new door to the kitchen. She waited at the window, peering into the bright green blur of garden. For a moment, Delaney thought Grace would turn and run. She didn't. They went into the shed and eased past the bicycle. Grace took a breath, then gently pushed open the screen door and stepped into the garden. Delaney stood behind her.

In the far corner, they could see the boy's back and Rose to his side. They were planting watermelon seeds. Rose looked up, and Delaney saw uncertainty in her eyes.

"Carlito?" Grace said.

The boy stood up, his skin coppery from the sun. There was no expression on his face.

"It's me, chico," Grace said. "Su mamá."

He suddenly looked frightened, staring at this strange woman. He slipped behind Rose and held on to her hip. Delaney thought: I've seen this look before, but not on the boy. Grace took another tentative step. Delaney did not move. The boy peered around the fleshy shield of Rose's hip. Then he eased away from her. He was squinting. Rose took his hand.

"Come on, boy," Rose said. "It's your mama."

She led him forward, but the boy held back stubbornly and seemed to get smaller. Rose smiled widely at Grace, and Delaney thought: Goddamn, she is tough.

"He's a little shy sometimes," Rose said. "Come on, boy, give your mama a big kiss."

Grace stepped closer, as if restrained by caution.

"Ven, m'hijo," she said. "Come."

The boy pulled away from Rose and ran to the farthest corner of the garden. Tears were flowing from his eyes. He squatted in fear.

"No," he said. *"No no no NO."*

Rose looked from the boy to Grace, whose face was forlorn. Delaney did not move.

"Take off the hat," Rose said. "Maybe he —"

Grace whipped off the beret and dropped it on the grass. She walked cautiously to the boy, but he was bunched up like a puppy expecting to be punished. Delaney hurried past her and lifted the boy and held him tight.

"It's okay, boy. Don't worry, boy. You're not going anywhere. Don't worry —"

"I want Rosa," the boy said, in a croaking voice. He curled his fingers in her direction. He was sniffling and turning his head away from the stranger. "I don't want to go. I want Rosa, Gran'pa."

"I got an idea," Rose said. "Let's eat."

In the kitchen, the boy sat next to Delaney. Rose smiled and said to Grace: "Welcome home."

"Thank you, Rose," she said. "Let me help."

"No, you sit down, Grace. It's already done, I just have to heat up some stuff." Then to the boy: "Show your mama your fire engine, boy."

He sneaked a look at this woman he didn't quite know, and went off slowly for the fire engine. Delaney tried to read the look on Rose's face. Determined? Tough? Or was she producing a special version of a last supper? The boy came back, pumping the fire engine, but there was no energy in the effort. He wasn't playing. He was performing.

"Your old room is all set," Rose said over her shoulder. "It's a new bed too. And Carlos is in the room where you used to paint. Dr. Delaney told me all about that."

Delaney wondered where Rose's own things were. Her clothes, her new boots, her dictionary and notebook full of English words. Then she called to Carlito.

"Okay, boy, time to eat. You know what!"

"Braciole," he said, and for the first time since Delaney had arrived with his mother, the boy smiled.

"He loves this stuff," Rose said to Grace. And Grace smiled in a tentative way and looked down at the food.

Grace insisted on washing the dishes and the pots and Delaney dried them with a dish towel. Grace thanked Rose for a delicious meal, and Rose shrugged in a polite way. The boy glanced at his mother, listened to her voice. Delaney thought: It's only six months, but it could have been six years.

"He usually takes a nap around now," Rose said. "Come on, I'll show you."

She led the way up the stairs, the boy directly behind her, followed by Grace and then Delaney. Grace ran fingers over the banister, and touched the familiar walls, and squinted at some dark paintings. When she put a hand on the boy's shoulder, he pulled away. Then they were on the top floor. The door to Molly's old room was wide open.

"Here's your old room, Grace," Rose said. "The mattress is new and pretty good. Plenty of room for your stuff." Then she stepped next door. "Here is Carlito's headquarter. He loves those Babar books and that one about the Wizard of Oz."

"That used to be mine," Grace said. "I loved that book."

"Him too," Rose said. "It must be in the blood."

Delaney held back as she showed Grace the bathroom and the yellow cheese box. But it was clear that this had become Rose's house too. She was showing it off. Then they stepped through the open door of Molly's room, and now Carlito was hanging back. Rough paintings by Delaney and the boy were leaning against the half-empty bookcases.

"These two guys come here and paint," Rose explained, and added in a dry voice, "The boy is better than the dottore."

Grace hugged the boy. "These are great, Carlito. Just terrific!" And turned to her father. "And Dad? I thought you'd never pick up another brush."

"An objective person would say it was a terrible mistake, Grace."

Grace looked around for a silent moment, then said: "My mother used to play her music here."

"Him too," Rose said, nodding to the boy. "Carlito, play something for your mama."

"No," he said. "I don't want to play the piano."

Rose raised her brows and said nothing. Grace looked wounded. She turned to Delaney.

"Where are Momma's books? And her pictures? And the music scores?"

The question was like an accusation. "Boxed up," Delaney said. "Safe and dry and sealed, down in the basement."

"So she's gone from this house," Grace said. Rose backed away, squatting to whisper to Carlito. Delaney could hear the word "mama."

"Yes, Grace," Delaney said. "She's gone."

A muscle quivered in her face. She said, almost to herself, "God, there's no end to the sadness."

It was time for a nap. Rose put the boy to bed and was showing Grace the closets when Delaney went downstairs and into his bedroom. There in a corner was Rose's cheap suitcase, with the black dress laid across the top on a hanger and her hat on top of the dress. She had not gone yet, but she was ready. He closed the door and removed his shoes, with every part of his body demanding sleep. But he was afraid to sleep. Afraid Rose would go. He removed his shirt, still damp from the river morning and the long walk. She can't go. He removed his trousers too, and his socks, and put on a robe. This is her house too. He drew the curtains and stretched out on the bed and fought off sleep. He could hear the murmuring voices of Grace and Rose on the landing outside the bedroom door. Almost surely removing clothes from Grace's suitcase. Both women returning upstairs on stockinged feet. He heard the sounds of traffic. And kids laughing. He did not hear Carlito's voice. He, at least, must have fallen into numbed sleep.

Delaney was dozing when the door clicked open. He could smell Rose before he saw her outline in the muted light. She sat beside him on the bed, and he spoke before she did.

"You'd better hang up your clothes," he said. "Before they get wrinkled."

"I don't think so," she whispered.

"There's plenty of room," he said.

"Not enough for me and Grace."

The bed sagged slightly as she got up, and then he heard her undressing. He thought: I've never seen her naked in the light. I know every inch of her body, but have never seen it all. She went into the bathroom and closed the door. Water ran. The toilet flushed. Then she was slipping beneath the covers beside him. He inhaled her fragrance of sweat and oil and roses. She touched him.

The next morning was glorious with sun. All of Delaney's rage had been purged. He felt oddly empty and hoped that in his anger he had put no permanent marks on Grace. Casey the undertaker sent a car for Delaney and Grace. Rose stayed behind, watching with the boy from the areaway as they eased into the car. Three kids walked by, eating ice-cream cones. Both Delaney and Grace waved good-bye, and the car followed the hearse to the Brooklyn Bridge.

"Do you think he'll *ever* remember me?" Grace said, her tone lighter.

"Of course. Little by little, and then pow! He'll remember. It could be tonight. It could be tomorrow. But he'll remember."

"I wish I could believe you."

"Grace? It happened once to you."

They were quiet as the two cars entered thickening traffic on the great bridge over the East River. The sun had risen, as always, in Brooklyn, and when Delaney looked behind him, the towers of lower Manhattan were gilded by its rays. Grace followed his look and turned to see.

"You know, when I was away, I saw this view in my head all the time," she said. "You brought me here when I was about ten. Remember? We took the subway to the Brooklyn side and then walked back. Then you took me to Chinatown."

"I remember," he said.

"It was like a gift," she said. "I want to give the same gift to Carlito."

"There's plenty of time."

"I hope," she said.

Traffic clogged again as they came down off the bridge into Brooklyn. The driver knew the way, of course. When Delaney visited the graves of his parents, he was almost always alone, and took the BMT to Twenty-fifth Street and walked to the cemetery. Molly would never come with him. At least once, in the days of money, he hired a taxi and had it wait. Now Grace peered out the windows as if visiting a foreign country.

"Do you dream about Momma?" she whispered.

"Sometimes," he said. "Do you?"

"Almost never."

She didn't elaborate.

"I want to remember her happy," she said. "Lost in music. Playing away in that room. Filling the house with chords and melody."

"I want to remember her that way too."

"Then she'll live, right? She'll live on."

"For a few people, yes. Not for Carlito. Not for Rose. They never knew her. But yes, for us."

She went silent again.

"Is it over with Santos?" he said. "In your letter —"

"Yes. For me. It's over. I was such a goddamned fool." She smiled in a bitter way. "I thought he might die as a heroic revolutionary martyr. You know, *for the cause.* But to give me up, and his *son,* too, for some . . . some woman." She laughed. "Jesus. What a friggin' cliché. What a bad movie." She slammed the leather car seat with the flat of her hand. "Karl Marx — played by Harpo Marx! Jesus!"

Delaney laughed too. Ahead of them now, the hearse was aimed at the stone gates of the cemetery. Father and daughter were quiet as the ridges of tombstones came into view. As always, the terrain reminded him of the Argonne.

"I like Rose, Daddy," Grace suddenly whispered. "I like her very much. I want you to know that."

Rose. Oh, Rose. The hearse went on ahead of them into the great necropolis, but a guard stopped their car just beyond the gate. He leaned in and told the driver to pull into the parking lot on the right.

"Yiz'll have to walk," the guard said. "But it's not far."

Delaney knew why the cemetery insisted on this routine: they needed time to place the coffin in its rectangle of earth. He and Grace stepped out of the car. A breeze combed the tall oaks and sycamores. Birds were winging. Everything was green except the stone path and the tombstones. Away off they could see the glassy shimmer of a pond. There were no other living people anywhere in sight. He imagined the scene when Frankie Botts was laid to rest. The vows of vengeance. The performed grief. He imagined Eddie Corso strolling alone in a graveyard in France.

"It's very beautiful," Grace said.

"It is," Delaney said.

The path began to rise, and he could see the undertaker and the gravediggers lounging a dozen feet above him. They knew their melancholy trade, all right, and timing was part of it. He took Grace's hand and they approached the grave with its surrounding berm of fresh black earth. Big Jim's grave was to the left, his wife Bridget's to the right, with the fresh grave right beside hers. Delaney knew there was room in the plot for at least two more coffins, one of which would be his. The undertaker, Casey, came over, looking solemn.

"We'll leave you alone for a while," he said. "If you care to say anything. Take as long as you want."

"Thanks, Mr. Casey."

He walked off. Delaney leaned over and took a handful of earth and dropped it on the coffin. Grace did the same. The earth made a lumpy sound against the plain pine top. Then they stepped back.

"Good-bye, Molly," Delaney said.

"Good-bye, Momma," Grace said. "Rest in peace."

Neither said another word. Then Delaney brushed the remaining dirt off his hands and took Grace's hand, and they walked between the graves of strangers to the peak of the hill. Grace gasped. The entire harbor was spread out in the distance, with the sun bouncing off its glassy surface, One freighter moved slowly north, a tug alongside. The Statue of Liberty seemed tiny, the skyscrapers like toys from Billy McNiff's window. New Jersey and Staten Island were distant smears.

"It's very beautiful," she said.

"Over there to the left," Delaney said, pointing. "That's the Narrows. That's where they found her."

She said nothing, perhaps thinking that she had passed her mother's bones on the way to Spain. Or perhaps just struck by the beauty. Delaney took her hand again.

"Let's go home, daughter."

• • •

The car turned into Horatio Street and stopped at 95. As they got out, Delaney noticed Mr. Cottrell sitting on his own stoop, his feet in the areaway. He was wearing a straw boater, a long-sleeved blue shirt, and dark slacks. His face glistened with oil. He was sitting on a green cushion. In all the years on Horatio Street, Delaney had never seen the man sit on the stoop. Cottrell gave him a stiff little wave.

"How are you feeling, Mr. Cottrell?"

"Better." He paused. "I'm alive."

"Just take it easy."

Then Cottrell cleared his throat. "If you're looking for the woman and the boy, they're not home." He paused. "They went out a couple hours ago."

Delaney felt a tremor of uncertainty.

"Did they say where they were going?"

"I didn't ask."

Delaney looked at Grace, and she tried to read his tense face. They started into the house. Cottrell cleared his throat again.

"Dr. Delaney?" he said. Then squeezed out a word. "Thanks."

Delaney nodded, then went to the gate and unlocked it.

Inside, Delaney pulled open his necktie, removed his suit jacket. He could feel Grace staring at him. He hurried up the stairs into his bedroom, glanced at Rose's suitcase, removed his shoes and trousers, and opened the closet. Her dress was hanging in the space he had cleared for her, and her hat was on the shelf. The rest of her clothes remained in the suitcase, over by the closed sliding doors. He put his suit on a hanger and dressed in street clothes. It was done. Molly was buried. That part of his past was buried with her in the Green-Wood. Molly in life, Molly in the time of numbness and solitude. Gone. Ahead was the future. Ahead was no-man's-land.

He went down to the kitchen, and Grace poured two glasses of ice water. She had changed into a blouse and dark skirt. Her face was distracted, her brow furrowed.

"I can't stay here, Dad," she said.

"Why not?"

"It's not fair to you," she said, staring at the ice water. "Or to Carlito." She paused, then looked at him. "Or to Rose."

He was silent for a moment. She was growing up fast. Then: "You can stay as long as you want, Grace."

"It might be a few days, Dad, or a few weeks. But I have to find my own place in this town."

"I understand," he said, and did: she had to be free, living an unobserved life, free to paint too, free to imagine. Above all, she had to have her son. Delaney suddenly pictured the house with all of them gone: Grace, Carlito, and Rose. All gone. Rose came here because of the boy, and loved him as the child she couldn't have, and when the boy goes, she would surely go too. And Delaney saw himself again in the mornings, with Monique handling the daily traffic, the war vets and the marriage vets, the endless casualties of the night, the addled and the lonely; then a hurried lunch; and off to house calls among the battered, hurt, desperate people of the parish; and then at night, solitude and numbness, and the dream of snow.

No. He could not go back. No. Goddamn it. No.

"Let's go outside," he said.

Mr. Cottrell was gone, but there were more people on the street. Kids were returning from the beach, red and sandy. One of the shawlies passed, and Delaney thought she was as mossy as a river piling in a black dress. The afternoon sun was heading for New Jersey. A breeze rose from the North River.

"Did Rose plant those irises?" Grace said.

"Yes," Delaney said. "I don't know about gardens." Grace grabbed his good arm and hugged it.

Then Grace leaned on the fence, gazing at the life of the street, a long way from the Plaza Real. Delaney sat on the stoop and looked at his hands and clenched and unclenched his fingers. In another week, the olives in the back garden would be edible. Rose said so. All the curtains would be washed and fresh. Rose said that too. Up ahead was the Fourth of July. Maybe he could take Grace and Rose and the boy to a ballgame. Maybe they could go to Coney Island together. Or down to the Battery. Or take the ferry to the Statue of Liberty. To be caressed by harbor winds. Maybe Grace could paint Rose.

Then away off at the distant corner, he could see Rose crossing the avenue, holding the boy by the hand. He stood up.

"I see them," he said.

He began walking quickly, stepping around some kids, slapping away a spaldeen hit foul. She didn't see him yet. He passed some men shooting craps. He dodged a kid on a bicycle. She saw him now, her eyes wide, and stopped. She smiled her beautiful smile. He reached her, wrapped her in his arms, and whirled her around, as if they were dancing.

"Where is Mamá?" the boy said.

An hour later, the boy was explaining the garden to his mother and how olives were growing on the tree and how watermelons would soon grow right there in the corner.

"We're going for a walk," Delaney said, with Rose beside him.

"Okay," the boy said.

"See you later," Grace said, and smiled.

They went out together and paused awkwardly in front of the house.

"I don't want to go to the river," Rose said. "That's where you used to go with, you know . . . with your wife."

"We'll just walk," he said. "Away from the river."

"That's better," Rose said. Her face was tight.

They walked without touching until they were out of the neighborhood. Then they saw a small triangle of park near Eighth Avenue, and he took her hand and led her in silence to a bench. A half-dozen pigeons gurgled around the next bench. An old woman was feeding them crusts of stale bread. A grizzled wino in a long army coat stretched upon another bench. Traffic was sparse.

"She's moving out, of course," he said.

"Maybe . . ."

"She needs to be on her own."

"Maybe not yet."

"And she's taking Carlito."

"If she goes, she better take him. He's her son."

There was acceptance in her voice, but no bitterness.

"But . . ." She paused. "But I keep thinkin', maybe I can make it easier for everybody. Grace doesn't need me around, watching her, watching the boy. . . . Maybe *I* could go. Then she could stay with the boy."

"Rose —"

"No, listen to me, Dottore." She turned away, then returned to him, her eyes glistening. "I'll always love that boy. The rest of my life, I'll love that boy. He gave me what I missed. A boy. A son." A pause. "But he gave me something else too. I came to take care of him, and I met you, Jim. That was one of the best things ever happen to me." A longer pause. "But I don't want to be the woman that made you lose your daughter and that boy. He has his mother now to take care of him. You don't need me."

"Yes, I do," Delaney said.

He saw her press her upper teeth into her lower lip.

"Don't play with me, Jim," she whispered.

"I'm not playing with you, Rose," he said. "I love you."

She leaned against him as if melting. He felt oddly lighter now, the words finally said.

"God damn you, Dottore," she said.

He kissed her hair, inhaled her fragrance.

"Let's go," he said.

She suddenly stiffened. "Let's go?" she said. "Go?" She shook her head, and her voice darkened. "To where? To what?"

He hugged her. "Wherever you want to go, Rose," he said.

She went quiet, fumbling for words. Then she said: "I want to go where you go, and be with you."

"I want the same thing, Rose."

"Then let's go home," she said.

They stood up. Delaney waited for the fine print, but there wasn't any. Rose looked behind her. The old woman was still tossing bread crusts to the pigeons. The wino did not stir. Rose took Delaney's hand and squeezed it, and they started walking west, to the river.

ABOUT THE AUTHOR

Pete Hamill is a novelist, journalist, editor, and screenwriter. He is the author of nineteen previous books, including the bestselling novels *Forever* and *Snow in August* and the bestselling memoir *A Drinking Life.* He lives in New York City, where he is a Distinguished Writer-in-Residence at New York University.